Haters

alisa valdes-rodriguez

LITTLE, BROWN AND COMPANY

New York ๛ Boston

Little, Brown and Company

Hachette Book Group USA
1271 Avenue of the Americas, New York, NY 10020
Visit our Web site at www.lb-teens.com

First Edition: October 2006

Library of Congress Cataloging-in-Publication Data

Valdes-Rodriguez, Alisa.
  Haters : a novel / by Alisa Valdes-Rodriguez.— 1st ed.
     p. cm.
  Summary: Having tried for years to deny her psychic abilities, high school sophomore Paski has disturbing visions about the popular girl at her new high school in Orange County, California.
  ISBN-13: 978-0-316-01307-9 (hardcover)
  ISBN-10: 0-316-01307-2 (hardcover)
  [1. Psychic ability—Fiction. 2. Interpersonal relations—Fiction. 3. High schools—Fiction. 4. Schools—Fiction. 5. Los Angeles (Calif.)—Fiction.]
  I. Title.
PZ7.V2158Hat 2006
[Fic]—dc22

                                        2005037283

10 9 8 7 6 5 4 3 2 1

Q-FF

Printed in the United States of America

Book design by Tracy Shaw

dedication

To Samantha Morris, who happens to be a teenager now, but who will always be one of the coolest people I know at any age. I am blessed to be Sam's aunt, and prouder of her than words can say. And to my brother Ricardo and sister-in-law Susan: You raised an incredible child, because you're incredible people. I love you all.

acknowledgments

Thanks to my agent and buddy, Leslie Daniels, for suggesting I write for a young audience and making this book happen in a big way once I did. Thanks to über-editor Cindy Eagan for her sensitivity and intellect, for championing this book from the start, and for fighting so hard to bring Paski-de-Taos to her very happy home at Little, Brown — all while recovering from one of the worst ice-slips in recorded history. Hello? Who cracks her skull and still manages to be the finest editor in teen lit? And to Miss Phoebe Spanier, an assistant editor I envision taking over the world someday because she is brilliant, meticulous and kind. To everyone at Little, Brown who read this book and helped shove it into shape — dudes, if any of you wears a ring, I shall gladly kneel to kiss it. (No tongue, I promise.) Finally, thanks to the sixteen-year-old me, for keeping such detailed diaries, from which the current me was able to borrow. Don't think I coulda done this if my inner teenager had not been a writer, too, connecting with me now through time and space with thoughts (and loves) I'd long since forgotten I'd had. . . .

And I ask myself: Who do I want to be?
Do I want to throw away the key
And invent a whole new me?
And I tell myself, no one, no one
Don't want to be no one
But me . . .

—Aly & AJ

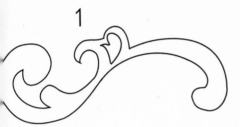

1

You know it's bad news when your dad comes back to Taos from a two-week business trip to Los Angeles wearing designer sunglasses and a velour Juicy men's tracksuit.

Oh, and by the way? He's got a goatee, too, and wears the giant sunglasses on his head like a girlie headband. Well, it's not exactly a goatee. It's like he tried to sculpt his facial hair, like he's trying to look like a twenty-year-old pop star. I'm not sure what he's got going on his feet. I think they're supposed to be trendy athletic shoes, but they're, like, *way* too shiny and, if I'm not mistaken, a little on the high side. High-heeled sneakers and a goatee, with sunglasses — at *night*? Uhm, hello?

Basically, my dad looks like an idiot.

I'm not the only one who thinks this, just so you know. We're standing in the hot blast of air in the entry of the Apple Tree restaurant, and even the overdressed Texan tourists stare at my dad like he's some kind of freak. Keep in mind that the Texans are wearing poofy little ski-bunny clothes with cowboy boots, as skiers from Texas often do. They think this is what people in Taos, one of the best mountain ski towns in the world, wear. (We don't.) Anyway, the tourists look sorry — but not as sorry as my dear old dad, apparently. This tells you more or less exactly how sorry Dad looks. It's like he's on meth or something.

"Two for dinner?" asks the big-eyed hostess. She looks up for a second, smiles blankly as if she's never seen us, and then does a serious whiplash-causing double take. "Mr. Archuleta? Is that you?" She looks at me like we're in the middle of an emergency together and she doesn't know what to do, like she's in a panic. I shrug to let her know it isn't my fault.

"Hey," says my dad, smiling at the hostess, narrowing his eyes as he tries to remember who this person is. He doesn't know the girl's name, I can tell. He smiles the same way every time one of his old art students recognizes him. Dad, a cartoonist, teaches art at the middle school when his money runs low. "How are you? Still drawing?"

The hostess looks Dad up and down, and I swear to God it looks like she's trying not to laugh. She, like me, is used to seeing him in jeans and a stained T-shirt. She, like me, doesn't know what to make of this new Rudolfo Archuleta. There's a good spot in heaven for me, for having a dad like this. I'll tell you that much.

Anyway, the hostess tells Dad she's not drawing anymore, which, I should say, I might have guessed from the fact that she's working here. Then she tells Dad he looks "different." Yeah. That's one way of putting it.

Dad and I get to our table, sit down, and look over the menus. I decide on the chiles rellenos, because they are basically the only halfway normal thing on the menu here. Dad rubs his goatee thing and tells me he's going to have the fish tacos.

Now I know I'm in trouble.

The other couple of times we've been here, Dad has ordered the tempeh. Tempeh is this vegan cake thingy that looks like bad skin and tastes like moldy cardboard. It was the kind of thing that went really well with my dad the way he used to be, like, last week. Last week my dad was a struggling artist who hung out with other local artists and complained about how conservative National Public Radio was getting. He was the kind of guy you might call "granola" as an adjective. Crunchy. Taos is a funky little artist-heavy town in the Rocky Mountains of New Mexico. The houses and buildings are almost all single-story brown mud squares, adobe. It's really pretty here, actually. The town sits in a valley with mountains rising all around. In the summer it's very green, with wild strawberries growing everywhere, and you almost want to skip over the hills yodeling or something. In the winter — like now — the city is usually covered in a layer of snow that looks like frosting on the old adobe buildings. The air smells clean, laced with smoke from people's fireplaces. We burn pine logs up here, and they smell really good.

Me and my dad live in a lopsided two-bedroom adobe off the plaza that's about four hundred years old, and every inch of every wall inside of it is covered with his drawings of superheroes. Oh, I forgot to mention Dad's not just a cartoonist — he's got a couple of graphic novels and a comic book series. So the house is decorated in sketches of Squeegee Man; Squeegee Man's archenemy Prince Flatulence; the always buxom sadist Darkleena, queen of the underworld; and the pure and willowy She-Nha, who, if you ask me, is a little too influenced by the wrong kind of Japanese animation. But nobody asks me. Anyway, my point is, until recently, my dad seemed to realize he was a hopeless geek. Then he got a call from a Hollywood movie studio that wanted to option Squeegee Man for a movie, with Dad as one of the animators. He went out last week to meet them, and now here he is, a changed being. You see what I'm getting at here?

Fish tacos? I didn't know you could put fish in a taco. I didn't know anyone would want to. I don't know who this man is.

"Dad?" I say. "Are you okay?"

Dad grins at me, and I swear his teeth look whiter than they used to.

"Did you do something to your teeth?" I ask.

Dad closes his mouth and puts a hand over it. I swear it looks like he's blushing. He pushes back his upper lip and touches a couple of teeth with the tips of his fingers. Eew? I know he doesn't smoke ganja like lots of other artist parents, but I swear he looks baked.

"Are you on drugs?" I ask him. He gives me that "ha-ha, very funny" sarcastic look and ignores the question. He thinks I'm too grown-up sometimes. I wish he were more grown-up sometimes, so I guess we're even.

"I had them laser-whitened while I was in California," he explains. He bares his teeth like a cornered coyote. I think he's trying to smile. Then he talks through his teeth like his jaw is wired shut. "What do you think?"

I shrug, because it wouldn't be polite to tell my dad what I think right now. What I think is: I recently got highlights in my shoulder-length brown hair, and that was a big deal for me. I'm not sure how I feel about it. It's fine to better your appearance, but I thought my dad's teeth were fine before, for a dad.

Thankfully, the waitress comes. We order, and then I start to whistle and look around the restaurant for something, anything, to distract me from the disturbing sight of my father falling into what I think is a midlife cartoonist's crisis. His latest girlfriend just dumped him, and I think this all has something to do with that. I think it was a blessing, her dumping him, because she was completely postal. She thought we were, like, best friends or something, and always came crying to me after they'd had a fight, like I was her therapist or something. One time she started to talk about how my dad gave the best massages, and I was, like, "Hello? Shut up? You're making me sick?"

"Pasquala," says my dad, with full-on heavy-duty Spanish accent. He does that when he thinks there are lots of "gringos" around. It's totally lame.

"Paski, please," I say. I hate my name. Pasquala. What kind of sixteen-year-old has a name like that? I've only ever seen that name in abandoned graveyards in northern New Mexico. Oh, and it gets worse, just so you know. My full name? Are you ready for this? Here goes: Pasquala Rumalda Quintana de Archuleta. Bunk, right? My mom and dad, at the time they named me, were on this whole Mexican power trip, and they thought it was okay to name me like that. Mom's not in the picture anymore. Actually, since I was ten, she hasn't been in the picture.

My dad's cartoons from back then are nothing but a bunch of bald-looking guys in long shorts with long socks, and *chola* women in skinny stilettos. Me? I don't care one way or the other about Mexican

5

power. I don't know why my dad is all "I'm Mexican" when he doesn't even know how to speak Spanish, but you can't argue with him about it. To me, people are people, and some get better names than others. You know which side of that I fall on, anyway.

"I have to talk to you about something serious," says Dad, totally ignoring my request for a name correction. Usually, Dad's a pretty good listener, one of those touchy-feely parents. He's raising me alone because my mom, sort of an art groupie who wanted to be a singer, had her midlife crisis and took off with a biker dude. She's a mess, my mom. I don't think about it too much because I don't see the point. Some people get moms that care. Some don't. I happen to be one of the ones who got a mom that didn't care. I mean, she did care, but not about me. She cared about boyfriends and pot and drinking. And that's about it. Dad, as you might have guessed, has bad luck in the lady department. I think he should stop picking the kind of lady with shoulder tattoos and tube tops, but does he listen? Nope. Not my fault.

I sip my iced water and wait for Dad to talk. The last time I felt scared like this was when he told me Mom had left the state without letting us know. There's never something good coming when Dad tells you there's something "serious" to talk about. There is no less serious dad in the world than a cartoonist.

"You know I went to L.A. to meet with the movie studio," says Dad. I nod. "Well, it went really well." He smiles, happier than I've seen him in a very long time. I hold my breath. "I mean, really good, Paski."

I nod and look around the restaurant some more.

"Hey. Look at me. Over here." He's pointing to his eyes with two fingers, like I don't know how to find them. Dad's a nut about eye contact. I look at him and wince. He belongs on that show *Jackass*.

"They want Squeegee for a movie," Dad says. "They aren't the only ones. The studios all wanted it. We had a bidding war, Paski. And they're talking sequels."

I have no idea what he's talking about. Dad leans forward across the table with a crazy smile. "It's my big break, Chinita," he says in a low voice, as if the Texan tourists are listening and might, what, report it to the government or something. Chinita is one of the many dreaded nicknames Dad uses for me, because he thought I looked "Chinese" as a baby. "They want me to head up the animation team."

"So?" I ask. He's gloating, and I hate it. I don't know what the big deal is. And honestly? I'm sick of him wanting me to congratulate him all the time on everything he does. Isn't that what Grandma is for? It's his job to congratulate me. Sometimes the whole parent/kid thing gets blurred in our house.

"So, we're moving to L.A.," he says.

I choke on my water. "We're what?"

"Moving to Los Angeles," he says, like I might not have understood what "L.A." meant.

"Why? When?"

"Because I have to live there to do the show. As soon as possible."

I feel a pit open in the center of my belly. Moving? I can't move. I'm having my seventeenth birthday in less than a month, and I was planning to spend it with my best friends at a concert in Santa Fe. I'm the editor of my school newspaper and the co-captain of the school mountain bike team. Granted, there are only three of us on the team, but still. It's January, the start of the new semester. They need me. Then there's Emily and Janet, my two best friends. I love them like sisters. How could I live without them? And then, after months of wondering whether he actually liked me or not, I just got asked to go to a party by Ethan Schaefer — only the hottest-looking guy in the eleventh grade at Taos High School. You can't leave town with Ethan Schaefer falling in love with you! That would be way crazy.

"I can't go with you," I say, knowing as I say it that I probably don't have a choice. Actually, I know I don't have a choice. I've had this weird feeling for the past couple of days that something big was going to happen to me, but I didn't know exactly what it was. I've been dreaming about a huge yellow pyramid, and the dreams have felt scary. I've known something bad was coming.

"You have to go with me. I'm your dad." Oh, really? And all this time I thought he was my pet. My father, the master of stating the obvious.

"I'll stay with Grandma."

My father looks hurt. "But it's California, Pasquala." He says "California" as if everyone in the world wants to live there. He sits up and smiles. "Beaches? Sunshine? Surfer dudes?"

I shake my head. Taos is fine with me. I love the mountains and the sky here. In my free time, weather allowing, I ride my bike in the mountains. And not just any old ride. I ride forty miles at a pop. I'm what you'd call a serious cyclist. I go up the sides of things nobody should go up the side of on a bike, and somehow I stay on. I jump things. I spin the bike in the air. I call it bike-dancing. You blast your iPod and go. I like the solitude here. Dad looks like he might cry, which would be pathetic. He might stain the velour. Wait a second. Did he really just say "surfer dudes"? I can't deal.

"Your grandma's pretty busy with her business," he reminds me. "And you know how she is now. She can't really take care of you."

I look around the restaurant some more. He's right. I was bluffing anyway. I wouldn't want to live with my crazy grandmother and all her spirit friends.

Spirit friends? Yeah. My grandma is sort of a local celebrity astrologer, tarot-card queen, witch doctor, communicator with the dead. People come from all over the world for her readings and cleansing and God knows what else. She's even been on *Oprah* for helping the local police solve a murder one time. That's the "business" Dad's talking about. I think Dad uses words too generously sometimes. As a newspaper editor, I am very specific about the words I use. My grandma and "business" don't match. At all.

My grandma. Basically, she's a sweet new-age guru lady who thinks every little thing you do is super significant. I love her to death, but if you think my dad's open and funky, you have to meet his mother. It's a little much for me sometimes. She's also got about six boyfriends, all of them these crazy artists or diehard hippie guys who smell like something died in their pants. And, worst of all, she thinks I'm a psychic like her, just because I've had a couple of dreams that came true. She's always, like, "You have the gift, you are the chosen one." Blah blah blah. This is why I never tell her my dreams anymore. Oh, and she wears only purple. You see what I'm saying, anyway. She's adorable, but I'm pretty sure she's a little Looney Tunes. I'd go insane living with her, now that I think about it.

"I know," says Dad. "It's going to be hard to leave your friends. I don't want to leave my friends, either. But we have to go, Pasqua — Paski."

"We don't have to," I say. "You could just stay here."

"No," he says, adjusting the sunglasses on his head. "We have to. I already signed the deal, and I got us an apartment. It's really nice. And I already registered you at Aliso Niguel High School."

"What?"

"You won't believe how cool this school is."

"What?"

"We have to start on the movie right away. Do you have any idea how long it takes to make these animated movies? Even with computers?"

I shake my head.

"That *Finding Nemo* took more than four years."

I stare at the top of the table. I'll be twenty years old — almost twenty-one — in four years. Twenty? That's halfway through college. I want to be a lawyer, though, so that's halfway toward law school. Wait a minute, back up. Did he just say he registered me at a high school already?

"We'll come back to visit for holidays. I promise."

The waitress brings our food, but I've lost my appetite. Dad, though? Mr. California parts his pearly whites and chomps down on those nasty-looking fish tacos like they're the best thing he ever tasted.

2

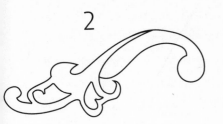

It's a snowy Saturday afternoon, gray and dreary, and Dad is home with Don Juan, our one-eyed orange tomcat, and a couple of Dad's artist friends, packing the last of our things into the U-Haul. The cat lost his eye when one of our idiot neighbors shot him with a BB gun. My dad, though, he lost his mind when he went to Los Angeles.

I should let you know that he is going to pack the stereo at the very end, because he's got it blasting while he works. He's listening to Gwen Stefani's *Love. Angel. Music. Baby.* Can I just say he's scaring me more and more every day? Seriously. There is nothing on earth scarier than seeing your dad sing along to "Harajuku Girls," doing his arms like serpents.

Oh, and Dad's not just singing along, okay? Singing along, dancing around, and wearing a big Phat Farm hockey shirt and too-long jeans that drag over his awkwardly trendy shoes. I mean, he's going bald, okay? Bald. Get a clue. Go gracefully into that good night, I say. I swear on everything I consider holy and dear that when I get to be thirty-eight years old I will not act like that.

Anyway, he's letting me use the car to go around saying goodbye to everybody I love. He says we're going to have to buy a new car after we get settled in L.A., because he's embarrassed to show up in this one to Hollywood parties. That's what he said. Does he not realize animators probably never get invited to Hollywood parties? Poor Dad. There's nothing wrong with this car. It's a dark blue 2000 Toyota Corolla with a CD player. It runs really well. But lately, Dad's all into saying, "a Beemer, I have to have a Beemer." Even his artist friends are confused.

First stop? Taos Bakery, to say goodbye to Ethan Schaefer. I know, I should go to see Emily and Janet first; they're waiting for me at Emily's house. Then I have to go to Grandma's after that. I'm on a tight schedule here, because Dad wants to get the car hitched to the U-Haul and leave before dark. In case you were wondering, my dad's a vampire. He only works at night, and he thinks I can sleep in the truck while he drives. I'm, like, ho-tel, okay? But whatever.

I can't stop thinking about Ethan, about how I'm never going to see him again. Or, if I do see him again, how he's probably going to be in love with someone else by then. It's not like I even know him that well to be all stupid about leaving him behind. It's just that he's the first guy I've known who makes me feel pretty. I like that feeling. I never thought I was all that pretty until Ethan started telling me how beautiful I was. I'm nothing exceptional, just a normal-looking New Mexican Hispanic girl, five-five, longish dark brown hair with very recent reddish highlights that don't look that great because Emily and Janet did them for me. I've got kind of pale olive skin, and I guess my eyes are big and very dark.

I'm not flashy, either. I stick to jeans, T-shirts, and sweaters mostly. There's no Urban Outfitters in Taos — or anywhere in this state — but I order things from them online twice a year, fall and summer, and that's pretty much my wardrobe. I like shirts with funny slogans on them, and I keep a diary where I write down slogans I think would look good on a T-shirt. I came up with a new one last night: IT'S MY DAD'S FAULT.

I don't do a lot of makeup, just some lip gloss and mascara. I see all these movie stars and singers, like Lindsay Lohan or whatever, and they're so beautiful and glamorous with their fake lashes and starving bodies. I'm nothing like that. I mean, I'm not fat. I'm strong. I like to eat the right things, and I ride my bike a lot. You can see a lot of definition in my calves and thighs, and one time when I was walking around in shorts last summer, this construction worker whistled at some other girls but when he saw me slapped his buddy on the arm and said, "I'd hate to piss her off. She's got some strong legs." I don't know what that meant, really, but I'm the kind of girl who takes it as a good sign that disgusting construction workers are afraid of me.

Because I don't have a mom around, I never had much of a chance to learn about too many girlie things. Emily and Janet have taught me everything I know about makeup and pulse points. But Ethan's all "Your cheekbones are so structured" or "Your body is amazing" and "You have the darkest brown eyes I've ever seen." He tells me all the guys at school talk about how pretty I am, but that's news to me. None of them ever talked to me before, until now. Ethan, meanwhile, looks just like Jesse McCartney. No, I'm not kidding. Exactly like him. So you see why I don't want to leave town. Just yesterday? On the phone? He's all "You should be a model, Paski." Yeah, right! Models are tall, and they wear, like, a size zero. I wear a size eight, and I'm not very tall. Personally, I'd rather be a professional cyclist than a model anyway, someone like Dede Barry. I'd rather spend my life training in the fresh air of the mountains than walking on a runway for a bunch of German men with cat's-eye glasses. Ethan's kind of corny, now that I think about it.

Anyway, I have never had so much in common with a guy before. We've been talking on the phone every night, and even though we haven't kissed or anything it's pretty clear he likes me. We like all the same bands, same food, same everything. It's cruel to pull me out of my life here with this happening, right?

I park in front of the bakery and go in. Ethan works here on the weekends for a little extra money, making cookies. I think it's cute. I mean, how many hot guys can bake, when you think about it? Let me count, uh, let's see: none. I talked to him on the phone about a half hour ago, and he said he'd go on break when I got there.

Ethan's at the counter, helping a fat lady with her order. She's getting boxes and boxes of pastries. Is that really a good idea when you weigh four thousand pounds? I don't know. People do what they're going to do. You can't stop them. Ethan looks up and sees me. He smiles and looks shy. I love that about him. Ever since he asked me out, he looks bashful around me. I used to think he wasn't interested at all, but he told me it's just that he was intimidated by me. That's crazy, right? A guy intimidated by me? Ethan tells me I'm beautiful. I'm going to miss that, too.

The fat lady pays for her poison and waddles out the door. Her thighs rub together in a way I think might start a fire.

"Don't you feel bad?" I ask, gesturing with my chin at the fat lady.

"Bad?" asks Ethan, taking the plastic gloves off his hands. "Why?"

"You might have just sold that lady a heart attack."

Ethan laughs. I love his laugh. It's like his voice has just barely changed, and it has a certain bell-ness to it. "You have a point," he says. "But if a lady wants to eat cake, I say let them eat cake."

"That's very feminist of you," I say.

"I am my mother's son," he says. Ethan's mom is a state representative, big on women's rights and water conservation. I like her almost as much as I like him. Before Dad decided we had to move, I wanted to get involved with water issues here in the state. We're running out of the stuff. Now I don't have an issue. Do they have issues in L.A.? Ethan starts to untie his apron. "Let me just punch out for break. I'll be right back."

I wait and look at all the yummy things in the pastry cases. None of them look as good as Ethan Schaefer.

He comes out from behind the counter in jeans and a striped button-down shirt. I notice he's put gel in his hair and wonder if it was to impress me. He's about six feet tall, with broad shoulders and a narrow waist. He's on the basketball team at school, and the coach thinks he'll get an athletic scholarship somewhere. He pushes a chunk of long blond bangs from his eyes.

"It's kind of bad weather," he says. "Wanna just sit in my car and talk?"

"Sure," I say.

We trot through the snow to Ethan's car. Yes, I said Ethan's car. He has his own, a 1994 Saturn bought with the money from his job. He rocks. We duck inside and close the doors. Ethan turns on the engine to get the heater going, and pushes a CD into the new stereo. It's our favorite artist, Gorillaz. We have the same tastes, me and Ethan.

He turns toward me, puts an arm up over the top of his seat, tilts his head to one side, and looks sort of sad. "So, you're leaving today, huh?"

I nod and try not to cry. I will not cry. I will not.

"That blows," says Ethan.

"Yeah, pretty much," I agree.

And then he does it. He leans in and kisses me. I've only kissed one other boy before, and it was pretty grotesque, like he was a vacuum hose with wet rubber lips. But Ethan has soft lips and sweet breath. I could kiss him forever.

"Wow," I breathe when we finish.

"You can't go," he says. "That settles it."

"I have to," I tell him. "My dad's packing the truck right now."

Ethan looks at his watch. "I've got ten minutes before I have to go back in there."

We spend the next ten minutes kissing, and then we promise to stay in touch through e-mail and phone calls. We get out of the car and hurry across the parking lot. He kisses me one more time in the snow, which feels colder than any snow ever. "I have to go now."

"Okay," I say, shivering. "See you later."

"No," he says with a big smile. "I'll see you soon."

I smile sadly.

"No," he repeats. "I mean it. I'll come visit you as soon as I save the money. I promise."

"Really?"

"Hell yeah!" He runs back toward me, kisses me again, and says,

"Don't worry about anything, okay? Things happen for a reason. I won't forget you."

I cry a little bit on the way to Emily's house and realize I'm ridiculous. Ethan's just a guy, right? There are lots of guys in the world. There are probably even guys in California. But I feel like Ethan understands me. He makes me laugh. I think he could have been that guy you always talk about your whole life as your first true love or whatever, like, the guy I lost my virginity to or something. But it's not going to happen, thanks to my psycho cartoonist dad. How stupid is that?

Emily lives in a pretty pink adobe house near the plaza with her mom and dad. She's one of the few people I know whose parents are still married. They're completely normal, too, her parents. They're, like, businesspeople or something. Almost everyone else around here is an artist or a tourist. Emily's parents do all the stuff I've never done my entire life, like go to church and have dinner together every night. My friendship with Emily started because I was jealous of her sparkly purple lunchbox back in second grade. I'm still jealous of her, the way her clothes are always clean, but now I like her, too. Our other best friend, Janet, is the prettiest girl at school, so I guess you could say we're the popular kids. I don't know. At Taos High School, I'd say we're pretty accepting of pretty much everyone. It's not like it's supposed to be on TV shows about kids.

I park in the driveway and ring the doorbell. The house looks like an iced strawberry cake in the snow. Emily's mom, Mrs. Sandoval, answers and gives me a hug. That's the kind of mom she is. She's petite, wearing slacks and an expensive-looking sweater with gold jewelry, and her red hair hangs in a tidy bob. I have no idea how it must be to have a mom like that. The house is warm and steamy with the smell of something cooking, and Emily's little brother is playing Monopoly with his dad in the family room. I have always wanted to have a family and a house like this, but seeing as I'm going to be a legal adult in two years, there's not much chance of that happening, like, ever. Unless, you know, I marry Ethan and we have kids and a nice house and everything like that.

"The girls are in Em's room," Mrs. Sandoval says.

I knock on the door to Emily's bedroom to be polite. "It's mee-eee," I call, so she knows it's someone she wants to let come in. The door flies open.

"Paski!" my best friends cry in unison. So you know, Emily is the tall one with the shoulder-length brown hair; Janet is the shorter one with the chin-length curly black bob and the super-pink cheeks. They grab me and hug me. We shut the door again. My friends stand to the side and smile at the bed, like I should look there. I'm surprised to see three beautifully wrapped gifts. I feel like crying. I've been through so much with these two.

"Open them," urges Janet.

"Yeah," seconds Emily.

I crawl onto the queen-size bed, and they tumble up next to me. I open the gifts carefully, slowly, because I want to save the shiny pink and purple paper forever. Inside the first box I find a pink velvet journal with lined paper, and a pink pen with a feather puff on the end.

"It's our friendship journal," says Emily. I open it to find that she's already filled one third of the journal with writing. I flip further through the book, and see that another third has been filled by Janet.

"The last part is blank," Janet says. "So you can put your memories of our friendship there."

I close the book and try very hard not to cry.

"Whenever you need us, you just read some pages from the friendship journal," explains Emily. She and Janet give me a group hug, and I tell them I love them and that they'll be my best friends forever.

"Open the other ones," says Emily, who is always the first to stop us from getting too sappy. We think of her as the sensible one. In one of the boxes I find a pair of sunglasses and some sunscreen. In the other box I find a tiny string bikini and the Blue Merle CD I've been wanting.

I hold up the bikini, laughing. "You guys are sick," I laugh. "I'm not wearing this. You know that."

"I hear there are nude beaches out there," says Emily. Well, sort of sensible, anyway.

"Uh, yuck?" I say.

"Well you have to do something to meet a guy," remarks Janet, who lost her virginity this year and hasn't stopped thinking about boys since.

"And we agree it's about time you, uh, stopped waiting?" Emily lifts her brows suggestively. She lost her virginity last semester. Neither of my friends can believe I still haven't done "it" yet. But they both have semi-normal families. When you have a promiscuous, crazy mother and a dad who draws voluptuous female cartoons that he drools over, um, let's just say you take your time. Rebellion takes many forms.

Anyway, I remind them that I'm not actually moving to Los Angeles. Nope. That would be too cool for my dad. Rather, I'm moving to someplace called Aliso Viejo, in Orange County. Dad says the schools are good there, especially the high school he already registered me in without even telling me. It is, in his opinion, the best place on earth to raise a child. I guess he forgot I'm not a child anymore. The only good thing about moving to something called Aliso Viejo, as far as I can tell, is that my new city will have a name almost as awful as mine. By the way, Aliso Viejo means "old cottonwood."

Janet stands up, grabs my arms, and pretends to stagger. "Take me with you! I want to go to the O.C." Emily stands and grabs my other hand, telling me to take her, too. As religious watchers of *The OC,* Janet and Emily believe my life is about to become as fabulous as the lives of the actors on the show. I have reminded them many times that television shows and movies are written by clueless grown-ups, and that those clueless grown-ups apparently look like . . . my father. "You are so so so lucky to get out of here," says Janet. "This place is so lame."

"I don't know," I say. "I don't feel lucky."

The three of us plop down to the floor around a bowl of popcorn. Emily pours me some Cherry Vanilla Dr Pepper in a plastic cup on a tray. I bet her mom brought all this in for us. Like I said, cool mom. They've been downloading songs from rhapsody to Emily's laptop, which also sits on the floor. Janet suggests we do a Mapquest of my new apartment and school and print it all out three times, one for me and one for each of them, so they'll know where I am and how to get to me if they need to. You can hit print on the laptop here and it will work from the printer in Emily's parents' home office. Emily's whole house is wireless.

My dad still does dial-up.

By the time I drag myself to Grandma's funky little mud hut, I'm emotionally drained. I actually cried at the end with Emily and Janet. They told me not to worry and said we'd see each other on holidays. They promised to keep me up to date on everything around here. Still. This is the suckiest day of my life, and all for what? So Dad can make movies? It's absurd. I need my grandmother right now. There's nothing better in the world when you're feeling depressed than going to see my grandma. The really cool part about seeing her without my dad is that she lets me ride her motorcycle. She has a Harley, and I love the way it feels. I want a motorcycle of my own, a little racing bike, but my dad is, like, no way, so whatever. The adventurous gene skipped a generation in our family. Just like the psychic gene. But that's another story.

Just so you know, my grandmother had her house designed to look like a snail. That's right, a snail. Like, the slimy little thing that lurks in your garden? Yeah. It's her animal guardian or something. So there it is. I'm opening the door to a snail, and the door is purple. The fun never ends. The good news is, the house smells amazingly good. Grandma knows her incense. And Grandma can cook.

She's seated in the red light of her living room, finishing up with a "client" when I arrive. I don't knock, because this is really like my second home. Grandma doesn't believe in locking her doors. She says she is watched over by spirits more powerful than any lock. Grandma doesn't notice me stepping into the living room, because she's in a trance. I can't believe who is here.

Grandma's wearing a silky purple robe thing, like a kimono or something, with her long crazy black witch hair frizzing out everywhere. I think she's fifty-nine or so. She's sitting at a card table across from the very same fat lady I saw at the bakery. Grandma's holding the lady's puffy hands; her eyes are rolling back in her head, and she's speaking in a language no one has ever heard before. It sounds totally fake to me, but it probably isn't. Grandma is unusual, and some think she's crazy, but nobody denies she seems to really be able to tell the future and talk to people who've gone on to the other side. It's still a little embarrassing to see her all tranced out like that. I mean, I could probably do it if I wanted to, but that's just the point: I don't want to.

I sit quietly on the bench in the entryway and watch. The light is dim, but I don't think it's dim enough to make me see things. And what I'm seeing is impossible. As my grandma talks in this weird language, the fat lady shrinks. I don't mean she gets really small, like George in *George Shrinks*. She shrinks, like she's losing weight faster than any human being on earth has ever lost weight. Soon she's not lumpy anymore. She's voluptuous or something. And her hair is shiny. Grandma is speaking English again, and tells her she can see the real heart of this woman. The woman starts to cry. Grandma tells her the obsessive eating is coming from pain in another life.

So you know? I'm a little freaked out by this. I don't like when things make no sense — and when you're me, there are plenty of things, vision kinds of things, that don't make sense. So I don't stay to hear what marvelous predictions my grandma is making for this lady. Instead, I go right for the kitchen. I'm starving. And even if Grandma is a scary good psychic, she can cook. There's always something tasty in her refrigerator.

I find some enchiladas and pinto beans and some homemade tortillas. I heat them up in the ancient stained microwave and settle in at the little table in the corner. By the time I get to the last bite, I hear the front door closing. Then Grandma joins me at the table.

"M'ija," she says, with that intense, burning look she gets in her eyes.

"Hi, Grandma."

She takes my hand. "Did you like the enchiladas?" She asks this like it's a life-or-death question.

"They were great."

"Good." From the look in her eyes, you'd think she was sitting around planning the takeover of a nation.

Then, without cracking a smile, she's up and pouring herself a glass of water from the Brita filter pitcher in the fridge. The back of her kimono is all wet, like she's been sweating. Or peeing.

"That was so heavy," she says.

"What, your four-hundred-pound client?"

Grandma gives me an icy stare. "Her past lives. She's had such a long journey."

Bakery to grandma's? Not such a long journey if you ask me.

"But enough of that," says Grandma. She closes her eyes and pretends she's got invisible ropes sticking out of her body. Then she uses her fingers like scissors and cuts them in the air. "Release," she says. "Release, release." She does this to disconnect from her clients. If she didn't, she tells me, she'd be emotionally drained. When she has finished cutting the cords, she comes back to the table. She still has the intense look, but slightly softened. We look a lot alike, me and my grandma. In fact, I look more like her than I look like either of my parents. She smiles at me and gives me a huge, mashing hug.

"I'm sorry you're hurting, sweetheart," she says. "I'm hurting, too.

I am going to miss you so much. I don't know what I'll do without you. I'm not going to say it's going to be fine the way everyone else is, either."

"I don't want to go with him, Grandma."

"I know. I know. I wish you could stay."

She stops hugging me and takes my hands in hers, looking hard into my eyes. I feel like my entire soul jumps out of my body then jumps back in. And when it's back, I feel instantly better.

"How's that?" she asks. Tears quiver in the corners of her eyes.

"You're amazing, Grandma," I say. "How do you do that?"

"I have something for you." She smiles. Grandma hardly ever answers questions the normal way.

"You do?"

"Come with me."

I follow Grandma to her bedroom. It's never a good thing when she wants to take you to her room. Her room has freaked me out since I was very small. It's painted dark red and has incense going all the time. It's full of weird art that looks like photos uploaded directly from the dead zone — ghoulish things from Mexico, miniature sculptures of skeletons and skulls that she tells me are in celebration of the afterlife. Grandma's good but trippy.

"Here." She takes a necklace out of her jewelry box and hands it to me.

"I can't take your jewelry," I say.

"It's not mine, it's yours," she says. "I made it for you."

It's a long, thin black rubber string with a bright turquoise stone attached. The stone is carved into the shape of some kind of bird. I think it looks like something you'd call an amulet, but I've never actually seen an amulet, so I can't be sure. It has that amulet feel to it, though, like something you'd read about in a science fiction book.

"It's, uh, very nice," I say. And that isn't totally a lie. It's actually kind of cool.

Grandma pulls me over to the bed and sits me down next to her. "It's not nice. It's *powerful*. This necklace is going to protect you."

"Protect me? From what?"

"It's a water bird. The water bird is very important to the Pueblo Indians. It represents distant travel, long vision, and wisdom. When you need guidance and I'm not there, seek it in the necklace."

She pushes the water-bird stone against my palm and curls my fingers around it. Her hand is hot. Grandma stares into my eyes. "You are entering turbulent times." She closes her eyes. "I see a yellow pyramid and a cement river." Her brows knit together in a scowl. I get goose bumps, but I don't tell her I've had dreams lately about the pyramid. Grandma opens her eyes and says, "What you are heading into won't be easy. But I think you know that."

"Please don't tell me I'm going to die at the yellow pyramid."

Grandma laughs. "No, sweetheart. Nothing like that." She stares a moment. "Actually, it will be like a *part* of you dies. So you're not completely off. And if you don't honor your vision and gifts, well . . . I just don't know."

Great.

"But you're not going to die *physically*." She grins at the panic she must see on my face. Then she hugs me again. She's trembling. "You'll be safe if you do the right things. I'll miss you so much. You're not going to die, okay? Don't think like that, okay, precious? It's not like that. I have blessed this water bird, and the spirits have blessed it. And

25

I feel that if you honor your gifts, you will find success beyond your dreams. The spirits have spoken, and this is what they told me."

Oh *goody*. The spirits. I hate the spirits. They scare the you-know-what out of me. Why they chose me as one of their therapists — yes, they like to talk to me — I will never understand.

"Wear it whenever you think you need a little extra guidance, and we'll be there, okay? Don't be afraid of the power of the water bird."

I stare at the stone and rubber and wonder how many people have a grandmother who says things like "Don't be afraid of the power of the water bird." There must be some who live by the beach some-where, where water birds poop on the cars, but other than that, none. Just me. Lucky me.

"I know you think I'm crazy," says Grandma. She's crying with a smile. I think it's almost harder for her that we're moving away than it is for me and my dad.

"I don't think you're crazy," I say.

"Listen to me. If you would just stop fighting the power, if you would just let it flow through you, you'd see what a great, great gift you have been given."

"I already told you it's a nice necklace."

"That's not the gift I'm talking about." Grandma laughs. "I'm talk-ing about this." She taps my heart. "And this." She taps my forehead, right between my eyebrows. "You are a seer, Pasquala. I know you saw my client transform in there."

"I didn't know you saw me," I say.

"I see all," she jokes.

I look at my watch. I don't like when we start to talk about my "powers." I don't want powers. I want a normal life, a date now and then. "Okay, Grandma. Thanks. I'm going to miss you. Dad wants me back soon so we can hit the road." I don't want to stay any longer, because I know I'll start to cry like a baby. I love my grandmother.

"You've forgotten what a great gift you were born with, just like your mother forgot about the gift of you."

I shudder at being compared to my mother. I mean, let's see. Irresponsible drug addict or honor student. Hmm. Nope. No comparison there.

"Allrighty then," I say. "I hate to eat and run, but . . ."

Then Grandma's face turns fierce. "You don't want to believe what I'm telling you, Pasquala. But if you continue to reject your powers, there's no telling how badly things might turn out."

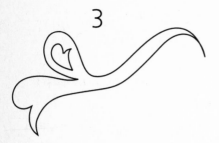

3

Dad has his Gwen Stefani CD blasting in the U-Haul with the Toyota
in tow behind us. Did you even know U-Hauls had CD players? Me
neither. But at least he's wearing his old clothes again, jeans and a
T-shirt. We just listened to my Alkaline Trio disc, and now it's Dad's
turn. He lives in a highly democratic universe. I mean, I can tell he
doesn't really like the music I like. But he tolerates it and never complains. He wants to *understand* me. So why is it that he misses how
scary I find it that he thinks he's Gwen Stefani? Anyway. I'm in sweats,
just in case I want to fall asleep, but how can anyone sleep with my dad
singing along to Gwen Stefani? Maybe that weirdo magician David
Blaine could do it. But not me.

Behind the seats, in his carrier, Don Juan howls in cat terror, as
he's done for the past two days. It's not even like a meow. It's like a
baby in a vise. I'm seriously about to lose it. This is two straight days
of Dad singing "Rich Girl," two straight days of the cat screaming, and

there's only so much a girl can take, you know what I mean? And then there's the whole thing of having to share a hotel room with my dad, who snores like a sick giraffe.

"Can I turn it down a little?" I ask.

Dad looks at me like I've insulted him. "What's wrong, Punkin?" he asks. "I thought Gwen was da bomb."

Here's how much I hate that nickname: I'd rather be called Pasquala than Punkin. I can't deal with the fact that my dad just said "da bomb," either. So I look out the window and say nothing. In the past hour, the flat, endless desert of eastern California has slowly turned into a flat endless assortment of tract homes. Out the window, it's house after house, square stucco things with pitched roofs done up in red tiles. Everyone has a little patch of struggling green lawn. Everyone has a white door. I guess it's supposed to be charming. I still don't want to be here. I miss home. Well, I miss Ethan, anyway. And the mountains. And my friends.

"What's wrong?" Dad has this habit of repeating himself until you answer him.

"Nothing's wrong," I say. Like I'm really going to tell my dad I think I'm in love for the first time? No way. He'll find it adorable. He'll call me Punkin again. He'll say I'm da bomb. This is the same dad who took me out for ice cream when I got my first period, and actually asked the staff to sing a congratulations song. Sometimes he's *too* understanding and supportive. I haven't had a scoop of mint chocolate chip since.

"We're almost there, Paski!" Dad takes an overly excited sip from the mammoth cup of Coke he got back in Barstow. It's got to be hot and flat by now. Foul. But that's the thing with this new version of my dad. Everything's "awesome" to him. He keeps using that word, too. By the way, don't ever go to Barstow. It's like a giant RV monster took a dump there.

"Yay," I say, sarcastic. "We're almost there."

"Cheer up." Dad rolls down the window on his side. "Look!" He sticks his head out like a too-happy dog, then ducks back inside just as this massive semi truck passes us and nearly chops his head off. Dad doesn't notice, of course. "It's warm out there! You feel that? It's like summer in January!"

I turn down the volume on the stereo and try not to look impressed by the beautiful weather. I'm actually pretty psyched about it. Speeding semis? It's not just the semi, either. The closer we get to our new home, the crazier people drive.

"Look!" Dad shrieks. I follow his pointing to a road sign for the turnoff from Interstate 15, which we're on, to California Highway 91. "Toward 'beach cities,'" he reads, pushing me playfully. "Did you see that? 'Beach cities,' kid! We're going toward *beach* cities! It's a whole new life for us. You'll see."

"But I didn't *want* a whole new life. *You* did."

I have to admit, but only to you and never to my dad, that there is something sort of exciting about moving toward beach cities. I know as well as anyone that what you see on TV is pretty much geared to fool and brainwash you. But you have to admit, California is a pretty cool place. In theory. I'm not going to get too excited yet.

Dad takes the turn onto Highway 91, and I'm surprised by a couple of things. First, it's really hilly here. Second, it's pretty. It's like nature here. I mean, it's no Taos, but there's a lot of nature around. I didn't expect that. I could do some serious mountain biking here. You see high-rises and stuff on television. I didn't expect mountain peaks with snow on them. You never hear about those. All you hear about is the beach and Beverly Hills.

I shrug. "I guess it's pretty here."

I cringe as I feel my father smiling at me. I don't look at him, but I know him well enough by now to know that he's happy I said something nice. I haven't said anything nice for days. I can't stand the way he smiles when he's proud of me but thinks he's *won.*

"That's better," he says. "You'll see. It's gonna be awesome."

After about a million other interchanges and tolls, we wind up on something called Moulton Parkway. I think of a lava lamp, and this reminds me of Emily, who has two. We're in Orange County. In case you're wondering? Yes, it's beautiful. There are flowers on the medians of the freeways, big splashes of them in purples and reds. Grandma would like the freeways here. And yes, everyone has a nicer car than we do. Well, not *everyone,* but lots of people. I have never seen more BMWs, Lexuses, and Infinitis in one place. And Hummers, which I hate on principle. I don't get it. How can so many people have luxury cars? How can so many people have that many important things to talk about on their cell phones? How can people drive so fast without crashing all the time?

"Huge," I have to tell you, does not *begin* to describe how big it all is. Everything goes on forever. The freeways, the parkways, the lawns, the malls. The sun is bright, and the air, when I roll down my window, smells like I remember the ocean smelling from a trip we took to Florida when I was younger. It's the same smell from my dream, like salt and car exhaust, clean and dirty at the same time.

Dad looks at his map while he drives, and almost crashes the U-Haul about forty times. He's singing, too, "'If I were a rich girl, na na na na . . .'" People are honking at us and I want to hide. I'm, like, yes, this is my dad; he can't drive, he can't sing, he's not a rich girl. Yeah, he's lost. He's going the wrong way.

"Sorry," says Dad, fumbling with the gearshift. "I know it was around here somewhere."

It? The apartment. You know, the place we're going to *live*? It's already three o'clock, and Dad tells me we only have until five to unload everything. After five, there's no moving in or out of the apartment building. Outside, everything looks like a mini-mall. And the weirdest part is that nothing is natural. There are plenty of trees, flowers, lots of grass, but it all looks like someone arranged it by straightedge. The whole world is manicured like a movie set here.

Finally, Dad finds what he's looking for. He's been promising me for days that I'm going to love this place and its racquetball, volleyball, tennis courts, gym, and swimming pools. It's not just an apartment, he's reminded me, it's a *luxury* apartment.

The St. Moritz Resort Apartments aren't what I expected. I thought, you know, apartment building. In Taos, that means just what it sounds like. A building. With a parking lot. Made of adobe and falling apart. Usually there's a drunk guy in the parking lot or something. But *this* thing sits at the end of a fake cobblestone driveway behind big iron gates. It looks like a college campus. There are buildings, lots of them, and acres of lawns with walking paths and palm trees.

The buildings are stucco, like almost everything else I've seen so far, in pretty peaches and browns. People have flowers on their patios. A few people walk past, and they are fit, with tans and tennis racquets thrown over their shoulders. It does look like a resort. Pine and palm trees tower over everything. Impressive.

"Wow, Dad," I say. "Not bad."

"I told you," he gloats, happy to be winning again.

Dad drives the U-Haul to our building and parks on the blacktop in front of a small white garage door. Then we walk to the office to get our keys. The clubhouse has white walls and navy blue carpet, with luxurious sofas and potted plants everywhere. There's fresh coffee and tea for guests, and chocolate chip cookies. I down a cookie. I hadn't realized until right now how hungry I was. The place is huge, like everything else in Orange County. Except the women.

The saleswoman who greets us looks like a model from way back in the 1970s, real blonde with blue eyes. We don't have a lot of people who look like that in New Mexico, unless you count the Texan tourists, which I don't. She looks healthy. So do the other two saleswomen who work in the office. Dad tries to flirt with them, which basically makes me want to barf. Even barfier? They flirt back, and he laughs like he's *da bomb*. I'm, like, it's their *job* to flirt with you, Dad, but I don't say it. I just think it. Dad likes to believe he's a stud. Let him.

We return to the apartment, and Dad opens up the garage and takes me inside to show me around before we start unpacking. It's a three-story townhouse, with a garage and storage on the ground floor, a living room, dining room, kitchen, and half-bathroom on the second floor, and three bedrooms and two bathrooms on the top floor. The walls are cream-colored, the carpets beige. It's very clean and new and smells good. Basically, it's nothing like the apartments I've known in my life, which were these dumps where my mom used to smoke cigarettes and play blackjack.

"You can have any of the bedrooms you want," he tells me.

"Even the master?" I ask. It's big, with an attached bathroom and its own private balcony overlooking a vast green lawn with walking paths and palm trees.

"Yep," says Dad.

I pick the master, of course. Far as I'm concerned, Dad owes me, big-time.

An hour later, we have the U-Haul unloaded, and I'm starving. Dad forgot to mark the boxes, so we have no idea where the dishes and pots are. It's chaos in here. I go out on the balcony of my new bedroom for some fresh air and to get a look around. Dad finds me there and tells me he's going to return the moving truck and pick up some burgers on the way back. I've never had In-N-Out burgers, and Dad swears I'm going to love them. And then he's gone.

I'm alone.

I wander around the townhouse for a minute or two, trying to let it sink in that this is my new home. Don Juan is walking around with nervous cat legs, sniffing everything and flicking his tail. He doesn't know what to make of this, either. It's definitely nicer than the house we had back in New Mexico, which was old and kind of run-down. I mean, I thought my house was fine, but now I'm not so sure. Maybe I've been too negative about all this. Maybe it'll be okay.

I realize I have to pee again, and head to the master bathroom. My bathroom, thank you very much. It's got a big counter where I can put my makeup and stuff. I never had that back home. Whoever lived here before us left some toilet paper on the roll, and it's a good thing because not only do I have to pee, but God has decided this is the moment I'm going to get my period. Great. I don't know where the box is with my supplies in it. I wad up some toilet paper and stuff it in my underwear. Gross, I know. But you do what you have to do.

Finished with that nightmare, I go back out on the patio. On the patio next door sit two pimply, goofy-looking guys who are probably a little younger than me. They're not ugly or anything, but they certainly aren't cute. I'm surprised for a second, because part of me believed all guys in California would look like movie stars. I look away from them, because I don't like giving guys the impression I like them, especially when I don't. I also can't look directly at them because I have a weird feeling about them — it's not a bad feeling, just unusual. I feel like I really like them and want to protect them or something, but it's not exactly me feeling it.

One of them startles me with a hello. I mean, I *think* it's a hello. What he actually said was "'Sup."

"Hey," I say, to be polite. The cramps are starting. Yep. There they are. Just my luck. I look at the guys briefly, and the sound rushes through my head. It's like the sound of my own blood, only really loud. I hear voices in the middle of the noise, and crying. Great. There's something creepy going on already. I think of my grandmother and realize I've left the stone necklace in the U-Haul. I should probably take better care of it, but whatever. I hope my dad gets it out of the ashtray. I have a feeling I could use it right now.

"You just move in?" one of the guys asks. He talks through his nose. I keep hearing a thunking-boing sound and wonder if it's part of the white noise in my head, but then I see it's just a basketball. He's got one and he's dribbling it, even though both guys are sitting in lawn chairs.

"Yeah, we just moved in today."

"Cool," they say in unison. I look away again because the wave of sound is coming back. What is that crying? It's awful. It's like a little girl.

They ask me my name, then tell me theirs: Keoni and Kerani. They ask me where I'm from, and I tell them. I don't ask them anything because I don't really feel like talking to possibly hormonal male strangers with my dad gone, and I don't want to encourage the weird noise to come back.

Then they ask me if I'm Asian.

"No," I say, surprised. I look at them, and the voices come back, clearer this time, speaking a language I've heard before but don't understand. *Dandan kowaku naro!* It's a shrieking voice, a little girl. *Dandan kowaku naro!* Then a man's voice, deep and menacing inside my head. *Utsubuse ni natte kudasai.*

"You look Asian," says one of them, I think it's Keoni but who knows.

"I'm Hispanic," I say. "Mexican."

"We're Japanese and black," says the other one.

Japanese. I feel a tingle in my spine and realize that's the language I'm hearing. There's a little girl pleading in Japanese, and the man is yelling at her. Have you ever felt like you're going completely crazy? That would be me right now. I must be tired. I don't like to tell people about the "voices," because I know they'd think I was insane, even though I know I'm not. It's like listening to people talking in another room, only that room is in a different universe.

I don't say anything in response to the guys' ethnicity because I'm not sure why they've told me this or how exactly I'm supposed to respond. They ask me if I'm going to be going to public school. Back home, pretty much everyone goes to public school. I tell them my dad has me registered at Aliso Niguel High School and that I'm supposed to start tomorrow.

"That's where we go," one of them says. He doesn't look happy about it. Then, as quickly as it started, the noises stop.

I finally look at them longer than a second. They're wearing baggy basketball shorts and white undershirts with skinny black neckties. They match completely, down to their dirty, unlaced basketball sneakers. One of them keeps dribbling the basketball on the patio floor, which makes me think of Ethan. I miss him, but right now I can't really even remember what he looks like. I realize with a shock, that my new neighbors are twins. Duh. I should have figured that one out before. Anyway, one has longer hair than the other, but they are otherwise identical, down to the zits on their foreheads.

"You like it there?" I ask of the school.

"It's okay," they say in unison. Then the one on the right says, "Niguel's a good place if you're popular."

The two boys look at each other sadly, and it wouldn't take a brain surgeon to guess they're probably not the popular type.

"If you're *not* popular," the other one says, "you hear from the haters."

"Every single day," says his brother. They look depressed.

"Haters?" I ask.

"Yeah. The school's full of them," says the one with longer hair.

"And if you're not one of them?" asks the short-haired one.

They say the last part in unison: "Aliso Niguel blows."

4

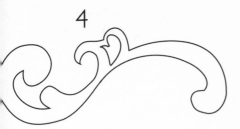

Dad gets home with the In-N-Out burgers half an hour later. I'm actually relieved, because I've run out of things to say to Keoni and Kerani Jackson. They only want to talk about chess, a "sport" over which they get entirely *too* excited, and some video game called *Conker: Live & Reloaded*. I could care less about Xboxes, and it seems like that's all these two care about. The more I talk to them, the more I hear that Japanese man's voice, too. *Utsubuse ni natte kudasai.*

"Pasquala Rumalda Quintana de Archuleta! Your *delicioso* burger is getting cold, *Chinita*!" calls my dad. The twins look at each other like they want to laugh. I wouldn't blame them if they did. I'd like them better, actually. Anyone who laughs at my dad is okay with me. They have a sense of humor. That's a plus. If I'm going to have to see them all the time, they might as well be funny.

"It's my full name," I say. "I have to go." They look down and shrug, which I assume is an Orange County goodbye from guys who like chess and wear ties with T-shirts. I'm just guessing here, but ten-to-one, social skills aren't their strength.

I enter the house-o-boxes. I feel like I just shrank and fell into a toy chest of wooden blocks at a preschool, or like that mouse in *If You Take a Mouse to School,* when he makes a house for himself. How will we ever get these unpacked? I have to start school tomorrow, too. Where are my *clothes*?

I find my father dancing around the kitchen with white paper sacks in his hands. I'm not sure, but it sounds like he's whistling "Toxic" by Britney Spears. "'Don't you know that you're tox-ic?'" he sings. Yup. Good guess on my part. I am now certain my dad is singing "Toxic" by Britney Spears. Moments like this make you wonder if there is a God. Don Juan circles Dad's ankles, crying for food. Don Juan is always hungry. He thinks that every time someone goes near a kitchen, that means it's time to open a can of food for Don Juan.

"What?" says Dad, looking at me. He examines himself like he thinks he might have something gross on his shirt or pants. Then he looks at me again. "What's wrong?"

"Nothing," I say. I'm not about to tell him I'm hearing terrified girl voices in Japanese, or that I just met two of the goofiest kids I've ever met. I'm not about to tell him I miss my house, my friends, my life. I mean, I told him all that already, but did it help? Nope. Better to be quiet.

Dad turns away, dancing, and sings, "'And I love what you do, don't you know that you're toxic?'" He rolls his hips on the "toxic." Oh. My. God. I would like to think of something smart and annoying to say, but I'm speechless. My psycho dad thinks he's a Backstreet Boy.

"What?" he asks again. "What's that face for?"

"Nothing," I say. Britney Spears? My father is singing Britney Spears? At least Gwen Stefani was somewhat cool, but Britney? "Did you get my necklace out of the ashtray in the U-Haul?" I ask.

Dad stares at me with a blank look. "Did you ask me to?"

"No. But I left it in there."

"Paski!" he says. He's got the disappointed-father face going now. "Why didn't you tell me? I can't read your mind!"

"I forgot."

Dad finds the phone and dials 411. He asks for the number of the U-Haul place and then waits on the line while he's connected. After about ten minutes of sighing, waiting, and explaining over and over what we're looking for, he hangs up. "They have it. You're lucky. I'll get it for you tomorrow."

"Cool," I say.

"A thanks would be nice," replies Dad.

"Thanks." I try not to sound sarcastic but fail.

"You need to learn to take better care of your things, Paski."

"Please don't lecture me right now," I say.

"I'm not lecturing. I'm offering fatherly advice."

"Same thing."

"Wanna eat on the balcony?" he asks. This is Dad's way of trying to change the subject. Just talk about something new. Pretend we weren't just arguing, sort of. I think of Kerani and Keoni.

"Uh, no. How about right here on the floor? We could use this box as a table."

Dad shrugs and goes along with me. He does that a lot. Sometimes my dad is very easy to get along with. "I know something's bugging you, though, for you to forget about the necklace like that," he says as he sits cross-legged on the floor across the box from me.

"Nothing's wrong," I respond.

"Whatever," says my dad. He actually puts his thumbs together to make the shape of a W with his hands. It has to be a midlife crisis. There's no other excuse, really. He opens the bags and unloads the food. There are two enormous burgers with everything gooped on them, and two giant orders of fries that smell like a heart attack. He's also gotten me a Diet Coke, gigantic size. "Dig in, Punkin," he says as he unwraps his burger. "I am telling you, these are the best hamburgers you've ever had."

I eat the food. It's as good as my dad said it would be, but I don't want him to get all superior about it, so I keep my thoughts to myself. The meal has also made me feel majorly, hugely fat. What I really need right now is to get out and ride my bike. I've been tucked up in the moving truck for days. I'm full of grease. The cramps from my period are getting pretty bad, and I've found that the best thing for that is to work out. Plus, I want to get a look around this town — without my dad.

"Can I go for a ride after this?" I ask.

Dad looks at me like I've asked if I can walk to the moon. "Bike riding?"

"Yeah, you know, a bike? It has pedals, handlebars, wheels, I think you've seen them before. Bi-cy-cle."

Dad gives me the "ha ha, very funny" face. "But we just got here. Where would you go?" He chews like a bull, the food going round and round forever. He's got a mustard smudge on the tip of his nose, but I'm not going to tell him, because I know he is trying to manipulate me right now.

See, most parents would just say no, right? Like, "No, you can't go bike riding." But not *my* dad. He's got this strategy where he thinks he can get me to do what he wants me to do by asking me a million questions and letting me come to my (his) own conclusions about things. He has no clue that I see right through him.

"I want to ride to my new school," I say. "I need to know how to get there tomorrow."

Dad's eyebrows shoot up in surprise as he realizes I'm making sense. "That's true," he says. "I was going to take you tomorrow, though."

"I don't want you to take me."

Dad holds a french fry up to the light and turns it over, as if it were a scrap of gold he found at the bottom of an archaeological dig. "Are these not the finest fries you've ever tasted?" he asks the fry. I assume he is talking to me, however.

"They're very good. So can I go riding?"

"Do you know where the school is?"

"Emily and I did a MapQuest," I say.

"A what?"

"Online. You put in addresses and they give you directions."

"You can do that?" he asks. Dad is not what you'd call techno-savvy. He's like a kid who was raised by wolves and brought back to civilization, always surprised about things.

"Yep."

He shrugs and nods, impressed. "Go ahead," he says. "But wear your helmet. And be careful. And get back here before dark. Take my cell phone. Call me if you need me."

"I don't know the number here."

"Ah." He jumps up and digs through some boxes until he finds a phone. Then he plugs it into the jack in the kitchen and calls the operator to ask her what our phone number is. He's lost the paper where he wrote it. He scribbles it on a napkin from the burger place and hands it to me. Our new area code is 949. I can just hear Emily saying, "You're kickin' it in the 949." She'd say something like that.

"Be careful out there," Dad says. "You're the most important thing in my life, and I don't want anything to happen to you."

I smile at him and pop another fry into my mouth. "Watch out, Dad," I say.

"Why?"

"You almost sounded like a real parent for a second there."

Dad smiles at me. He looks like he's going to cry through that smile for some reason. I realize that even though he's a total loser, I'm pretty lucky to have him.

5

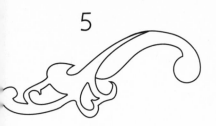

After dinner, I dig through the boxes until I find one with my clothes (and tampons, thank God!) in it. I fix my leak and put on a pair of cycling shorts I haven't worn since the summer, along with a long-sleeved red T-shirt Emily gave me. The shirt is from a Canadian company called Roots that Emily loves. It feels cozy and fits just right. Emily dresses like someone on a college campus in a movie. She's very preppy but cool at the same time. I put on my old army-green fanny pack and bring Dad's cell phone, the map to my school, and the napkin with our new home number. I pull my fingerless cycling gloves over my hands, snap my cycling shoes onto my feet, pull my hair back in a low ponytail. I clomp down to the first level of the townhouse and find my dad unpacking a box of kitchen stuff. He tells me to be careful and gives me a hug. He makes a point of hugging me at least once a day.

My bike is in the trunk of the Corolla, in the garage, with the quick-release front tire popped off. I put it together quickly and find my helmet and pink iPod Mini inside the trunk, too. I'm a little tired of the mix on my iPod. I need to upload some new songs, but now that I can't borrow Emily's high-speed connection, it's going to be tricky. Maybe I can talk my dad into getting cable and a high-speed Internet connection, you know, now that he's a *mack daddy* and all. He used to be all "no TV in this house," but now I don't know. Now he's Mr. Hollywood.

I stick the speaker buds in my ears, hit play, and the Black Eyed Peas' latest comes on. I like upbeat, funky music for when I'm riding, something I can lose myself in. Something that inspires me to take on the hard slopes and bumpy paths. I'm happiest when I'm challenged, and I'm proud to say I've never had a bad fall. I have crazy good balance, one of my gifts — the others being an ability to draw and the whole thing with dreaming about things that actually happen later on.

This song *jams.* I'm good to go.

I've memorized the map. Northwest on Summerfield toward Aliso Creek. Left on Aliso Creek to Terrace View Drive. End at Wolverine Way. Less than two miles in all, a breeze of a ride for me. I'm used to riding at least ten miles a day, even in the freezing cold, and usually a lot farther than that.

I take Summerfield out of the apartment complex up a slight hill. I stick to the sidewalk in the shade of big trees. The intersection at Aliso Creek is huge. It looks like a freeway to me. But this is just a *street* here. Like I said, everything is massive. There are six lanes and so much traffic I'm afraid to cross against the light. I press the walk button and wait for the white walking-man light to come on, and then I cross Aliso Creek to wait again to cross Summerfield. I ride slowly and take it all in. To my right is a big mini-mall, which, signs tell me, is called the Aliso Viejo Town Center. But unlike Taos, where the town center was historical and sort of charming, this thing is brand-spanking-new and all about shopping. There's a big Barnes & Noble and a PetSmart. It's all very pretty but so shiny and new and perfect I almost don't trust it. Compared to the majesty of Taos, this place feels like it lacks a certain kind of soul.

Five minutes later, I spy a mountain range to the left. There's a layer of smog over the mountains, and I can barely see them. As I ride, I feel blasts of cold, moist air gust over the small hills to my right, from the ocean I have yet to see but which I know is very close. I wonder if there's anywhere in these mountains or hills I could ride. I'd hate to break my training. I have plans to compete professionally one day, and I don't want to get soft riding on flat land.

My iPod mix shifts to a Spanish-language song by Maria Matto, a new singer my dad turned me on to but who I really like. She's soulful and makes me think of home. The song, *Me Siento Perdida,* makes me want to haul, to cut loose and free, but I don't see anyplace here where I might do something like that; just asphalt and traffic lights. Maybe once I get to the school, there'll be walls or something to jump. I've got days' worth of pent-up energy in my bones. I need to get it out.

I get to Wolverine Way and turn left toward the school. I know from the map that it's close to here, maybe two blocks. But what I *didn't* know from the map was that the school was two blocks away down a super-steep hill. Yeah, boy! I lift off the seat and let the bike go, zooming. I love the feel of the wind on my face — along with Maria's big, strong voice, it makes me feel free. I know this hill and I are going to be mad good friends, man. As I zoom down, I pass steep hills on the right, landscaped and leading to what looks like apartments or condos. I could have some fun on those hills, too, and I think that on the way back I'll give them a shot.

I round a corner and see Aliso Niguel High School at the bottom of the hill. It's huge, like everything else around here. The main building is brown and gray brick, with the usual barracks on one side and endless playing fields all around. I gasp as I see a huge yellow pyramid behind the school; some kind of a business building built to look like a pyramid. I get chills. That's exactly the building I dreamed about.

I take a quick look behind me, see that no one's coming, and jam across the street, hopping the curb with a little wheelie. I stop on a bluff and look down at my new school. It's pretty, with green grass flowing everywhere. Because it's Sunday, there aren't a lot of kids around, but there are a few. Some boys with skateboards do tricks along the walls and steps, in clear defiance of the signs that say NO SKATEBOARDING. Some kids sit in parked cars doing things they don't want people like me to know about, so I don't look too hard. I see guys practicing on what looks like a football field behind the school, and a couple of girls playing tennis. The school is well equipped. It looks like a college campus or a private school. The cars the kids drive are nicer than the cars grown-ups drive back in Taos. I get the sense that this is a school for the rich girls Gwen Stefani and my dad sing about.

I check out the hill I'm standing on top of, a scrappy bit of nature, wild with grasses and an old overgrown dirt road. I don't know what used to be here. I could take the street down, you know, the easy way? But I'm feeling *pumped*. I need the feel of the bike bucking under my body like some kind of wild animal. I need the rush of uncertain arrival. I look around for some kind of authority figure who might try to stop me. Nobody's around. Perfect.

I hit replay on the Maria Mattos song, check the helmet to make sure it's on right and tight, and crank the song. I'm *taking* this hill, suckers, and I'm landing on that campus in *style*. "This is for Em and Janet," I whisper to myself. "Paski in the house, representing Taos."

I point my bike into the weeds and grass, right down the hill. It's steep but nothing like what I'm used to in the Rocky Mountains. I can feel eyes on me, I don't know where from, as I jump and hop the bike through the plants, over a couple of big rocks. Bike-dancing. I love the feel of my muscles as they flex in symphony. I think my ability to see things in my mind helps me do this kind of thing without disaster, because I just *feel* where to go. I don't *look,* exactly. It's hard to explain. But I do know for sure that I never feel as alive as I do when I'm taking on the world this way. And I've never fallen. Not once.

I squeeze the hand brakes so I can hop the bike sideways down the hill in time to the rocking song. I know I'm good at this, that I'm showing off, but that's how I am. If I have to go here, I want to *own* this freakin' school. I'm not going to let these California kids with their fancy cars and fancy school tell me who I am. That's what I'm feeling as I zip and flip down the hill. I'm like a top someone set loose. I'm like a wild horse. Almost to the bottom of the hill now, I pull one of my wildest tricks and spin the bike 180 degrees, riding backwards for a moment before flipping it again and doing a wheelie all the way down. I feel heat blast through my abs. *Yeah, girl.* This is what I'm talking about.

The smooth surface of the road next to the school feels wimpy after the wilds of the hillside. I'm pumped. I loved it. I turn the bike and scale the hill again to repeat my performance. I'm in my element, rocking. I've forgotten all about the cramps, my dad, the whole nightmare I'm living.

After the second run, I get off the bike and walk it to the school. I love the power I feel twitching through the muscle fibers in my legs. No matter what happens here tomorrow, no matter how much of an outcast I end up being — and don't new kids always get cast out somehow? — they won't be able to take from me the power I feel on my bike. I take off my helmet, yank the rubber band out of my hair, and shake it loose. I remove the ear-buds and stand still to take a look around. The silence is embarrassing. You forget when you're listening to your iPod that the rest of the world can't hear what you're hearing. I listen to the wind. And the other sound, a low constant drone, metallic, motorized. What is it? Traffic. It occurs to me that with all the huge roads and parkways and whatnot here, this low groan must be the backdrop to everything all the time.

"Hey, you," someone calls. A male someone. I look around cautiously, thinking there's no way someone is going to be talking to me. I don't see anyone. "Hey," I hear again. "On the bike. I'm over here."

I look as casually as I can to the left and see a guy in faded jeans and a tight-fitting zip-front black sweatshirt, the kind with racing stripes on the sleeves and a turtleneck. The kind that shows off a young man's muscles if he has them, and this guy *does*. Wow. He's straddling a motorcycle, holding his red helmet like a football. He is *cute*. And not just *cute* but cute in a way I have *never* seen in person. He looks like an actor or a model. He has his chin held up high in kind of a cocky pose, but there's a small smile on his full lips and a big smile in his blue eyes beneath the dark brows. With all due love and respect to Ethan Schaefer, this motorcycle boy is the best-looking guy I've *ever* seen. Something deep in my belly responds to the look of him, and I try to stop my heart from thudding in my chest. My heart keeps beating hard. I'm afraid he can hear it.

"That was pretty impressive," he says to me. He nods in a sexy way and grins at the hill. "Real impressive, in fact."

I glance at the hill, too, and try to act casual. "What, that? Me?" I shrug and realize I sound like *such* a dork. I also realize that it might not be all that hard to forget about Ethan Schaefer.

"Yeah, girl," he says, stepping on the pedal to start the motorcycle. I was going to thank him, but I doubt he can hear me now. He doesn't put on the helmet. Rather, he eases the motorcycle closer to where I am, and once he's right next to me, he cuts the motor again. He looks me up and down with that cocky smile, and I feel like I'm going to pass out.

"You don't go here. I'd know if you did. No doubt."

He smiles, and dimples appear on either side of his pretty mouth. He removes his helmet. He's tan, with brownish black hair cut in a short style that he spikes up a little bit in front with gel or something. He smells like cologne and summertime. What is that? Coconuts? His hands are large and strong, with perfectly clean, round oval nails. He is gorgeous. I want to touch him.

"I start here tomorrow," I say.

His nice, friendly, sexy eyebrows shoot up in pleasure. "Yeah?" he asks. "Tomorrow, huh?"

I nod. He smiles and looks down at my belly with a satisfied smile.

His eyes drag slowly across my breasts and neck up to my lips. His gaze lingers there, and then he snaps his eyes up to my own. Oh. My. God. He is so confident. I've never seen a guy my own age this confident. My hand jumps to my front instinctively, and I'm horrified to feel that my shirt rode up and my belly button is exposed. I pull the cloth back down.

"Aw, don't do *that*," he says, flirty. One side of his mouth rises higher than the other. I can't breathe right in front of him.

"I don't usually show my stomach like that," I say.

"You should," he says.

"It's cheesy."

"Nah. It's a nice thing to see. Your belly. Believe me."

I blush and can't keep looking at his eyes. "Thanks."

"I'm Chris." He holds a hand out to shake, like a businessman, never breaking eye contact, and the whole time with that unbelievable grin.

"Paski," I say as we shake. His hand is warm and I feel prickles of electricity shoot through his hand to mine and up my arm straight to my chest. He is the most alive boy I've ever met. I can feel life force in people, creativity, passion, all of that, and this guy has it in excess.

"Paski. Cool name. You have a last name, Paski?"

"Archuleta." I pull my hand away because it seems like Chris wants to keep holding it. He's got a real seductive way of looking at me that leaves me nervous. I can tell you right now, this guy has girl experience, and he knows exactly what to do. It's terrifying. I love it and hate it at the same time, because this guy seems like he could have any girl he wants — and I bet he does, all the time.

"A *Latina*." He says the word in a pretty decent Spanish accent, not patronizing or anything. He smiles, and I see that his teeth are whiter than my dad's *new* ones, only this guy's are real. It's almost like they flash with lights. Like his mom never let him eat sugar. He points to his strong-looking chest and says, "Chris Cabrera." He pronounces his last name in the same strong and convincing Spanish accent, as opposed to my dad's strong *fake* Spanish accent. Other than that, his English is perfect. Perfectly perfect.

"Nice to meet you," I say. "You speak Spanish?"

"We summer in Barcelona." He uses "summer" as a verb? No one in Taos uses "summer" as a verb — none of the locals, anyway. "My mom's from there. My dad's from Mexico City, and we have a house near there, too, in San Miguel de Allende. The artists' colony?" He rolls his eyes like there's something wrong with San Miguel de Allende being an artists' colony.

"You have a house in Spain and another in Mexico?" I ask.

He nods and shrugs like this is no big deal. "Yeah," he says. "But that's it."

I don't bother to tell him my dad and I are lucky to have an apartment — one single little apartment — *here*. I ask him if he goes to this school. Chris nods, and I wonder if everyone at Aliso Niguel High "summers" and has more than one home.

"Where'd you learn to ride like that?" he asks me. I tell him I'm from Taos and that I trained in the mountains. He says his family skis in Taos sometimes, and then backtracks to apologize for making fun of artists' colonies.

"Taos is an artists' colony, right?" he asks.

"My dad's an artist," I say. It's sort of true.

"Really? My mom's an art dealer."

I don't say anything, because I don't know what to say. *Great, your*

53

people pimp my people? He licks his lips and asks, "You ever thought of riding motocross? You'd *rock* some motocross. I can tell."

I shrug. It's occurred to me to try my jumping skills on a motorcycle, but we don't have enough money for that. Chris asks about it as if everyone in the world has that kind of money. "My grandma has a Harley back in Taos." He laughs like I've told a joke. I wish I had. I guess not a lot of people have grandmas with Harleys. "No, really," I say. "I used to ride that around a little."

"Motocross is a lot more your style," he says. "You'd rock."

I wonder what jumps would feel like on a motorcycle. If we could afford it, I'd do it in a heartbeat, but I doubt my dad's going to spring for one anytime soon.

"What grade are you in?" he asks. He still looks cocky and cute. I tell him I'm sixteen, a junior. He tells me he's a junior, too, and grins like this means he wants to kiss me all over. I get shivers.

"You do motocross?" I ask. He nods, and I feel butterflies in my belly. In addition to sometimes seeing things that are going to happen in the future, my "vision" lets me know pretty quickly after meeting someone whether or not they're a good person. I get a very good, warm feeling about this Chris Cabrera guy, even though he *is* cocky. I have a flash pass my mind of him kissing me, of me on a motorcycle, but I can't tell whether this is just wishful thinking.

"Well," he says, looking around like it's time for him to go, "I know three girls who won't be happy to know a beautiful girl who rides like you is starting at our school tomorrow."

"What? Why not?" He thinks I'm *beautiful*? No. He did *not* just say that, did he? I'll have to die if he did. I'm too young to die. Poor Ethan. I shouldn't even be thinking about another guy like this.

He laughs to himself. "Nah," he says with a shrug. "Don't listen to me. I don't know that for sure. Don't let me scare you. I'm sure you'll have a good time here. It's a cool place." He looks like he might be lying. "Overall."

"I don't understand," I say, but I feel something dark inside me, as if what he has just said makes sense with the dreams I've been having.

"You'll find out soon enough," he says, putting on his helmet and starting the engine again. I notice that the motorcycle, his clothes, everything about him looks very expensive. Very shiny and new, all of it in just the right place. Like Aliso Viejo. "I'll look for you tomorrow, Paski Archuleta. I'll look forward to it."

"Yeah, okay."

He smiles at me as he drops the clear plastic face cover, then keeps smiling to himself as he pulls away on his motorcycle. I watch him go. He stands and leans in to the hill, his rear end perfectly sculpted in the jeans. Chris Cabrera is not just gorgeous; he's also graceful. A pro. Seductive, irresistible. My heart, which has recovered from the ride, is still pounding — for *him*. I can't wait to tell Emily and Janet. They'd die if they saw this guy. Seriously.

As the smooth roar of Chris Cabrera's bike engine fades up the hill, I stand alone on the empty campus of Aliso Viejo High School, the sky darkening overhead. The sun is setting. When did it get so late?

I blink up at the soft twinkling of the emerging stars overhead and feel a cold gust of wind come over me, a salty blast of chill straight from the heart of the ocean. Night is coming, and I want to go home. I just don't know if I'll ever feel at home *here*.

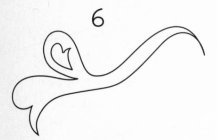

6

So, if my dad hadn't given me good enough reason to *resent* him yet —
you know, ripping me away from my life back home and all that — he
has, right now, just given me *another* really good reason.

"You *what?*" I demand.

I'm so angry, I feel the blood rush to my head. I've just finished
showering, and I'm in my white bathrobe at the dining table, eating
the oatmeal he made for both of us. It's mushy and cold. My dad sucks
at cooking. He's across the table from me, already dressed in his
FUBU shirt and baggy jeans. He has some kind of "studio meeting"
this morning, and he's leaving soon, stopping to pick up my necklace
on the way. It looks like he tried to put a red color in what's left of his
hair, but I don't have the energy to ask him. He's starting to remind
me of a really old pop star, like Bobby Brown, who's trying too hard
to connect with the youth.

"I arranged for you to have a peer mentor from school eat lunch
with you today." He takes off the black horn-rimmed glasses and

polishes them with his napkin. Is that an earring he's wearing? A little tiny diamond in his left earlobe. Oh. My. God.

"What does that *mean*? A peer *mentor*?" I ask. I've suddenly lost my appetite.

Dad sips his mug of coffee, crosses one leg over the other. He's got his laces untied like all the kids back home used to. The sneakers look like elephant feet all round. How sad. "It means that the administration has picked a cool kid from your grade to agree to eat lunch with you."

I choke on my orange juice. "What? Dad! How could you *do* that to me?" Doesn't he know that any kid the *administration* thinks is cool is going to *not* be?

"I was trying to help," he says. He uncrosses his legs and sets down the mug. He leans forward with his "listening" face on. He points to his eyes to get me to look at him again.

"Help?" I repeat. "You think that's helping? By getting some *weirdo* I don't even *know* to eat *lunch* with me? Why would you do that?"

"It can be really hard to start a new school," says my dad. He shrugs and plants his elbows on the tabletop. He's still staring into my eyes with that sensitive look.

"Great," I say sarcastically. I feel sick. "Now the whole school is going to know that I couldn't make a *real* friend. Dad! What is wrong with you?"

"They assured me it's very discreet. And I would appreciate it if you didn't talk to me that way."

"Have you never *met* high school kids?" I ask him. "This is *exactly* the kind of thing everyone loves to talk about. My God, Dad!" I fold my arms across my chest and use my feet to push my chair away from the table. I think I'm going to be sick.

"You should eat," says Dad. "Breakfast is the most important meal of the day."

"I'm not hungry. I can't go to school today. I'm sick."

"Paski, don't be like that."

"Like *what*? Wanting to have a shred of dignity on my first day of school? *God,* Dad. Are they going to make me wear a special tag, too, something like 'Loser new girl'? Or how about 'Kick me, I'm new'? That would be perfect."

"I'm sorry." He looks so hurt.

I say, "I *hate* this. I hate being here, this apartment, this breakfast, this city, everything."

"You don't mean that," says my dad. "You're speaking in anger. Count to ten and let's try to talk this out."

I glare at him. "You're wearing an earring," I say. Dad's hand jumps to his earlobe, and he blushes. "An *earring,*" I repeat, like an accusation.

"And?" he asks. "Your dad can't ice himself?"

Ice himself? No, he *didn't.* I stand up and turn toward my room. "Just do me a favor, ice man. *Don't* try to help me anymore, okay?"

"Okay," says my dad in such a small, sad voice that I instantly feel guilty. How does he do that? "I'm sorry, Paski. I was trying to help. I didn't *know.*"

"Yeah." I take the stairs toward my room so I can go get dressed for my first day of school, where, apparently, I have a date with my own doom. "Well, now you do."

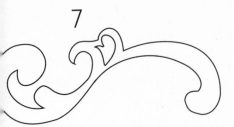

7

I'm wearing a pair of jeans and a simple black T-shirt, my usual outfit. I wear a pair of green Converse sneakers laced very loosely. I've got my hair down, a little messy, but messy in a styled way. I don't want to look like I'm trying too hard. Actually, I want to look like I've spent the day at the beach and I'm super-healthy and irresistible.

I ride the almost two miles to school, hungry but jumpy with nerves. I have a sick feeling about the peer mentor, but there's something else I can't pin down, a discomfort I can't name. I have a feeling Ethan has someone else already. There are times in life where you don't really want to know the whole story, like now. I don't need to know in my gut that Ethan already forgot about me. I need to have the illusion that he's still my boyfriend. Sometimes, being psychic sucks.

Basically, I don't want this day to go badly. Dad offered again to drive me and help me find the school office, where I'm supposed to go to check in, but I was like, "No, thanks. I'll find the office on my own." It's bad enough to have a peer mentor waiting to laugh at me. I don't need to give my "peers" any other reasons to make fun of me, like a dad with a FUBU shirt and "ice" in his ear, who tries out every new slang word that bubbles up from the bowels of BET. I really don't.

I get to the top of the hill on Wolverine Way and stop the bike to look down at the school. The parking lot is filled with cars, and my soon-to-be peers are walking toward the building, hanging out in clumps on the grass or sitting on low walls. So far they don't look like they dress all that differently from the kids back home. The usual stuff. Jeans and T-shirts. Sneakers. I see a few girls hobble past in hoochie outfits, but every school has those kinds of girls. *Las hoochies,* we called them back in Taos. They usually have issues. I think my mom was one of them back in her day, which is a big part of the reason I have always gone out of my way not to be one of them, but not to be mean to them, either. I feel sorry for them.

Cars ease down the hill past me, filled with more kids. A few of them turn to look at me, and I avoid eye contact. My heart pounds. From this height, they look like kids at any other school, but when you look at them in their cars, you can see that this is not your average high school. Kids drive past in BMWs, Hummers, Mercedes-Benzes, and all sorts of luxury cars. Back in Taos, we actually had kids who came to school on horseback. I don't want to be here. I don't know how to navigate this place.

I take the iPod earbuds out of my ears and remove my helmet. I shake my hair loose and take a deep breath. Instantly I hear very loud, very guitar-heavy music. I recognize it: "Shut Up," by Simple Plan, one of my favorite mountain-conquering songs. It's blasting from a car behind me. I turn and see a bright red convertible, a Lexus, with the top down and a beautiful girl driving it. Ugh.

My heart races in competition. I don't want it to, but it does. Law of the jungle. Two other pretty girls are in it with her, one in the front and one in the back. They sing along: " 'It seems like every day I make mistakes, I just can't get it right, it's like I'm the one you love to hate, but not today, so shut up shut up shut up, don't want to hear it . . .' "

The driver has a sweet oval face with very long brown hair cut in layers around her face, and it doesn't look like she's ever actually felt any of the things this song talks about. She wears a black ski-cap type of hat over her hair, which wouldn't look all that good on most girls but does on her. Her hair has golden highlights in it. She appears to be Chinese or Vietnamese or something, with large brown eyes and really pretty, healthy-looking smooth skin that glows in a perfect tan. It looks like she spends a lot of time in the sun, a total California girl. Her eyes seem brave and confident as they survey the other cars and the neighborhood. She nods her head in time to the dirty guitar riffs of the alternative rock song. She's an alternative chick, but a really pretty one. I can just imagine Ethan Schaefer's jaw hitting the floor if he saw her, and right now I'm glad he can't. Even if he is dating someone else already. I know he is. I feel it. Anyway, this is one of his favorite songs. It makes me hate her. It makes me hate him. I am filled with hate, and that's a super-unhealthy thing to be filled with, so I try to think about something else.

Usually girls are either grungy or pretty, but rarely have I seen them be both at once. This girl with the red Lexus pulls it off. With her ratty sweatshirt and perfect makeup, she's like the most beautiful tomboy in the world, and she looks like she knows it. Her eyebrows are the prettiest thing about her face, well tended, with a gentle arch in them. Her nose is cute, sort of round and small, and her full mouth curls up in a smile that looks like it could quickly turn into a snarl if you said the wrong thing to her. She looks like the kind of girl who bites. I know, without having to be told, that these are the girls Chris Cabrera warned me about. I *feel* it.

I don't want to have a vision right now, but it comes anyway, the driver girl in a cast, like she's broken her back or something. Suddenly I don't hate her anymore. I feel scared for her. I try to think of something else. I don't want to know things like this about people.

The other two girls in the car watch the driver closely and copy pretty much everything she does. They laugh when she laughs, sing when she sings. The one in the passenger seat has a colorful scarf wrapped around her head, with big wooden-looking earrings. Her hair is kinky, and her lashes might be artificial. She reminds me of Alicia Keys. The one in the backseat looks like she could be the long-lost sister of Britney and Jamie Lynn Spears, with tanned skin, big brown eyes, and straight blond hair that is so long I can't see the end of it. Something tells me these three girls are the Aliso Niguel High version of me, Em, and Janet back home. I gulp, because I know that if the three of us were lined up against the three of *them,* like in front of a panel of hipness judges, we'd lose. Big-time. These girls are beyond glamorous, beyond cool. They're like us on *steroids.*

I feel the clear, beautiful eyes of the driver turn toward me as she sings along to the song and beats time to the drums on the steering wheel. I try to look away before she catches me staring at her. Girls like her *want* to catch people staring at them. They live for it. I don't want to give her any more reasons to believe she's perfect. But I'm too slow. She sees me and looks me up and down with a mocking smile. She whispers something to the Alicia Keys look-alike, and then all three girls laugh at me. Great. I put the earbuds back in, strap on the helmet, and blast my own song just to get hers out of my head; it's a Gorillaz song that makes me think of home and Ethan. I take the hill in jumps and turns. It's pathetic to show off like this, I am aware of that. But I don't have anything else to defend myself with. That's how I feel right now, like I'm under attack by the pretty, rich girl in the Lexus. I can't afford a car like that, or clothes like that, or friends like that, but I can do *this*. That's what I tell myself. Money doesn't mean everything, does it? I've got other gifts. I try to smile like I don't care if anyone is watching me. I try to act like I don't care that I'm the new fish in this huge and apparently extremely wealthy pond.

I get to the bottom of the hill at the same time as the red Lexus. I remove the helmet, turn my head over, and shake out my hair. It's almost as long and shiny as the driver girl's. I stand up straight and look directly at the car. I will not look away. I force myself to keep looking. The Lexus has slowed to a crawl, and all three girls are staring at me. The two passengers seem worried; they look at each other like they're trying to figure out what to do. The driver girl looks angry for a split second, her cheeks red with rage, and then she turns the car toward the parking lot and laughs like she doesn't care.

Something tells me she *does* care.

Something else tells me that my life would be a lot better if she *didn't*.

8

I find my way to the office and get my schedule, locker assignment, and a map of the school. The secretary welcomes me to Aliso Niguel with an insincere smile, and then I'm on my own. My first class of the day is an advanced-placement English literature and composition course with a teacher called Mr. Big. No, I'm not kidding. It sounds like a bad episode of *Sex and the City*. I can hardly wait. Not.

I keep my earbuds in as I weave my way through the bodies in the hall. Crowded. That's what I notice first about this place. There are lots more people here than are at my school in Taos. I feel like a cow in a dairy. Except that the cows would have to be moving really fast. Everyone here moves a million miles an hour. They talk faster than they did back home, too. And for some weird reason, a lot of the kids look older than they should, or younger than they should.

I don't want to look too closely at anyone, but I do notice right away that this is a much more diverse school than mine, at least in terms of skin tone. There are kids of all colors here, and they all hang out with each other. This is contrary to what they try to show you in movies about kids our age. But somehow the thing that seems to matter the most here is *money*. There are kids of all colors, wearing expensive-looking clothes, hanging out together in clumps, and kids who don't look like they have as much money, hanging out together in clumps. At some point I'd love to sit back where no one can see me, and just analyze these people. I haven't figured out who's who yet, or who is popular, or whatever, but I will. Right now I'm focused on finding my classroom.

I can't find it.

I walk the way the map told me to, but there's no class there. The warning bell rings, and kids sprint past me in the quickly emptying hallways. Great. I don't know where I'm going. So not only am I going to be the loser new girl, I am also going to be late to class. I stand in the middle of the hall staring at the map with a confused look on my face, and hear a familiar voice.

"Where you trying to go?"

I look up and see one of the twins from next door, in a pair of basketball shorts, with a T-shirt and tie, just like the first day I met him. I show him my schedule and the map. He takes the map and crumples it up to throw in the nearest trash can.

"This is crap," he says. "I'll take you."

"Which one are you?" I ask. I can't keep them straight yet. He calls out "Keoni" as he walks, without turning to look at me, like he's used to answering this question. He walks without moving his arms, on the tips of his toes. His backpack is secured tightly over both of his shoulders, and he has Xbox 360 stickers all over it.

When we get to the room, Keoni stands to one side of the door and looks at the floor somewhere near my feet.

"This is it," he says. "If you want someone to walk home with after school, me and Kerani can wait for you by the front wall, if you want."

I thank him just as a tall, tan, gorgeous blond guy who looks like he just stepped off *The O.C.* dashes down the hall toward the room. Seeing Keoni, the guy goes out of his way to bump into him, pretending it was an accident. Keoni almost falls down.

"Uh, sorry, *chess* boy," says the Chris Carmack–looking guy. Keoni looks away just as the guy says, "Not!"

Keoni shrugs in my general direction and slinks down the hall. I follow the good-looking guy in and hunt for the teacher. I can't bear to look too closely at the students themselves yet. I really don't like what I just saw. Keoni's a geek, yes, but he's a *nice* geek. He showed me my room, even though it probably made him late for his own class. He offered to walk home with me, just because. He didn't do *anything* to that guy. Why did the guy push him?

I see a young-looking man sitting behind the desk, with brown hair and dimples. He looks like a Ken doll, or a recently retired member of a boy band. *This* is Mr. Big? Does everyone at this school have to look like a movie star? I'm starting to understand why my dad thinks he needs new teeth and an earring. Everyone in Southern California seems to try extra hard to look good.

I approach the desk slowly, trying to make sure this guy isn't really one of the old-looking students I've seen around here. The man looks up and smiles at me, which instantly tells me he's the teacher. No high school student would smile at a stranger like that. Besides, he has wrinkles around his eyes.

"Can I help you?" he asks in a boyish voice. I half expect him to say "dude" at the end. I explain who I am and what I'm doing here. He nods and tells me he's been expecting me. For some reason he looks at my schedule to confirm that I'm in his class, then asks me if I have stopped at the book office to get my textbooks yet. I haven't. I didn't know I was supposed to, even though as he asks, it makes perfect sense. It's just that the people in the office didn't tell me to, and I was running late. The teacher doesn't appear to mind. He seems laid-back.

"We'll just find you someone to share a book with," he says. He looks up at the class just as the final bell rings. All the other kids have taken their seats. I muster up all my courage and look at my classmates. Everyone is staring at me. Or at least it feels like they are. And they all — or almost all — look like models.

No! I instantly spot the girl with the red Lexus sitting in one of the rows near the wall, three seats back. She's holding hands with the boy at the desk in front of hers. He has his back to the front of the class, facing her, and they seem very much in love. The guy wears Oakley sunglasses on the back of his neck, like he's got eyes back there or something. I've seen this a few times in the halls here. I don't think I ever saw a guy in Taos wear his sunglasses backwards on his neck, right on the nape like that. They do it here as a fashion statement, but I'm not sure what they're trying to say, exactly. I get a weird feeling, like there actually are eyes back there. That neck looks familiar.

"Ladies and gentlemen," says Mr. Big. "I want to introduce a new student. So if I could get your attention, please." He cracks his knuckles playfully and clears his throat. "That's nice teacher-speak for shut up and pay attention, wankers."

The teacher has a way of speaking that is very youthful, like he's one of us, or at least like he thinks he's one of us. The weird part is that everyone seems to like and respect him. They all stop chatting and either take their seats or turn to face us. Mr. Big stands up. His khaki cargo pants are fashionably ripped, like they're from Abercrombie & Fitch or something, and I see that he, too, wears Oakley sunglasses backwards on the nape of his neck. What? Weird.

My heart does a somersault in my chest when the boy who was holding hands with the Lexus girl turns around and I see that it's Chris Cabrera, the wicked-cute guy from last night. He's wearing a black T-shirt, like me, with a beige zip-front hooded sweatshirt. The sweatshirt looks like it's made out of a really expensive kind of cotton. He looks at me, and I can see his face drop with disappointment, like he's embarrassed that I just saw him holding hands with that girl. Like he's *caught.* I am only sixteen years old, but already I am tired of the way males seem to think it's okay to have more than one girlfriend.

Okay, I supposedly have a boyfriend back in Taos, but I know in my heart I really don't, that I'll never be with Ethan again. I had a vivid dream last night about him and his new girlfriend. I even know her name. It wasn't just a dream, because in the dream her name was Stacey; she looked like a beagle and she just started working at the bakery. She was a college freshman at the College of Santa Fe. I saw her face and everything, and then I woke up and called the bakery and asked if a girl named Stacey who was a freshman in college had started working there, and the girl who answered said, "Yes, this is Stacey. Who is this?" I hung up.

Anyway, I'm disappointed that this Chris Cabrera guy has a girlfriend. Disappointed he's a jerk like Ethan. I don't think I'm going to be

able to trust another guy for a long time. This Chris guy was so stinkin'
flirty with me last night, and now he's here doing the whole public-
display-of-affection thing with that *girl*. That perfect, pretty, rich *girl*.
He shouldn't have started it with me if he was going to come to school
and nuzzle up to some hottie the next day. That's just plain tacky.

"Everyone, this is Pas . . . Pas . . ." Mr. Big tries to read my name.
How is he the *English* teacher? I wonder. Shouldn't he have slightly
better reading skills than that?

"Paski," I say. "Just call me Paski."

He looks at me and grins. He's not bad-looking for an old guy. I bet
he sleeps with students. I mean, I bet there's no shortage of willing
students. I mean, I wouldn't do him, obviously, but I'm sure someone
around here would. Not that I know he would also be willing, but it's
hard to tell. Back in Taos, there was a writing teacher sleeping with a
couple of students. They do that, some teachers.

"Paski," he says. "Paski Archuleta. She comes to us from Taos, New
Mexico, and this is her first day. I'd like you all to say your names so
Paski can get an idea of who we are. First and last. Andrew, let's start
with you."

The teacher points to the same boy who pushed into Keoni as I was
entering the classroom. The stereotypical surfer-looking California
boy who, I am starting to realize, doesn't look all that much like most
of the people around here. I think Janet would dig him, even if he
pushes geek boys around. Maybe if I didn't know how mean he'd just
been to Keoni, I might even think Andrew was hot. I mean, he is hot.
No question. But if he was nicer, I might be interested in him.

Andrew is *very* tall, probably six-two, and *very* buff, with a square jaw and nice cheekbones. He wears a blue-and-red-striped shirt and ripped jeans. His short sandy-blond hair is messy in a way that looks good. He and Chris Cabrera share a look that tells me they're friends. Of *course* they are. They also happen to be the two hottest guys at school. Or at least they're the two hottest guys I've seen so far. I wanted to think better of Chris, though. Now I can't, because not only is he a flirt behind his girlfriend's back, but he's friends with a mean guy who pushes defenseless chess geeks in the hall. Maybe my instincts about Chris — that he's very cool and kind — are way off.

Andrew smiles at me in a way that lets me know he thinks I'm cute. He winks. That's so cheesy. So why am I actually *flattered* by it? I'll write it off to the fact that I've got the first-day jitters. I can feel a couple of the girls in the class getting tense about Andrew's apparent approval of me. They want him. And he knows it.

"I'm Andrew Van Dyke," he says, like this should mean something to me. "And I'm very single."

Mr. Big interrupts. "You know, Andrew, it would be good if you could say a little something more useful about yourself, such as what you like to do, or a hobby, so Paski can have a sense of who we are as people."

Andrew Van Dyke laughs out loud and rubs his chin with one hand as he sort of wiggles his hips in his seat. His sleeves are rolled up, and I can see the muscles of his forearms tense and relax. Wow. He's got to be some kind of athlete. He says, "Mr. Big, I can't tell this poor girl what I like to do. It wouldn't be appropriate." He pantomimes pulling a girl's hips into his own, pumping his arms. Another cute guy, this one buff and Asian-looking with a big, strong chin dimple, leans across the aisle to Andrew and gives him a high five. The kids in the class laugh the way they do when a popular guy says something mildly funny, like they're afraid not to.

Mr. Big looks at me. "Don't pay attention to that, Paski. Andrew's a joker and a dork." To Andrew, he says, "I'll tell her something. How about that? I forgot you guys are scared of making asses of yourselves in front of each other." Asses? Did the English teacher just curse in front of his students? Back in Taos, a teacher could get fired for that. "Andrew here is on the soccer team," says Mr. Big. "And, for the record, I'm the soccer coach."

"And he *sucks*," says Andrew. Everyone laughs again. "Just kidding, Bigsy." Who calls their teacher Bigsy and gets away with it? Again, weird.

"We're regional *champions*," says Mr. Big. "Don't listen to Andrew." I smile like this champion garbage impresses me, because the teacher clearly wants me to be impressed. But honestly, I'm trying to figure out why schools always let the coaches teach subjects like *English*. Shouldn't coaches stick to coaching? It was the same in Taos. The wrestling coach was my math teacher, and he spent the whole time talking about competitions and stupid things like that. He always flirted with the cheerleaders, too.

"Who's next?" asks Mr. Big. He looks at the cute guy who high-fived Andrew Van Dyke and says, "Tyler?"

Tyler looks like that actor from One Tree Hill, the buff one with the cleft chin. At mention of his name, he sort of blushes, which I find adorable. "Uh," he says. "I'm Tyler Ma. I play soccer. I like the beach." He looks at Mr. Big like he doesn't know what else to say.

Mr. Big says, "Tyler's parents are from China, right, Tyler?"

"My grandparents," says Tyler. "But it's no big deal. Oh, I have a girlfriend, and I'm the only guy at this school that's not a player."

"Oh, please," says the pretty girl from the Lexus.

"Shut up, Jessica," Tyler says to her.

"Whatever," she says.

"Okay, that's enough of that," says Mr. Big. "Thank you, Tyler. Now you, Mr. Cabrera." He looks at Chris.

Chris Cabrera laughs to himself like he doesn't want to participate in this game of introductions. He leans back a little in his seat and spreads his feet a little wider. He smiles that cocky grin at me, his eyes bunching up like he's going to laugh, and I get a flash vision of me kissing his belly as he leans back like that. He is beyond hot. He's burning. I erase the fantasy vision from my mind, and he's still grinning at me. I don't want to feel like my heart melts in my chest, but I do. He is still the most attractive guy I've ever seen, even if he flirts behind his girlfriend's back.

"Me," says Chris, with a laugh in his eyes. Like he's embarrassed but loving it, if that makes sense. "I'm next, huh?"

"Yes, Mr. Cabrera," says the teacher. "Please amuse us."

Chris clears his throat and gives me a secret smile before saying, "I'm Chris Cabrera. I ride motocross, and I play on the soccer team, too." For whatever reason, he doesn't pronounce his last name with a Spanish accent this time.

Everyone waits in silence, as if they usually expect more from him.

"That's it?" asks Andrew, turning to look at his friend. "Dude, that *sucked.*"

"Dude," says Tyler to Andrew. They high-five each other again, and everyone sort of laughs. These must be the popular boys.

Chris folds his arms on his chest, shrugs, and lifts his eyebrows like he doesn't have anything to add. He's not bothered by Andrew's criticism, not one bit. Chris is the most confident being I've ever seen.

Andrew turns to me. "Here's what you need to know. Chris is the freakin' man. Every girl in the school wants him. That's what he forgot to tell you."

Chris looks embarrassed but handles it by saying, "That's just what Andrew tells people so they don't notice *he's* the one that really wants me." Chris makes kissy lips at Andrew.

Everyone laughs, even the teacher.

Weird. This place is so weird.

"Okay, next," says Mr. Big. He points to the pretty girl with the Lexus. She adjusts the ski-cap thing on her head and sighs. She glances at me like I make her tired. I can see her nostrils flare. She's blinking too fast, like she hopes I'll disappear if she flutters her eyelids hard enough. She sits up and purses her lips, like the last thing in the world she wants is to talk to me.

"Uh, I'm *Jessica*." She has a thick California-girl accent, the kind of accent my dad would call "Valley girl." She says "Jessica" like "Jessicaaaahh," the last part coming out like something a crow would say.

"Jessica Noo-yen," says Mr. Big. "But you spell it with a silent G, right, Jessica?"

"Yes," she says with a roll of her dark eyes directed to the teacher. She looks at me again and smiles insincerely. "I'm Jessica Nguyen." She reaches forward and touches Chris Cabrera's shoulder in a territorial way. "I race motocross, too. Like my *boyfriend,* Chris." She wants me to know that he's *hers* and hers alone. Chris leans forward until her hand falls off of his shoulder.

"You've probably heard of her," says Mr. Big with a smile of admiration. "Jessica here is the national motocross champion for her age group."

I get the sense that Mr. Big is in love with her. Or at least in lust.

"Wow," I say. I am impressed, though even as I say it, the vision of her in a body cast or traction comes back to me. What is *up* with that? I close my eyes and concentrate the image away. I hear sirens, too, emergency sirens. Like I'm supposed to tell her to look out. I'm not ready for it. I don't even *know* this girl. I usually don't see violent events unless it's someone I know well. Or if it's super-important. I say of her fame, "That's really cool."

Jessica nods. "I know," she says with a toss of her hair. "It's *very* cool."

"Modest, she's not," says Tyler. He rolls his eyes at Jessica.

"Shut up, Tyler," Jessica tells him.

"Forgive them," says Andrew. "They have issues."

"Oh, please," snaps *Jessicaaaaah*. "I'd have to care to have issues with Tyler."

"Okay, children," Mr. Big inserts. "Moving on."

Andrew says, "Tyler's just pissed that Jessica dumped him for Chris. That's the secret here. That's why he was all 'Oh, look at me, I have a girlfriend,' because he wanted to piss her off."

"Please, dog," says Tyler, screwing up his face like he smells something foul.

"Guys, chill," says Chris. "You're friends, remember? Jesus."

So, Chris, Andrew, and Tyler are buddies. The hot trio. Does everything here have to come in threes? Anyway, I can tell you, if three seriously hot guys who looked like Chris, Andrew, and Tyler showed up at Taos High School, I can't even *imagine* what all the girls would do. There aren't guys like that in the entire state of New Mexico, much less three in one class. I feel like I've landed in a parallel universe.

Chris stares into my eyes with that weird half-smile and doesn't say anything. It's like he isn't even paying attention to what these people are saying. I can almost hear his thoughts, and they're not clean. His thoughts involve me and him, our lips, together. I like his thoughts. Sometimes it's a blessing to be able to feel what people are thinking about.

Mr. Big gets the rest of the kids to tell me their names and their stories, but I don't pay much attention. I keep looking back at Chris, who stares at me without flinching, transmitting his nasty thoughts like a radio tower. He blinks at me slowly and with passion and conviction. I have the uneasy, pleasant sense that Chris Cabrera is looking into my soul, right in front of his girlfriend.

Before I know it, everyone has introduced themselves, and Mr. Big says, "Okay class, now that we all know each other, let's get to the reading assignment. Do I have any volunteers to share books with Paski?"

For a moment, I'm terrified no one will raise a hand. Like they're going to have to call up my peer mentor and ask him or her to share with me. But almost as if on cue, Chris raises his big, perfect hand. As he does, Jessica's mouth drops open. Chris looks at her and shrugs. "I tried to tell you," he says to her. Her face reddens in anger.

"Chris," says Mr. Big. "Hey, thanks, buddy!"

The teacher helps me move a chair toward Chris's desk. I don't want to feel the whole butterfly-in-the-tummy thing as I approach him, but I do. I'm way attracted to this guy, even if he's a jerk. I avoid eye contact with Jessica, but I know she is glaring at me. I know because I can feel her ice in my veins.

9

I have physics before lunch, and the teacher tells me to wait in the room for my peer mentor. She has the decency to tell me in a written note, so that the other students who are packing up their books and leaving the room won't have a reason to laugh. I consider not waiting, because I don't want to start my new life with the reputation of being the chick who needed a peer mentor. But then I think of the terrible way that guy Andrew Van Dyke treated poor little Keoni, a kid who was just trying to help me, a guy whose only crime was that he liked chess, and I realize that if acting like Andrew is what it takes to be popular at Aliso Niguel, I don't *want* to be popular.

I take a seat near the back of the classroom and pretend to be interested in the diagram on the blackboard. I didn't understand a thing when the teacher was explaining it, but I haven't quite figured out how to tell her. Our physics class back in Taos was somewhere else in the universe, apparently. Not sure what to do with this stuff. The teacher looks up at me like she really feels sorry for me, which is awful. Even the teachers know that kids who need peer mentors are losers.

A couple of minutes later, a very tall, very skinny, very pasty and pale girl peeks her head in the door. She's wearing all black, trench coat included, and reminds me of a ghost from a Harry Potter movie. Her hair is a very Bismol shade of pink and sticks out in little spikes all over the place. She has so many holes and metal objects in her face and ears that I think she knows what it feels like to be a pincushion. She has a big white anarchy symbol stenciled onto her black backpack, and a large drawing pad under one arm with something scribbled on it in pencil. She wears purple combat boots. At least they're not black. How nice, eh? The administration took one look at my father and decided that the best match for me was Little Miss Vampire herself.

The teacher looks up and smiles at the girl with no small degree of fear. "Hello, Tina," she says. "Can I help you?"

"Uh," says Tina. She looks at a piece of paper in her hand. "I'm supposed to meet a girl named Pasquala here." Tina has a deep voice. Amazingly, she says my name right. She even uses a slight Spanish accent. The teacher points toward me.

"That's Paski right over there," she says. "Waiting for you."

Not knowing what else to do, I wave weakly at Tina the Human Pincushion. "Hi," I say. Tina smiles. I don't know why this surprises me as much as it does. You don't think of Goth kids as the smiling type. We only had a few of them at Taos, but I have to confess I never bothered to get to know any of them all that well. They sort of scared me.

"I'm Tina," she says. I notice that in spite of all the unfriendly clothing choices, she is a really pretty girl. And even though she's pale, there's something about her that seems black to me. Something about her face reminds me of Halle Berry. Like maybe Tina's an albino black girl or something.

We nod at each other. She takes a seat in a desk near mine. We're awkward, and neither of us can seem to think of anything to say. Finally, I break the silence. "So, thanks for agreeing to do this."

"No problem," says Tina.

"You don't have to," I add quickly. "Anyway. It was my dad's idea."

"I want to," says Tina, surprised. She smiles again, and I can't believe a nice person lurks beneath that *outfit*. "I'm all about building bridges, in the Eric Wolf sense."

"That's good," I say. What else is there to say, really? Oh, I know. "Who's Eric Wolf?"

"One of the most brilliant anthropologists of all time." She gets a distant look in her eyes. "Famous because he didn't believe peasants were insignificant. He believed everyone mattered and that it was only the powerful ruling elites who wrote the theories that effectively wrote the powerless out of history, even though they were there all along, contributing just as much as everyone else."

"Oh," I say. *Huh?*

"So you could say I'm the Wolfian Wolverine," she says. I stare blankly at her. She smiles to herself and explains: "The Wolverine is the Aliso Niguel mascot."

"Ah," I say.

"Don't tell me you haven't seen the hideous wolverine-vomit mural on the front of the school?"

I remember it now. The wolverines in it look anorexic and drunk. "Yes," I agree. "It's pretty bad."

"I'm an artist," states Tina, holding up her drawing pad. "Bad art pisses me off, especially in public."

"I can understand that."

"I'm an artist and an anthropologist. Like Gauguin, only I won't sleep with underage girls."

"Yeah," I say. I have no idea what she's talking about.

"So I'm all about respecting everyone, peasant and ruler alike, at this school, which, if you think about it, is just like a microcosm of the nation, or the world, and history."

"Uh-huh."

"People don't realize it, but human nature doesn't change all that much no matter what you do. There are those who rule and those who get ruled. The most you can hope for in life is that if you're the ruled, you can change social castes before it's over. Your life. Before you die, I mean."

I nod and try to think of something to say. There's nothing, however. Well, nothing polite. I'd like to say "Please come back to Earth now," but that seems awfully direct.

"So, you wanna get some lunch?" she asks, all at once cheerful.

"Yeah," I say. "I'm actually starving. I couldn't eat this morning."

"Nervous about your first day?" She has a listening face that reminds me of my dad's. She *leans* in to her listening, like she really, actually cares what people are saying. She's so nice now that I can't believe I was afraid of her a minute ago.

"Actually, sort of," I admit. "I didn't know what to expect."

"Come on," she says as she stands up. She raises her arms over her head to stretch, and she looks like a ballet dancer. "Let's go see what to expect. I'll fill you in on everything around here."

I stand and follow Tina, the multiply punctured Wolfian Wolverine, to the cafeteria.

10

The Aliso Niguel cafeteria is a lot like the Taos High cafeteria, only bigger. This has been my experience all day. That everything seems somehow familiar but larger than life. The cafeteria smells like Tater Tots and cheap pizza. Does every school dining hall have to smell like that?

As we enter the room, students turn to look at us. There are kids who look rich, kids who look too trendy for their own good, kids grouped by language (I hear some speaking Spanish, some speaking something like Russian, and some speaking an Asian language I don't know), and there are cheerleaders huddled in their skirts and sweaters, hip-hop kids, long-haired kids, and no shortage of boys who think they are Usher. It's the same as back home, but with more kids who seem to be from other countries. The rich kids and geek kids are multiracial. I see a lot of different kinds of people, and I can't imagine how I would ever find a group to fit in with here. I'm not trendy. I'm not typical, I guess, for anything.

When I see everyone bunched together in cozy cliques, I am glad to have Tina, even if everyone probably thinks she's a little strange. She's probably one of those people other people look at and then turn away and laugh together about. Even so, the other kids all seem to have a certain respect for (or fear of?) her. As we walk, she greets almost everyone we see by name, with a friendly hello. She acts almost like a grown-up. She knows a lot about a lot of kids, asking about their hobbies, their sisters and brothers, their sick parents, puppies, whatever. Things like that. It doesn't matter if they look like preps, glamour queens, skaters, or geeks, Tina is nice to everyone, and she introduces me to as many kids as will listen to her.

We get in line for lunch and I panic for a second that I don't have any money. How much would that *suck*? But I remember the ten bucks Dad gave me before he left for his meeting. I pick a personal-size pizza and a side salad. The food here looks better than it did back home, like something you could actually *eat*. Tina gets a veggie burger and tells me that she's a vegetarian for ethical reasons, then lectures me on my choices. It makes me look at the pepperoni on my pizza a little differently when she tells me that pigs are smarter than dogs, and that they have not only saved each other but have, on more than one occasion, saved a human being, too. Tina's nice but weird. Something tells me that after a while, it might get kind of hard to be around her.

We sit down at a far end of the cafeteria, and I start to nibble my food. Tina pulls out her drawing pad, squints at the assembled people, and her jaw tightens as if she's thinking. She starts to draw without looking at the paper, something that my dad does sometimes.

"Okay," she says. "Now, don't turn and look right now, but the most 'popular' — and I say that in quotes — girls in the school just walked in. I don't buy in to the whole popularity thing, but I think it's important you know the hierarchy, even if it's just to say 'screw it.'" She lowers her voice to a whisper. "Okay, so, Paski. Listen. Turn very slowly and casually so it doesn't look like we're talking about them."

I do as she has asked, and sure enough, see Jessica Nguyen and the two girls who rode with her in the Lexus this morning. I can see their outfits now. The blond one who looks like a younger Britney Spears or an older Jamie Lynn Spears wears tight long jean shorts with long black socks and checkered beige and white sneakers with a big E on the side. She wears a tight beige sweater that shows off her big boobs. With her tiny waist, shapely legs, and firm butt, she has a body like a porn star.

"They're not real," says Tina.

"What?"

"Brianna's boobs."

I look at Tina, amazed that she knew I was even looking at Brianna's boobs. Amazed and embarrassed.

"Don't worry," says Tina. "Everyone stares at them. I think that's the reason her mom got them for her sweet-sixteen present."

"Really?"

"Yeah. She was here one week, flat as a board, and then — boom — she goes to 'Greece' for a 'family vacation' and comes back with enormous knockers. It's kind of funny or kind of sad. I haven't decided yet."

"Yeah," I say. I've never known anyone my own age to get plastic surgery, much less as a gift from her *mother*.

"Brianna's family is from Greece," Tina tells me. "Brianna Sarantopoulos."

"That's cool," I say, hating myself as I say it. "Cool" is one of those words you use when you can't think of a better word.

"Yeah? Well, that's probably the only truly cool thing about her. Her dad made his money building tract houses and charging way too much for them. Her mom's a trophy wife. Brianna's about as original and exciting as the houses her dad makes. She's popular by default. The other two are talented and smart, they have something interesting about them. But Brianna? She's just a hanger-on."

I say nothing, surprised by Tina's venom. I thought she would be nice to everyone, but apparently she has her favorites, like everyone else.

Tina looks at me and backtracks. "I shouldn't make it out like she's useless. You're right. It's not fair."

"I didn't say it wasn't fair."

"You thought it."

I say nothing.

Tina continues, "Brianna plays volleyball pretty well, but in all honesty, not *that* well. She looks good in a bikini when she plays, especially with all that saline bouncing around, so the guys are all, like, drooling over her. That's the value of having Brianna around, basically. Guys like her. A lot. The fact that she's smart as an eggplant doesn't bother guys. You know how they are."

I shrug and think of Ethan Schaefer, who actually likes smart girls. I don't think Ethan could date a stupid girl. Stacey must be very smart. He'd get bored otherwise, wouldn't he? Then again, if she had huge fake boobs like Brianna Sarantopoulos, he might make an exception. You never know. Thinking of him makes me realize again that

I've lost him. I have to call him later and just ask him, point-blank. That's the best way.

"Okay," says Tina. "So, the one with the turban on her head?"

I nod and look at the girl who reminded me of Alicia Keys. She wears a frilly skirt made out of something like yellow gauze; it rides low on her hips, showing off a flat belly and a hip with a tattoo of a snake or something on it. The skirt falls just above her knees. She has on a short T-shirt, the kind with sleeves but that shows the tummy anyway. The girls out here seem to like showing off their tummies. The colorful shirt is striped and has a V-neck that she's filled with a bunch of wooden beads in different colors, like a hippie friend my grandma has. Her earrings look even bigger now than they did before. She has that turban around her hair and a color/kind flower stuck behind one ear. She wears flat shoes with open backs, round toes, and shiny beads all over them. She looks like she just stepped out of a music video.

"Haley Williams," Tina tells me.

"She looks like Alicia Keys," I say.

"Yeah, and that's not all. She's a musician. She plays guitar and she sings and writes songs like Alicia and sounds as good."

"That's cool." I am really starting to hate how I keep saying this word. Tina is smarter than me, and I'm not doing much with my vocabulary to redeem myself. I stuff pizza in my face and try not to think about all the brilliant little piggies who died for my lunch.

"No, you don't *understand*," says Tina. "She's *really* good. You have to hear her. She plays at assemblies sometimes. And she has a job playing at a café in Laguna Beach on the weekends. They say she had an offer from a couple of record companies to make some records, but her mom wouldn't *let* her."

"That's *crazy*," I say.

"No. It's sane, actually. Her mom is a singer who used to do backup for Mariah Carey. She's, like, this white studio singer who everyone says sounds black. Her dad actually *is* black. He's a big-time record executive who used to work with Babyface and has his own company now. Haley's parents were all 'No, you can't take the deal, because the music industry sucks and they'll just eat you up and spit you out by the time you're eighteen, and you'll be *done.*' They want her to wait until she's, like, twenty, to get her record deal, so she has a chance at surviving as a real artist. I actually respect them for that."

"Yeah." I stop short of saying it's cool. My head is spinning. In Taos, the closest we got to a celebrity was a kid whose cousin's friend's sister had dated a guy on a WB show. But he wasn't really even like a cool guy. He was, like, one of the supporting characters. Then there was the girl who once met Jared, the formerly fat guy who does ads for Subway, at the airport. That's about it.

Haley catches me looking at her, and I look away fast. I don't want them to think I'm looking, but it's hard not to look at these girls. They command attention. Everyone is staring at them, even if they don't want to. Haley leans over to Jessica and whispers something, and they all look at me. Great. Now I'm on their radar.

"They're looking at us," I say.

"Let them," says Tina. She sips her water like she doesn't care. I admire her for it, but I wonder how sincere she is about not caring. I feel her fear.

I concentrate on my salad and take a bite but manage to dribble white ranch dressing on the front of my shirt. *Great.* Now I look like an idiot. I mean, like more of an idiot than *before.* Tina eats and pretends to look around the room like she isn't talking about anyone specific.

"Now, Jessica *Nguyen*," she says with a flinch, like it hurts to think of her.

"I know about her," I say. "She's in my English class."

"What do you know?" Tina looks like she is obsessed with Jessica in a way that she hates. Her eyes narrow.

"I know that she's into motocross."

"Yeah, only the national *champion*," says Tina, like this is a bad thing. Tina has a jealous streak I don't like. "She has endorsements like crazy, and a couple of months ago there was this documentary on her on one of those kid networks, one of the Disney networks, and some big athlete saw it and gave her a crapload of money for her life story."

"Really? Who?"

"Someone like Shaquille O'Neal, some old basketball star. I can't remember. I'm not big on sports. I'll find out for you."

"That's amazing," I say. I sneak a look at Jessica, and she looks at me right as I'm looking away. She gets this look like she's amused that I was watching her, like she thinks she is perfect. It's like she turns in slow motion toward me and I can't get away. She's still wearing that hat and the low jeans with the sparkly belt. Her jeans are so low you can see ass cleavage. Her body is perfect, trim but strong, with not an ounce of fat anywhere. She wears pink jeweled flat thong sandals, like a girl who isn't trying that hard but looks incredible anyway. I've noticed that a lot of people wear this kind of flip-flop sandals around here.

Tina says, "No, listen to me. That's not even the tip of the iceberg with Jessica." She gives a sarcastic smile, like she thinks about Jessica way, *way* too much. "The other thing you need to know about her is that she's the richest girl at this school."

"Really?" That's saying something, considering the cars and clothes I've seen around here.

"Yeah. Her dad is some big-time businessman. They wrote about him in the *Orange County Register* a while back as one of the richest guys in the county, and none of the other kids here had parents on that list. They said he's worth over two hundred and fifty million dollars. People were all, like, 'Jessica, is it *true?*' and she was, like, 'Of *course.*' Can you believe that?"

"Two hunderd and fifty *million?*" I choke on my Pepsi.

"Yeah. Isn't it disgusting?"

"What does he *do?*"

"He's a 'venture capitalist,' whatever that is. That's what the article said."

I sneak another look at Jessica. Her clothes look nicer now than they did five minutes ago.

"No, there's more," Tina continues. Her eyes dance with a wicked sort of pleasure mixed with bitterness. "Jessica's mom used to be a *model,* right? In Vancouver and Hong Kong. But the lady's super-*smart* and good at designing clothes, so she's come up with this line of racing clothes for girls called "JessWear."

I gasp. I've *heard* of JessWear. Emily wanted to order some shorts from the company online after she read about it in *Seventeen* and we realized, as we often did, that we couldn't buy the clothes anywhere in the state of New Mexico. "That's *hers?*" I ask.

"It's her *mom's,* but I heard Jessica has half the company in her *name.*

The racing stuff was so popular they branched out into regular clothes, like tops and shorts and skirts."

"I've heard of it."

"Okay, so you know. They sell the clothes in Macy's. It's insane. All the Harajuku girls in Japan like it, too. She's a phenomenon in Japan. Like they weren't rich *enough,* now Jessica's making a ton of money with her racing, like, every time she wins a race, she gets a boatload of cash, and now her mom is raking in the dough with the clothes named after her, and Hollywood's knocking."

"That's unbelievable," I say.

"Yeah, well, once you see the girl ride, you'll understand. It's hard to hate her, even though you want to. Even though she herself hates everyone who isn't her slave."

"She's good?"

"God, yes," says Tina. "She's hot on a bike. It's pretty amazing to watch. I hate her."

"She's really pretty, too," I say.

"Yeah, well, that's the *crappy* part. She gets to be rich, talented, with parents that adore her and think the world revolves around her, and she's just, like, the most beautiful girl in school." Tina looks at me and grins. "Or she used to be."

"What?" I ask.

"You're as pretty as she is."

"No, I'm not," I say. Is Tina insane?

"You could be. With some makeup and the right clothes, you could look like a Mexican Rachel Bilson."

"I could?"

Tina nods, then glances at Jessica and her friends, who've taken a table near the door. They aren't eating. They sip water and laugh too loud, like they're making fun of everyone. Tina says, "You look exactly *like* Rachel Bilson, Paski. You just don't know it. And that makes you *prettier* than the hater girls."

I wonder for a second if Tina's a lesbian or something but thank her anyway.

"And I'm *not* gay, don't worry," says Tina, like she read my mind. "I have an amazing boyfriend. Cesar."

"How did you know I was thinking that?" I ask.

Tina shrugs, stuffs the remainder of her veggie burger in her mouth, and says, "It sounds crazy, but I have really good people instincts. Too good sometimes."

I look up and see Andrew Van Dyke leaning down and flirting with Brianna. Brianna's all, ooh, look at my boobs, sticking them out. Yuck. Jessica whispers something to Andrew, and he looks my way. They all laugh, and then Andrew starts to walk toward me and Tina like he's on a mission.

"Uh-oh," I mutter. Tina sees the same thing, and it looks like she braces her body for a blow.

Under her breath, Tina says, "Andrew Van Dyke. Major womanizer. Typical rich white boy who thinks he was born to rule the world, which, if you examine history and so on, he unfortunately was. Youngest of three brothers. Filthy-rich family, the dad's a surgeon of some kind and heads a hospital or something, but I'm pretty sure he cheats on the mom." She stops talking and tries to look like she hasn't said anything.

"Hey, Paski, right?" says Andrew. I nod. Andrew sits down with us, taking a look back at the popular girls. What's he looking for?

Approval? Why? He stares into my eyes with a grin that's not even close to being as charismatic as Chris's. But still; he is cute. "So, like, I was wondering if you had a boyfriend back in Mexico."

"*New* Mexico," I say. "It's a state."

"Hello, Andrew," calls Tina, waving like he might not have noticed she was sitting right there next to him.

He sighs and looks at her. "Tina. What's up."

"That's better," says Tina.

Andrew looks at me again. "So. You got a man?"

"Kind of," I say. I think of Ethan, and I hate to admit it, but my feelings for him are already fading. I can't really remember what he looks like anymore. I mean, I know what he looks like. But it's like my brain doesn't want to remember him right now. Whenever I try to think of him, all I can see is Chris Cabrera's sexy smirk. I shouldn't be attracted to Chris. He's the kind of guy who will break a girl's heart. I am pretty sure of that, plus he's got a girlfriend. But I can't help it.

"That's too bad," says Andrew, "because I was gonna invite you to Trent's party with me and my friends. You know, Chris Cabrera and Tyler Ma, those loser dickheads from English." At mention of Chris's name, my heart surges. Tina looks at me with a warning in her eyes. I'm, like, I know. In my head I know. But the heart isn't the head, and that's all there is to it.

"When is it?" I ask Andrew. "Can Tina come too?"

"This weekend." He tries to look casual and comfortable. I can feel the eyes of Jessica and he friends on me.

"I'm busy," says Tina. Andrew ignores her and says, "Give me your number, and I'll call you."

I blush. "I don't know my number yet." How *lame* am I? "We just moved here."

"That's cute," says Andrew, looking over at the popular girls like he's bored with us already. Jessica and her crew seem to be laughing at me. Andrew smiles back at them, I have no idea why. He says, "I'll give you my digits, and you ring me when you know your number. How about that?"

"Okay," I say. "But I have to ask my dad."

"That's cute, too," says Andrew, like he never has to ask his parents for permission to do anything. He pulls out a business card and flips it toward me. A *business* card, okay? This is a high school junior with his own business card. It has his picture on it and about a thousand numbers and e-mail addresses. Apparently Andrew has his own website and blog, too.

"Call me," he says, doing his hand like a hang-ten phone at his ear, all suave. Why do people do that? Aren't the words "call me" enough? Anyway.

Andrew joins the other girls. Tina shakes her head and blows air out of her mouth. "Paski," she says. "You should let me teach you about these people before you go to a party with them."

"Why?" I ask, thinking I was popular back home, there's no reason I'm not going to be popular here. I know Tina's nice, but I don't want her to be my only friend.

"Because Andrew's a jerk," she says.

"I know." I sigh. "I saw him push a kid today."

"Just one?" she asks. "Usually he's pushing whole flocks of children."

"I thought you were all about building *bridges,*" I say.

"I am. With people who *deserve* it. But there are some people who *don't* deserve it, and Mr. Model Van Dyke is one of them."

"Andrew's a model?"

"Well, *duh*," says Tina. "*Look* at him."

I shrug and finish my drink. "All he did was ask me to a party." A party with Chris Cabrera in attendance. The sexy, dangerous Chris. What's wrong with me? I'm going to a party with a jerk. A party with Chris there. A party where I can see Chris. I shouldn't be so happy about that, right? It's not smart.

"I know that's what it looked like to *you*," Tina says. "But you have to trust me. There are some serious haters at this school, and there's nothing more dangerous than haters in groups. That's what a 'party' will be, okay? Especially at Trent's house."

"Who is Trent, anyway?" I ask

"He's a football player."

"Is he nice?"

Tina looks like this is a philosophical question. "I don't know. Are any of them nice? I don't know. For your sake, I hope so. My guess? They've got a joke planned, and you, fresh meat on campus, are going to be the punch line."

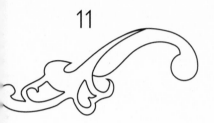

11

I get home from my first day of school before my dad. I stash my bike in the garage and head upstairs to start unpacking the boxes in my room. Can I just say this: I *love* my room! It's *huge*. I can't even believe I have so much space. I don't know what to do with it, but I'm thinking I'll paint the walls. Do they let you paint apartment walls? I can draw, like my dad; I just never want to, mostly because he draws. I don't want to give him any reasons to get more vain than he is, and thinking I'm *just like him* would do that.

I stop unpacking when I find the memory diary Emily and Janet made for me. I sit down on the carpet (it's so new and beige and soft!) and read through the diary again, even though I ought to be doing something else. As I read, remembering the times we spent together, I feel the tears begin to swell. I want to talk to my friends. I *have* to talk to them. I know I shouldn't make a long-distance phone call without asking my dad first — he can't deal when I do something like that without asking — but some things you just have to *do*. Follow your heart, as Dad would say. I'm sure he'll understand.

I call Emily's house. My fingers fly over the phone number; it has been the same since grade school, and I've called it, like, millions of times. I will never forget this phone number for as long as I live. Em answers with "Paski!" (caller ID) and squeals at the sound of my voice. She tells me Janet is there, and Janet runs to get on another extension so we can all talk. They sound like home. I love their voices. I want to crawl into the phone line and get away from here. The more they tell me, the more I miss them. They ask about my new life. I tell them all about the town, the school, the crazy people here. I tell them about how, after school, all these *moms* come to pick up their *kids* and the moms look younger than the students.

"How?" asks Emily. "What do you mean?"

I say, "No, *listen* to me." God, I sound like Tina. I hate how the people I'm around influence me like that. "Seriously. Listen. There are all these totally skinny little moms who've had so much plastic surgery they look younger than their own kids."

"That's crazy!" says Emily.

"And they dress all hoochie. It's like they share clothes with their daughters."

"Eew!" my friends shriek together.

I say, "Oh, and there's this girl at school with fake boobs, too. They're *huge*. She looks like if Pam Anderson and Britney Spears could have a baby." My friends and I have this game where we like to say who people look like, as if they are the baby of this person and that person. It's funnier when you do it with two guys or two females.

"How do you know they're fake?" asks Janet, who has told us all once or twice that some people mistakenly thought her rather large breasts were fake, and she's, like, really *proud* of that.

"Everyone *knows* they're fake," I say. I don't mean to sound California, but that accent is wearing off on me already. "This girl *brags* about it." I don't know for sure if this last part is true, but I say it anyway.

Janet tells me that it's snowing again in Taos, and she says that they miss me. She probably wants to change the subject because she doesn't like to think that anyone our age might have bigger, better boobs than hers. Some guys in school took a poll once, back in seventh grade, and voted Janet the best boobs in our class.

I ask about Ethan, and there's a silence. Someone coughs. I hear the silent noise between my brows that I get when I'm about to "see" something in my head.

"He's good, I guess," says Emily. I know her well enough to know she's lying.

"We haven't talked to him, have we, Em?" adds Janet.

"No," says Emily. "But he's good. I mean, we've heard he's good."

"You can tell me," I say. "I had a vision about it. About that Stacey girl." Emily and Janet know about my visions and accept them.

Again silence. Then Emily tells me Ethan has been holding hands with a horsey-looking older girl from work. "We didn't want to tell you until you were settled in better over there," she says. "We didn't want this to be any harder on you than it has to be."

"I'm fine," I say.

"We hate Ethan," says Emily.

"Hate him," Janet reiterates.

"He's just a guy," I say. "So, is it true about Stacey?"

"Yes," says Emily. "She's way old. I don't get it. They're all over town together, kissing in public. She could get arrested for that."

"You're so strong," Janet pipes. "Paski, don't worry about it."

"It's not that," I say. "It's that I already met someone." I know Chris has a girlfriend, but I still have a really good feeling about him.

"Who?" they chorus.

"Just a guy. There are lots of them here. You would not *believe* the guys here. Oh my God. They're all *way* hot. It's *so* not normal how many hot boys there are here."

"I *told* you!" screams Emily. "Why didn't you take me with you? I am so tired of Taos boys. They all have hay in their hair."

We talk a little more, and even though I don't want to see it, I get a mental picture of Ethan holding hands with that Stacey girl. I get a knot in my belly as I realize he's been intimate with her. He's in love with her.

"I got invited to a party with the most popular kids in school," I tell them.

"Already?" exclaims Emily.

"See? Girlfriend wastes no time," says Janet.

"Are they snotty like the kids on *The OC*?" asks Emily. "Do they all have pools and big Hummers?"

I'm about to answer, but I'm interrupted by the most hideous noise, two noises, actually, coming from the parking lot downstairs. The first is a horrible screeching. The second sounds like a polka. It's awful, and I am pretty sure I know exactly what it is, at least the polka part. It's a really, *really* loud version of that stupid song "*Frijolero,*" an obscene joke of a song my dad *loves* by the Mexican rap group Molotov. Dad listens to it and sings along, dances around with his Chicano-tough-guy face on — you know, when he's not dancing to Britney Spears or *whatever*. I can hear the sarcastic lyrics being spit over the top of the accordion lines. "'Don't call me a gringo, you fucking beaner, stay on your side of the goddamned river, don't call me gringo, you beaner . . .'"

"Oh my God," I say.

"What's wrong?" asks Emily.

"My dad has *flipped*."

"Is he still acting all Mr. Hollywood?" asks Janet.

"Yes," I groan/admit.

"Your dad is so cool."

"No! He's not. He's getting worse the longer we're out here. He has an earring now."

"See?" says Emily. "My dad would never do that. Yours is way cool."

I sigh. "Guys, can I call you later?"

We say our goodbyes, and I rush onto the balcony off the living room. Don Juan, who has been sunning himself out here, runs inside and hides in a closet. He doesn't like this noise, either. The music is *so* loud I can feel the bass in my sternum. I hope to *God* it's not my dad who is responsible for this, but of course it's him. Who else would be blasting a Mexican rap group in the middle of Aliso Viejo?

Yes, ladies and gentlemen, my dad is home, blasting Molotov and singing along with a big smile on his face and some old cholo sunglasses on. "'*No me digas beaner, Mr. Puñetero, te sacare un susto por racista culero . . .*'"

Oh. And I should tell you. He's *not* in the Corolla. He's sitting behind the wheel of some gigantic, scary convertible that looks really old, like from the fifties or something. It looks like the Batmobile, if the Batmobile was falling apart, rusted out, and a really disgusting color of puke-yellow-green. The car is the source of the screeching noise, like there's something wrong with a belt somewhere in the engine. The booming Molotov polka blares from the car *stereo,* which appears to work better than the car itself.

But *that's* not the worst part.

Just so you know, the *worst* part is that Dad's not alone, and the guys he's with look like total Hollywood *gang* members. There are three of them, two with shaved-looking heads and those shirts I call wife-beaters but that my dad asks me not to call wife-beaters because he finds the term anti-feminist and offensive. The other one has a beret and a braid of hair down his back. My dad's friends always look like these guys for some reason. They've got sunglasses like him, and they look like total *cholos.* How has my dad already made friends with three *cholos?* We just *got* here. I haven't even made three friends yet, but here's my dad like cruising with a bunch of stinkin' *vatos.* I see that one of them has tattoos all down the back of his neck like an inmate. I swear to *God.*

My dad looks up and sees me. He waves with a big old smile on his face, real proud of himself and his stupid car.

"Hi, *Chinita!* What do you think?"

I stare at the car with a frown. I don't bother answering, because he wouldn't be able to hear me anyway.

He motions for me to come downstairs. "Come check it out!" He says "check" like "sheck," the way he does when he's trying to sound like a street thug or something. It's embarrassing. I think he's trying to impress his new friends. Lately it seems like my dad is always trying to impress *someone.* But the more he does, the less he impresses me.

I turn to head back inside but see Keoni and Kerani on the balcony of their apartment with their mouths hanging open. They are peering down at the disaster of my father like he's amazing. Like they *like* him.

"Wow," they say in unison. "Cool."

"No," I correct them. I feel like crying. "It's not *wow*. It's not *cool*. It's *awful*."

"Can we go see it?" one of them asks me. I recognize him as Keoni.

"You want to go down there with the crazy people?" I ask. I'm baffled.

They nod. Keoni begs, "Please, Paski? Take us with you?"

I hear the engine cut out, but the music continues, only now it's some song by that band Ozomatli that my dad loves. I see a blond lady peeking out of her apartment window with a scared look. My dad and his friends start to sing along like a homie barbershop quartet: "'Dib dob, socialize, get ready for the Saturday night . . .'"

Oh my God. I can only imagine what the neighbors think of this. My dad's going to get us thrown out of here.

"Fine," I say to Keoni. "Meet me downstairs."

I go down, open the garage door, and, flanked by the neighbor boys, I greet my father.

He jumps out of the driver's seat and hugs me. "What do you *think*, kiddo?" he asks. His face tells me he expects admiration.

"I think you should ask me about my first day of school before asking me about this weird *car*," I say. I cross my arms over my chest. You know what? I'm *glad* I made that long-distance call now. I should have stayed on longer. I should have made a random long-distance call to, like, *Bombay* and stayed on the phone for an *hour*. I should have stayed inside. I should have ignored this nightmare. Maybe it would have gone away.

Dad hits himself on the forehead and gets that face on like he feels he's a terrible father. "I'm sorry, *Chinita*." He staggers around and puts an arm around me with the sensitive-dad look on his face. "How was school?" he asks. "I totally should have asked you that first. Damn. I'm *sorry*. Here, let's go upstairs and talk. You want to do that, Punkin?"

"No," I say. How can he go from being like a fake old gangster to being the most sensitive father on earth? My dad must be bipolar.

"Hey," he says, digging in his pants pocket. He pulls out Grandma's amulet. "At least I didn't forget this!" He holds it out to me like he wants to be congratulated on his fine parenting skills. I take the necklace. It's cold at first, but as it makes contact with my skin, it begins to almost vibrate and grow warm. Eerie. I put it in my pocket but can still feel its warmth. I try hard not to look at my father because I know he wants me to. Dad touches my arm. I ignore it. He points at his eyes with his fingers. I look at him but only because I don't want a scene here in front of the neighbors. "Well?" he asks. "How was it? Did you make any friends? How are your teachers?"

"It was okay. I made a friend." It's sort of a lie. Tina isn't exactly a friend. Neither is Andrew. "And my teachers are . . . teachers. They're the same everywhere you go."

"She already got invited to a party with the popular kids," says Keoni to my father. Kerani nods. I look at Keoni and see he's lighting up a cigarette. He smokes? That's crazy. My dad notices, too, and seems as surprised as I am.

"How did you know about Trent's party?" I ask Keoni. I like how when I say "Trent's party," it sounds like I already know Trent. It makes me feel important, because everyone seems to always talk about him.

"Word travels fast at Aliso Niguel," he says with a sad shrug. "Just don't turn hater on us. We thought you were good peeps."

"'Sup, boys," Dad says to the twins. He waves away the smoke dramatically. "What's the shizzle dizzle today?" What? Shizzle dizzle? Please tell me my dad didn't just say "shizzle dizzle." Please?

"That's a really cool car, Mr. Archuleta," says Keoni. He hands his cigarette to Kerani and lights another one for himself. I am starting to think Kerani never talks unless it's in unison with Keoni. Maybe he's a mute. Maybe the smoke is some kind of therapy for boys without voices. Keoni points to the car and asks my dad, "What is it?"

I laugh even though the question probably wasn't intended to be funny. My dad answers, "A 1958 Edsel Citation, almost mint."

"An *Edsel?*" I ask. "Didn't they *ban* those or something? Where's the Corolla?"

"I traded it in," crows my dad. He flashes his big fake teeth at me like I should be happy about this news.

"You *what?*" It takes everything I have not to cry. "Dad, there's a reason they don't make Edsels anymore."

Dad looks confused. "Well, I wanted to get a Beemer or something like that, the way all these other people out here have, but we can't afford it right now, and then I decided that it would be better to have a memorable car that nobody else had. This is it."

I look at the guys in the car. "Did the Chicano posse come with it?" I say in a low voice. "We don't have enough room in the garage for them. Unless you stack them up."

My dad gets a guilty face again. "Oh, man. Sorry. Paski, these are my new friends Lalo, Sleepy, and Bartolomeo." The *cholos* wave. "Lalo's a Chicano playwright from L.A. who used to know your mom back in the day. He's got a show Off-Broadway in New York, and he won a bunch of awards. He's heavy."

"Nice to meet you," says Lalo, far more gentlemanly than you'd expect from the tattoos on his neck. His voice is really, really deep, like a movie announcer's or something.

Dad rubs his sideburns, which, now that I look at them, seem to be newly sculpted into strange little curls. When does he find the time to do this stuff? It's crazy. What the heck is wrong with my dad? I *swear*.

He says, "Sleepy's an artist like me, a friend of Lalo's. He's going to help paint the mural."

"The mural?" I ask. Dad is one of those people who thinks you have to have murals to be a real Chicano.

"On the hood," Dad explains.

"Oh my God." I feel sick.

Dad continues to introduce his friends. "Bartolomeo here's an attorney who went to Yale. He works in the state attorney general's office now, but back in the day he was a lowrider. Bartolomeo, I'm telling you, Paski, he can *really* fix cars."

The attorney in the beret grins and shakes my dad's hand in some elaborate way that reminds me of an old movie starring Edward James Olmos. He's even got old acne scars like that actor. I stare at the three wannabe hood rats — four if you count my dad — and try to get my mind around the fact that these men are *professionals* in their thirties or forties, really *old*. I might be imagining it, but it seems like in other eras, old people just acted like old people. Now it's like they all want to be young forever.

"They're here to help me work on the car," says Dad. He slaps the hood, and I hear something fall off the bottom of the engine and clatter to the ground, like he knocked it loose. I don't want to laugh. I try not to. But I laugh anyway. "And you can see it needs some work," Dad acknowledges, embarrassed.

Kerani, the silent twin, bends down to pull the piece of metal out from where it fell. He hands it to my dad, who hands it to Bartolomeo.

"The Corolla didn't need work," I point out. "It was fine." To myself, I add: And I could drive it in public. There is no way I'm driving this piece of garbage in public, unless there's, like, a tsunami and I have to get to higher ground really fast or something.

"I *know* the Corolla was fine," says Dad as his buddies get out of the car and start to unload cans of spray paint and crazy-looking tools from the trunk. "But the Corolla did *not* have one thing this baby's got." He gets into a superhero pose with one fist up in the air and the other over his heart. "A fantastic future as the *Squeegeemobile!*"

Dad grins like a maniac, pulls a drawing pad out of the backseat, and holds up a drawing he's done of a car very much like this one, except in bright colors, with a figurine of his Squeegee Man mounted on the hood. It looks like a *Lowrider* magazine wet dream, complete with the hot cartoon ho leaning over in her high heels and Daisy Dukes. Blech? I take the drawing and look closely at it. There are slogans and weird little things drawn all over the car, and the fins in the back look even bigger in the drawing than they do in real life.

"What *is* this?" I demand. I have a horrifying image of my father dropping me off at the party this weekend in *that*. I can't go now. Not unless someone gives me a ride. That's all there is to it. I don't want to see Chris Cabrera outside of school *that* badly. From what I saw at the school today, everyone else has parents with clean, shiny, quiet Volvos, Infinitis, and Lexuses.

Dad bounces on his toes the way he does when he's really excited about something. "*That* is the Squeegeemobile once we finish with her. Is it not the coolest thing you've ever seen?"

"No," I say. "It's not."

"I think it's *cool,*" says Keoni. Kerani nods and smokes.

"Who asked you?" I snap. To myself, I think that it is *very* bad that the goofiest kids in school love the Squeegeemobile. My dad's friends loiter in the parking lot and tap their toes to the music. I can't be sure, but I think that Sleepy guy is making eyes at me. Eew. Is there no end to the indignities?

"Come on, Paski," says my dad. "Where's your sense of *fun?*"

I turn to go back inside, leaving my dad to brag about his stupid car with the cancerous chess twins.

I think of Emily and Janet and my grandmother. I think of Taos Mountain, how it always welcomed me away from the chaos of my life. I don't know where to go now. There's no escaping my crazy father. I'm homesick. I want to cry.

"I don't know," I answer to myself as I walk into the garage. "I guess I left my *sense of fun* back home in Taos with everything else I love."

I go upstairs, and even though my instincts say I shouldn't, I call Ethan and ask him if he's dating that Stacey girl. I use her name and everything. He sighs and says he knew it was just a matter of time before my "stupid friends" told me about it. I hang up on him. Emily and Janet are not stupid. They believe me. They don't judge me for it. And that's the thing about Taos, usually. It's a city that loves different kinds of people. Ethan Schaefer seems like a million years ago anyway.

Then, maybe to massage my ego a little, I call Andrew and give him my phone number. He tells me he'll pick me up for Trent's party on Friday, and I give him my address.

"Are there houses over there where you live?" he asks. As he speaks, the amulet heats up even more in my pocket, until it feels like it's going to burn a hole in my pants. It hurts. I reach in, yank it out, and it nearly burns my flesh. I throw it to the floor.

"It's an apartment," I say.

There's a moment of silence. "Uh, okay." He sounds uncomfortable, like he's embarrassed for me. "I'll pick you up at your . . . apartment."

So obviously apartments are bad as far as the popular kids are concerned. Whatever. I hang up and pick up the amulet. It's cold now. I put it in my underwear drawer. I don't want to wear it. It freaks me out. I don't want to lose it, but I don't want to own it, either. Kind of like how I'm starting to feel about this California business. I look at myself in the mirror over the dresser, wondering what other surprises Orange County has in store for me.

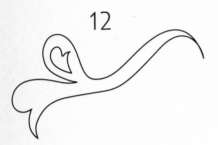

12

For the next three days, Chris Cabrera doesn't come to school. Mr. Big tells the class that Chris is traveling with his mother in Europe, shopping for art for her gallery. Like it's nothing. Andrew tells everyone not to worry because "the stud" will be back in plenty of time for the party. He pronounces party "par-tay." The party, just so you know, is all anyone can talk about. The popular kids are talking about who will be there and how much fun it will be; everyone else talks about how stupid it is.

Tina goes out of her way to eat with me every day, and I find her interesting, but I have to admit I'm not thrilled about the way everyone looks at us like we're queer or weird. She has attached herself to me without my permission. She's an intense girl, committed to her politics and anthropology stuff, but to the point that it's *all* she talks about. The popular girls are nice to me, saying hi in the halls, but it's not sincere. I figure that out pretty fast. After I've worn jeans and a T-shirt three days in a row, Jessica pulls me aside and says with a smile, "I really like the way you go for consistency in your wardrobe. Are you actually *changing* clothes or is it, like, the *same* clothes over and over?"

"We hear you live in an apartment," says Brianna with a stupid smile. The other girls flinch, like they don't like it when she speaks. She doesn't notice. I wonder if she notices much. I wonder if she would notice if she, like, stopped breathing. "Do they have laundry rooms there, or do you have to, um, go to the Laundromat or something?"

Haley gives me a sympathetic look and tells her friends, "Come on, you guys. Be nice. Apartments are nice. There are some really great ones out there." Jessica rolls her eyes. She flinches like she feels sorry for me. Great. I've gone from a school where I was one of the popular kids to a school where I'm the kid the popular kids like to make fun of and feel sorry for. My dad comes to L.A. and gets to be a big shot. I come and get to be a nothing. Life's fair.

I decide I'm going to have to ask my dad for some money for clothes. They're much more important here than they were back in Taos. It's like one of those nature shows on PBS, where the narrator talks about how a certain kind of bird sizes up all the other birds by the way they display their feathers. Orange County is full of human birds that strut and preen. I figure Dad has been spending money on his new image; the least he can do is help me hone my own. And when I do, I'm not going to exactly copy the popular girls here, but I'm going to try to fit in. I'll do this because they look good, not because I feel a need for their approval. Okay, that's a lie. But I'm not going to tell anyone that.

In English, Mr. Big tells me that the first paper I've written for class is pretty good. I tell him I've had a lot of practice at my last school, being on the newspaper and all, and he suggests I go to the counseling center to find out more about the paper here. "They can always use new people," he says. I don't know why I hadn't thought of it yet. I guess I've been mostly worried about getting to class on time and trying not to get lost.

It's Thursday now, and after school I check in at the counseling center about the school newspaper. They give me the name of the teacher in charge of it and tell me that the next meeting of the *Wolverine* staff is tomorrow, after school. I make a mental note to go and head toward the bike rack.

As I'm unchaining my bike, I see Tina lurch out of the school with her drawing pad under her arm. She always seems to be looking for me. I feel like she's clinging to me now. I think she just volunteered for that peer-mentor stuff so that she could prey on someone new for a best friend. As far as I can tell, she doesn't really have any other friends at school. She knows everyone, but everyone seems to steer clear of her.

"Hey, Taos," she says. She's started to call me this all the time, like it's cute or special or something. I realize Tina is one of those people who thinks everyone should have a nickname. She'd get along with my dad. "Where you headed?"

"Riding," I say. I changed out of my jeans into my cycling shorts in the girl's bathroom, in the hopes of getting some training done today. I also put on the amulet, just in case.

"You have rider's legs," she tells me. She totally acts gay. I know she said she wasn't, but she totally is. "You're pretty serious about the whole bike thing, huh?"

"I used to train in the mountains back home."

"You know there's a bike trail right behind the school here."

"I didn't know that, actually."

Tina points to the football field. "Yeah. It's right there, on the other side of the chain-link fence. It runs along the creek, and if you take it that way"— she points to the right —"it goes to this nature preserve thing and you can go on all these mountain paths and stuff. You'll like it."

"Really?" I'm psyched. I thought I was going to have to adjust to riding on cement all the time. I mean, the cool thing about Orange County is that all the streets are really new, and they all seem to have bike lanes. But up till now I'd thought it was uncool that you had to ride on streets.

"Yeah, I think you can ride all the way to the ocean, through this wilderness park with bobcats and rattlesnakes everywhere."

"Wow!" I exclaim.

Tina looks at me like she doesn't trust me, then smiles to show that she's kidding. "You're the only girl I've ever met who would get *excited* about bobcats and rattlesnakes, Taos." She draws on her pad. I look at it and see that she's actually pretty talented. She's doing cartoons of corpses walking around with cups that say "latte" and "fashion Nazi" on them. Nice. She's the daughter my dad always wanted. Oh well.

"I'm gonna go check it out," I say. "Thanks for the tip."

"After you're done, you should stop by the Starbucks on Alicia Parkway and Pacific Park."

"Starbucks? Why?" I am afraid of Starbucks. For some reason, I feel like only very pretentious high school kids would go there. It's not the kind of place we would have hung out in Taos. Starbucks? It's like the *devil,* as far as my old dad used to be concerned, though lately he's come in the apartment with Starbucks cups. He used to complain about how they exploited people and were taking over urban America, but now he seems to think you need to have a Starbucks cup in your hand as, like, an accessory. But for me? I don't know. The shop is probably full of girls with better clothes than me. Girls with Lexus cars. Girls who tell me I look like I wear the same thing every day, which I do, but *still.* I don't need the stress right now.

"I work there after school and on weekends," Tina tells me, as if sensing my fear of Starbucks. "My boyfriend works at the Rubio's. You can come hang, I'll give you free coffee or whatever you want, and you can meet Cesar."

"Cesar?"

"My boyfriend. He has some cute friends." She says this last part suggestively, like I might want to meet one of his cute friends. Or like I might want to be seen hanging around Starbucks because my friend is an employee.

"Okay," I say. "Thanks. I'll try, but I might have to get home, uh, for dinner." Honestly, I don't even know if my dad is going to be home for dinner. Lately his idea of dinner is having takeout with his pro-*cholo* posse while they mess with that stupid car in the garage. I had never realized how much I counted on Emily's family to be like a family for me, or how much I counted on going over to my grandma's for food. Until now. Now that my dad seems to live off fast food and paint fumes.

Tina looks like she knows I'm lying, that I don't really want to hang out with her and her boyfriend, Cesar. I don't know why I don't want to be around her more, exactly, except that she seems almost too nice. I don't trust people who are too nice. The hurt look on her face makes me feel bad.

"I'll really try," I say.

"Nothing like a Frappuccino after a hard ride," she says, half joking. I don't even know what a Frappuccino is, but I'm too ashamed to say so.

"It's a cold coffee-shake kinda thing," says Tina.

"So, how do I get to that path?" I ask, trying to change the subject.

She laughs to herself, tells me that if I go behind the barracks, through the little park there, that I'll hit the bike path. I thank her, put my earbuds in, my helmet on, and start toward the path.

I should really go home and call my dad on his cell, the way he's asked me to do every day after school, but right now I have so much energy I need to get out that I don't want to go back. I want to ride. I want to ride with my music on, as far as I can go. Dad won't notice anyway. He's been so busy with his important meetings and his stupid car that he doesn't have time for me.

I cross the parking lot, the barracks, the park, and find the path. It runs along the back high above a creek, and as soon as I get on it, it's like I've entered another world. A natural world. I can't believe it's right here, in the middle of all the perfect manicured yards and landscaped malls, this wild place. Across the creek I see a skate park full of kids in helmets doing tricks. Next to it is a public soccer field with what looks like a bunch of grown-up men in bright uniforms; they yell at each other in Spanish. I should tell my dad about it. He loves soccer and has always wished he had more athletic friends so he could start playing.

I crank up my iPod, increase the tension in the gears. *Yeah*, boy. I *love* this path. No traffic lights. Nothing to stop me. A couple of skinny men in cycling shorts and shirts pass me with a wave and a smile. This is now officially my favorite place in Orange County. For the first time since I got here, I feel at home. All it took was a good path through natural land and a cool breeze. It's almost like being back in Taos in the summer, only it's California in the winter. I think I could get to like it here.

I pedal under a bridge, and then — boom — right there in front of me are these big round hills, so big they might qualify as small, soft mountains. They are wild and undeveloped, covered with long wild yellow grass and flowers. The bike path ends for a little bit, but signs point me down a quiet side road to this nature preserve area. There are wild plants, and the hills are crawling with everything, the way nature meant it to be. I *love* it here. I haul along onto the paved trail, past the ranger station, amazed that a big city like this can coexist with a seriously challenging nature trail. I see rabbits and a roadrunner on the path, and hear water flowing alongside the path. A *roadrunner*? I didn't even know they had those out here! This looks so much like New Mexico I can hardly believe it. Southern California is full of surprises.

I pump my legs in time to the music and feel my mouth curl up in a smile. I forget all about the way Jessica made fun of my clothes. I'm happy. I go about five miles into the canyon, and pretty soon there's no trace of human beings at all, no more tract homes, nothing, just me and some soaring birds.

Seabirds.

I feel the amulet around my neck grow warm at the sight of them, but I can't be sure it's not just my imagination and the heat of exertion. I see a dirt path off to the side and instantly decide to take it. Up

I go, standing and leaning in to the steep hill, following the birds to the spot where they circle. Higher and higher I go, until I'm at the top of the hill. My legs are spent, burning with all the effort. I know a lot of people complain about exercise, but to me there is no better feeling in the world than this burn. It means power and health, and those things are important in connecting with whatever forces in the universe make us live.

I stop at the top of the little mountain, panting, and look up. The birds circle here. A large tree grows out of the top of the hill, and I park my bike beneath it. I take off my helmet and remove the earbuds. It's so quiet here. The air is clear and clean, nothing like it looks when you're on the freeways and see nothing but haze. If I listen closely, I can hear the far-off roar of something, either cars or ocean or both. I close my eyes and take a deep breath. I feel the amulet vibrate on my neck, and I put my hand to it. I can feel a tugging at me from the spirit world, and even though I usually resist this feeling, I can't right now.

I open my eyes and feel a shock of energy shoot into my legs from the earth beneath my feet. I look around at the hills and valleys of the canyon and feel like I'm in a dream state. I know I'm awake, but I still feel things that come from somewhere else. It's hard to explain. It feels a little bit like a night terror, only without the fear.

On the wind, I hear a piercing howl. I see some people on bikes down below, and they don't seem to have heard a thing. I listen again, my body still and waiting. The howl comes again, shrill and familiar. Coyotes. The lone cry is met by others, yipping and yapping the way they do when they've found something to kill. I feel the flesh on my arms pucker into goose bumps, and the howling is joined by a thundering drumroll of noise. I look to a hill in the distance and see a large herd of buffalo come running over the top, spilling down the hill. I see a couple walking hand in hand on the path, and they hear nothing, see nothing. I breathe deeply and witness. That is all I can do at these times. None of this is in my control.

The buffalo pound their way down the hill, across the bike path, right through the people there, and then they turn up my hill, toward me. I don't feel the need to flee. I'm not sure why. I stand still and face them. One of the buffalo is bigger than the others, with a diamond shape in white fur on its forehead. The herd follows this leader. They rush toward me and slow as they draw near. The herd stops before me, and the lead buffalo and I look into each other's eyes. This is no ordinary animal. It is intelligent, more intelligent than I am. It says nothing, just stands unmoving, looking at me. I have the eeriest sense. I can't explain it. In the same way, I know that the animal is gentle. I have the sense that this creature knows me, maybe even better than I know myself. I am comforted by the steady gaze, though there is an element of danger in what the animal is trying to tell me. Behind it, the other buffalo all turn their heads toward the source of the coyote shrieking, which has begun anew. A few of them stomp and shift, nervous, eager to leave. The lead buffalo senses the others' discomfort and bucks its head the tiniest bit to let them know it is still with them. But it continues to stare into my eyes for another thirty or forty seconds, filling me with peace and strength. Then, as the wails of the coyotes grow closer, the buffalo blinks slowly, with great kindness, and turns back to the herd. As one, they charge down the hill, leaving me in a haze of ghost dust. I have no idea what I've just witnessed, or why, only that all of the fear and panic I have been feeling about being here in Orange County have left my body. The fear I had has fled on the buffalo hooves.

It's a good thing, really, because as soon as I realize I am brave, strong, and ready to take on whatever the world might throw at me, I hear a low, sickening growl. I turn slowly, with my heartbeat slow in my chest, and look. The coyotes are here, about twenty of them in a semicircle on the other side of the tree, looking right at me. Their yellow eyes glow, and their skinny bodies seem to vibrate with a wickedness I cannot name. They are hungry, ferocious.

The coyotes have a leader too, a bigger animal, with a deeper gaze, and I am drawn to her eyes. She growls low, and moves toward me. I am frozen in place, not so much by fear as by curiosity. I watch her approach me, knowing that she wants something. She circles me one time and comes to stand before me. She yips and yaps and drops her front legs so that she is submissive, on her belly. The other coyotes do likewise. I'm confused. Why are these creatures bowing down to me? I don't want to be superior to them. I thought I was going to be *supper* to them.

Taking my cue from the animals, I bend to my knees and let them know that I respect them. The lead dog rolls onto her back in an even more submissive pose. What is she trying to tell me? I have no idea. But I know she will not allow me to be equal to her. It is clear in her eyes that she is here for me, at my service in some strange way.

I stand again and nod slowly at the lead coyote. I acknowledge her power and do my best to thank her for her gift through my eyes. Satisfied, she stands again. The others join her, and then, like the buffalo, they turn and run. I am left with shivers, cold and hot at the same time. I'm filled with a vibration that is impossible to name, connected to the many layers of the universe we inhabit in a clear and certain way that is impossible to explain to people without having them look at you like you're completely insane.

I wait and let the chill evaporate from my flesh. I stand in the tangy yellow warmth of the sun and watch the bikers and hikers down below. None show any sign that they might have heard or seen anything unusual. Then, with the quirky solitude that comes with being Pasquala Archuleta, daughter of an artist, granddaughter of a psychic, I mount my bike, put on my helmet, stick the earbuds in my ears, blast my music once more.

I take the wild way down the hill, off the path. I barrel through the grasses and past the rocks and cacti with the grace of a coyote, jumping and leaping as I go. I am a coyote, the wheels my paws. With them, I sense the texture of the sand. With them, I tap the earth, fearless in my animal movements, sensing the rabbits hiding in their holes. Down I ride, powerful, unafraid, on my way back to civilization, away from these dreams. I ride back toward the path below, the path along the creek, the path that will return me to my new world, minus my fear.

I am fearless. I am going to Starbucks.

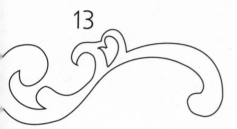

13

Here is what you need to know about the Starbucks where Tina works. It's in a very upscale mini-mall with fountains and fancy tables outside, and little kids hang out there.

No, I'm not kidding.

I've just walked in, sweaty from my ride and feeling not all that glamorous, and three little boys laugh at me. I mean *little* boys, like ten years old. Maybe younger. They sit at a table in the corner, without any adults that I can see anywhere near them, sipping coffee or something that looks like coffee. They wear ratty shorts with big suede sneakers that no longer have laces. The boys have skateboards, and apparently, this is where they come for fun. Or for *making* fun. I don't know why they're laughing at me, exactly, but I suspect it has something to do with the fact that I don't look anything like all the other high school girls in here.

That's the other thing you need to know about this Starbucks. Older kids hang out here, too. There are a dozen or so kids my age, and all the girls look like fashion models: impossibly thin, with low pants and bellies exposed, and super-trendy and beautiful clothes. I'm in cycling shorts, with my hair in a ponytail, and I need a towel to dry all the sweat.

While the little boys laugh, a few of the pretty girls turn to give me the once-over, which, now that I know the coyotes have my back, doesn't bother me one bit. I smile at them, and they turn away. This is the weak spot in mean girls. They don't know how to deal when you're actually nice to them. They expect rivalry and nastiness, and if you aren't willing to go head-to-head with them on this stuff, they're lost. I realize that Tina, for all her weirdness, knows this too.

Speaking of Tina, I see her standing behind the counter, pouring a drink for someone. After she's done concentrating on her task, she looks up and sees me. She smiles and waves. "Hey, Paski! Looks like you had a good ride. Did it rock up there or what?"

"Yeah," I say, coming to the pastry counter. I'm starving, and all the chocolate cakes and scones look amazing. The sight of the baked goods makes me think of Ethan. Or at least the Ethan I kissed in the car on the day I left Taos, which feels like so long ago.

"You want something in there?" asks Tina. She points to the pastries. I shrug, and she smiles like she knows I really do want something. "How about a brownie?" she asks.

"Okay," I say. "But I don't have any money."

I hear someone behind me laugh. I turn to see some girls I don't recognize, but they look just as pretty and well dressed as everyone else.

"My treat," says Tina. "How about something to drink?"

"I'd really just like some water." I'm extremely thirsty.

Tina takes a brownie out of the case and puts it on a white plate and tells me to grab a bottle of water from the cooler. She says she's going to try to get her break now, so we can talk. I take the food and water to a table by a window and watch the fountain outside. It's like a Spanish town square out there, with metal tables and families eating dinner, kids running in the grass. It is, overall, very pleasant here. Overall. That's the word Chris Cabrera used the other day. I can't explain why, but I feel him powerfully in my heart. Like I know he's thinking of me, which is crazy, but I feel it. I notice that the families here are well dressed and all look wealthy and attractive. Almost all of them are thin. It's strange to have landed in a place where so many people seem to put so much importance on looking good. There's something nice about it, but something oppressive about it, too.

I see a bin with newspapers and grab an *Orange County Register* so I'll look like I have a reason to be at a table all by myself. A story on the cover of the local section catches my eye. It's a society column with a photo of some glamorous-looking people at a fund-raiser. It's a mom and dad and daughter. The daughter is that Haley girl from school. The caption says that her parents donated money to a cancer charity. I can't imagine what it must be like to have parents with enough money to give some away like that. My dad is usually asking for a loan from his friends, and my mom has been known to be completely homeless a few times. I am so not of this place.

I feel a hand on my shoulder and look up to see Tina in her black Starbucks apron. She's really happy I'm here, or at least that's what it looks like. She sits at the table with me, and I try not to notice the way the girls our age look at us like we're total losers. They don't seem to have any problem whatsoever laughing at us. At least the little skateboard boys are gone now. They've been replaced by a group of three dorky-looking kids playing cards. I can't believe that most of the people in here are kids. My dad would freak if he knew about it. Or at least he would have back in Taos when he still boycotted Starbucks.

Tina asks about the ride, and I tell her it was great. I don't get into details. I'm still feeling confident, but the power of the coyotes is fading a little. I look down at the empty plate, embarrassed that I've scarfed the entire brownie like nothing.

"Good?" Tina surmises.

"Yeah, it was."

"You wanna meet Cesar?" she asks. I don't, but I shrug because I can tell she's proud of him. She says his name all Spanish, like "Seh-sar." I think she truly is the daughter my father never had. He would love her.

Tina leads me out of the Starbucks, across the patio area to a taco place called Rubio's. I look at the posters in the window. It's all about fish. Fish tacos, the things my dad came back from here loving. Everyone eats them around here. There's a really long line, too. I walk into the restaurant, expecting an awful fishy smell. I'm surprised when it smells really good.

"That's him," says Tina. She points to this tall, handsome dark-skinned guy working the register. He reminds me of a Mexican Orlando Bloom. He looks old, though, like too old to be in high school.

"He's cute," I say. "How old is he?"

"Twenty-six," Tina replies. I gasp. "It's not a big deal," she continues. "It's just ten years' difference. I'm very mature. I think he's extraordinarily immature, so it works out."

Cesar looks up and bucks his head at her. She smiles and grabs my arm. "I'm in *love* with him," she tells me. For a moment I feel like I'm back home with Emily or Janet. Then Tina says, "We totally did it on the beach last weekend. It was intense. But beach sex is way overrated. You get sand in places you really shouldn't have sand. Not easy to extract." Suddenly I'm not with my friends anymore. I'm back in Orange County.

We wait in line like everyone else, and when the two girls in front of us comment about how cute they think Cesar is, Tina beams at me. We get to the counter, and she introduces me to her older, underemployed, immature boyfriend. He says hello in a thick Spanish accent. I guess I like him, but I can't figure out why he's dating an underage girl, other than that he's probably a jerk. Tina orders an orange soda, and we take a seat at a table nearby, where she can swoon over him.

"He's *Mexican,*" she says, breathy, like this is scandalous news. "My parents would *freak* if they knew."

"I'm Mexican," I tell her. I don't usually say that. Usually I'm lecturing my dad about how we're not really Mexican because we don't speak Spanish, and he's always, like, lecturing me back about how "Mexican" is cultural, not linguistic.

"No, you're not," says Tina. She honestly looks like she feels sorry for me for being so confused. "I mean, you're not from *Mexico,* are you?"

"No." It's like talking to myself.

"I didn't think so. You're, like, Mexican-*American,* right?"

"Yes," I say.

"Me, too," she says.

"Wait a minute," I say. "You're Mexican and your parents don't like Mexicans?"

"Yeah, stupid, I know. But we're not like Mexican from over *there.*

We're from Arizona originally. I mean, my parents are. I'm from here."
She looks at me and bites her lip. "I didn't mean to offend you. My
parents would be cool with you. It's just people *from* Mexico they have
problems with. They have this thing where they don't think I should
socialize with them. My parents are stupid that way. Well, that way
and a lot of other ways." She looks sad. "I don't want to get into it
right now."

I say nothing but silently thank her for not getting into why her parents are stupid. I am dumbfounded by the Mexican thing. Back in Taos,
we didn't really make a distinction between Mexican-Americans and
people from Mexico. At least my dad didn't. We were all Mexicans to
him. The people who thought they were above us liked to say they
were "Spanish." It's all retarded, if you ask me.

"*My* dad would freak more that Cesar is really *old*," I comment.

"Old and *experienced*." She smiles. She wags her eyebrows. "He is *so*
good in bed. Absolutely *incredible*. It's like in *The Kama Sutra*, where
they talk about your souls meshing together."

I smile awkwardly. What is there to say? I don't know what makes
a guy good in bed or bad in bed. I know a little bit about *The Kama Sutra* only because my dad has a copy of it stashed somewhere. It freaked
me out when I was a little kid, and I never looked at it again. All those
drawings of weird blue people doing the nasty, and then the whole
idea that my dad read it. Ugh. I only know about kissing guys, and that
I would like very much to kiss Chris Cabrera.

"Uh-oh," Tina says. "You're a *virgin*. I can *tell*."

I shrug. "So?"

"No, nothing. No biggie. That's just rare around here," she says.
She doesn't seem to pass judgment on me for it, thank God. "But

knowing this about you now, I have to say again, be careful at Trent's party tomorrow."

"Why?"

"Are you still going? Please tell me you changed your mind."

"I'm still going."

Tina frowns. "Well, just be prepared for some freaky stuff."

"Like what?"

"You'll see." She looks at her watch. "My break is almost over. I should head back."

"Okay."

As we walk back, she puts her arm around me and leans in. "Whatever you do, don't let them know you're a virgin. Just play cool, like whatever they're doing, you've seen it all before."

"Why?"

"Just don't act shocked if you see people screwing around. Act like you're way above it all. That's my advice. Be a snob. I've heard brutal things about those guys."

"Even Chris Cabrera?"

"I don't know that much about him, actually." She looks at me like she senses something. "You like him," she says. I shrug and try not to blush. "He seems okay, except that he's been dating Jessica forever and they're such the perfect couple it makes you want to vomit."

"Okay," I agree.

"See you later, Taos," says Tina.

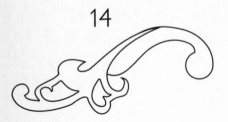

14

It's Friday, which means: A) I've survived a whole week at my new high school; B) Chris Cabrera, the hottest boy on earth, is going to be back at school today; and C) My dad and I both have parties to go to tonight.

Yes, that's right. Dad's a party *animal.* It goes with his new identity as a cool-geek animator *cholo* with a stupid car. As I sit at the table across from my father, eating a bowl of Kashi while he slurps at the breakfast burrito he made for himself, he tells me about the party in Santa Monica that he's going to.

"I wish I could be here for you," he says. "I know you'd like to use the Squeegeemobile to get to your own party." As *if.*

I shake my head and wonder to myself if the outfit I picked out seems like I'm trying too hard to look different than I usually do. I'm wearing a polka-dotted miniskirt that Emily gave me last year and a couple of my Urban Outfitters T-shirts. (I'll put bike shorts under the skirt to ride to school.) But unlike usual, I have my shirts layered one on top of the other, the way the girls do it here. I've also loosened the laces on my K-Swiss sneakers so that they're practically falling off. My dad hasn't noticed anything different about me, or if he has, he's too nice to point it out. "No, that's okay, really. I have a ride."

"With who?" asks my dad.

"A kid from school."

"A *boy* kid or a *girl* kid?"

"A boy kid."

Dad gives me a look that means he's not happy.

"He's harmless," I say, even though I'm not even sure if this is true.

Dad frowns, gets up, and goes to his room. He comes back with a bag from Best Buy and hands it to me.

"What is this?" I ask.

"Open it," he says.

Inside, I find a T-Mobile cell phone with a few different snap-on face plates so you can do different colors if you want to.

"Your first cell phone," says my dad.

"This is *mine*?" I exclaim. It has text messaging and everything.

"Yeah. It's already turned on. I wrote your phone number on the box."

I take it out and try it. "Wow. Thanks, Dad. Why'd you do this?"

"Because you're riding to parties with 'harmless' boys, that's why."

I smile.

He looks guilty. "I'm on the road so much, and you're so far from my work, I just thought it would be good for us to be able to keep in touch better. Back home it was easy. I always knew where you

were, and you knew where I was." He pauses. "Things are a lot different now."

I look at the phone in my hands, and for some reason, I feel like
crying. "Yeah," I say. "I know."

"You okay?" asks my dad.

I nod, but I don't make eye contact with him because I know that
if I see that concerned-dad expression on his face, I'll lose it.

"You don't look okay," he says. "Been a hard week?"

"Kind of."

"I'm sorry, kid. Can I do anything to help?"

I stare down at my hands. "I could use some new clothes."

My dad looks like he's embarrassed for missing another really important part of being a parent. I'm actually embarrassed for him. I'm
tired of having to remind him all the time that I need lunch money or
clothes. It's not that he doesn't want me to have these things. It's just
that he's always so busy and thinking about his work and his own image that he forgets I depend on him for just about everything I have.
He hits his forehead with the palm of his hand. "God, I'm so sorry,
Paski. I should have thought of that. A young woman in a new school
needs trendy clothes, right?"

"I don't need them to be trendy, exactly," I qualify. "Just I'd like to
fit in better."

"Of *course* you would." He looks truly tormented by the fact that
he hasn't realized this sooner. "I have been so selfish, *Chinita*. I'm so
sorry. God, I'm an idiot."

Don Juan wanders in and meows in agreement.

"You're not an idiot," I say, wondering for the millionth time why it's always my job to make my dad feel better when he should be the one who's there to make me feel better. In truth, I agree with Don Juan; I *do* kind of think my dad's an idiot.

"No, I am. I am an *idiot,*" he moans. He pulls out his wallet and starts to riffle through it. I see wads of receipts, no cash, and a few credit cards. I'm familiar with the contents. Bleak. I think you can tell how responsible a father is by the state of his wallet. Emily's dad, the businessman, has this neat, crisp wallet full of cash and shiny platinum credit cards. My dad's wallet looks like a bunch of pieces of old linty cardboard all stuck together.

"How about I give you my charge card and you go get yourself some clothes?" he asks.

"I don't think anyone will let me use it. They usually want an ID?"

"Oh, okay. Right." He looks at the digital time display on the face of the microwave. "How about we play hooky today and go shopping for you? I can call in sick. I'll call the school for you."

I think of Chris Cabrera and how I've been looking forward to seeing him for days. "No," I say. "I can't miss school, Dad. I just started. God."

He looks guilty again. "That was a stupid idea. Sorry."

"It's okay."

"Bad parenting. God. I'm an idiot."

"You're not an idiot," I say again. Yes, you are.

"How about I go get some cash and leave it here for you and you can go shopping after school?"

I shrug.

"How much do you need?"

"I don't know." I *hate* this. I *hate* that he is always asking me things like this, making a big deal out of things that don't seem to be a big deal for *normal* parents, people like Emily's parents. Her parents take her shopping for school clothes and don't apologize about the fact that they forgot about it. Oh, wait, that's because they *don't* forget about it. Normal parents like Emily's always remember to get her what she needs, and she always looks great. For *my* dad? Everything has to be a big production, like he wants me to stand in awe of the fact that he's actually acting like a grown-up.

"Five hundred dollars?" he asks.

I gasp. That is more than he has ever spent on clothes for me in one shot. At most, he's given me fifty bucks and dropped me off at JCPenney's. "Yeah," I say, excited. "Can you afford that?" There I go again, acting like a mom to my own dad.

"Punkin, I wouldn't offer if I couldn't." He smiles like he's the big shot now. "I'm making a lot of money now, *Chinita*. We'll probably get a house in the next six months." I'm so angry at him for having money and not telling me about it, for forgetting that I might need clothes, for being a dad when what I really need is a mom. I wonder if my dad has any plans to do something psycho with his newfound money, like get "ice" implanted in his front teeth. God, that would suck, to see my dad flashing his teeth like Mike Jones. He'll stop calling it a mouth, and he'll call it a grill. Just watch.

"What's wrong?" he asks.

"Nothing." I try to erase the image of my dad smiling through a grill full of ice.

"You don't want to go shopping?"

"I *have* to go shopping. I *need* clothes."

"You want more money? Is that it? I know these girls out here put a lot of time and effort into their threads."

Threads? What is he now, a has-been extra from some old show, like *The Fresh Prince of Bel-Air*? "No. It's fine."

Dad looks hard at me, like he's trying to figure out a top-secret code. It creeps me out. He asks, "Do you think I'm neglecting you? Is that it? You want me to stay home tonight? I can do that. We can rent movies and stay in and have a dad-daughter night. I don't mind. Hey, we could do microwave popcorn now that we have a microwave."

He *seriously* needs to get over the whole microwave fascination. "But you just said it's a bunch of people you should know," I say. I don't want to stay home with him. I *want* him to go to a party. I want to be alone.

Dad shrugs. "It is. But none of them — none of them — is as important as you are to me. Okay, Paski? I want you to understand that. I want that absolutely clear."

"I know."

"You are my life. I know I forget things now and then, but you're everything to me. You got that?"

"I know." I get up and rinse out my bowl and stick it in the dishwasher. It's nice to have a dishwasher, though I'm not all in awe of it, like my dad is with the microwave. We didn't have either one back in Taos because my dad, in his former incarnation, was Mr. Nature. Now he's all about the radiation. It's alarming. Back in Taos, it took, like, twenty minutes for the water to get hot. Here, it's instant. Life is almost too easy in Orange County. I can see how it'd be real easy to forget about things like conservation and nature here. The rules of nature don't seem to apply.

"You are my world, girl," says Dad. He looks mopey and sad. I think he needs a girlfriend. Or a dog. Antidepressants. Something. He really does. I don't *like* being his life besides work. I think he needs something else in his personal life, so that I can have a life of my own. It's too much pressure to be another person's life. Especially when that other person is your dad.

"Just go to your party and have a good time," I say, heading upstairs, sounding like a mom again.

"So, I'll see you when we get home later?" calls Dad.

"Yeah," I call back.

"I want you home by midnight," he instructs. "And I want that harmless boy's name, parents' names, and phone number before you leave."

"Okay," I say. "You be home by midnight, too."

"I don't know if I can do that. Traffic is pretty bad around here."

"I was *joking,* Dad," I scream down the stairs. "I am the *kid,* remember? I don't set your curfew." *God.* What is *wrong* with him?

"Right. Okay, well, just call me if you need me."

His voice sounds so small and sad downstairs. I close the door, go to the bed, and start to cry into my pillow. I don't know exactly why. I'm trying to be alone with my misery when the Japanese girl's voice suddenly comes again. I want it to stop so I can sob in *peace.* I don't want to hear voices, and see coyotes, and whatever else happens to me. Then I'm startled by a light thumping on the wall next to my bed. I hear a muffled voice call out: "You okay over there?"

I stay still and say nothing and hear it again. It is not a spirit voice. It's human. From the apartment next door. It's Keoni.

"You want me to come over?" he asks. "I'm a good listener. If you have a problem."

Great.

His room is directly on the other side of the wall. He's practicing his good listening skills without my permission, through the *wall*.

15

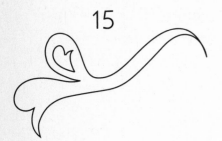

Half an hour later, Dad has gone to work, and I've called Emily and Janet to complain about my weird father. Talking to my buds always makes me feel better. What I'd love more than anything is if they could visit me here.

I leave the apartment through the garage. Kerani and Keoni wait outside for me, with concern on their faces.

"You okay, Paski?" asks Kerani. He talks. He talks! I try to calm my surprise enough to answer.

"I'm fine. Why?"

"We heard you crying," the twins say in unison. Keoni speaks next. "We wanted to let you know that no matter what, we're here for you."

Kerani speaks again: "Whatever you need. We'll listen."

The twins look at each other and then back at me. Keoni says, "We know what it's like to be sad."

"Thanks," I reply softly. I feel exposed. Sometimes I think it's a bad idea to share walls with people you don't really know. There's something to be said for separate houses.

"Want to talk about it and walk to school with us?" asks Keoni. As soon as he's spoken, I hear the Japanese voice, the little-girl voice. I hold my hands over my ears, but it doesn't help, of course, because this kind of voice doesn't come from the real world. I wonder occasionally if I need medication.

"What did we say?" the twins ask in unison.

"It's not you," I say. I tell them about the voices I hear, hoping that they'll decide I'm too weird to hang out with. I'm not a big fan of smoking or the ties with T-shirts. I'm sure they're really nice guys, but there's also the way they keep looking at my legs and my chest. They're horny. I don't need that right now. Not from them, anyway.

The twins listen to my story about the voices and tell me it doesn't sound weird to them at all. They tell me that their mother prays to dead ancestors all the time, and that in Japan they even take the bones out of the dead and clean them off. Then the twins ask me to tell them what I'm hearing now. I listen to it again and try to repeat the Japanese words.

"There's a girl saying, '*dandan kowaku naro*,'" I say. "And a man's voice answers, real mean, '*Utsubuse ni natte kudasai.*' And then I hear the girl screaming and crying really hard, and it's horrible. I hate it."

The boys look at each other and shrug. "Go get Mom," Keoni tells his brother.

"Yeah, okay," says Kerani. He goes back up the stairs to his apartment and I notice that in the right light, these guys actually aren't totally bad-looking. You always hear about actors or singers who are really hot in their twenties and they always say they were fat or geeky in high school. I think these could kind of be like that, if they get a little taller and lose the baby fat and the zits.

A minute later, Kerani comes down the stairs with his mother. This is the first time I've seen her, and I'm totally surprised to see that she's one of those young-looking moms you see around here sometimes. She's wearing a Juicy T-shirt and terry sweatpants with flip-flops. Her hair is cut in a chin-length bob that is long in the front and sort of short in the back, at an angle. It's got pretty highlights in it. She is beautiful. She smiles at me and I say hello. She tells me her name is Melanie and asks if I like Aliso Viejo so far. I lie and say I think it's great. What else do you say? That I want to go home? That I don't think I'll ever be rich enough or cool enough to feel as comfortable and confident here as I did back home? That my best friends are the coolest people on earth and now, unless we all go to the same college, I won't see them forever, or at least for another two years?

"How is your dad?" Melanie asks me. Is it my imagination, or does she seem to think my dad is all that? She has a crush on him. I can feel crush energy powerfully sometimes, and this pretty woman finds something of interest in my weirdo dad. *She* must need medication. Or maybe she takes too much already. Whatever it is, something's not right, not if she digs my dad.

"My dad's fine," I say.

"Mom's an artist, like your dad," says Keoni.

Melanie looks embarrassed. "I make my living building custom cabinets and shelves, things like that. But I like to sculpt."

"Oh," I say. I hear the voice again and try to ignore it, but it's a damn unsettling voice that doesn't want to be ignored. Melanie notices my concerned expression has shifted, so she changes the subject.

"Kerani tells me you have some Japanese words you want me to translate?"

"Uh, yeah," I say. I repeat the words for her, and her face gets pale. Her mouth opens, and she looks at me like I've said something frightening.

"Oh my God," she says.

"What is it, Mom?" asks Keoni.

"You said the second part is a man screaming at a little girl?" Melanie's eyes are filling with tears.

"Yes," I say.

"The first part is a cry for mercy," she explains. "The second part is a man telling her to lie facedown."

As she says this, I hear a new phrase. "I'm hearing 'hahaoya' now, and crying."

"How?" asks Melanie. "How are you hearing this?"

"I'm crazy?" I joke. But by now she is completely crying. "What? What did I do?"

The twins are as confused as I am. Their mother touches my arm and says, "My mother was a little girl in California during World War Two. She and her parents were rounded up and put in one of those internment camps. Do you know about those?"

"No." I respond solemnly.

"I'm not surprised," says Melanie. "They don't teach about it in schools here. During the war, the government here rounded up everyone they thought was Japanese, or who looked Japanese, and they put them in concentration camps."

"Like the Nazis?" I ask.

"Not that bad. But it was still pretty awful. My mother never really talked about it, but she did tell me that she remembered being in the camp when some soldiers . . ." Her voice trails off. She regains her composure and goes on, "Basically she saw soldiers rape her mother right in front of her."

"Oh my God." My chest hurts with the pain of what that must have been like, both for the child and for the woman.

"She was six years old."

"I didn't know that," whispers Keoni.

"Holy crap, Mom," says Kerani. "How come you never told us this?"

She shakes her head. "It's a sad chapter of our lives that I would rather forget, and my mother never wanted to talk about it, so out of respect for her, I have tried to forget about it. But she used to have nightmares, and she'd scream those very words that you're hearing now."

"Do you think it's Grandma talking to Paski?" asks Keoni.

"Is she still alive?" I ask.

"She died when I was a teenager," Melanie explains. "She never got to meet my children."

"I'm sorry," I say.

"I pray to her every day, and I've prayed that I'd hear from her. I have so many things to ask her. I think you're communicating with her. I don't know how or why, but you are."

I feel the flesh on my arms rise. I don't want to be communicating with the dead grandmother of these guys. I don't want to know about the fact that she saw some men rape her mother when she was six years old. It's horrible. I hate this gift. My grandmother is completely wrong. It's not a gift. It's a curse.

"Do you hear anything else?" Melanie asks me, taking my hands in hers.

"No," I say, adding silently, *and I don't want to.*

"If you do, tell me," she says. "Tell her I love her."

God, I think. That is a huge responsibility. Communicating love between the living and the dead, between family members. Mothers and daughters. I get chills and feel so sorry for Melanie and especially for her mother. I just want to hold the little girl she used to be in my arms and comfort her and protect her.

"Mom, we have to get to school," says Kerani.

Melanie looks at her son and smiles. "You guys are right about her," she says. "Our new neighbor is very smart and special."

I'm not really sure how to feel since I know something so intimate and revealing about this family I've just met. Part of me just wants to get away.

"See you later," I say. Then I add, "I'll let you know if I hear anything from your grandmother." I don't hear the Japanese voices right now, and I'm grateful for that. I look at the boys, who seem sad. So I say, "For what it's worth, your grandmother loves you very much. She wants you to be happy. She thinks you're great."

Melanie wraps her arms around the boys and smiles. "Thank you, Paski," she says. "You have no idea how much this means."

I ride to school in the cool wind, listening to my music and trying to get that awful story out of my head. Sometimes I just wish so much I could be a normal girl.

As I'm locking my bike outside the front doors, I hear a familiar motorcycle engine. I look up just in time to see Chris Cabrera coming down the hill. My heart jumps, and I run my hands over my clothes and hair to make sure I don't look totally dorky. When he steers the bike right up to the curb near me, I feel my breath leave me. He stops the bike and takes off his helmet. He's smiling and looks like he got a bit of a tan, wherever he was. In short, he looks awesome.

"Hi," he says.

"Hi," I say casually. "Welcome back."

"Thanks. You look good."

I try to shrug like I didn't put any effort into it, but that's a lie. I worked hard figuring out the clothes, and I even did a little makeup with a photo of Rachel Bilson next to the bathroom sink, thinking of what Tina told me. I feel self-conscious about it. I'm hoping the effort will pay off, by at least getting Jessica to keep quiet about me.

"You look good, too," I say to Chris. I blush, and he grins.

"Andrew tells me you're going to Trent's party tonight with him?"

I shrug as if it hasn't been the main focus of my entire week. "I don't know yet. I have to see how I feel."

"You should come."

"You going?"

"I wasn't planning on it, but now that I know you're going to be there, I'm going. Trent's 'rents are out of town. It's gonna be wild."

"Cool," I say.

The first warning bell rings. We've only got a few minutes to get to class. "I gotta go park this monster," says Chris. "See you in Big's class." He eases the motorcycle toward the parking lot and around a corner.

I head straight to the girl's bathroom to check my makeup. I've stashed mascara and lip gloss in my backpack, but they're kind of old. The other girls here have new cosmetics, NARS and that other brand I keep seeing everyone use around here, M•A•C. I'm embarrassed because I got my gloss at the drugstore, and the looks on their faces tell me that they know it. I don't think many girls around here get anything at the drugstore, except condoms, if they use them.

I smile at them, but they don't smile back. I act like I don't care and busy myself fixing my hair, trying to make it look messy but cool. I rub fresh deodorant on my armpits and hope I don't smell too gross. I spritz on the vanilla body spray I got at Walgreens. I see the other girls sharing a hot-pink bottle of Ralph Lauren Cool perfume. I wish I had something like that. I've never had a real bottle of perfume. I always borrowed Emily's. I'd like to smell expensive. As it is, I think I smell a bit cheap. As the other girls spray themselves, one of them complains because the Mini Cooper her parents just got her for her sweet sixteen was the wrong color. "I wanted red," she says, almost in tears. "I told them, like, a thousand times I wanted red. And they got me black. Black! It's awful. I hate them. I have to take it back."

I try not to stare at them, but I can't believe what I'm hearing. I'd kill for a black Mini Cooper. She has no idea how lucky she is.

As I'm walking to Mr. Big's class, I feel someone bump into me. I turn to find Jessica and her friends laughing.

"Oh, sorry," says Jessica with a fake smile. "Did I do that? I didn't mean to."

I keep walking and notice that Haley looks embarrassed for me again. She seems like a nice person who is caught being friends with the wrong people.

Jessica bumps into me again, and this time, when I look at her, she holds out a piece of folded paper.

"For you," she says. "Special delivery."

I take the note, and the girls sashay down the hall. I stand to the side and open the note. In bubbly letters with circles for dots on the letter I, I find these words: *Chris is mine. Don't mess with him or you'll have to deal with me. Destroy this note or we'll destroy you. I mean it.*

I fold the note and stuff it in my backpack, my gut in knots of fear. I don't need this. I really don't. At the end of the hall, I see Jessica toss her shiny dark hair and laugh, like she's just heard the funniest joke in the world. As I watch her, I get the noise in my head, the noise of warning. On my neck, the amulet grows warm. In that instant, I see the vision again. Jessica in a body cast and flowers all around. I can't tell if she's dead or alive, and I don't want to know. Then I see myself in a mirror and my face is covered with huge bloody cuts. I shiver in fear and fight my desire to run away, go home and crawl into bed. *What does this mean?*

I manage to make it through the rest of the day without any more harassment from Jessica, mostly because I avoid her. If I see her coming, I turn and scurry away. I pity myself for being so afraid, but it's not just Jessica's power that scares me. It's the feeling I get around her. Like she is purely evil.

During lunch, I take off on the bike trail instead of waiting around for Tina. I don't know why, but the thought of Tina today makes me depressed. I call my grandmother from my cell phone and tell her about the Japanese grandmother. She listens without saying anything. Then I ask about the visions of Jessica.

"The universe is trying to get you to help that poor girl."

"Poor girl?" I ask with a laugh. "Grandma, this is the richest girl in *school*."

"That's not what I meant," says Grandma. "I mean poor as in *spiritually* poor."

"Oh, *please*," I retort. "She's one of the meanest people I've ever met. She's a total spoiled *bitch*."

At the word "bitch," my grandmother goes silent. After a moment, she says, "Please don't use that word to describe other girls, Paski, you know better than that."

"I'm sorry. It's just, you don't know what it's *like*."

Grandma laughs lightly. "I don't know exactly what it's like for you right now, no. But I have a feeling."

"I want to come home."

"I know, honey, but everything in life happens for a reason," says grandma. "You're there for a reason that isn't clear right now but will be. Just remember, do not ignore your gift or —"

"Or bad things will happen," I finish. I roll my eyes, even though she can't see me. How many times does she think she has to tell me this?

Grandma ignores me. "Whether Jessica is nice or mean right now, as a teenager, is not important. Few of us remain the way we are as teenagers once we've grown up. It's hard for you to understand, but there is a bigger purpose for you being where you are right now."

"What do you mean?" I ask.

"I can't tell you. All I can do is encourage you to make peace with your vision about Jessica Nguyen."

"I don't want to make peace with it. I want it to go away."

"Oh, Pasquala." My grandmother heaves a deep, heavy sigh. "It won't. Please take my advice and honor your gifts."

"I don't want gifts. Other than clothes and maybe nice perfume. Those are all the gifts I want." I start to whine. "I just want to be *normal*."

Grandma sighs again. The guilt sigh. She's very good at it. "Honor the vision," she says. "Try to understand what it's telling you. Pay attention to the voices, sweetie."

"No. I don't want to. I want to forget all about Jessica Nguyen and her stupid friends."

"Well, you can try. But I don't think I have to tell you that when we try to run from our spirits, they only work harder to find us."

I get chills. "Yeah, well I don't want spirits. I want clothes. And I want a boyfriend who doesn't cheat on me. I want a car that isn't embarrassing. I want a normal family."

My grandmother laughs. "Okay, Pasquala. Keep your chin up, and have faith that it's all what it is meant to be."

I look at my watch and I have to get back for the end of lunch. "I'll talk to you later, Grandma."

I go back to school and muddle through my last two classes. I don't want to have anything to do with Jessica. I don't want to honor the spirits that are trying to warn me about her. If I'm supposed to help her, I don't want to. I want my own life. Maybe that's a selfish way to be. I don't know. Probably. But what if I didn't have this "gift"? No one would warn anyone about the things I see. And life would be what life was supposed to be.

After school, I go to Miss Munn's room. She's the senior English teacher who oversees operations of the school newspaper. About ten kids are working at different tasks on computers and desks around the room. I like the look of these kids better than I've liked the looks of most kids at this school. They seem normal — well, all except the one who's breathing through his mouth. He might be a little abnormal. That or he's got allergies.

I introduce myself to Miss Munn and hand her a folder with copies of the school paper from Taos, so she can see that I'm serious. She shakes my hand, asks me if I'd like a bottle of water, and invites me to have a seat next to her. She doesn't sit at her desk. She sits with the students. She almost looks like a student. I like her. As I sip the bottle of water, she reads through my clips.

"These are great," she says. Then she asks me to go talk to someone named Sydney. Miss Munn points to a chunky girl with a black ponytail and funky red eyeglasses. "She's our editor. You can check with her to see what she thinks."

I approach Sydney. She's focused on her computer, biting her lower lip as she taps away, and doesn't seem to notice me. I know I shouldn't look at what she's doing, but I peek at the computer screen anyway. It looks like she's doing layout for an entertainment page, with a photo of the singer Jesse McCartney and the headline: TALENTED, OR JUST HOT? I answer the question in my head: talented, but he reminds me too much of Ethan.

I tap Sydney on the shoulder. "Excuse me," I say. She turns her head. Her eyes are dark black, with long lashes, and they look amazing in her glasses. Few people can pull off a good look with glasses on, but this girl does it. She has milky-white skin and very pink cheeks. She's pretty, but I can see how the average hot boy around here might overlook her because she's a little overweight.

"Can I help you?" she asks with a smile. I can tell she's friendly and I am *so* relieved by her friendliness. I tell her who I am, and what I want to do. I tell her I used to edit the paper at my school and all that, and she doesn't get territorial, which is excellent. I think that if it were me, I'd probably get a little nervous if some new kid showed up saying she was an editor, too.

"That's awesome news." Then she makes a funny face. "No pun intended. I was just sitting and wishing we had another reporter around here."

"Really?" I ask.

"Sure. If you don't mind reporting. I know you probably want to edit."

"No, it's okay, I just want to work at the paper."

"That's great, then. I was just trying to think of someone to do a sports feature I've been meaning to run for a while."

Sports? Like, scores and plays and all that? Uh-oh. Better to be honest and let her know I'm clueless about organized sports. "I don't really know how to cover games," I say. "I didn't do any before."

"Oh, this isn't a game. It's a race. Motocross. You know, like, motorcycle racing. Jessica Nguyen. She's —"

At mention of Jessica's name, I feel my pulse accelerate. My grandmother's voice echoes in my head, about how when you run from the spirit voices, they just work harder to catch up to you. "I know who she is."

"Oh, okay, cool," Sydney responds with another smile. "So then you know she's a pro motocross racer?"

I nod. But I don't want to do any kind of story about Jessica. I really don't.

Sydney lowers her voice, with a secretive look, and I lean in to hear her. "I mean, around here everyone seems to think Jessica is all that. But it might be cool if, during the course of the race, you interviewed some of the other racers to see how they feel about her. See if she's all that to them, too, or if there's another side of Jessica that nobody here knows about."

Great. I'm new at school, and my first assignment is to do an expose on the most popular girl who totally hates me. Maybe I shouldn't be a reporter. "What if she turns out to be nice?"

Sydney shakes her head and laughs. "You are new here. For now just cover the race. But later, we'll get you or someone else to dig around for the dirt on Nguyen. What if she turns out nice, you ask?" Sydney laughs. "And maybe the earth is actually flat."

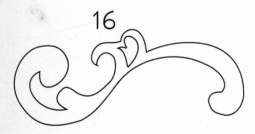

16

After I've met all the people on the Wolverine newspaper staff, I ride my bike back to the apartment to get the money Dad promised me. It's already almost five P.M., and Andrew Van Dyke is planning to pick me up at eight, so I better hurry. I know there's an Old Navy in the same mall where Tina works, so that's where I'm planning to go. I don't know of any other stores yet, and even if I did, I don't have transportation.

I find a pink envelope stuck to the refrigerator door with a United Farm Worker magnet. I pour myself a glass of milk, get some graham crackers out of the cabinet, and sit down to eat and look over the *Orange County Register*. I open the pink envelope and find a card inside. My dad is the master of cards. He leaves them for me all the time, congratulating me on everything, telling me how much he loves and respects me. His middle name should be Hallmark.

The card has an inspirational saying on the front with flowers, and inside, my dad has written the usual stuff. Oh, and there are six hundred-dollar bills, crisp and neat.

Six hundred dollars?!?

I hold the crisp bills in my fingers and rub them together. They're almost like sandpaper, they're so new. It's a fortune. I have never known my dad to have this much money. And usually, the money he *does* have is crumpled and sweaty at the bottom of his pants pocket. He's unrecognizable, this new version of my father. I don't know what to do with all this money, so I set it down on the table and place it in the shape of a fan. It's so pretty.

Oye Chinita,

I remember the day you were born like it was yesterday, and I know that's a cliché but I truly do. I will always think of the moment you first opened your little brown eyes as the most incredible spot in time for me.

I want you to know that I am proud of you. I know I'm not around as much as I should be, and as I get my new career off the ground in Los Angeles it's going to be like this for a while. But I want you to know that I am your dad, and I love you, and that no matter what you need I'm here for you, to listen, to talk, to be your biggest fan.

Every day you grow into a more incredible and interesting young lady. I am honored to be your father. There were times, raising you on my own, when I didn't know if I was doing anything right. But to see you now, so strong and confident, so funny and self-assured, even in those times when you argue with me and talk back, I feel great knowing that you turned out exactly as any parent could have hoped.

You are the greatest kid in the world. Have fun shopping. I can't wait to see what cool clothes you pick out. You have your mother's looks but my taste — thank God.

Be careful tonight, and call me with the "harmless" boy's phone number and information. You forgot to leave it for me earlier today. I'm not mad, I just want to make sure we're on the same page and I know where you are. I want you to know that I trust you to make good decisions in life, and I do, but I am still your dad and I still need to know who you're with and what you're doing. I worry about you and want you to be safe. That's what dads do.

Love,
Dad

I look closely at the ink, and I can't be sure, but it looks like it might have gotten smeared by a couple of drops of salty water. I guess he hasn't changed in some ways. Another thing about my dad? He's sappy, so his eyes tend to leak.

*   *   *

I finish my snack, tuck four of the hundred-dollar bills into my underwear drawer, and haul ass to Old Navy. My iPod battery charge is running out. I'll have to recharge it when I get back to the apartment. There are just too many things to remember right now.

Top on the list is what I came here to buy. I had a list in my head of what I thought would look good but not *so* good that it might seem like I was trying to impress anyone. There is a fine line between wanting to look cool but not wanting to seem like I want to look cool, if that makes sense.

I chain my bike outside, on a trash-can stand, and head inside. I see a couple of girls I recognize from school browsing at the front of the store. They see me and we kind of say hi, like we recognize each other and respect the fact that we're all here shopping. It's the first time I've felt like I'm starting to be a part of the school. When girls you don't really know say hello to you because they recognize you, it's a good sign.

I get a rolling cart, the kind they usually have in grocery stores, and start to look around. The clothes are so new and cute! The only thing I wish is that Emily and Janet were here to shop with me. We would have a blast. They're so crazy, I bet they'd try to get inside that display-truck thing in the middle, with the fake dog. I don't think you're supposed to go in it, but I can just imagine Janet doing just that.

I *love* the smell of new clothes. I actually stop and pick up the corner of a long beige peasant skirt and hold it up to sniff it. I don't know what that smell is, but there's no way to get it back once you've washed the clothes. I look at the prices. Things aren't very expensive here. Four hundred bucks could go a really long way, actually. I think

I'll just get a couple of things for the party tonight and save the rest of the money for later.

Even though I don't want to, I keep thinking of Jessica and her friends and the clothes they wear. They always look cute. I want to dress like them. I don't want to *want* to dress like them. But I do anyway. No one has to know.

I pick out a couple of cute skirts, short and flirty. Most of my pants are blue jeans, so just for some variety, I force myself to get some pink pants and a pair of black capris. I get some tank tops with sparkles around the neckline and some T-shirts. I get a sexy spaghetti-strap top, black like the pants. I have no idea what to wear tonight. Andrew mentioned there'd be a swimming pool, but I don't think I like the idea of Jessica looking at me in a bathing suit. She wouldn't be very nice about it. I'm not fat or anything, but around Jessica, I feel fat.

Now for accessories and shoes. I find a straw hat, sort of like a cowboy hat but way cuter, and try it on. It looks good. At least I think it does. I need my friends here to check me on this stuff. Emily and Janet never let me go out looking like a dork. They always saved me from myself. You don't realize how important that is in life until you don't have it anymore.

I find a little sequined handbag that's only twenty dollars, and I throw it in the cart. This is incredibly fun! I love shopping where you can actually feel what you're buying. Out in Taos, for cool clothes the only real shopping option was online. I always ended up sending something back. This is way, way better.

I find some bracelets and earrings and beads. I even find some shiny, strappy gold sandals. They're flat, but they wind all around the foot and ankle in a real sexy way. I might actually really look hot. This is too cool.

I head to the register and pile all the stuff onto the counter. I see a tube of the sparkling lip gloss like the one the girls had at school today. I want it but somehow feel like I've already gotten too much stuff. Like I don't deserve it. I've gotten way more than I thought I would, and the cashier, a boy I recognize from school, looks at me with sad eyes. "Find everything you were looking for?" he asks.

I realize in that instant that he probably has to work for spending money and he must think I'm one of the shallow rich girls around here. "I did," I say. Then I blurt, "I have never bought this much stuff at once in my entire life."

He misunderstands my apology and seems to think I'm bragging. He blushes and looks hurt. "Must be nice," he says with a shrug. There are more apartment kids around here than I realized. In fact, I bet we're the majority. But maybe it's like Tina says: The few rule the many until the many stand up and fight back.

I grab the tube of lip gloss and put it in the pile and apologize to the boy. I'm not sure why.

17

The doorbell rings at exactly — and I mean exactly — eight o'clock. Andrew might be kind of a cute jerk, but at least he's punctual. I'm actually on the phone with Janet, who's trying to tell me how to act with Chris to get him to notice me. Some of her advice is good, but sometimes she's a little crazy. Like she thinks I should pretend to fall on him. That's nuts. I tell her I have to go, and after I promise to call her later to tell her *everything,* we hang up.

I breathe deeply to calm myself down and take one last look in the mirror on the back of my door. I decided on jeans, the tight, low ones with the rhinestones on the back pockets. I can't believe I'm down to a size six. I guess the stress of the move has made me lose some weight.

I wear two tank tops, a plain white one underneath a pink one with sparkles at the neckline. I thought about wearing the straw hat, but it looked like I was trying way too hard, so I went for some dangly earrings and loose, curly hair instead. I've done my makeup as much like Rachel Bilson as I could, with strong emphasis on my eyes. I outlined them in black liner and did charcoal eye shadow with lots of mascara. I'm wearing a shimmery body lotion, Jergens, all over my body. I've got on the strappy sandals, and I even had time to put red polish on my toenails. I put on a little of the lip gloss, and spray myself with the cheap spritzer. I would have gotten real perfume, except I didn't have time to go to a department store. I've read that boys really like citrus smells. Anyway, I look at myself and I'm surprised by how much I'm starting to look like a girl from Orange County. At least I think I do. I don't know what the people at this party will think.

I open the door and find Andrew looking taller than usual, extremely cute and well groomed in his Abercrombie shirt and scruffy shorts. He has amazing legs, with little blond hairs all over them. He wears a couple of gold chains around his neck, and I can smell his acidic cologne from here. His hair is perfectly rumpled. He looks like the model that he is. He would look just right in a magazine ad for messy preppy clothes. He's got an arm up on the wall next to the door, and he's leaning in all casual, like he does this all the time. But as he sees me, the cool look on his face changes to one of mild surprise.

"Wow," he says.

"Hi," I say. I blush because I can tell he likes what he sees.

"Daaamn, girl, you look *hot.*" His voice cracks on the word "hot," like it's still changing. He steps back and looks me up and down like a piece of meat. "I mean, I knew you were cute, but I didn't know you were *hot.*" He smiles and nods with enthusiasm. "Daaaammn. You're hot, *mamacita.*"

Mamacita? Why did he call me *that*? I don't know if any of this is supposed to make me feel good, but what it actually does is make me feel naked. At the same time, I'm totally flattered, in a sick way, and loving it. "I'm ready to go," I say, clutching the shiny gold handbag to my side. I wish I could take out my new cell phone and send his photo to Emily and Janet right now. They would die.

"Yeah, let's go, shorty," he says. We start down the stairs, and I'm horrified when, as we go down, we run into Keoni and Kerani on their way up, with a pizza and a liter of Pepsi. They are dressed exactly alike again, this time in plaid shorts and ties with tank tops. Not. A. Good. Look. I notice that Kerani is carrying a stack of library books. I glance at the titles on the spines: They're about Japanese internment camps in the United States during World War II. I feel a strange sense of peace that he has these books, like it would make their grandmother happy. I want to ask him about it, but now's definitely not the time.

"Hi, guys," I say.

They glare at Andrew and say nothing. They look at me all betrayed, like I'm some kind of traitor or something.

"Have fun staying in practicing your chess moves, *geeks and freaks,*" Andrew tells them. "Fucking weirdos," he turns to me. I feel personally struck by this insult. I want to protect the twins, and I can feel their grandmother trying to talk to me. I tune her out because I don't want Andrew to think I'm a total weirdo.

"Be careful, Paski," Keoni says after we've passed.

"*What* did you say, dickwad?" asks Andrew, turning to look up at them.

"I told Paski to be careful," says Keoni. His voice sounds like it's shaking with fear. My heart pounds with the tension in the air. I don't want to see a fight. I really don't. That would be so stupid. What is it about guys that they're always ready to fight each other? I hear the Japanese words come in and out, like a radio not quite tuned to the right station, in the grandmother's voice: *Naze desu ka . . . kudasai . . . Ikimasho.*

"Come on, Andrew," I say. "Let's go."

"Yeah, whatever, loser, okay?" says Andrew to Keoni. He puts his arm around me and kisses the top of my head. "This chick is in very good hands. Don't you worry about her. I'm going to make her *very* happy tonight."

I feel filthy as the twins give me a sad, disappointed look. He's going to make me *happy*? What the hell is he *talking* about? Why is he acting like I'm some kind of skeezer girl who's going to have sex with him?

The inside of Andrew's shiny black Porsche smells like cherry cough syrup. I notice that he has a red air freshener hanging from the rearview mirror, and I figure this is the source of the smell. My dad always says those things are cheesy, and I have to say I share that opinion. It makes my throat hurt to smell it.

"Nice car," I say.

"*Word,*" he says. He puts on blue-tinted Oakley sunglasses, and as he turns the key in the ignition, he looks me up and down again and whistles through his teeth. "Damn, I had no idea. I mean, I really had no idea."

Andrew revs the engine a few times, and I can see the twins looking out at us from their balcony. From this safe distance, they're actually laughing at us. That's not good, is it? They aren't bad people. They're nice guys, actually — just a little odd, but I'm not exactly one to talk, right? I don't like that I've become hilarious to them. What do they know?

Andrew cranks up his stereo and adjusts the controls on a black iPod until the bass booms so hard I feel it in my bones; he's got a device that broadcasts the music to the FM dial. It's a Fat Joe rap song, and he chants along, using all the offensive words. He smiles over at me like I might be impressed by this. I'm not impressed, but I have to admit that being in such an expensive car with such a hot guy and such a booming stereo is a *little* bit exciting. Okay, a *lot* exciting. I've only ever seen things like this on TV. I like the idea of where I am right now. I just don't know if it's good that Andrew is so vulgar. Maybe it's all a front. Maybe he has a soft side somewhere.

Andrew revs the engine a few more times and blasts the a.c. With only one hand on the wheel — and the other over his crotch — he looks over his buff shoulder and backs out of the driveway very fast, so fast that I clutch my seat and the grab bar over my window. As he drives, he licks his lips and raps: " 'Mami tell me do you like it, I know you like it, it's written all over your face, don't fight it, you like it, more than I like it, so put it all over your face don't bite it.' "

He notices that I'm afraid. "Hey, chill, shorty," he says. "I'm a hell of a driver."

"Okay," I say. I don't "chill," however. That's because I'm afraid of more than Andrew's driving. I'm afraid of *Andrew.*

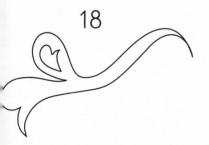

18

After a scary fifteen-minute drive on freeways where everyone seems to drive a million miles an hour while sipping Starbucks and chatting on a cell phone, we pull up to an iron gate leading to a street that winds up a hillside. Everything is shaded by giant bright green palm trees. They're so well manicured they look like toys. The houses on the other side of the gate all look exactly alike, pink with red tile roofs. It looks comfortable and safe, like somewhere I'd never live.

"Wow," I say. "This is really nice."

Andrew looks surprised. "You *think?*"

"It is."

"Bunch of freakin' *McMansions,*" he says. He rolls down his window and tells the guard that we're here for the party at Trent's house. The guard looks at a guest list, then waves us through.

Andrew cranks the stereo, driving too fast down the streets, and as we get near the end of a cul-de-sac, I see a bunch of shiny new cars, some of them the very expensive kind, parked along the curb. Andrew hits the brakes so hard they squeal against the blacktop. He parks behind the nearest car, and we get out. I can hear rap music blasting from a huge, beautiful "McMansion" at the end of the cul-de-sac. We're about half a block away, but I feel the music in my feet, it's that loud. Andrew looks smug and dances with some lame-looking hip-hop moves while looking at my body like he owns it.

The yard at Trent's house is full of tall brightly colored flowers, and the porch has these folksy pots and signs with smiling cats and rag dolls painted on them, like his mom is Little Miss Homemaker. I always wished I had a mom who put things like that on the porch. Heck, I always wished I had a porch.

The front door is wide open. I see kids inside and in the yard, sitting on each other's laps, drinking what looks like beer. A few of them smoke cigarettes with their eyes half closed. The song roars out the door and washes over us. I see some guys get out of a white Mercedes SUV and start walking toward the party, a bunch of pampered-looking boys. When they hear the music, their heads start to bob and they twist their hands up all stupid, in imitation of the thugs they've seen on MTV. They think they're tough. It's almost funny to see these rich boys pretending to be gangsters or something. One of them sees Andrew and waves. Andrew responds by pointing to me with both hands and lifting his eyebrows, like he's saying. *Look at this big hunk o' meat.* Eew?

"Not bad," calls one of the boys, like I'm on display just for them.

"Not *bad*?" calls Andrew. "*Fuck* you, dog! You wouldn't know good if it bit you on the *ass*." The boy turns and pulls his shorts down to moon us with his hairy rear end. Lovely.

As soon as we enter the house, Andrew is swarmed by a different group of guys in Abercrombie clothes, almost all of them attractive in some way, and I'm left standing there. Andrew talks to them for a minute and then introduces me. "She's new at school," he says. "She's an *apartment* girl."

The guys seem to think this means something. Something funny. They laugh. I don't like how I'm feeling. Why should it matter that I live in an apartment? I excuse myself and wander through the house. It's beautiful. A winding staircase with a black iron banister leads to a spacious loft on the second floor. There's art on the walls, and expensive-looking sculptures in these tiny nooks with their own lights on them. I wonder what Andrew's house must look like that he thinks this house is a McMansion.

I find what I think is the great room. There are a bunch of kids in there, their bare arms and legs spilling all over the beige leather sofas. They appear to be drinking and screaming. Oh, and smoking. Weed. I smell the green smoke of marijuana, a familiar smell from the limited time I spent with my mother. Yuck. A couple of preppy-looking boys light the most enormous joints I've ever seen, inhaling deeply until their faces turn purple. Everyone is huddled around the center of the room in a group. The whole group roars with laughter and screaming. I try to see what's going on that's making everyone laugh so hard. A loud Missy Elliott song comes on the stereo, and everyone starts to bob and weave in time. "'Music make you lose control, music make you lose control . . .'"

One of the girls in the circle backs up and runs off, looking a little green and dizzy, like she's going to throw up from drinking too much, and I can see into the circle of kids. In the middle I see two pretty girls I recognize from school, in tight low jeans and tank tops. I'm in shock over how many pretty girls there are around here. Back home, there were a few, but in Orange County it's almost like every single girl you see is pretty.

One of the girls puts something that looks like a cherry in the other girl's belly button and slurps it out with her mouth. Then the girls *share* the cherry by kissing each other and biting it in half, while all the stupid drunk guys watch and yell and laugh. The girls stop and look around like they're waiting for everyone to be impressed.

"Encore!" one of the boys screams. His voice hasn't quite changed yet. Everyone looks *way* baked. The girls kiss again, then one of them turns around and bends over for the other one to spank her.

"Oh, *shit!*" cries one of the guys. "*That's* what I'm talkin' 'bout, yo." Why do they all speak like a rap video?

I turn toward a door that's open to the backyard and try to make my escape. This isn't exactly my scene. No, let me be very clear. This isn't my scene at *all*. I don't drink or do drugs because, probably unlike most of these kids, I had a mom who did all that for me, and I was lucky enough to see exactly how messed up someone's life can be because of it. But before I can take two steps, I hear a guy call out: "Hey, you!"

I look behind me to make sure he doesn't mean someone else. "You! The new girl. Come here," he says. I shake my head and smile, because I don't want to seem unfriendly. But it's no use. Some girls from the group have already broken away and rushed over, giggling and stinking of alcohol. They grab me and drag me into the middle of a circle, where they try to dance with me like we're hoochies from some rap video.

The guy who called for me shouts over the music: "We're trying to decide which of the two chicks here would make the best threesome for me. I vote for you and Amber."

I've barely had time to wonder who Amber is when I find out. I'm spun around and pushed into the center of the circle. Everyone yells and laughs, boys and girls alike. A super-pretty girl from school is in the middle with me. She has long reddish hair and big brown eyes that remind me of a baby deer. She wears super-short jersey shorts with the word "Juicy" on the butt, and a tight tank top with the Baby Phat logo in jewels over her boobs. She doesn't wear any shoes and has rings on a few of her toes. She looks totally *baked* and happily numb. She smiles at me and comes over to put a hand on one of my breasts. She makes a face like "oooh," like she really likes touching me, only I can tell it's a total act for the benefit of the boys. I don't know what to do. I feel trapped, but everyone's laughing like this is normal and harmless. I see a TV on one side of the room. A porno movie is playing, and the actress is making the exact same face as this girl.

"No," I say. "I don't *think* so." I try to get away, but there are hands all over me, pushing me back into the circle. Some of them touch me in places I would rather they didn't.

"What's the problem?" cries Amber. She stumbles and laughs and grabs me behind the neck and pulls me in to kiss her, like she's not going to be rejected. I have no choice. I have only ever kissed two other people in my life, both of them boys. I don't kiss back, and I try to get away. I feel like a kid who hates getting kisses from a crazy old aunt or something. The boys start to boo and push me really hard. If I don't kiss this girl, I think they might actually *hurt* me. Survival instinct kicks in.

I look at her and close my eyes. She kisses me again, and for some reason I don't even understand, I give that kiss everything I've got. I hate myself for wanting these losers to like me. Who am I? The boys whoop it up. Part of me is totally embarrassed, but part of me finds it interesting that this is so *normal* and so not a big deal to these people. Amber sticks her tongue in my mouth, and it just lies there like a dead fish. It's totally gross. She has bad breath. Then I feel her hands, or someone's hands, on my rear end. Okay. That's enough. Game *over,* freaks.

I pull back and smile and dance my way out of the group while all the boys yell and clap. By now the boozers have happily moved on to one of the other girl couples who wait for their approval. I am totally creeped out and practically run into the backyard. I have no idea where Andrew is, and I don't really care. It's not like he'd be any help in this situation anyway, right?

I find more kids out here, some of them much calmer than the animals inside. The mellow kids stay outside, apparently. They sit in tight groups on the lawn and on the pool chairs, talking and laughing. Some of them actually look cool, like people I could hang out with. There's a huge keg at one end of the patio, and this is where I find Andrew. He's filling a plastic cup, then guzzling everything in it while some other boys grunt to encourage him, and then he's filling it up again. Beer spills all over the front of his shirt. He reminds me of a thirsty old dog at a bowl. Sloppy. Uh, do I really want this guy to drive me home? *Not.* I feel in my handbag for the cell phone my dad gave me. It's there. Good. I just might need to call him to come get me. Not that I'd want the Squeegeemobile to be seen by anyone on earth, especially people who go to my school, but it beats, like, ending up at the bottom of some canyon in a heap of twisted metal, pinned under a crushed Andrew.

Andrew sees me and waves. Not knowing what else to do, I go to him. I pretend to be happy to see him. I mean, he's the closest thing I have to a friend here.

"Beer!" he says, handing me a clear plastic cup full of the stuff. Thanks, I think. I never could have figured out that this was beer without the insightful description.

"No, thanks," I say. "I don't drink."

Andrew laughs like I've told a joke. Then he seems to get it that I'm not kidding. He pours the cup of beer on the grass and asks if I'd like a soda instead. I say yes, and he goes into the house. I can't be sure, but I think I hear him shouting Jessica's name, and I think I hear her awful laughter. A couple of minutes later, Andrew comes out with a plastic cup of Coke for me.

"Thanks," I say. I take my cup and sit on an empty patio chair. The yard is kind of small but neat and clean. The pool takes up practically the whole area. I see some kids climbing the trees. They probably aren't supposed to be doing that, but I guess they're very in touch with their inner monkeys.

I look around the yard for any sign of someone I might know, specifically Chris. As soon as I think about him, I hear Andrew scream his name.

"Chris fucking Cabrera, yo! What up, dawg?"

I look up and see Chris and Tyler come through the open door from the family room. Tyler's head is turned because he's looking at the scene in the center of the sofas — I can only guess it's, what, a couple of girls Frenching? Ugh.

Behind them I see Jessica, Brianna, and Haley. They all look amazing, like they just stepped off the pages of *CosmoGIRL!* I feel my body tense up with envy. I don't want to be envious of them, but it's impossible not to. I should ask Jessica about the race I've been assigned to write about for the school paper, but this probably isn't the right place to do that. It seems like everyone worships her anyway. The kids out here look at them and act all submissive, like the coyotes in the canyon. Everyone might as well bow down to these girls. They are worshipped.

Chris wears jeans and a simple ringer shirt, but he looks *way* hot. He seems bored, until he sees me. Then he smiles, and I feel lightheaded, like I'm drunk or something, even though I've only had a couple of sips of warmish soda. Chris has a natural masculinity that makes me crazy. He is the finest guy in the world. Tyler, who is totally gorgeous, too, wears khaki cargo shorts and a striped button-down shirt, like a prep. He heads straight for the keg with a weird smile. Andrew shakes hands with Tyler, and they start to look at me and whisper and laugh.

Jessica wears a tiny white skirt that rests very low on her firm, narrow hips, with a blue-and-white-striped shirt that falls off one shoulder, all retro. She has on big white earrings, and these cool wedge sandals. Her legs look glossy, like she's got something syrupy on them. She could not look cuter if she tried. She makes me feel big and clumsy. Brianna wears super-low jeans and a short Juicy T-shirt that's *really* low-cut — you can practically see her nipples poking through. Her boobs stick out like a couple of small blimps, and all the guys are, like, *hell-o.* Haley looks the most normal of the three, but even she's a glamour girl. She's got on a long skirt, peasant-style, beaded at the waist, with a tank top and a small sparkly sweater and sandals. She's the only one of the girls who smiles when she sees me. I get a good feeling about her, even though I'm starting to feel a little dizzy and weird, like I just got off a roller coaster. I take a deep breath and try to get control over my head. I have to stop being so tense.

Chris takes a cup of beer from Andrew, who seems to have made it his mission to give everyone alcohol. Then Chris heads directly over to me. Jessica watches him from the keg, where she and the other girls are getting their cups filled by Andrew. Brianna and Haley watch Chris as he sits next to me, and they look at one another like they're worried about something. Haley shrugs, and Brianna elbows her.

Jessica looks at me, throws her head back, and laughs again. It seems like she does this a lot, and I have a feeling she's only doing it so I'll think she's having a better time than she actually is. Why is she so committed to making me think she's all happy? She puts her arms around Andrew's neck and acts like she's totally into him, but she keeps looking over at Chris to see if he notices. He doesn't. He's too busy. Busy looking at me.

"Hi, there," he says. He has a coolness to him that rises above every other guy here, like he really doesn't care what people think. He holds his cup out to toast with me.

"How are you?" I ask. I'm not sure, but I think I'm blushing.

"I'm glad to see you." He sits next to me, and I can smell that spicy cologne he wears. I love it.

"Me, too. I mean I'm glad to see you."

"So, what do you think of Trent's party? Great, huh?" He seems sarcastic, like he doesn't like it.

I shrug. "It's okay."

He looks into my eyes and smiles with that laugh right below the surface. "Yeah? You think? Really? Look at these people. They're insane."

I shrug again.

"You guys have parties like this back in Taos?"

"No," I say. I blush again, but I'm not sure why. I miss Taos. My friends there felt like real people. Not like this.

"Good for you," he says. He looks around the yard. "I'd probably like living in Taos for that reason."

"You don't like the party?" I ask. I'm surprised. For some reason I thought everyone would like this party. Or at least if they didn't, they would try to hide it, like I do.

"I'm not a party boy," he says.

"Why not?"

"No, I mean I like parties. Parties with a purpose. Like, my parents have parties, and people talk about ideas. They tell stories, they talk about places they've traveled to. It's interesting. *This* shit, though . . ." He looks around and shakes his head like he's just heard something really funny. "Pssh. *Whatever.* You know?"

"Yeah," I say. "I know."

We sit there looking around. The guy from the family room, the one who made me kiss that Amber girl, comes out with a crazy look on his face. He's running around in a way that makes me think of a small dog. He doesn't look very smart. He says hi to Chris and Tyler and comes over to me and says, "Okay, new girl, the guys and I were just talking inside, and we agree that you have to kiss Jessica Nguyen next."

"What?" I ask.

"What?" Chris asks me.

"Dude," says the guy, "you should have seen her swap spit with Amber, man. It was fucking hot."

"You kissed Amber?" Chris asks me.

"They made me," I say.

"Chris, dude, do you *not* agree that it would be totally hot to see Paski and Jessica kiss?"

I look at Chris. "Help me?"

"Trent, dude, calm down," says Chris. Trent? This is Trent? This nerdy little guy is the one holding the *party*? That explains why everyone does what he wants. But how the heck is he a football player? Aren't they supposed to be bigger than this?

Trent starts to jump around and says, "That would be the most amazing threesome of all time, those two and me. Damn, come on, Paski, do a nigga a favor!" *Nigga*? Did this little white boy just call himself a *nigga*? How disturbing. On so many levels.

"Maybe later," says Chris. "We were talking about something right now. We'll find you, okay, bro?"

Trent makes a face like he's just been dissed or something, and he runs over to Jessica and starts to talk to her. She looks over at me with the most disgusted expression. "Oh, *hell* no," I hear her say. "I don't *kiss* girls, okay? And even if I did, I wouldn't kiss *that* one."

Why didn't I stand up to him like *that*? Why am I acting like such a wimp?

"How was Amber?" Chris asks me.

I blush one more time and look at the ground.

He lifts my chin with his finger and grins at me. "I would have liked to see that."

"Yeah, sorry you missed it." I try to sound as sarcastic as I can.

"There's someone I think I'd like to see you kiss more, though."

"Yeah? Who?"

He touches my bottom lip with his thumb, very lightly. "Me." This is the part where a normal guy would, like, try to make a move on a girl. But not Chris. He just sits there and stares at me with the laugh that never seems to actually come out. The feel of his thumb has filled my body with a powerful longing, like it feels to take my bike down a really steep slope. Excitement.

"Don't you have a girlfriend?" I ask. I look over at Jessica. She's laughing again, this time with Tyler. She's jumping onto his back so he can give her a piggyback ride around the yard. In her tiny white skirt? Guess she likes people to see her undies. She pretends to whip him like a horse. "Yah!" she shouts. "Yah!" People laugh and clap like this is high entertainment.

Chris watches them for a second. "I guess, I suppose I have a girl-friend."

"What's the deal with you guys?" My head is feeling light again, and I shake myself.

Chris takes a deep breath and sips his beer, watching Jessica over the rim of his cup. "I've been trying to break up with her for a while."

"Really?" This makes me nervous. If he breaks up with her, she'll blame me. And God only knows what Jessica would do to me if she thought I took her boyfriend. On the other hand, it makes me really excited to think about the possibility of dating Chris.

He nods, and the laugh finally comes out of his mouth, a small, frustrated chuff. "The only problem is that you can't really do things that piss off Jessica Nguyen and expect to *live*."

I look at him to see if he's joking or not.

He smiles. "She doesn't want to lose me."

"She's smart," I say, wondering as I do if this is too forward and inappropriate. "I mean, if I were her. You know." I guzzle the soda because I don't know what else to do.

"I've tried, like, four or five times, and she always gets me to come back somehow."

"Like how?"

"She calls me up crying and begging," he says with a shrug. "One time she said she was going to kill herself."

"Really?" Somehow I can't imagine Jessica doing any of those things. She seems way too aloof for that kind of needy emotional stuff.

"Oh, yeah. I shouldn't tell people about it, actually." He looks like he regrets opening his mouth. "It's her own personal stuff. It's kind of disrespectful to tell you about it. I'm sorry. She's a good kid. She's just a little . . ." He looks at me.

"What?" I ask.

Chris stares at me and says nothing.

I feel my heart expand in my chest. I want to say something back, but there's nothing to say. I am so falling in love with this guy, and it's so wrong in so many ways, I can't even tell you.

"She knows how I feel about you," he says.

"She does?" I mean, *I* don't even know how he feels about me. How unfair is it that Jessica knows but I don't? This might explain why she hates me, by the way.

"I told her about you the first day I saw you. I called her on the phone, and I was like, 'Jess, don't get pissed, but there's a girl who rides as well as you do, and she's pretty, and she's cool, and she doesn't seem to have an attitude problem.'"

"You said that?" I'm not sure I like being compared to Jessica, even favorably.

He nods. "That's the only bad thing about Jessica. She's got major attitude."

"I noticed."

"I told her that's why I wanted to split up. Her freakin' attitude. When you know her, you realize it's just because she's insecure, but it doesn't make it any easier to deal with. It's a nightmare."

"Why would Jessica be insecure? She has everything."

"People are complicated," he says. He brushes the side of my face with his hand. I feel chills, and it's like my body fills up with something sweet and warm. "She wants attention, I think. But she also wants to feel like she's just like everyone else. She's never really fit in anywhere. She's always been different somehow, you know?"

"Because she's Asian?"

"Vietnamese. No, not just that. I don't think that has anything to do with it. More like because she's *really* rich and pretty and kind of mean, and she just stands out. I don't think she realizes she's being mean, either. It's just her personality."

"She looks like she wants to stand out," I say as Jessica flashes her panties to the world and whips Tyler like a mule.

"Yeah," says Chris. "I don't know. Whatever. It's complicated, like I said. People are complicated."

"Are you complicated?" I ask.

He laughs. I like his laugh. I don't think he laughs a lot, but when he does, it's like bells ringing. "Yeah. I guess I am."

"How so?"

"Let's see. I've got a girlfriend I can't get rid of. I want this other girl instead. She's remarkable."

"That's pretty complicated," I say.

"Doesn't have to be."

"It doesn't?"

"Nope."

I look at him and feel like my soul is showing through my skin, naked. "I guess," I whisper. I want him so much I can hardly breathe.

He says, "If you want it simple, I mean. Like me and you. One plus one. That's pretty simple."

"I always liked that equation."

"That simplifies things," he says. "I'm not complicated anymore."

"You're not?"

"I'll tell her tonight when I take her home."

"Tell her? Tell her what?"

"That we're over. That I don't want to be with her anymore. I actually broke up with her a week before you got to our school, but she guilted me back into being with her. But this time I'm really going to do it. And then, you know, I'll ask you out."

"Oh," I say. I remember the note from Jessica and imagine the horrible things she could do to me. I should stay away from this guy. Then again, Jessica isn't the one who decides what I do. And Chris rocks.

"I mean, I'll ask you out if you're not, like, going out with Andrew Van Dyke or something now."

I make a disgusted face. "No!"

Chris laughs. "What's wrong with Andrew?"

"Nothing. He's just kind of, like, I don't know. It's like he thinks he's a player or something."

Chris laughs some more. "Yeah. But you know what, Paski? It's like with Jessica. Andrew's just a mixed-up, insecure guy like the rest of us."

"Are you insecure?"

He smiles. Nods. "It's the human condition."

Jessica is finished with her piggyback ride, and she's running over. She stands in front of us with her hands on her hips. She looks hateful, but I try to remember what my grandmother said about her needing my help, and what Chris just said about her being insecure like everyone else. I remember how Emily and Janet told me I should warn her about the accident, no matter how much I think I don't like her. I don't know, though. I don't totally buy it that she's got issues and she's just, like, a poor little rich girl or something. She actually looks like she's going to kill me. Is that something poor little rich girls do? Kill girls?

"Did you read the note I gave you, apartment girl?" she asks me. She does that awful fast blink she does.

"I did," I say. "Why does everyone call me that? What's wrong with apartments?"

"*What* note?" Chris asks me.

I consider my options. I can stay quiet and be nice, or I can tattle on her and, like, *not* be nice. I'm finished with the cup of soda, and I have to admit, I'm not feeling all that nice. I'm feeling a little nauseated, truth be told. What's wrong with the Coke?

I looked at Chris and say, "The note where Jessica told me to stay away from you or suffer the consequences."

"What?" Chris asks, looking at Jessica. "You *did* that?"

174

"No," lies Jessica. She narrows her eyes at me, and I can practically see the steam coming out of her ears. "I think apartment girl's had a little too much to drink."

"I'm drinking soda," I say.

"Guess you're a real lightweight, then," Jessica replies, with a cruel smile. "Either that or just stupid."

As I look at her, I'm overcome with the vision about her again. I'm feeling a little woozy now, sick actually, like I need to lie down, and it's harder to resist the vision. I see the whole thing at last, start to finish. I see Jessica in her lavender and white racing clothes on her motorcycle. She has a white helmet with a big yellow rose on the side. It's pretty. I see a banner, NATIONAL MOTOCROSS TEAM REGIONALS. The start flag comes down, and she's off, on a track, jumping and flipping, just like I do on my bike, only faster and higher. She's beautiful. So graceful. I gasp. She makes it through two impossible turns, way out in front of the pack, and then, on the third turn, she hits a rock and her tire spins out underneath her and she wipes out. I see her lying on the ground, her helmet cracked. She's not moving. People scream. There's blood. I can't stand it. I feel sick and sad. It's horrible, the most vividly horrible vision I've ever had, and I'm overcome with the urge to warn her, but then I realize she's not dead, and I think that maybe it would be okay to keep it to myself. She'd only say I was crazy if I told her about this, anyway. She'd use it against me somehow. I hate this "gift," and I want it to go away, and maybe if I just stay quiet this time then the spirits will finally realize they chose the wrong person and they'll move on. I know, I'm selfish. But sometimes the visions don't come true, and sometimes you have to protect yourself, especially from venomous haters like Jessica.

"Paski?" Chris leans over and waves his hand in front of my face. "Hello? Anybody home? Are you okay?"

"Huh?" I shake myself out of the vision state and look at them. Jessica is laughing at me.

"Guess she doesn't hold her soda very well," Andrew laughs, walking over. Jessica looks over at him and grins. His eyes stray to me. Jessica says, "Cuckoo, cuckoo," and laughs at me.

"No," I say. "That's not it." Well, maybe that's part of it. But still. If I'm nuts, it's not by choice, it's genetics.

"You feeling okay?" asks Chris.

I take a deep breath and brace myself for what I'm about to do. Do? I'm going to warn Jessica about the wreck. Kind of. I mean, enough so that I can sleep at night but not so much that she'll turn the world against me for being some kind of dial-a-psychic nutjob.

The room is spinning. "Jessica," I say. My voice sounds really far away to me. I'm sick. This is more than just being tipsy. What's going on? "I have to tell you something important. Okay? I mean, I know you don't *like* me. You don't really even know me, but that's okay. You don't have to like me. I don't care. I mean, I *do* care. I think my life would be a whole lot easier if you liked me. But anyway."

"What the F are you talking about?" asks Jessica. She sits on Chris's lap and smirks at me. He gives me an apologetic look. Andrew asks me how I'm feeling. "More soda, apartment girl?" he says. I don't answer because I'm focused on telling Jessica what I need to tell her; in fact, I don't really even hear him ask me anything until after I've started talking again. It's weird, like time is moving differently, like I'm floating somewhere outside of my own body.

"Okay. Here's the deal," I say. "All my life, ever since I was really small, I've had these dreams that, like — okay. I mean, sometimes I have dreams that come true."

"Oh, how sweet," says Jessica, all sarcastic. This isn't going well.

"Very sweet," Andrew agrees.

Jessica gives him a strange look and says, "Dreams can come true? How adorable."

I need to get my point across. I shake my head. Nothing makes sense right now. "No, not like that. I mean I see things. Things that happen before they actually happen."

"Oooh!" Jessica is totally laughing at me. She looks at Chris. "Did you hear that? She sees *dead* people."

Andrew chimes in: "And Bruce Willis? Can you see him, too?"

"Shut up, you guys," says Chris. "Let the girl talk."

Jessica remains quiet.

"Talk," says Andrew. "I'm sorry. Was I behaving badly again?"

I ignore him and say to Jessica, "Okay, so you don't have to believe me. But the thing is, ever since I moved here, I've had this vision of something bad happening to you."

"That's funny," says Jessica, looking at Andrew. "I had the same vision about you just now, when I saw how you were looking at my boyfriend."

"No, listen to me." I put my hand on Jessica's arm.

She slaps me away. "Don't fucking *touch* me, okay?"

"Okay," I say. I give up. I told her something bad would happen. That's enough, isn't it? She's horrible. I've warned her, just like Grandma said. That's all I needed to do. "I won't touch you. Sorry."

"Let's walk," she tells me. She stands up and holds her hand out like we're friends now.

"Walk?"

"I want to talk to you alone for a second," she says. Chris looks at me with fear, but I'm not going to let her scare me anymore. I'm not.

"About what?" I ask.

"About Chris," she says.

"Jessica," says Chris, "leave Paski alone."

"No," I say, "it's okay. I can handle it."

"Shall we?" asks Jessica.

"Fine." I stand up and walk with her. She takes me to a part of the yard next to the pool, where there aren't many other people. She smiles so that anyone looking at us would think we were friends or something.

"You're a sick bitch," she tells me.

"What?" I say.

She's still smiling sweetly. "Stay away from Chris or you'll be very, very sorry," she says. Still smiling. She puts her hand on my shoulder and turns her head to one side as if she's offering me friendly advice. "And stop talking about bad things happening. I don't like psycho girls who threaten me."

I feel dizzier now than I did a minute ago, and my legs are weak. "It's not a threat. It's a dream." There's something very wrong with me. "There's more I should tell you about the dream. It's not just a bad thing but a specific bad thing."

"Come whisper it in my ear." Jessica comes close with a sickening smile on her face and wraps her arms around me. Then, with a strength that surprises me, she lifts me up and throws me in the pool. As I go down, I feel a crack against the side of my head, like I hit the concrete. Then the shock of the water clears my head, and I struggle back up to the surface. I can't breathe. I kick my legs frantically and can't feel my arms. I'm in the deep end and can't feel the bottom. The yard and the sky spin above me, purple and green with flashes of light. I look up and see Jessica laughing with her stupid head thrown back. "Sweet dreams, apartment girl," she howls. "Time to wake up!" Lots of kids rush over, and they seem to be laughing, too.

I see Andrew reach his big, tanned hand out to help me, but he's laughing. Why is he laughing if he's trying to help? I try to swim toward him, but I can't move right. His hand seems to ripple and waver. I'm going under, swallowing water. It's like there are weights on my legs. Oh my God. I'm going to drown. My head is killing me. My nose, too. What's wrong with my nose? Did I get water in it? Why can't I swim? I'm a good swimmer. I taste rust in my nose and mouth. It stings. I'm under the water, sinking, when I hear a loud bubbly swoosh, the sound a splash makes when you're under the water. I feel hands on me, and terror floods throughout my body. Is Jessica in the pool, holding me under? Is she trying to kill me? Why does she hate me so much? I feel like I'm going to throw up.

I feel myself move through the water, like I'm being pulled, and then I'm out in the air again. Everything is a smear of lights and sounds.

"Hold on to me," says Chris.

Chris?

He's in the water, holding me, and paddling toward the shallow end of the pool. He spits water out, struggling, too. He releases me when we get to a part where I can touch bottom. I try to stand but stumble. He catches me, and I throw up, right into the pool water and on him.

"Fucking *gross!*" someone yells. I feel like there's fire in my guts, like I'm going to die.

"I want my dad," I say. I am so scared. "His number is programmed into my cell phone. Please, I want my daddy."

"Paski? Paski? Look at me." Chris holds me. I look at him.

"Oh my God," he says. "Someone call an ambulance! She's bleeding everywhere! Oh, shit!"

Bleeding?

He touches my head and my nose with his hand and pulls it back covered in blood.

"Why?" I ask him. I can't move or hear, or see. It's like there's Vaseline in my eyes. Why am I bleeding? I feel him lift me up and gently place me on the grass. I sit up, leaning against him, and he holds my head against his chest. I see Jessica come over, and Chris looks up at her.

"We, you and me, are *over!*" he yells at her. "You understand? Don't *call* me. Don't *talk* to me. Don't even *look* at me." He stares at me just as I feel my eyes start to roll back into my head. "Someone call an ambulance!" he shouts. "How many times do I have to ask? Jesus Christ!"

"Call 911!" someone shrieks. Then I hear everyone screaming to call 911.

"They already called," someone says.

"What's happening?" I ask Chris. I feel faint.

"Hang in there," he says softly, near my ear. "Help is coming, Paski. Hold on."

Why is the yard spinning? Why does it feel like I've swallowed a thousand knives? Why is Jessica still laughing at me? Why is Haley shrieking at Andrew, slapping him, asking him what he put in my soda? "How could you do that to her, you stupid motherfucker?" she screams. "Haven't you learned *anything*? My God! What is *wrong* with you guys?"

Why does Andrew look so scared? Why is he running into the house like he's being pursued? Why have all the faces that were laughing a second ago turned so scared? Why does the sick hyena sound of Jessica laughing sound so, so far away? Why am I passing out?

Why is this happening to *me*?

19

I wake up in a hospital room. I haven't been in one of these since my mother overdosed on cocaine a few years back and we all drove from Taos to Santa Fe to visit her and try to talk her into going into rehab. My father sits in a chair next to the bed I'm in, with that very same face that he had then. My stomach and head hurt so much I can't stand it. I groan, and Dad uses a cool white washcloth to dab my forehead.

"Dad," I whisper. "What happened?"

"Shh," he says. "Just rest."

I feel my stomach lurch. "Oh God. I have to throw up."

Dad holds a pink plastic tub up to my mouth, and I vomit into it. "That's good," Dad says. "It's the medicine they gave you to make you purge the drugs."

"Drugs?" I ask. He wipes my mouth and looks at me with a mixture of love and pity in his eyes. "Dad, what happened to me? Why am I here?"

I look around the room and see that Chris is here. No! I don't want him to see me like this. Why is he here? Please tell me he did not just see me hurl. No, wait. I have a memory of hurling on him earlier. Oh, my God. For some reason, Haley is with him. There is also a nurse in the room. She checks my chart and watches me carefully.

"Hi," says Chris with a strange, sad smile.

"What happened?" I repeat.

My father looks at Chris and Haley, and then Haley answers. "Andrew put something in your soda, Paski."

"You don't know for sure it was Andrew," says Chris.

"Like what?" I ask.

"The date rape drug," says Haley.

Now my dad speaks. "According to your *friends* here, one of the boys at the party put something in your drink so that he could try to have sex with you without you remembering it." My father says the word "friends" sarcastically, as if he can't believe these people care about me, as if he *hates* them.

"Oh my God," I say. "Tina warned me."

"Who's Tina?" asks Dad.

"A friend," I say. For the first time, I realize that she really, truly is a friend. She might be the only friend I've made, and she tried to warn me. I shouldn't have put my need to be with the popular kids ahead of my loyalty to the nicest girl in school, the only one who went out of her way to make me feel welcome, the only one who tried to protect me from Andrew. Well, almost the only one. Chris saved me. I remember that now. He jumped in the pool and pulled me out. And Keoni and Kerani told me to be careful. I have to thank them for that. They're good guys. They really are.

"My poor girl," says Dad, dabbing my head again. Okay, now the whole washcloth thing is getting annoying. Dad is kind of clumsy with these real gentle tasks. It makes me wish I had a mom, so bad.

"Why would Andrew *do* that to me?" I wail. "What did I ever do to *him*?"

"It's not the first time," says Haley. "It's not you, it's him. He's got issues with girls. Big-time."

"What do you mean?" Dad demands.

"Andrew's done this to girls before. He thinks it's funny."

My dad looks incredibly disturbed by this, and disgusted. He turns to me. "Why are you hanging *around* with people like this?" He points to Haley and Chris. I feel like I'm going to be sick again. He can tell by the look on my face and holds up the bucket. The smell of the vomit that's already in there makes me throw up again. He wipes my mouth when I'm finished. This is the worst I've ever felt. I don't want to be here. I hate this.

"That kid Andrew should be arrested," says my dad. "He should be in prison."

"He's not the only one," says Haley. She looks like she wants to say more but doesn't.

"Thanks for saving me," I say to Chris. He shakes his head like I shouldn't be thanking him. "Dad," I say. "Don't be mad at them. They were the only ones who helped me."

Dad gives Chris and Haley a suspicious look. "Don't talk about it right now," he tells me. "Just try to get some rest, Paski."

"Am I going to be okay?" I ask.

"You'll be fine, honey," says the nurse. "You're lucky this guy here had the frame of mind to call an ambulance when he did." She smiles at Chris; but he looks worried and angry.

"Can I take her home soon, you think?" my dad asks the nurse.

"In a few hours. We just want to make sure we get everything out and that she's hydrated before we release her."

Get everything out?

What the *hell* was put in me?

20

The hospital sends me home with instructions to stay home from school for a couple of days and eat bland food. Oh, and I'm supposed to drink plenty of water. Chris and Haley have gone home, and it's now close to two in the morning. My dad called Emily and Janet and let me talk to them, and they're really concerned. I don't want them to be concerned. I want them to be here. With me. I need them.

I'm glad Chris isn't here anymore, to see me all doubled over and queasy, climbing into the Squeegeemobile. My dad is uncharacteristically quiet on the drive. The top is down — honestly, I don't even know if my dad can get the thing up — and the cool air feels good on my skin. I feel guilty for some weird reason, even though I know I didn't do anything wrong.

"I'm sorry," I tell my dad at a stoplight. When I look at him, I see that he has tears on his cheeks. "Why are you crying?" I ask him. Like I mentioned before, my dad is a weeper sometimes.

"It's my fault," he says. I should have known my dad would find some way to bring this all back around to his favorite topic lately — himself.

"You weren't even there," I say.

"That's just the point. I *should* have been. It's not easy doing this alone, you know that? Raising a kid on your own. I have to be mother and father to you, and I don't have enough time to do everything I'm supposed to be doing. So I should be the one saying I'm sorry here. I'm sorry for letting you down."

"Dad, please, it's not your fault." Why am I comforting him now? Isn't this, like, my time? Of all the times that are my time, shouldn't this be a big one?

The light turns green, and we drive the rest of the way to the apartment in silence.

Later, once I've changed into my favorite long flannel nightgown — it's a granny nightgown, I know, but back in Taos you need these things, trust me — I crawl into bed and my dad knocks on my door.

"Can I come in?" he asks.

"Yeah," I say.

He comes and sits on the floor next to my bed. He's stopped crying, but he still looks really sad. "Are you okay?"

"I'm fine."

"Did anything else happen that you want to talk about?"

"No."

"I know that when I was your age, I wasn't very comfortable talking to my mom about sex and all that."

"Nothing happened," I say.

"Are you sure?" He looks concerned.

"I'm sure."

"Okay," he says. "I trust you to make good decisions, Pasquala, I always have. I know what happened tonight wasn't your fault. I want you to feel like you can talk to me about whatever, okay? I'm here, you can tell me anything, and I won't judge you or go crazy, okay? I just want you to know that even though I'm not around that much, you can count on me. I know sometimes you probably feel like you don't have a lot of people to hold on to, but you have me. That's all I want you to know, that you have me, and you don't have to find love or attention anywhere else." He looks like he's going to cry again.

"Okay, Dad," I say. "Can I go to sleep now?"

"Oh, God, right." Dad looks guilty again, like he should have known I wanted to go to sleep. I was actually just trying to lighten the mood a little and make him smile, but it looks like I sent him back into the crisis of bad parenting. "I'm so sorry," he says. "Good night. Go to sleep. I'm just right in the next room if you need me, okay? You call me. I'm going to leave your door open so I can hear you."

I stare at him in a most unfriendly way.

"Unless," he adds with a nervous shrug, "you want it closed."

"Closed, please," I say.

"Right."

Dad, looking like he's still surprised by his own bad suggestions, turns off the light, closes the door, and I'm left staring up at the blackness of the ceiling. There are no visions, no voices, no sounds. Just my breath, in and out, small and weak. I replay the events of the night and try to figure out what happened. I start to doze off but am jolted back to consciousness by a light, irritating tapping.

A muffled voice on the other side of the wall says, "Paski? You up?"

It's Kerani, eavesdropping. "What do you *want*?" I ask. I am starting to understand what's wrong with apartments. At least this apartment. The walls are too freakin' thin.

I hear his voice again. "I just wanted to say good night. Your dad's way cool. You're lucky."

I don't say anything, and he doesn't speak anymore. Soon enough, I can hear Kerani snoring in the apartment next door.

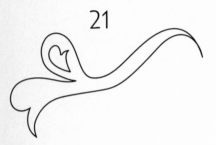

21

I'm on the sofa watching a movie on HBO. Did I say HBO? I *did*. My dad, feeling guilty that I had this horrible experience with the supreme popular haters of Orange County, has rushed out and gotten digital cable so that my recovery time at home might be more enjoyable. I like it, but the more I flip through the stations, the more I realize I really wasn't missing anything.

Dad is in the kitchen trying to make green chile stew with the frozen chile Grandma sent us from Taos. It smells pretty good. And makes me very homesick. I can't even imagine someone slipping me a mickey, as Dad puts, in Taos. I'm not in Kansas anymore. I've actually never been in Kansas, but I bet it's nothing like this.

I hear a knock on the door. I feel fine, actually, so I try to get up to answer it, but my dad rushes over. He's all "No, no! Sit down. Don't move!" I try to tell him I don't think there's any of that drug left in me, that I feel totally normal, but I think he's enjoying this chance to play Mr. Mom all day. He's called in sick to work the past couple of days to stay with me, and his bosses are very cool about it. They've sent him some stuff over the Internet, and my dad's all "Wow! I didn't realize you could do so much with e-mail!" I'm, like, what *rock* did you crawl out from under that you don't *know* this already? But whatever. Dad is just getting familiar with all these computerized animation techniques, too. He used to be what you'd call a throwback. He did everything the old-fashioned way.

Dad opens the door, and I see Tina standing there with her pink hair sticking up and her big black sunglasses on. She looks like a tall Kelly Osbourne. "Hi," she says. "I'm Tina. I came to see Paski."

My dad lets her in and gives her a big hug. She's looking at me over his shoulder like, "What is your *dad* doing? Is he a *pervert?*"

"Thank you for trying to warn my baby about those boys," he says. "You saved her life." Actually, Chris saved my life, but my dad can't accept that any hot guy who had beer on his breath and was at that party could possibly be innocent and good in any way. He won't even let me talk about Chris. He has told me that if he sees me with Chris, I'll be grounded. I wanted to ask him how he'd know if I was home, seeing as how he's never home except for the past few days, but I didn't say anything. Sometimes, my grandmother taught me, it's better to stay quiet.

"Boys and girls," says Tina. "Haters come in all genders."

"Thank you," says Dad, releasing her.

"You're welcome, Mr. Archuleta."

The force of my dad's embrace has knocked the ever-present drawing pad from under Tina's arm. It splays across the floor, revealing some of her creations. I see something that looks like a spider with a human face. Tina is still weird, but I like her. My dad looks at the pad as she scoops it up, and after he apologizes again (does my dad ever *stop* apologizing anymore?), he tells her that he would like to get a better look at the drawings if she wouldn't mind.

Tina shrugs and hands the pad to my dad, then she comes over and sits by me on the sofa. "Hey, Pasquala," she says. *"¿Como estás?"*

"I'm fine," I say. I don't know what the big deal is, really. Why does everyone look at me like I'm roadkill? Do I look *that* bad? Tina reaches out and touches the stitches on my forehead. Did I mention I have *stitches* on my forehead? Well, yeah. I *so* do. I look like the bride of Frankenstein. When Jessica threw my drugged butt into the pool, I seem to have smacked my head and nose and chin on the side of the pool. How I managed that, I will never know.

"Does it hurt?" Tina asks.

"No, it feels great," I say, sarcastic.

She smiles. "Sorry, dumb question." She looks over at the television. I point the remote to turn down the volume. "You know," she says, "you're quite the cause célèbre at school these days."

"I'm what?"

"Everyone's talking about you."

"Good or bad?"

"Mostly good. They all feel really bad for you. The whole school is way pissed at Jessica Nguyen for what she did."

"What about Andrew?"

Tina shrugs. "You know how it is with jock boys."

"No, actually. The jock boys back home were pretty normal."

"Okay, well around here, no matter what they do, society forgives them because they are jock boys. It's like being a soldier. You can rape and pillage, you can disembowel babies, but if you're a soldier, they throw parades for you when you get home."

She sounds like my dad. I look over, and he's grinning at Tina's drawings. Tina looks over, too. Dad nods in approval. "These are good," he says of the drawings.

Tina shrugs like it doesn't matter, but I can tell she's happy someone noticed. "Thanks."

"My dad's a professional cartoonist," I say. It does not escape my notice that the phrase "professional cartoonist" is hilarious. "He should know." I am trying in a weird way to make Tina feel good, out of guilt for not being sure I liked her. She's a good person, and I am really starting to understand that good people come in all styles, even weirdo and geek.

Tina's face completely changes with this news. I mean, totally changes. She is no longer a morose, brooding girl who has come to fix me and the rest of the world. She is now a normal, curious kid.

"You are?" she asks my dad. He nods.

"We moved here so that my dad's comic book could be turned into a movie," I say.

"I am a comic book *junkie*," says Tina. "Which one did you do?" Dad tells her about Squeegee Man, and she jumps off the sofa like someone in a baseball stadium whose team just hit the most amazing home run of all time.

"No way!" she shouts. "You're Rudolfo Archuleta?"

My dad gets this smug look, as if he wants me to understand that he's not just, like, my stupid parent. That he has fans. "Please, call me Rudy." Uh, *puke?*

"I love Squeegee Man!" cries Tina. And then they start talking about all the obscure, weird things my dad's characters have done over the years. As Tina and my dad talk, the phone rings. I answer it, and a woman asks for my father. I ask her who she is so I can tell him. She identifies herself as a reporter from *People* magazine and says she's been asked to do a feature on my father and his work.

Really?

I hand him the phone, and as he listens to her spiel, his eyes grow very, very wide. "You want to profile *me?*" he asks.

To Tina, I mouth, "*People* magazine."

Tina drops her jaw to show me she doesn't believe it. "You guys are *so* cool," she gushes. "Nobody at school has a *clue* how cool you are. You know that? You know your dad's about to become a *millionaire,* don't you?"

I turn off the television and look around the apartment. Is he? He hasn't mentioned it, but now that I think about it, Hollywood, *People* magazine, a feature film. Hmm. Maybe so. I listen as my father goes into the kitchen and begins to tell his life story to a reporter from the most popular magazine in, like, the world.

"And you know what else?" Tina asks. I just look at her. I am still thinking about the fact that my dad is about to become a millionaire. I shudder to think how many Squeegeemobiles he'll buy with that kind of money. I'm happy for him, but part of me is, like, great, you know? He waits until I'm almost on my *own* to get rich. I won't really even be able to benefit from it, except that maybe now I won't have to worry about paying for college. That would be cool. I want to go to Harvard. I don't know anything about it, except that I really want to go there because it's famous. Then I want to go to Yale Law school. God, what if we could actually afford that? What if I had my own car when I went to college and then Emily and Janet went to Harvard, too, and we drove all over Boston looking way hot and blasting our music? That would *so* rock.

Tina says, "The haters won't be able to call you 'apartment girl' anymore. That will be amazing."

"Do you live in an apartment?" I ask. Tina nods. "So it's kind of personal for you, too?" She shrugs, but I'm right. She knows it and I know it. I wonder what the haters did to her and how long they've been doing it.

She narrows her eyes and says, "I *so* want to be there the day you drive up to school in your new car." Her brown eyes gleam wickedly. "What would you get?"

I shrug. "Not a Porsche."

"Oh my God. Andrew's car is so cheesy, isn't it?"

"It's nice, but a little macho."

"Who the hell drives a Porsche anymore?"

My father sticks his head in to interrupt. "Don Johnson," he answers.

Tina howls with laughter. "Your dad's hysterical," she says.

"Who's Don Johnson?" I ask.

"This old guy from this show *Miami Vice* my mom used to like."

"Oh."

Tina claps her hands together and actually rubs them, like a cartoon villain. She says, "I want to see the looks on their faces when they realize that your *dad* created the most popular character since *Spider-Man*. They're going to be eating crap out of the palm of your hand, girl."

I smile, but it's hollow. I'm only half listening. I'm thinking about the kind of car I'm going to get when — if — my dad gets to be a millionaire. "Tina," I say. "I really don't care what the haters call me anymore. It doesn't matter. I don't need anyone to eat crap out of my hand."

Tina leans back and blows air out of her mouth, very comfortable here. Almost too comfortable. "That's where you're wrong, girlfriend," she says. "You might not *want* what they think to matter. But this is Southern *California*. Look around. Money and power will *always* matter here. In fact, I would bet that money and power are just about the only things that will ever matter here. I mean, it's certainly not the environment or poetry."

"Don't forget surfing," I say. "That will always matter here."

She laughs. "You and your dad crack me up. Can I move in?" I get the feeling she's only pretending to joke. "Okay," she says. "So, money, power, and surfing matter here. And what matters here ends up mattering around the world eventually."

I wish I had the strength of conviction to argue with her. But the truth is, she's right. I *hate* it that she's right. But she's right anyway. I'm sorry to admit this, and I'm only going to think it, but I would really like to be an overnight millionaire with my own car and better clothes than Jessica. Well, at least better than Brianna. Or as good. I'd like to roll up in my own little Infiniti or something and see their faces. How shallow, I know, but inside every deep, psychic girl, I would bet you there's a shallow moron just waiting to come out.

"The only thing you can really do about Southern California," Tina says, "is surround yourself with people who will care about you no matter where you live or how much your dad makes."

I smile at her and think of Emily and Janet. I miss them. But maybe Tina's beginning to grow on me.

22

I guess I'm still a little sick, because when Tina leaves and my dad heads out to the grocery store for more of everything I want — even Diet Pepsi, which he never used to let me have, owing to his deep-seated hatred for everything American soda companies represent — I fall asleep on my bed. I didn't mean to fall asleep. I meant to read my physics textbook in hopes of learning something. But boom. Asleep.

It's a weird sleep, the kind where you aren't even sure you are asleep. I have a lot of these. My grandmother told me that they're called night terrors, where you feel awake but like you can't move, and there's a sense that you're not alone in the room. Yeah, well, I get that. I get a night terror. Just when I thought nothing else bad could possibly happen to me — you know, statistically speaking — this. I try to resist it. Usually there are spirits that want to talk to you in a night terror. And more often than not, those spirits are bad. Really bad. So bad that you're better off making yourself wake up and do something else.

I fail. I can't wake up, and I can't turn away. I know that I am awake but also asleep, and then I feel like I'm rising out of my body. I mean, I am rising up. I don't have a body anymore. I hate this. It's terrifying, frankly. There is nothing scarier in the world than this sensation right now, which makes my blood feel thick and frozen, like melting ice cream. I turn and see myself asleep on the bed. I wonder for a second if I'm dead. A long, scary second. Then I hear a voice say, "Don't worry. You're still alive."

It's a familiar, high-pitched voice. I turn toward it and see a little girl sitting on the chair in my corner. She looks Japanese. She wears a dirty dress, and I want to feed her. "Who are you?" I ask.

"I'm Yuko," she says. Her manner is not the manner of a little girl. She looks at me like a grown-up and moves her hands like a grown-up. I am getting very freaked. You've seen scary movies, right? Well, this is a million times scarier than the most frightening moment of a scary movie. Trust me. I don't think I can deal. "I'm your future grandmother."

"What?"

I'm not really talking, not in the usual way people talk. It's like we're communicating telepathically. I mean, I know that the little girl is probably speaking Japanese, but for some reason I totally understand it. It's like the symbols of the words are gone and all I see are the feelings and thoughts they are meant to represent.

"I am Keoni and Kerani's grandmother," she says.

"I am not going to marry those boys," I say, wondering as I say it if it's even true.

The little girl laughs. "No, you're not. But your father. . . ."

"My dad is not going to marry those boys, either," I say. I wonder why I can still be a smart-ass, even when I'm in a scary, creepy dream state, floating above my body and communicating telepathically with a dead woman who appears to me as a little girl. I think it's a coping mechanism. I can't deal with this horrifying situation any other way.

She laughs. "My daughter likes your father very much. She notices him, and even more important, I like him."

"You like my dad?" I ask. She pulled me all the way to the spirit realm to tell me this? She needs to get a life. Er, a death. Whatever. Something.

"Your father is a great man," she says.

"I'm sorry," I say. "I thought you were talking about *my* dad."

"I would appreciate any help you can give me in helping them find each other."

"Is that why you keep trying to talk to me?"

"No," she says. "I have another reason."

I wait for her to tell me.

"I watch my grandsons suffer at school, with all those mean boys and girls, and it makes me very, very sad. I thought we had to sacrifice and suffer in this country, all the discrimination, so that our children and grandchildren would not have to. But I realize now that discrimination takes many different forms."

"What do you mean?"

"Well, for us, it was because we were Japanese, or Asian. For my grandsons, it is because they're not rich, or because they aren't what others think they should be with their clothes and interests."

"That's why you want to talk to me?"

"Yes. Because I want you and my other grandchildren to remember what my generation went through."

"I don't understand."

"It is important that you and Kerani and Keoni all stop listening to those hateful children and start to love yourselves for the amazing human beings that you are. Stop letting other people make you who you will be. That is the most dangerous thing in the world."

"Peer pressure?" I ask. "I'm sorry, but I don't see how peer pressure compares at all to what happened to you with the internment camps."

"When you meet a person one-on-one, it is very unusual for a person to discriminate. The usual way people behave, human nature, is to try to find common ground in order to get along and help each other. It is when people become insecure and act in the context of a group that danger exists. So it is that your peers put pressure on each other to harm less popular children and those who are different from them in the same way that people in nationalistic, xenophobic societies put pressure on each other to treat foreigners and other people who are different from them badly."

I think about this. It makes sense, and it reminds me of someone. "You sound like my friend Tina."

"Tina is a good girl," she says. "I am happy my future granddaughter has such a good friend."

"Why do you keep calling me your granddaughter?"

"Don't you get it?" she asks. "Your father is going to marry my daughter."

"He is?"

She nods and smiles. "If I get my way. And I'm not leaving until I do."

"Why does it matter so much to you?"

"Because," she says. She is starting to fade, and I feel myself slipping back into my body again. "What my grandsons need is the love of a father figure. They are becoming men now, and they need to have a strong man around who can guide them and who, through his own brightness, can teach them that it is okay to shine with their own beautiful light."

Once she totally disappears, I am happy. Happy that the terrifying situation — a little-girl ghost talking like a grown-up? — is over. Or kind of over. I'm still thinking about what she said. And I can pretty much forget sleeping. What was she talking about? Shine their own beautiful light? Strong man? She might be long dead, but I still suspect she's been smoking crack.

I pick up the phone and dial the number of the only person on earth who will understand exactly how I'm feeling and what I'm going through: my grandma.

23

So, it's the weekend. Sunday, to be precise. I get to go back to school on Monday. Dad has decided to blow off Sleepy and the other Homie Doll–looking guys to stay in Aliso Viejo all weekend hanging out with me. We're not your typical religious family, so there is no church or anything like that. Not unless you count the Squeegeemobile, which my father appears to worship. I spend as much time as I can avoiding him and talking on the phone to Emily and Janet. Things sound interesting back home, with Emily starting a new relationship with a guy from Española I've never met. Janet assures me the guy is super-hot. I'm sure he is. Emily doesn't go for any other kind. Then I hang up and I'm back here, with stitches.

There's just me and Dad all weekend, renting movies (last night) and driving around looking at houses (yesterday) that Dad would like to buy. He says it's "bonding time." Is he *baked*? Hello? The time to bond with your kids is when they're infants. I'm *sixteen*. This is seriously *separation* time. But Dad needs bonding, so, you know, I'm down. At least I'm pretending to be down, because I'm feeling nice and I want to get on his good side for when he starts making the millions and buys me my own Infiniti, only now I've changed my mind and I don't want the Infiniti, I want a Mercedes, because even though they used to be way wack and old-fashioned, they've got a bunch of new ones that are slick.

"You ready to go?" Dad asks me.

First we're going shopping for bathing suits and towels, even though it's the middle of winter. I don't see a lot of locals going in the ocean right now. Sometimes I don't think my dad pays a whole lot of attention to the world around him. It's like he lives in those drawings he does. To him, California is warm, and warm means beach time. I'm telling you, he's gonna be the only loser out there on the beach in a Speedo or something. Me? I prefer to follow the rules of conduct for the place we're in. Dad, Mr. Super Trailblazer — or Rain Man, I haven't decided — wants to go swimming. I think he's nuts, but whatever. He didn't ask me, and he's been acting so goofy lately that I just let him do what he wants. I'm counting the days until I turn eighteen and graduate and go to college and start my real life — with my Mercedes.

We go to Target for the swimwear. I don't like any of it, so Dad takes me to something called Sports Chalet. Can I just say I *adore* this store? It's *amazing*. We don't have stores like this in New Mexico. We barely have stores in New Mexico, but that's another issue. Anyway, the Sports Chalet has all the usual stuff you'd expect from a sporting goods store, but lots of other stuff, too. Really cool clothes. Lots of them. Dad encourages me to browse and tells me to get whatever I want. He even brings me a shopping cart to load it all in. I look closely at him to make sure he's my real father. Yep. It's him. Just *baked*.

We go home after shopping and put on the swimwear. I wear a Nike yoga outfit over my one-piece bathing suit (I am not going to wear that tiny bikini Emily and Janet got me, puh-lease!) because I know for a *fact* it's going to be freezing cold at the beach. My dad got these floral Hawaiian-looking trunks and a big T-shirt. It's way better than the thong Speedo I was expecting. I suggest he wear a jacket, but he looks at me like I'm crazy.

"This is Southern California, Punkin, not Alaska," he says, tying a bandana around his head. Yes, I just said my dad is tying a bandana around his head, like a gangster from a movie. Or J. Lo in a video where she's pretending to be Ciara. I am so embarrassed, and we haven't even left the apartment yet.

He's been doing some serious work on the Squeegeemobile — seriously *weird* work, like the kind that might land him in the loony bin, but *whatever* — and people stare at us as we drive through Aliso Viejo toward Laguna Beach. You'd stare, too, if you saw it. It's not puke green anymore. It's cherry red, with flames licking the sides. It's got the mural on the front, some Aztec-looking guy and the floppy Mexican hottie in his arms, and a picture of George W. Bush with a big red circle around it and a line through the circle. Dad's stuck a big plastic sculpture of Squeegee Man on the hood, the squeegee held aloft like a saber. It's crazy to look at, but from a completely artistic standpoint, it's not that bad. It would look cool in a museum or in a photograph. When it *doesn't* look cool is when I'm sitting *inside* of it. Or at least it makes *me* look *so* not cool. I'm surprised that most of the people who stare at us seem to really like the car. A few guys give Dad the thumbs-up, and two of them ask him about the car at stoplights. I can tell he's super proud of it. He blasts Green Day's "American Idiot" song over and over, like he thinks he's making some kind of a statement. I look at him funny, and he says, "This is a Republican county, they need to be schooled." I actually kind of agree with that part. Maybe I don't appreciate my dad enough. He's one of a kind, anyway.

We get to the beach, and Dad finds parking about five blocks away. As we walk, I point out that the only people in the water are those wearing wet suits. The wind is freezing, just like I thought, and my dad knows I'm right but doesn't want to admit it. He hates to lose. I love to win. I think I get it from him.

We find a bench near a playground and sit down.

"I didn't want to swim anyway," he says.

"Yeah, right."

"No, I didn't. I really just suggested this because I thought it would be a good chance for us to have a talk."

"Oh." A talk? No, thank you. Anything but that.

Dad looks nervous. "I don't know how to bring this up. But I'll do my best." He looks like one of those people on *Fear Factor*, about to jump into a tub of scorpions.

Uh-oh. I try to think of what might come next. Dad looks so awkward and scared. Did he knock someone up? Am I about to have an illegitimate baby brother or sister? Do I need to tell my dad about condoms?

"I know we had that birds-and-bees talk a couple of years ago," he says.

"It was *six* years ago," I say. "When I was *ten*. When I got my period." And you took me out for ice cream and humiliated me, I think.

"Six years?" He looks at me like I'm lying. Maybe it's just that the bandana is cutting off circulation to his brain.

"Yes, *Dad*. Six years."

"God, where does the time go?"

"I don't know, Dad." Funny. To me it feels like eternity.

"Well, I realized after this whole thing with that little bastard Andrew and the 'party' that there's more I need to talk to you about than the basic biology of the whole thing. Things I haven't talked to you about because I've been too anxious or lazy. I didn't want to give you any ideas or make you grow up too fast. It was stupid, and I should have brought all this up sooner, but anyway, better late than never." He's all sweaty. "So," he says. "Tell me what you know and what you don't know."

"Huh?" What is he talking about now?

"I mean, I don't know where to start. Fill me in."

I think about what he said a minute ago, and I ask, "If I don't *know* something, how can I tell you about it?"

"What?"

"You just told me to tell you what I know and what I don't know, but I don't know how I'm supposed to tell you something I don't know. It's not logical."

Dad looks confused. "You know what I meant."

"No, I don't. I really don't. What are you talking about?"

Dad sighs, and I instantly feel guilty. How does he do that? How can he make me feel guilty just by breathing? Is that a special gift parents have? "I mean *boys,* Paski. And —" he pauses and gulps. I can actually hear the gulp, like a sound effect. My dad is turning into one of his characters. That's what's happening here. "And sex." He chokes on the last word, and his face turns dark red.

Oh my God. My dad brought me to the beach to have a *sex* talk with me? Why couldn't he humiliate me in the comfort of our own home? Why does he have to do it out here in the open where everyone can see me?

"I'm going to be very frank with you now." Dad clears his throat, and I realize he doesn't want to be here, either. "Have you . . . I mean, are you still . . ." He has to wipe his brow. Only he doesn't exactly wipe it. He pulls a piece of the bandana down and sops it up. Eew. "What I'm trying to say is, I am, I'm wondering —"

"No," I say. "I haven't done it yet."

Dad looks relieved, then suspicious. "You don't have to lie to me about it if you have. I'm not one of those dads who's gonna get all mad about it and tell you you're ruining your chances at marriage by not being a virgin or anything *pendejo* like that."

"Okay," I say. I didn't even know there *were* dads like that anymore. Are there?

"But I'm not going to be this dad who's encouraging you to drop your pants, either."

"Not even to go to the bathroom?"

Dad doesn't smile. "You know what I mean."

"Good," I say. "Then I guess we don't have anything to talk about."

"So, have you?" he asks me.

"Have I *what*?"

"Had . . . intercourse with a boy."

"No, Dad! I just *told* you that!"

"Well, I wasn't sure you were being honest. I wanted to make sure you felt safe being honest with me, and now that you feel safe, or at least I hope you feel safe, I wanted to ask you again and see if your answer had changed."

"I told you the truth the first time." Baked. Totally baked.

"Okay, well I saw this study in *Details* magazine that said the average age an American girl loses her virginity in the United States is sixteen, and this lightbulb went off in my head and I realized the clock was ticking because I hadn't talked to you about it yet."

"Dad," I say. "First, I think you need to stop reading *Details* magazine. Second, I don't think we need to have this talk." I mean, what is he going to tell me about sex that I don't already know? I know all about sex in theory. I've read about it, and Emily and Janet told me everything, even if I didn't want them to.

"I wish we didn't have to have this talk," says Dad. "Trust me. I do. I hate this. It's *pinche* embarrassing to have to talk to your teenage daughter about this stuff."

"Yeah," I say. "Especially now that you're getting to be that age where you need Viagra and everything."

For the first time since he started this conversation, Dad's mouth turns up in a smile. "You are *such* a pain in the ass, *Chinita,* you know that?" he asks with affection. He looks out at the ocean. "You are so much like me. God. How did you end up so much like me?"

"Bad genes?" I offer.

Dad laughs out loud. "Yeah, bad genes."

"Speaking of bad jeans," I say, "you should stop wearing them so baggy, Dad. It's, like, so last decade. Did you learn that in *Details*?"

"Very funny."

"So are we finished with 'the talk' now?" I ask.

"No! You keep messing up my train of thought. I had this whole speech all planned out." He takes a piece of folded yellow paper out of his pocket, the kind with lines on it, and opens it. His hands are trembling. *He wrote a speech?* What is this, an inauguration or a heart-to-heart? "Okay," he says with a deep breath. I can hear the paper rattling. "What I wanted to say was — oh, hold on. Wait a minute." He turns the paper over. "I wrote two speeches. One for if you weren't a virgin anymore and one for if you were."

Oh my God. It is so creepy to hear my father speaking like this. It makes me sick, actually. I want this to stop. It's like I used to feel in haunted houses when I was a child, waiting for the end, afraid that something horrible was going to scare me to death around the next corner.

"Dad, you don't have to read me your speech," I say.

"No, no. I want to. Here." He clears his throat. Sniffles like he's going to cry. Oh my God. He's put so much work into this whole thing. I sink down lower on the bench and pray no one can hear him or see us. I wish for powers of invisibility. "Pasquala," he reads. He sounds all robotic when he's reading. My dad would not make a good actor. "As you enter this time in your life . . . uhm . . . Okay." He takes a deep breath and looks like he wants to hide. "As you enter this time in your life, you are going to be feeling many strong feelings about boys, and they are all completely normal. No matter what anybody says, girls are by nature just as sexual as boys, and they aren't just there to be used by boys."

"What?" Where did he get this?

"And I want you to remember that no matter what anyone tells you or tries to make you think and feel, nature doesn't screw up. And nature is what made all human beings have a sex drive. That's why there are so many people in the world. Billions of us. We all have these feelings. They are completely healthy and normal."

Ooookaaayyyy . . .

Dad takes a deep breath and continues. "We live in a puritanical society that will try to shame you at every turn, but you have to remember that your body is your temple and you are just as entitled to enjoy it as you are expected to take good care of your health and make good decisions that you won't regret later and that won't ruin your life or even kill you."

"Dad! Shut *up!*"

He frowns at me. His hands are still trembling. He says, "I'm not done. By 'good decisions' I mean condoms. I am going to assume you know what they are. Do you?" I laugh. "I'll take that as a yes," he says. "When that day finally comes and you have found a boy you love and who respects you, I know that you will make the right choice and choose to protect yourself from disease and pregnancy in this most sensible of ways. I have made an appointment for you at the local Planned Parenthood office —"

"You *what?*"

"— because I love you, and I want you to be informed and protected out there. It's what any good liberal parent would do. I don't want to sit here and preach abstinence to you, because I was sixteen once, and there is nothing scarier than the hormones of a sixteen-year-old. At sixteen, people are rather insatiable that way."

Oh my God. My father has lost his mind.

He looks like he's thinking about something. "No, wait," he says and keeps reading. "There *is* something scarier than the hormones of a teenager. Sex in the absence of love is scary. It is one of the ugliest forces in the world, and I don't think you are foolish enough to place yourself in a situation like that. Sex with love is the divine expression of our beauty and potential for connection as human beings, and I would say that if you love a boy enough to trust him not to hurt you . . ." Dad gets his crazy *cholo* face going.

"This is like torture," I interrupt. "Here." I hold out my hand. "Just take my fingernails off with tweezers. That'd be easier than listening to this."

He ignores me. "So, without going into details about technique — that's half the fun, learning as you go —"

"God, Dad! *Enough!* I surrender! Leave me alone!" I cover my ears with my hands.

Dad grabs them and pulls them off. "I will just say that I salute your blossoming adulthood, and I know that you will make smart, mature decisions about your health and future. I also know that if you have any questions about any of this, you will feel safe and comfortable coming to talk to me, your dad, like as if I were your mom — well, not *your* mom exactly, but *a* mom — or a good friend, because I love you and I want you to be around for many years to come, with a college education, and good health, none of which will be possible if you have unprotected sex and get AIDS and have a baby as a teenager."

I stare at him in disbelief. Dad folds up his paper again and stuffs it in his pocket. Speech over.

"Any questions?" he asks. He takes off his glasses and rubs the bridge of his nose, a thing he does only when he's really worn out and stressed. I will never, ever, when I grow up, take off my glasses and rub the bridge of my nose in the presence of my child. It will make him or her feel guilty and awful, and I'm not going to do that.

"No." I say. "No, wait! I have a question."

"Okay." Dad puts the glasses on again and stares out to sea with a serious look on his face, as if bracing for something painful. "Shoot."

"Can we go home now?" I ask. I need to call Janet and tell her about this. She'll freak. Her parents *never* talk about this stuff with her. I need someone to laugh with about it, I *so* do. Maybe Emily, too, but Emily thinks my dad is way cool, and she'll tell me to appreciate his openness. I would bet you anything that Tina, if I were to tell her about it, would say the same thing. All these people think my dad is cool. Weirdos.

I'm freezing, and after hearing him talk about sex and humanity, my nausea is back with a vengeance.

24

I still have the stitches in my forehead, like these tiny, raw train tracks, but I don't think that's the only reason all the kids in the hall at school are staring at me. I feel like a celebrity, but not a *good* celebrity. I feel like Mary-Kate or Ashley, whichever was the anorexic one, on the way to the clinic where they're going to force-feed me with a tube. I feel like Paris Hilton after an unfortunate intimate video incident. Exposed. Pitied. Laughed at. Like people might have once thought I was sort of cool, but now they all think I'm tragic.

Basically, I've become *that* kid.

By the way? Every school has one — a *that* kid. Back in Taos, it was the geek boy with the uneven bowl cut and the short pants who tried to kill himself. Everyone ignored him for years, made fun of him, and then one day he went home and sliced up his wrists with a bread knife. Then, all of a sudden, everyone knew who he was, and felt really bad for having teased him. We all went to visit him, and he got popular for the totally wrong reason. Over in Española, *that* kid was a boy who shot both of his parents after they told him he couldn't stay out past eleven. Every school has *that* kid who does something weird and gets schoolwide attention. That's me now, only I didn't do anything so much as I had something done to me. How is it possible? I haven't even been here two weeks, and I'm *that* kid.

A few people smile with their shoulders up by their ears, like they can't finish a full shrug about me, but mostly they just stare. Some of them lean in toward each other and whisper. The nicer ones wait until they've passed to do it. When they see that I've noticed them whispering about me, they turn around and pretend to be looking for something in their lockers. It's stupid. I know why they're freaked. I'm the girl who got drugged and almost got killed by Jessica Nguyen. In other words, I am exactly what every girl in this school is afraid she might be one day. Everyone lives in the menacing shadow of Jessica.

I get to Mr. Big's class and take my seat. I pretend to read my textbook, because I can't deal. In truth, I keep reading the same chapter-end summary over and over, without really comprehending any of it. People come in, talking loud like usual, but as soon as they see me, everybody shuts up. Some even say, "Oh my God." I hate this. I don't want to look at them. Most of all, I don't want to look at Jessica. She comes in wearing tight jeans and a white leather blazer with what looks like black lacy lingerie beneath it, and then it really gets quiet in the room. Chris comes in with his shiny motorcycle helmet tucked up under one arm, wearing jeans and another extra-soft hoodie sweatshirt, in dark blue. He takes an empty seat far away from Jessica. He's called me at home a couple of times since the party, to see how I was doing.

For the record, Chris told me he totally broke up with Jessica and she cried and acted like a big baby about it. Actually, he didn't say "baby." He said, "She wailed like a banshee." I had to look "banshee" up. Just so you know, a banshee is this mythical Irish fairy that shows up and shrieks to warn families of bad things to come. Great. Jessica is a shrieking banshee warning of bad things to come. I don't like the sound of that. Chris said he wants to take me out, but he wants to make sure I'm totally better first. I told him that my dad won't let me see him, and he said he wants to come over and talk to my dad "man-to-man." Yeah, like *that* would go well.

The truth is, I don't really know if I want to date Chris. I mean, I want to, but I don't know if it would be a smart thing to do. I'm a little down on the whole trusting-people thing right now. Especially guys. And Jessica. First Ethan swears his undying love for me, then he falls in love with the first thing he sees after I leave town. Then Andrew drugs me and I almost die. You might say I'm a little boy-scared right now.

Anyway, about Chris coming to talk to my dad? Bad idea. Somehow, I don't think my dad would like that very much. Anyway, I told Chris that I don't care if my dad doesn't want me to see him. It isn't up to my dad what boys I see. It's up to me who I see, and I'm not sure I want to see anyone. Except that I really do want to see Chris. I just wish I didn't really want to. See what I mean? As far as I'm concerned, my dad has made more than enough decisions for me lately, like moving here. Oh, and the Planned Parenthood thing. God. I almost forgot about that. The appointment's two weeks from Saturday.

The bell rings, and the ever-suave Mr. Big comes in the room, wearing khaki shorts with a stylishly frayed hem and a loud Hawaiian shirt. There's total silence. I feel everyone's eyes on me, even the people who aren't looking directly at me. They all know I'm here, and they know Jessica's here, and no one knows what any of it means. I count myself among those who don't know what's happening.

"Hello, everyone," says Mr. Big. "Good to see we've got a full class today. Everyone's here except Andrew, who is going to be out for a couple of weeks." He claps his hands the way teachers do, and asks, "Do you all know where he is?"

No one answers. I look up. Mr. Big is looking right at me with sympathy in his eyes. Then he looks right at Jessica without sympathy. I hear someone clear his throat. It's Chris. I turn, and he smiles in a reassuring way that makes me feel a lot better. I'd like to think he's a solid guy, but things have already been so messed up since I got here and it's only been, like, a week.

"Andrew's parents sent him to an intensive counseling center where they work with kids who have emotional problems," says Mr. Big. People look at each other out of the corners of their eyes but sit as still as rabbits afraid of a noise. Mr. Big continues, "So, as you all know, we've had a busy week here. I'm not going to mess around and pretend I don't know about it. I don't think you should, either. It's been in all the papers and on the news. It's no secret, Paski, that you had a terrible thing happen to you last weekend. I want to say I'm very sorry that this was your introduction to Aliso Niguel High School."

I feel my heartbeat get faster. It's like a bird heart. Boomboom-boom. I feel heavy in my face, and the stitches throb with the increased blood flow. Ouch. This so sucks. I don't want him talking about this here! Why is he doing this to me?

"So, today I thought we'd have a change of pace, and instead of talking about the reading assignment, I want us all to put our desks in a circle."

No one moves.

"Come on," says Mr. Big. He claps his hands again, even louder. "Move your desks. Let's go!" He sounds every bit like the soccer coach he is.

We put our desks in a circle. Chris puts his hand right next to mine. "How you holdin' up, kiddo?" he asks me. Jessica gives him an evil stare.

"I'm okay," I say.

Mr. Big walks around the outside of the circle, handing us all photocopies. One is a magazine article about date rape drugs. Another is a newspaper article about the influence of pop culture on girls and women today. Then there's another one on why girls are so mean to each other when they should be sticking up for each other at this incredibly hard time in their lives. It reads like my dad wrote it, I swear to God.

Mr. Big gives us all fifteen minutes to read the articles. After everyone is finished, he starts a discussion. At first no one wants to talk. But Chris takes the initiative.

"I agree with everything in these articles," he says. "And I'm not afraid to say it. Andrew was a friend of mine, but I am disgusted by what he did."

"Thanks, Chris," says Mr. Big. "What about the rest of you? Do you think it was okay for Andrew to do what he did?"

Everyone shakes their heads. Even Tyler.

"How about you, Jessica? What do you think?" asks Mr. Big. He sits on the edge of his desk, crosses his legs, and folds his arms across his chest, defensive. Don't tell me the teacher is even afraid of her? That's whack.

Jessica looks at her hands with a scary little smile and doesn't say anything. Then, slowly, she lifts her eyes and stares him down. "I think I don't want to talk about this. If you don't mind, 'sir.'" She says "sir" sarcastically, to drive home the fact that she has no respect for his authority.

"Is there a reason?" asks Mr. Big.

Jessica stares at him with hate. "No," she says. "There's no reason. But I think you should stop pushing me about it, unless you want me to bring up another topic that might interest the class. A topic you and I have discussed before."

Mr. Big looks nervous all of a sudden, and Jessica smiles.

"Here's the topic," she says. She leans forward and smiles like she's crazy. "Teachers who flirt with their female students. Oh, and soccer coaches. I think that's having a really bad impact on the self-esteem of high school girls, don't you, Mr. Big?"

Mr. Big blushes, and moves on to another student. I realize there are more layers of sickness at this school than I know — or want to know.

25

After school, Tina, dressed in black pants, black shirt, and black jacket like a vampire with pink hair, bobs down the hall next to me. School's out for the day, and I'm going to the newspaper. Earlier, she cracked the knuckles on her long, skinny fingers and told me she didn't think I should go alone. Tina said that she knew I'd feel slightly strange, because my assignment to write about the race looks a little bit *different* now that everyone in school knows Jessica tried to *kill* me. "The homicidal wench," Tina concludes.

"She didn't try to kill me," I say as we walk through the hall.

"Hello? Hospital? Intravenous fluids? Were you not *there?*"

"I know, but I don't really *believe* Jessica tried to kill me."

"It's official, then," says Tina. She shrugs in defeat.

"What's official?"

"You're officially in denial."

We enter the bright room and look around. Lots of plants and maps. When she's not doing the newspaper, Miss Munn is the senior

English teacher. I suppose it's nice of Tina to be here with me. She's, like, the only person in school who hasn't changed the way she looks at me or talks to me because of this whole stupid thing. I love her for that. She's what my grandmother would call a keeper, someone you cherish because they will never let you down.

All the newspaper kids sort of stop what they were doing and look up at me. Then, like everyone else I've come into contact with today, they flinch or fidget or look away like they don't know what to say. I see Sydney, in the kind of elegant pants and sweater grown-up lawyer women wear, *way* focused on her computer, tapping away. She hasn't even noticed we're here. She's a good editor. I like the way the papers turn out here, and I'm impressed by how dedicated and smart Sydney seems. She's one of those kids who don't seem to care what people think of her. Tina wants to be that kind of kid, but I think she cares as much as the rest of us. Her whole thing with trying to look Goth and countercultural still seems to acknowledge what is acceptable, if only to go against it. Sydney doesn't even know what's acceptable, or if she does, she cares so little that it doesn't affect her life at all. She's already figured out who she is and what she wants.

I walk over to her desk, and Tina follows. I tap Sydney's shoulder, and she swivels her head. Unlike the other kids, she smiles like nothing is wrong with me. She's got on a new pair of funky glasses, sort of square-shaped, black with gold flecks.

"Hey, Paski," her voice chirps. "How are you?"

I tell her I'm okay, and she looks at me long and hard, like she's trying to figure out whether or not I'm telling the truth.

"Hi, Sydney," says Tina. To my surprise, Sydney smiles and gets up to hug her. I didn't realize they were friends. "Have you thought about that cartoon strip anymore?" Sydney asks.

Tina shakes her head. "Nah."

"Oh, come on," says Sydney with a friendly fake punch to Tina's arm. "You totally have to do it. You're so funny."

I look at Tina like I want to know what they're talking about, and she tells me that Sydney has asked her to draw a comic strip for the paper, about kids who are kind of like the kids at school.

"You should!" I think it's a great idea.

"Nah," says Tina again.

"C'mon!" pleads Sydney.

"I'm not comfortable with it," Tina says.

"But why? You could have a huge impact here."

"I don't *want* to have a huge impact here," says Tina. "I want to wait to get out in the real world to have my big impact. *Here* is a place I just want to get out of. Like Alcatraz."

Sydney shrugs at me, like she's tried all she can. I can tell she isn't giving up, though. I like that about her. "So," she says to me. "I know all about what happened with the party. I'm not going to say I'm sorry, because I know that's not what you want to hear."

I see some of the other kids in the room listening to us, and it seems like they all really respect what Sydney has to say. I realize that even though Jessica and her friends are the most obviously popular girls in the school, there are many layers of popularity, and kids can be popular in different cliques for different reasons. Sydney the smart, funky newspaper editor is exactly the kind of person I would like to be friends with.

"So, anyway, all I'm going to say about it is that you don't have to do that motocross race story if you don't want to."

"I don't mind doing it," I reply.

"Okay, but I have to ask if you think you have a conflict of interest now."

"A what?" I ask.

"A conflict of interest is when, as a journalist, you don't think you're going to be able to do a fair job covering a story because your personal feelings or experiences about it might get in the way."

"Oh," I say.

"Do you have bad feelings about Jessica that might get in the way?" asks Sydney.

I consider the question, and the truth is . . . *no.* I know that I should dislike her, obviously, but it's like someone planted another feeling in me. It's this weird sense of peace, and I know that it's coming from the same place the spirit voices and invisible coyotes have come from. Trust me, I don't like that I feel this way. It's like I wish I could be angry about it, but I just feel neutral.

"I'm okay with it," I say.

Tina looks at me in shock, grabs me by the shoulders, and stares at my eyes, close up. "You're crazy," she says. "In a good, Walt Whitman sort of way. But crazy."

"Are you sure about this?" Sydney asks me, but Tina thinks the question is for her.

"I am completely convinced she's insane," she exclaims.

"I'm not sure Jessica knew what she was doing," I say. "I think the bigger problem for me is with Andrew, or whoever put that stuff in my soda."

"Okay, then," says Sydney. "I like that you're being open-minded about it. That's a must for reporters."

Sydney opens a file box on the floor next to her and pulls out a white envelope. She hands it to me. "This is your press pass for the race this weekend. Use it wisely."

I stuff the envelope in my backpack and try to ignore the awful, bloody vision of Jessica crushed under her own motorcycle in the third turn. I tell myself I've done all I can to warn her, but in my heart I know the truth: *I should have tried harder.*

26

I open the door from the parking lot to the garage, and in the half-dark, I see the hulking shape of the Squeegeemobile. I *smell* it, too. Oily. Like spray paint and CK One. You know that new-car smell? Well, whatever the *opposite* of that is, I think it smells like *this*. Dad's back early. It's Friday, and we have plans, me and Dad, to go to a movie. It's been a long time since we did that. Ever since the party, Dad has been coming home earlier than before and spending less time with his pro-*cholo* posse.

I stash my bike in a corner far from the "car" and head upstairs. When I open the door to the apartment, I hear a muffled gasp of surprise and look up to see my dad and Melanie, the twins' mom, jumping away from each other on the couch with these guilty red faces. No. Way. *Please* tell me I did *not* just walk in on my dad making out with the lady next door. Please tell me I'm hallucinating. Don Juan, sitting near them, points one of his back feet up toward the ceiling like a ballerina and proceeds to lick his butt. I want to ask him what's going on, but he'll just walk away like he always does, waiting for a can of food to get the butt taste out of his mouth.

"Hey, Punkin," says my dad in a sort of high-pitched tone. He looks at his watch, way awkward. "I didn't realize it was this late already. Wow."

I smile tightly but can't find my voice. I don't know what to say. I just stand there, all stupid and frozen.

"Hello, Pasquala," says Melanie. She's adjusting her shirt. *Adjusting her shirt.* Eew. Please tell me my dad was not the cause of her shirt's disorder. Oh. My. God. Dad is feeling up the neighbor lady. Puke?

"We were just sitting here . . . talking," says Dad. Melanie laughs with her hand over her mouth.

"Yeah, okay. I'll be in my room if you crazy kids need me," I say. I dash up the stairs before they can stop me. I don't mean to slam the door, but that's what happens anyway. Wham! Like I'm angry, which I'm not. Sickened and angry are not the same thing. I pick up the phone from my old dresser and punch in Janet's number. I need to talk to her about everything.

Janet tells me all the latest gossip from Taos High, including the fact that she has a crush on a boy I used to think she liked. She denied it back when she had a boyfriend, but now she says she thinks he's cute. She also finally tells me that Emily is getting hot and heavy with the dude from Española.

We laugh about my dad making out with the lady next door. I tell her I have had weird visions about them getting married someday. Janet gets all excited and asks me what I envision for her and her new crush, and I tell her I have no idea. I have never been able to have a vision on *demand*. They just come when they feel like it, and it's my job to figure out why and what to do with them. Janet asks about Chris Cabrera, and I tell her I've sort of been avoiding him because of my dad.

"Don't *do* that," she says.

"I know." It's not like my dad has a lot of ground to stand on. He's the freak who's downstairs molesting the neighbor lady.

"You're his daughter, not his slave," Janet says. Thank God for friends.

"You think I should go out with Chris if he asks me?"

"Duh," says Janet. "He's hot, he's available, he saved your life. What part of perfect do you not understand?"

At that moment, the call waiting beeps. I look at the caller ID. *Cabrera.* I tell Janet I'll call her back, and I switch the call over. My pulse races.

"Hello?" I say, like I don't already know who's calling.

"Paski?"

"Yeah?"

"It's me, Chris. Cabrera."

"Oh," I say, pretending to be surprised. "Hi. How are you?"

"Fine. You?"

"Okay. I mean, I just walked in on my dad making out with the lady next door, but other than that . . ."

He laughs. "Your dad's a character."

"I guess that's why he draws them," I say.

He laughs again. I love his laugh. "So, I'm calling to see if you have plans tonight."

"I'm supposed to go to the movies with my dad."

"Oh. Can you get out of it?"

226

"Maybe. Why?"

"It's a beautiful evening," he responds. "And I'm dying to see you ride a motorcycle."

"I don't have a motorcycle," I point out.

"I know," he says. "But I do."

"I don't know how to ride."

"What about your granny's Harley?"

"I can't ride *your* motorcycle."

"I'll teach you."

I get goose bumps when he says this. It sounds amazing.

Come to think of it? There are *lots* of things I'd like Chris Cabrera to teach me.

"Let me see if I can get out of this thing with my dad," I say. I might be making a mistake, but after you've been through what I have lately, what's one more little problem?

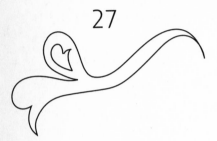

27

My dad seems relieved when I tell him Tina invited me to go to the movies. It's a lie, of course. I'm going to meet Chris at school, leave my bike there, and he's going to teach me to ride his racing motorcycle.

Yes, I just said I'm going to learn how to ride a motocross *motorcycle*. Can you *believe it*? Me, neither. You have *no* idea how excited I am. Not just to learn to ride, but to go for a ride, too, behind Chris, where I can wrap my arms and legs around him and hold on. You have to curl around the driver on the back of one of those things, right? It's, like, a requirement. So I won't be a *hoochie* for it. I'll just be *safety*-conscious. Very convenient.

I can't exactly tell my father what my plans are, though. I think that on any other day, he would have noticed I was lying. He's usually pretty good at that. But today he's embarrassed about making out with Melanie in our apartment. It's not like I really care. I'm happy for him. No, seriously, I am. I want him to have someone besides me to tell him how great he is. And if he had a girlfriend, it would make my leaving for college a little easier.

Melanie is still in the living room when I ask Dad if he minds that I go with my new friend instead of him. "I mean, no offense. It's just, Tina's really cool."

"She's awesome," he agrees. Awesome? Why is my dad still using that word? He sounds foolish. "You should meet this girl, Mel," he says. "She's dope." Dope? The only dope here is my father.

"What movie are you going to see?" asks Melanie.

I panic. I hadn't thought of a movie. Nice. How *stupid* am I? I try to act cool and say I forgot the name of it. "Something about aliens, I think."

Dad stands up. He's feeling guilty. He needs medication or something for that. "You need money? You want to take the Squeegeemobile?" I say yes to the money and no to the Squeegeemobile. I mean, *hello.* "But how will you get there?" he asks.

"Tina works until seven," I lie. "I'm meeting her at her job, and she's driving."

"Okay," says my dad. "But I want her phone number and her parents' phone number. And no parties."

"Okay," I say.

I go back up to my room and close the door behind me. Again, I don't, like, *mean* to slam it, but it slams anyway. That's because these are thin white doors made out of some kind of flimsy metal grained to look like wood with six panels. They feel like they're hollow. I stare at the door and sigh to myself. I've taped a million photos on it of the jagged purple mountains and tangerine mesa sunsets from *New Mexico* magazine, to remind myself of my misery. I miss my home state the way you hear about amputees missing limbs. There's an itch from it on my soul that makes me want to cry all the time. I'm going back there someday. Not for college but after that, when I'm a lawyer. Maybe I'll be a district attorney, or better than that, a child-rights lawyer who will pass laws making it impossible for single dads to remove their kids from the state without the kids' approval.

I turn from the landscapes on the door and look around the room. A square, decent size, with one window and a mirrored closet door, new carpet. The shades on the window are hard white plastic strips about four inches wide that hang from the top and wag in the breeze from the air vents. Don Juan likes to walk between these shade-thingies and twists them up. They're curved a little bit in one direction, and once one is turned backwards, it doesn't close right with the others. I go over and turn each one back into place, even though I know it's a losing battle. Don Juan will be back soon, weaving in and out of the shades, messing them up. It's fun for him in that one-eyed-cat woo-hoo kind of way. At least Don Juan's life is sadder than mine.

I need new bedroom furniture. The stuff here is old. I've had the same twin bed since fifth grade. The rest is plain brown furniture for a random room. I've decorated the dresser with stickers over the years, changing my mind and ripping them off as my tastes changed, leaving behind these white smudges of sticker glue and paper that refused to come off. I'm sure once Dad makes his millions, I'll get something else, if I still live here. I grab the cordless phone from my desk and flop on the bed to call Tina and tell her I need her as an alibi.

Tina seems excited about this. She likes to buck the system. She tells me she's going out with her man friend tonight, and she'd like to use me for an alibi, too. Even though I think she should look for a guy her own age, I agree to do it. If her mom calls my cell, I'm supposed to tell her Tina's in the bathroom. Ditto for my dad. And then we promise to call each other's cells immediately with the message to call home.

"Gotta love cell phones."

"Yeah," I agree.

"Chris Cabrera," she says, like she's thinking hard about his name. "*Muy lindo.* Have fun, Taos."

"Thanks."

"I have a really good feeling about him."

I don't want to say anything, but I have a good feeling about Chris, too. Almost too good to be true. And like most things that are too good to be true, I think, he probably is.

28

Okay. So I've been here waiting by the bike rack at school for Chris, and now he's here, pulling up in front of me with a crazy cute grin on his face. Oh my God. I wish I could trust him completely. I wish I didn't feel scared and excited all at once. I never wanted to be one of those loser girls attracted to bad boys. Hopefully I'm not.

He stops the motorcycle and takes off his helmet. He has very good posture and beautiful eyes. He says hello, tells me I look hot, and hands me a helmet he's brought.

"Let's ride," he says.

Maybe I'm an idiot, but I lift a leg and climb onto the motorcycle. So now, like, I'm officially sitting behind Chris on the narrow black leather seat of his apple-red Honda motorcycle, wearing the helmet he brought for me. I feel the engine ignite with a tiny boom beneath us, the steady, healthy roar of the motor, the warmth of Chris in front of me. He wears jeans and a black leather jacket, both of which hug his lines and bulges with artistic perfection. This body? This perfect guy's body? It is so not what I need right now. I mean, I need to be focused on learning how to ride, not focused on wanting to kiss him. He is *beyond* solid, so strong, so perfectly formed it seems almost unfair to the rest of the guys in the world.

As he steers the machine out of the parking lot and up the hill, I feel his expertise in the solid, smooth way we move along. I can also smell his scent. So totally yummy. It's not just the cologne he wears that I love. There's something else, a scent that is completely Chris. God, I love this smell. It makes me feel happy and safe to breathe him in. The motorcycle feels confident and muscular going up the hill, past the peach and pink stucco houses with their green manicured lawns and thick, well-watered palm trees. Power. There is a big, strong Orange County power to all of this, the bike, the cute guy, the homes and cars, the hazy blue of the sky. It's thrilling in the same weird way riding down massive hills on my bicycle is thrilling, but someone else is in control here. I hate to admit this, but I kind of like it. I never thought I'd be big on giving someone else control, but it's not bad if that someone else is Chris Cabrera.

Just so you know, Chris is not a showy rider, not here, anyway. I'm happy about that. I wouldn't want to get on a motorcycle with a psycho macho show-off kind of guy. He's solid, safe, considerate of me. A gentleman, basically. I mean, how many guys would think to bring the girl a helmet? He's thoughtful. So maybe I *can* trust him. Maybe he's not a dangerous liar the way Andrew is. Maybe I can be myself and relax around Chris. Not all guys are the same, right?

That's how I feel about it, like it's totally okay to be here. My instincts tell me. The guides, if that's what you want to call them, tell me. It's not like when Andrew pulled out in his Porsche, all testosteroned out. I'm sure Chris has plenty of testosterone — maybe that's the smell I love? — but he doesn't let it rule him here. It's not that he's riding gently but that he's riding intelligently. As we turn the corner onto El Toro Road, I wrap my arms more tightly around him and press my front into his back. I breathe in the fresh musk of his neck. Yeah. I feel safe here. I can't wait to tell Emily and Janet about *this*.

From El Toro, he stops at Laguna Canyon Road and leans back to say, "We're gonna head west, toward the beach. Then we'll take a ride down to San Diego County, to Barona. There's a track out there, and I'll let you take over, okay?"

I nod and feel the center of my body melting at the sight of his smiling eyes on the other side of his helmet. He is wise. Gentle, wise, and strong. The thought hits me: Old soul. That's what he is. He's been here before. Certain people have that wisdom to them, that connection to the world. I wonder if he realizes how special he is. Probably not.

He pulls a left onto Laguna Canyon, a winding, narrow road that has hardly any cars on it. It looks like one of those roads they use on car commercials, a black snake of pavement twisting through this golden, rolling, sun-swept canyon. It's beautiful here. On either side of us rise the hills, long blond grasses waving in the breeze. The sky is bright blue, away from the inland smog, and the air smells salty and fresh. Seabirds circle high up in the sky. Seabirds. I think of the amulet and wish I hadn't left it at home. It reminds me of here.

Chris increases the speed a bit, and I instinctively grip his legs with my knees and thighs. I feel a rush from the speed and from the closeness of his body. Our bodies on top of the motorcycle move like one, and this makes me curious about other ways our bodies might move nicely together. Bad girl, me. But sitting on the back of his (vibrating) motorcycle in my tight jeans, holding him with my entire body like this, doesn't help ease the longing I am starting to feel. I have never felt a longing for a boy the way I feel for Chris Cabrera.

As we speed along, I feel free. I feel in touch with who I am, with a voice inside of me that is trying to direct me toward my own best self. I realize in this instant that even though we came to California for my father, we were also meant to come here for me. Chris is important, and I want to be his girlfriend, but there's something else. I can taste it on the wind. Something powerful.

We crest the canyon, and suddenly the ocean rises into view. It's so huge it takes my breath away. Such a perfect shade of blue, with the sun glinting on the tops of the waves. The ocean makes me feel the same way the desert does, like the earth is alive and I'm a part of it.

"Wow!" I cry. Chris nods and gives a thumbs-up. This moment is as close as it gets to heaven here on earth.

We ride this way, sailing along the coast, in and out of canyons, all over Orange County, almost like we're flying, for what must be over an hour, and finally arrive at the training track. Chris has some sort of membership here and shows a card to get in. He parks his bike in a dusty dirt parking area, and we get off, removing our helmets. He chats with one of the workers, and they take us to a parking area where another bike waits, this one a little smaller than the one we've been riding, used but clean and well loved.

"It's my old bike," Chris tells me. "I let a friend of mine's sister use it. They brought it up here for you."

"Really?"

He nods, takes one look at my crazy mess of helmet hair, and grins. He's a little messy, too. He reaches out and rubs my head in an affectionate way. "You look so cute," he says.

I reach up and grab his hand out of my hair and hold it for a long second. Can't believe this guy. He found a motorcycle for me? "You're not too bad, either," I say. I reach out and mess up his hair. He smiles and runs his hands through it to smooth it down. Then he takes my hands in his.

"Chris?" I ask. He looks at me, waits for the rest of what I'm about to say. "Why did you go out with Jessica? I can't imagine that a nice guy, like a really truly nice guy, would put up with her."

"You saying you think I'm just pretending to be a nice guy?"

"I don't know. That's what I'm asking. Are you nice?"

"Yes."

"So why did you go out with Jessica?"

He sighs and makes a smile that looks almost like a frown. "I don't know. No, that's not true. Probably because she's popular and all the other guys wanted to go out with her. She's hot-looking. Sometimes guys are stupid about that. Peer pressure, right? Stupid. I know. Then, after I realized how messed up she was, it was more like guilt. Or like I wanted to help her. Only she can't be helped."

"Help her?"

"Like, show her that she didn't have to be the way she is."

"Did it work?"

He looks me straight in the eye. "Am I still with her?"

"Is that a rhetorical question?" I ask.

"I suppose it is. What's your answer?"

"No. You're not still with her."

"So I guess that answers your question."

"Yeah."

He smiles. "Did you like the ride?"

He moves in closer and looks at my entire face, lingering on my lips. The skin of my entire body feels like it is being lightly tickled with the tip of a feather. I get chills.

"Yeah," I almost whisper. "I liked it a lot."

"Me, too," he says. I can tell that he wants to kiss me. I want to kiss him, too.

"Come on." He points to the track. "Let's go watch for a minute. Then I'll teach you to ride."

I follow him to the track, doing my best to keep my eyes off his amazing body. He slows down to wait for me, and we walk side by side. We bump into each other.

"Sorry," I say.

He looks at me with a half-grin. "Don't be." He bumps me again and bites his lower lip with a naughty look on his face, a look my grandma likes to describe as "impish." "We're like magnets," he says over the roar of nearby motorcycles. "Can't stop the pull."

We stand at the top of the hill in the dry, warm breeze, and Chris places himself right next to me. Our arms touch. I want to squeeze him, or at least touch him. I see the tracks below us. It looks like there are two, maybe more, and I can hear the buzzing of the motors as people on bikes race around, leaping over mounds of dirt, pulling stunts and tricks that take my breath away. The noise is deafening. My heart races at the thought of jumping like that. I want to do that almost more than I've wanted anything. I want it even more than I want Chris, and at this moment, trust me, that's saying a *lot*.

"Wow," I say.

"It's the most amazing feeling in the world." He looks over at me with that grin and tilts his head, like he is reconsidering what he's just said. "But I bet there's maybe something that would feel better."

My eyes lock with his. "Yeah?" I ask. "What?"

I don't know why I *ask*. I *know* the answer. He's thinking that kissing me — and maybe doing other things with me — would feel better. I can *feel* him thinking this, and I can see it in his eyes. He doesn't answer, because he knows that I know. He touches my hand with his, lightly, just runs his fingertip along my palm. It's a tiny touch, the slightest of scratches with a short stab of fingernail, but it sends shivers through my entire body.

"Let's ride," he says. I gulp and nod. I pretend he means the motorcycle, and so does he.

Chris asks me to follow him, and he walks the bike to a relatively quiet area that I assume is meant for beginners. Most of the people here are little kids. I'm talking ten, eleven years old. They look like lollipops with their huge round helmets. I didn't even know parents *let* kids this small ride motorcycles. They're barely off tricycles, right? It's crazy. The parents totally shouldn't do that, should they? Let their kids go out on a machine like this?

"Here," says Chris. He straddles the bike to demonstrate, then gets off and says, "You try it."

"Okay." I stuff my head back into the helmet, take the motorcycle from him, and feel his big, strong hand brush against mine as we make the trade.

"This is how you turn it on," he says after I'm situated on the seat.

He leans over me, and I smell him, feel him. He knows how to turn things on, that's for sure. "Just step down on the pedal."

I stomp the pedal once. It catches, grumbles for a moment, and sputters out.

"Try it again," says Chris. He stands back, and this time, certain he's not going to be in the way, I really stomp on it. The motor roars to life. I feel the vibrations in my hands, along the seat of the bike. Powerful. I like it. I am starting to crave power, and this scares me a little.

"Good!" shouts Chris over the din. "Now the rest is pretty straight-forward, like your grandma's motorcycle." He moves in close again and shows me how to brake, how to steer. "Awesome, Paski. That's perfect. Just let your instincts do the rest."

"Okay," I say.

"Cool. Now, let's see. Just hold on. Don't move anything yet." He moves alongside me and adjusts my wrists, my hips, the way I'm sit-ting. Bit by bit, he massages my body into place on the bike. I look at his face as he does this, and our eyes meet. I feel a shock of electricity in my spine as he communicates with me without words. I can't be sure, but I think he's, uh, saying he wants me. Whoa.

"That's it," he says, shifting my thigh and letting his hand linger there longer than he has to. I love the feel of his hands on me and don't want it to stop. I don't just mean right now, either. I have a strange and scary feeling that I don't *ever* want Chris Cabrera to stop touching me. Okay, I know. Let's tone it down a bit. Let's just say I want Chris to touch me for, like, the rest of the afternoon. That would be very cool.

"Stay there," he says. He holds up his hands like a traffic cop. Like

I am going to *go* somewhere? Please. He says, "I'm going to get my bike. I'll be right back. Don't take off, okay? Just wait there."

"Okay," I say. Amazing how willing I am to follow his instructions. My father would be stunned that I'm capable of such obedience. Chris walks a few steps backwards, admiring me on the bike, then turns to trot back up the hill. Nice view, the back of Chris. The back of Chris's jeans, with Chris in them. Very nice.

I straddle the motorcycle and try not to notice the way all the little lollipops stare at me. I think they're laughing, but I can't see past the helmets to their faces. Maybe they aren't children but aliens. Or midgets? I giggle out loud.

Soon Chris comes jogging back toward the baby track with his own bike in tow. It looks a lot bigger and more muscular than the one I'm on. I want to ride his bike. That would rock, too. When he gets to where I am, he hops on the bike and says, "Follow me."

Chris leads me slowly around the simple track. I loosen my muscles and try to just let the motorcycle bob up and down and side to side beneath me. I like how it feels, a little like my bicycle, a similarity to the balance. It also feels something like Grandma's Harley, but a lot lighter under my hands and feet. I rev the engine a bit, just to see what happens, and the bike bucks forward like a rodeo horse. My pulse surges, too. Whoa! This bike could really go fast. Chris looks back at me over his shoulder as I release the gas and let the bike slow back down.

"Sorry!" I call out. "I had to try it."

"Be patient!" he shouts back. He's smiling, though. I rev the engine again and this time manage the buck a bit better.

"Paski!" he shouts. "There are little kids here. Be careful."

Yeah, I think, but those little kids are zooming past me, laughing at my old-lady pace. I want to fly. But I obey Chris again and lumber around the baby track. I am careful the first few times around, but then I feel that sense of rightness. That voice. And I listen. I just let go and ride. You know that feeling you get on a carousel, as it speeds up? That's how it is, the solid saddle beneath me, the world smearing past in almost electric bursts of color. I pass Chris and zip along. The hum of the engine pitches up, and my blood races faster to meet the sound. I ride well, and when I get back to Chris, he's stopped his bike and he is standing there in the tiny entrance area with his mouth open, shaking his head.

"I can't believe you, girl!" he says.

"What?" I ask, removing the helmet.

"I've never seen anything like it." The innocent happiness of his smile makes me think I don't have anything to fear with him. I can trust my instincts. This guy, even though he was dating the meanest girl in school, is actually really sweet. And tough. On him, it's a good combination.

"Like what?"

"You just did in ten minutes what it takes most people months to learn."

"I did?"

The laughter bubbles up from his chest, cool and calm. "You've just graduated to the intermediate track, girl. I *knew* you'd rock at this."

We switch to a harder track, and like before I feel at ease, completely at ease, after only a couple of loops. I listen to my heart, and I ride. I love the rush of adrenaline. I feel like I can't go fast enough. It's like all that training on the mountain bike, and all those secret rides on

Grandma's motorcycle (we could never tell Dad, he'd freak) have been building up to this. The wind cuts beneath my chin and I laugh with the rush of the ride. After fifteen minutes, I want more. I want harder. I want to dance on this motorcycle, lift off on it, twist. I want to *move*. I circle back around and stop to talk to Chris. He says he's speechless, which is impossible, given that he has just spoken to tell me so, but anyway. He's impressed. I am so excited I can hardly speak. The first man to walk on the moon could not have been more in awe than I am right now. I jump up and down and squeal like a silly . . . girl.

"I want to try the advanced track," I say.

"You sure?" Chris tilts his head doubtfully.

"Please!" I beg. He smiles at me, and then his face grows serious. He touches my face with his hand and moves close. Then his lips are on mine, and I feel the heat spread through my body. At first we kiss with closed lips, but then he nibbles mine and our mouths open. It's gentle, the way we explore each other's mouths with our tongues. He tastes good, clean and healthy. Warm. I could kiss him forever.

"You are amazing," he says when we come up for air.

"Does that mean you'll let me take your bike on the advanced track?" I blink playfully.

His beautiful mouth curls into a grin. "It means I'll let you take my bike — and me — anywhere you want."

29

The next morning I wake up early, full of energy, and stare at the gentle spray of sunlight through the slits between my shades. I can still smell Chris on my lips. I take a deep breath and exhale slowly. Life is good.

I come downstairs whistling to myself, dig around in the cabinets for a mixing bowl, wooden spoon, and pan. I open the shades on the small kitchen window, struggle with the lock for a moment, slide the glass open a crack, and then, with the Southern California birds — I have no idea what you call them — singing and a cool breeze whispering through, I make pancakes from a mix. I know. How very domestic of me.

I guess I'm feeling guilty for lying to my father. Dad is still asleep, and I could barely sleep, up all night thinking of Chris and motorcycles. I've been *up* up, like wide awake, since six. Last night, after an evening of riding motorcycles, as the world cooled down and the stars and crickets came out, Chris brought me back to the school, and we kissed for like an hour, first on this low brick wall outside the band room, and later on the cool, wet grass. We pressed our bodies against each other, and it was intense and rather urgent. I didn't want to leave. I wanted to spend the night there, with him, looking up at the hazy moon and the determined stars, listening to the gentle, salty wind in the trees. Talking. I feel like I can talk to Chris about everything. I told him all about my friends back home, and my grandma, even my weird mom. He didn't even seem freaked that I had a mom who abandoned me. Usually people feel too sorry for me when they don't have to. Chris simply listened to me talk about her and said the same thing I think, which was "With all her problems, it sounds like you're lucky she's *not* around."

Dad shuffles into the kitchen in his threadbare red plaid pajama bottoms and a gray T-shirt, groggy and happy, just as I discover a bag of blueberries in the freezer. Yes! Blueberries *so* rock in a pancake.

"Hey, kid," he says. He smells like secondhand cigarettes, like someone else must have been smoking at the party. The way my mom almost always used to smell when she'd come to visit me, back in the days when she used to actually, you know, come to visit me. Dad yawns, stretches, and asks, "How was the movie?"

Movie? Oh, right. The *movie*. Quick, Paski, think of something. "It was okay." I shrug for that surly-teenager emphasis. "You know, the usual shoot-'em-up aliens kind of thing." Dad nods, stretches, and yawns again, like he wants me to notice him stretching and yawning or something, then starts to wash out the coffeemaker from yesterday, to make more coffee, which, as it so happens, is his primary food group.

"Pancakes," he says, impressed.

"*Blueberry* pancakes," I correct him. "I'm going all out."

Dad pats me on the back, and once he's got the coffeemaker set up and dribbling its bitter brown brew into the pot, he shuffles out to our little square of front porch to fetch the newspaper. He comes back in shivering. "Cool out there. Nice. Smells all oceany. I love this place."

"It's okay," I say. Is "oceany" a *word*?

Dad smiles to himself, thinking he's won. Thinking that I love this place, too. I feel just guilty enough to let him believe it. He sits at the dining room table and opens the paper with all this drama, like he wants me to notice him opening the paper. I hate when he does this, because he usually sighs and then starts to read me all the awful news about how terrible the government is. Times like this, I wish Dad had a wife. Someone who would say something like "So what's new in the world today?" and actually, like, care. Not that I don't care about what's happening in the world. I just don't care to talk to my dad about it.

"So," he says, scowling at the paper. "What you got planned today, *Chinita?*"

"I have to cover that motocross race," I tell him. "Remember? For the school paper?"

Dad hits his forehead with his hand and gets the guilt face going again. There is now a smudge of black newsprint on his forehead. He has no idea, and I'm not in the mood to tell him. He'd just panic. "Oh, right. I'm sorry, Punkin. I didn't forget. I just — I need my coffee." He gets up to check on the brew progress. Bobs his head to try and speed up Mister Coffee. As usual, I feel like the parent. Like he hasn't figured out he can't control the speed of the coffee machine with his

245

head bobbing. It's the same with elevators. He likes to press the button over and over, like it will make the elevator come faster. Things like that drive me nuts.

I flip a pancake. I love the bubbles on the uncooked side right before they're ready to turn over. There's something satisfying about the hiss of the damp side on the surface of the pan.

Dad clears his throat. "Is this race something your dad could come with you to?" I feel my shoulders tense up as I scream silently inside my head. *No!* I mean, it is, technically. But I'm planning to meet Chris there. We're going to watch the race together and he's going to give me tips about the sport.

"I don't know," I say evenly.

"I hear you," says my dad. "At ease." He pushes my shoulders down and laughs to himself again. He nods up and down at me like he's some kind of detective who just found a super-important clue. He's real proud of himself for figuring out that he is *allowed* to go to the race but that I don't *want* him to. "Say no more," he adds with a pat on my back. "I'll stay here and do the laundry. You take the Squeegeemobile. She's all gassed up."

Ick. There's something about the phrase "she's all gassed up" that makes me ill. My dad has a real gift for making everyday things sound terrible. I flip the cooked pancake onto a white CorningWare plate. We've had these plates since I was a tiny kid. I can't remember ever using any other kind. Steam rises from the pancakes like a genie from a bottle. There's no better morning smell in the world than pancakes cooking, except maybe bacon frying. I wish we had bacon. That would have made the breakfast perfect. But as usual we don't. I think of the

Squeegeemobile and realize I am finally going to have to drive that thing. Oh, well. It's not the end of the world. It's not like I have an image to protect anyway. I'm *that* kid. And *that* kid always has a funky car. Or something messed up. I remember a *that* kid from middle school whose mom would pick her up in a weird station wagon full of trash and newspapers and dogs. They'd shove the girl in the very back, so you could see her big, pale face frowning through the smudgy glass as the car drove away. We used to laugh at her, but we were only eleven and didn't know that, you know, she might have feelings or something like that.

I give Dad some pancakes and sit down with a plate of my own. I'm feeling very hungry this morning. I feel like I want to consume everything in sight. Chris Cabrera has had that effect on me.

He makes me want to experience everything.

I stare at the table and hope that my dad can't hear me thinking about Chris. My thoughts are so clear and colorful that I can't imagine anyone not being able to tell just by looking at me what's in my head.

"What time is this race?" asks Dad, sticking a huge bite in his mouth. I mean huge. It's like half the pancake all at once, getting folded up into his mouth like a cardboard box into a trash can. He eats faster than anyone I've ever met. If it weren't considered rude, I think he'd hold the plate right up to his mouth and just shovel it all in like a dump truck.

"It's at two," I say.

"Cool," Dad muffles through his pancake. I look away from the mess in his mouth. "Then we have time to go throw a Frisbee around in the park or something."

Frisbee? Is he out of his mind? What am I, *seven*? Like I'd be caught dead throwing a Frisbee in the park with my *dad*? Please. "Actually," I say quickly, "I need to go get some clothes."

Dad swallows with a loud gulp. I don't think he chewed. He's like that snake from fourth grade, the one my teacher used to feed a live mouse every month. Ugh. I want to love him, but right now he sort of grosses me out. Dad needs a course in manners or something. "Oh, okay," he says. "Where should we go shopping?"

I look at him and feel like I could hold a pencil between my brows with all the angry skin folded up there.

"Ah," he nods. "I see. You'd rather go alone." He sops up some syrup with a look like a wounded child. I feel sorry for him again. He is so good at that, making me feel bad for him when I shouldn't. I mean, isn't it normal for a sixteen-year-old girl to want to go clothes shopping *alone*? Or with friends? Without her snake-mannered dad?

"I have plans with a friend," I say.

"Cool, okay, chill, no problemo." Dad forces another half a pancake into his mouth. Dad swallows and starts to whistle, which tells me he's up to something, I don't know what.

I think of calling Tina to go to the mall and the race with me, but I have a feeling she'll spend the whole time pointing out how shallow everything is. Tina's cool, but I can't exactly see her shopping. She'd rather read and talk politics. I remember that when I was in the hospital, Haley told me I could call her anytime if I wanted to hang out or talk.

"What friend?" asks Dad. He's trying to sound casual, but he's being a detective again. He trusts me, but I don't think he trusts any of the other kids in Orange County.

"Haley," I say.

Dad nods solemnly. "As long as it's not that boy, what's-his-name."

"Andrew?" I ask.

"No! I mean, of course you'd never hang out with that psycho. The other one. Cabrera."

"Chris?"

Dad frowns and chews with his mouth open. "I don't like him."

I avoid eye contact. "Haley's cool." I finish my pancakes and get up to put my plate in the dishwasher.

"Look at this." Dad points with his fork at a news story. "Damn shame. I can't believe they get away with it, bloodsucking bastards."

"Yeah," I say. I don't look at the story because I don't want to have sad news ruin my mood. I'm in love. I rode a motocross bike. I'm going shopping. "It's awful." I say this last bit just to placate my dad, because if I don't he'll take it as me disagreeing with his politics, and if I do that, I'm in for an hour-long lecture I don't have time for.

"The problem is that *la raza* don't vote," says Dad. "We need to get involved in registering them."

"Sure," I say. I have an overwhelming urge to run. "But right now I have to make a phone call. I'll be in my room."

Dad looks up, wounded again. Don't do this to me, I think. I don't need this right now. He looks like he's going to launch into one of his "la raza" sermons, but he notices my frown and stops himself. "Thanks for the pancakes," he says. "Blueberries were a good touch. I'm a lucky dad to have a teenager who still thinks enough of me to make me breakfast now and then."

Still avoiding eye contact, I say, "You're welcome. I'll be upstairs."

*　　　*　　　*

I shut the door to my room, fish Haley's phone number out of the purse I had on me at the hospital, and call. I flop onto the unmade bed and stare at the ceiling. At first Haley sounds surprised to hear from me. But she quickly warms up.

"I've actually been meaning to call you, Paski. How are you doing?"

"Fine," I say.

"That's great. So what's up?"

"This is probably weird, but I was calling because I need to get some new clothes, and I thought you might know where to go," I say.

"You are *so* calling the right person." Her voice gets louder and more animated. "I *love* shopping." Haley pauses, lowers her voice, and mumbles, "It's very unhealthy how much I love it, actually."

"Yeah," I say, like I might agree with her, except that I don't actually know what it's like to have enough money to shop so much as to have a problem with it.

"Uh, can you drive?" I ask her. "I mean, I don't know where I'm going around here." It's a lie. I mean, a half-lie. I don't exactly know where I'm going, but the bigger problem is my troubled relationship with my father's car. I don't want to be seen in it.

"I'm actually stranded right now. My car's in the shop — fender bender on the Five, you know how it is — and Mom and Dad have things to do today. You have a car?"

"Kind of," I wince.

"Great. You come get me, and I'll show you where the best shopping is in the OC."

She gives me her address and directions to her house. I write it down on the cardboard back of one of my spiral notebooks for school, all the while thinking that I would rather eat cockroaches than show up at Haley's in my dad's car/experiment. Oh well.

I hang up and congratulate myself for making the lie I told my dad this morning actually end up being true. I *am* going shopping with a friend. At least I think she's a friend. I don't know her well enough to know for sure, and this is Orange County, where many things — and people — seem to not be as they first appear.

I shower, put on a little makeup, and fix my hair. No use even trying to compete with the likes of Haley. Sigh. And then, in my usual boring jeans and T-shirt, I open my jewelry box to look at the amulet, but I hate to admit it looks kind of dorky. I'm worried I won't make a very good impression on Haley if I wear it. So, even though I know Grandma would not approve, I shut the lid and leave it there.

Then I zip past my dad, whose head is still buried in the newspaper, to the garage to make peace with the Squeegeemobile, *cholo* mural and all.

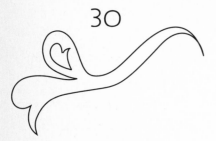

30

Haley lives in one of those large two-story peach-colored stucco tract homes with a red tile roof. I'm still getting used to the whole pitched-roof thing. Where I grew up, the roofs are all flat, and the houses are all adobe. Haley's house is on a little hill and backs to a green space with a walking path. It's really clean-looking and reminds me a lot of Trent's, where the party from hell was. I guess a lot of people have houses like this around here. I would also guess that there are many parties from hell, but what do I know.

I park on the curb in front of the house because there's a Mercedes sedan in the driveway. It's one of the newer ones, shiny and white, sculpted and round like a torpedo with an overbite. Of course Haley's family has a car like that. I'm the only weirdo in the OC with a car like *this.* But you know what? I think it's starting to grow on me. Surprisingly, I liked the attention I got driving here, even the confused glances and the muffled laughs. It's like driving a cartoon around. Mostly, I think people are impressed, if not with the car itself then with the guts it takes to drive it. And if I carry myself like I'm some kind of special artist or something, it's even better.

I ring the doorbell, and Haley opens the door wearing the single cutest outfit I have ever seen. Figures. I should be happy for her, but part of me just feels like an underdressed dork, even in my new Old Navy gear. She wears dark blue jeans, low, with a big belt that looks like it was woven together with a bunch of thin strands of soft beige leather. Her top looks like a big, colorful scarf that has been tied criss-cross over her chest, with a bow in the back. She has on a floppy hat and flip-flops with jewels on the straps. She's got those Orange County toenails, too, done in a French-manicure style. She smiles when she sees me, and her teeth are really white and pretty. She has warm, friendly eyes. I can see that she could be a star, the way Tina told me. She is *so* Alicia Keys, down to the beautiful eyes. As I look at her, I realize she's probably the most attractive of the three popular girls, but because she's also the nicest, she doesn't get the attention the mean one does. The mean one being Jessica.

"Hi, Paski!" Haley smiles with that certain energy celebrities have, where you instantly like her and want to know more about her. It's like you know she's drop-dead beautiful, but you don't hate her for it because there's a niceness to her that's even stronger than her beauty.

Haley gives me a hug and invites me in. She smells like dark perfume, the musk kind my mom used to wear. "I want you to meet my parents," she says. "They saw the piece on your dad in the paper."

"There was a piece on my dad in the paper?"

"Yeah, the *L.A. Times,* the arts section. All about his comic books and how he moved to the OC to make this movie. He's the top-paid Latino animator of all time, it said."

"He *is*?"

I enter the house and look around. I try not to stare. It's so fresh and well designed and white. Practically everything is white, except the trees and plants everywhere. The carpet is white. The walls, which extend up two stories, are white. The scalloped curtains draped over the large windows are creamy white, custom. Layers and shades of white, all of which seem very soothing and beautiful. But how do they keep something like this clean? None of my friends back in Taos had homes anything like this.

"Should I take my shoes off or something?" I ask.

"Nah. It's all coated with stuff that makes it hard to stain. I know. Freaky, right? People worry about getting it dirty, but it's like a regular house. Relax."

Haley leads me across the living room into the kitchen. More white, in the floors, walls, and counters, gleaming marble and tile. The appliances are silver. Somebody has a white fetish. It's actually starting to freak me out a little.

Standing at the stove is a man I assume is Haley's dad, a tall black man with short hair. He's a little overweight and wears a jogging suit. A white jogging suit. He seems to be frying onions and something else in a pan, or at least that's what I smell. Onions frying. Seated at the counter is a petite, beautiful white woman with long light brown hair and hazel eyes. She's wearing a red robe, and the brightness of the color is shocking. I see where Haley got her eyes, because they're just like her mom's. A boy of about six sits next to her, and she's nursing a baby. Haley introduces me to everyone.

"Welcome, welcome," says Haley's dad. He has a booming voice that sounds like bells clanging.

"Thanks," I say.

"We're so happy to meet you," says Haley's mom. "It's good Haley finally made a friend whose parents are in the arts like we are."

"Oh," I say stupidly. I don't know what else to say, and it doesn't feel quite right to say nothing at all. Seems like a strange thing for a mom to be happy about.

"Not that I have anything against her other friends," says Haley's mom. She has the same low-pitched voice as her daughter.

"Mom," interjects Haley, as if this conversation has been had before and annoys her.

"Well, it's just that sometimes we get a little tired of the whole young-Republicans-convention vibe at your school, baby doll," says her dad.

"We're going now," announces Haley, like she's sick of this discussion.

"Sweetie, can you pick up some Dior perfume for me?" asks her mother.

"Sure," says Haley. "See you later."

Haley and I leave the house, and when she sees the Squeegeemobile, she gasps.

"I'm sorry," I squeak. "It's my dad. I don't know. He thinks it's funny or something."

"Hold on," she says, excited. "I have to go get my dad. He'll freak."

She runs back in the house and returns with her father, who's still holding a big white spatula. He stares at the car like it's something amazing, and together they walk around it several times, grinning.

"Your *dad* did this?" asks Mr. Williams. They look impressed rather than frightened, so that's good.

"Yeah," I reply. I don't know why, but I'm feeling a little proud of Dad. Talk about a change of heart. "Him and his *cholo* posse."

"You and your dad have to come over for dinner," says Mr. Williams. "I have to meet this dude."

"Really?" I ask.

"He's nuts." Mr. Williams grins and nods like being nuts is a great thing.

"Okay, Dad," says Haley, rolling her eyes.

"Catch you later, baby doll."

"I hate that name," she says. "Please."

"Sorry. Haley. Catch you later, Haley."

We leave Mr. Williams and get into the car.

Haley bounces into the passenger seat. "This is such a cool ride!"

"You think?"

"Totally." She takes a CD out of her purse and asks if she can play it for me. "It's my demo," she explains.

I start the engine, and it rumbles ten thunderstorms. Haley gives me a thumb's-up. "You really think it's cool?" I ask as I pull away from the curb and ease the tank down the street. The CD starts to play, and it sounds like a real album, hip-hop and alternative.

"You don't?" She truly seems amazed that I wouldn't be, like, in love with this weird car.

"It's okay," I say. "This is you?" I point to the stereo.

"Yeah," Haley shrugs, changing the subject. "So we're totally going to Fashion Island. Take a right here."

As we drive toward the mall along the wide, smooth avenues of Orange County, past luxury apartment complexes bigger than the entire city of Taos, past mini-malls with Starbucks after Starbucks, Haley tells me that her family used to be poor when they first got to the area, when she was a baby. They lived in apartments, and she says she knows that money isn't a measure of a person's worth. I'm sure she's trying to be nice, but the whole thing makes me feel very weird, like she thinks I'm less than everyone else, or she doesn't want me to feel like I am because everyone else does, something like that.

"A lot of people around here don't understand that," she says. "Don't let them get to you. I mean, the paper said you guys are going to be making a lot of money soon, but some of the people at school are mean about kids from apartments."

"Yeah, I know."

"Well, I'm totally not. Just so you know."

"Okay," I say. I want to talk about something else. Anything else. Not me. Not my apartment. Not this freakin' car that everyone is pointing and staring at. I can tell by the way Haley sits up really straight and throws her head back that she likes the attention. "You sound great." I point to the stereo again. Haley smiles and nods, but without vanity, and thanks me.

"Okay, turn here," she says. We come over a hill, and once again, there it is. The Pacific Ocean, dark blue, a shimmering flatness that goes on forever. I gape at the sight of it. Do people here get used to it? Every time I see the sea I get chills.

"It's so beautiful here," I say.

Haley looks at the water and nods. "Totally," she says. "It's like paradise. Here, pull into that lot. We'll go in right there. Unless you want to valet?"

Is "valet" a *verb*? Like "summer"? "You can park valet like that at the mall?" I ask. But when Haley gets that confused look on her face, I regret having blurted it out. "I mean, I didn't see a valet stand, or whatever you call it."

"It's down there." She points absently toward the entrance to the parking lot.

"I don't mind walking," I say.

Haley smiles and squeezes my arm. "Great minds think alike, Paski. I totally want to walk all the time, and Jessica and Brianna are, like, no, we have to valet. Blah blah blah. They are *so* into valet. But walking is so much more healthy, right?"

I search the lot for an empty space, and it doesn't escape my notice that almost every single car here is new, luxurious, and expensive. "Right," I say. Fashion Island, so you know, is not an island at all. But it's right on the coast in Newport Beach, and so pretty I can't believe it. It's like a museum instead of a mall. Or like one of those seaside resorts you see in the travel section of the newspaper, in Italy or somewhere.

"Wow," I say.

"Pretty cool, huh?" agrees Haley. Out here in Orange County, people are surrounded by amazing beauty in everything they do, even going to the mall. It's not like back home, where the mall was all the way in Santa Fe and wasn't even very nice, tucked back in some dusty lot somewhere.

As we cruise along at a whopping three miles an hour in the parking lot with Haley's own funky demo CD blasting, everyone turns to stare at the car. Now I am horrified. I want to say, yes, yes, rich people of the world, I *know*. We're a freak show. Thank you very much. I'm mortified that everyone is looking, but Haley really seems to like it. And just so you know? Her CD rocks. She sounds like Jill Scott, throaty and soulful. She is so way better than any of the singers out there right now. And I'm psyched she's here with me, wanting to be friends.

I finally spot an empty space and do my best to ease the tank into the narrow opening. I have to back up and reenter the spot a few times to get it just right, and even then we seem too close to the other cars.

"Can you get out?" I ask.

"I think so."

Haley and I get out, and I stash my dad's car stereo in the trunk, as he instructed me to. "Can't you put the top up?" asks Haley.

"No. It doesn't go up."

"What do you do when it rains?"

"Swim?"

Haley looks at the sky. No clouds. "I think we're okay for now," she says. "Let's go shopping!" She loops her arm through mine and continues to sing the bluesy song about the "blessing of true love" that was on her demo.

"You have a great voice," I tell her.

"Thanks." She smiles in a way that tells me she knows it.

"Is that what you want to do, like, professionally?"

Haley nods. "It's all I think I *can* do. I really don't think I'm very good at anything else."

"I don't think you'll *need* to be good at anything else."

Fashion Island is mostly an outdoor mall, with large concrete fountains and slick, super-expensive little shops everywhere. There's music everywhere, too, like mall music, even though it's not a mall like an indoor mall. I wonder where they've hidden the speakers. As

I'm looking at the potted flowers and palm trees, I see a group of cute guys with skateboards watching us.

"Hottie alert," whispers Haley. She pulls me closer, lifts her head and ignores them as we walk past. They say hello, and when I answer with a hello back, Haley scolds me.

"You can't do that," she says.

"Why not?"

"You have to make them work for your attention. Don't you know that?"

We keep walking around, and I swear all the boys stare at us. Mostly they stare at Haley. With that snooty attitude of hers, I think they find her irresistible. But just so you know, a few of them look at me, too, even though I don't feel all that hot in my normal everyday clothes.

Haley takes me to a store called Bebe, where I love literally every single thing I see. She helps me pick some jeans — they are *so* sexy, with dark blue embroidery on the back pockets — and a few tank tops in different colors. I get a shrug sweater to go over the tanks, and some earrings. They sell shoes here, and I get some beige leather-and-mesh-striped sneakers. I also get a real bohemian-looking outfit, something that's more like what Haley might wear than me, but it's cool. It's a tiered skirt, blue with gray stripes that looks like webs, and a big leather belt and a maroon tank with a weird floral shawl. Haley kind of pushes me to buy the outfit, but I don't mind. It's very artsy, but I think I like it.

"Chris Cabrera is going to *die* when he sees you in this stuff," Haley declares.

I look at her, confused that she knows about him. I pretend not to know what she's talking about, mostly out of self-protection from Jessica.

"Please," Haley says as I hand my money to the cashier. "It's *so* obvious. You guys were made for each other. You see how he looks at you. Don't tell me you *don't*."

I don't know why, but I trust Haley. I tell her about yesterday with Chris, how he totally kissed me and how it was incredible. She listens with a smile and leads me to the food court. We get spring water in bottles and sit at a table. There's an atrium over our heads, and the whole place feels very luxurious. I could get used to this life. I really could. This is *so* not like Taos right now, I can't even tell you.

"I'm happy for you," she says. "Chris is one of the nicest guys at school."

"But what about Jessica?" I ask, somewhat confused. "She's your friend."

Haley nods. "Sort of. I've known Jessica since fifth grade. I like her. But she's starting to hurt people too much, and I don't like that. I'm torn."

"About what?"

"I don't know. Several things. She says she wants to get even with you." Haley pauses. "I feel like I had to tell you that."

"Even for what?"

Haley shrugs. "For being pretty and smart and good at riding a bike."

"That's it?"

"She's threatened by you. I want to have a talk with her. I think we can all be friends, but it's like my mom says — we have to be honest and talk it out."

I try to imagine Jessica Nguyen doing those things. Nope. Does not compute.

Then, I'm not sure why, I tell Haley about my vision of Jessica getting hurt at the race, and about how I've had these visions all my life and they usually come true. "I tried to tell her at the party," I say feeling anxious. "But she didn't listen, and then she threw me in the pool. I feel like I have to stop her before the race today. What if . . . could you . . . Could you go with me to the race, maybe, and warn her? Like, tell her to be careful?"

"Wow," breathes Haley. I can tell she doesn't really believe me. I hate when people look like that. I shouldn't have said anything at all.

"You think I'm weird," I state.

"No, no," she insists. "I was just trying to figure out if I could go to the race. I'm totally bummed that Jessica didn't call to invite me. It's today?"

"This afternoon. Like, in three hours."

"Can I come with you?" she asks.

"Yes! *Please.* I just invited you."

"Oh." She sips her water and looks guilty. "I was probably distracted by the whole 'I have visions' thing." Great. Now I know she totally doesn't believe me.

"Maybe you could warn her," I suggest again, this time firmer. "I know, it sounds crazy. But it really happens. This stuff really happens to me."

"Interesting."

"You don't even have to tell her it's because I had a vision about it."

"Vision," Haley repeats with a raised eyebrow.

262

"You could call her right now." I feel an intense urgency to tell Jessica about the accident, knowing the race is only three hours away. I feel it the way you feel like you need to pee after drinking a huge bottle of water. That kind of urgent.

"Call Jessica?" Haley asks.

"Please?"

She shrugs and digs a phone out of her purse. "And tell her . . . what?" She looks perplexed and dials.

"Tell her to be careful today." I hope "be careful" is enough. Maybe it is. Maybe Jessica will be extra careful and I'll still seem normal to Haley. Right now I just want to make things normal. Haley listens to the phone. She mouths "voice mail" to me and then says, "Hey, Jess, it's Haley. I wanted to wish you good luck in the race today and let you know I'm coming. I also had, like, kind of . . ." Haley looks panicked and uncomfortable.

"Tell her you have a bad feeling about it," I whisper in a rush.

"And I have, like, this sort of bad feeling about the race and I just wanted to say, well, just be careful. That's all. Love you, girl. See you later."

Haley hangs up quickly, and I get a flash vision of Jessica crashing again. I'm afraid a "be careful" won't cut it. I try to make the images go away, but they don't. They play themselves inside my head just like a slow-motion movie clip.

"Was that okay?" Haley asks anxiously.

"Yeah." I want to believe it is. "Thank you so much."

Haley makes a mocking face and puts her hands up next to her head, the way little kids do when they're trying to imitate scary monsters.

"Visions," she says, then suddenly laughs, and my heart sinks. I hate that she doesn't believe me, but more than that I hope nothing happens in three hours to prove me right.

"I know, it sounds so stupid. Just, just do me a favor, and if you can, tell her again to be really careful at the race when you see her today because you have a feeling. Something like that."

"I'll try," she agrees reluctantly. "But I can tell you right now, Jessica isn't the superstitious type. And, well, you know, she doesn't like you very much. I totally could not tell her it came from you."

"Don't tell her it's from me," I say. "Just tell her."

Then Haley's face brightens and she sits up straight. Like there's nothing wrong in the world. Like she has no worries, which she probably doesn't besides this seemingly minor matter. It hits me now that no matter what I do in life, no matter how hard I try, I will never completely fit in. I will never be like Haley. I will never be the kind of girl who says what she says to me next, and that is this: "Hey, you ready for more shopping? It's my biggest passion in life, after music."

31

I drive with Haley to the raceway and try not to think about the visions, or the crash, or anything. Maybe Jessica will heed Haley's warning and nothing really will happen. Maybe it was a totally false vision to begin with. Maybe I can truly be just like every other girl out there. Normal. Happy. Without worries. Not responsible if bad things happen by sheer chance to other people, particularly those who hate me. I don't want this gift, and I am going to start right here, right now, to renounce it. I passed along the message to be careful and now I am giving up. I quit. I am not going to be psychic anymore.

I park the Squeegeemobile and show my press pass to the people at the front gate. I tell them I'm covering the race for my school paper, and they tell us we better hurry, because the race is about to start. We rush toward the stands, and I see Chris already here with Tyler. He waves and shows that he's saved a spot for me. Haley and I join them. I remind Haley to warn Jessica again, but she's busy flirting with Tyler. Tyler says hello to me and apologizes for Andrew Van Dyke's bad behavior at the party. "I'm sorry about all that," he says.

Down on the track, I can see Jessica in her lavender racing outfit and the white helmet with the yellow rose. The announcer says this is the qualifying round for the upcoming regionals and that Jessica's team has an excellent chance to take it to nationals. Jessica waves to the crowd, and they cheer. I have a sick feeling. A sick feeling that is going to do its best not to let me think the warning was enough. I have an overpowering urge to get up and rush back down the bleachers toward the track myself. As I take off, Haley calls out, "Where are you going?" I don't have time to answer the normal girl. We non-normal girls don't have time to explain as we look even more bizarre in our erratic behavior. I don't want to feel like I have to get to Jessica, but I have to get to her. Simple, really. I have to tell her. Why didn't I just insist before?

I'm too late. Before I reach the track, the starting gun sounds and the race begins. The buzz of motors is deafening. I stand frozen, unable to move. I have seen it all before. The way the girl in the brown charges out front. The way Jessica hops the first hill like nothing, her body rising up off the bike like she's weightless. The grace of her as she rounds the first turn, then the second.

I want to cover my eyes as she nears the third, because I know what's about to come. I can't stop looking, though. And then, exactly as it has happened every time I've visualized it, Jessica hops the mogul, twists apart from her bike as the tires slip on the landing, and then, wham, she's on the ground and the motorcycle lands on top of her. It happens almost too fast to comprehend. She lies motionless on the packed wet dirt as the other riders hop the same hill and swerve to avoid her body. Sirens sound. Flags are waved. Medics rush the track. The race continues as they drag her limp body to the sidelines.

I stand and start to cry. I could have stopped this. I didn't try hard enough. I feel a hand on my shoulder, and I'm vaguely aware that it's Chris. Haley, too. I can hear them saying something.

"Holy crap. Oh my God, Paski, you were right." But I'm not really listening. I'm too numb. I am furious at the universe for giving me this curse of sight. I don't *want* to know these things. All I want to know is how to shop and go to the beach. I want to know what it feels like to have a big house in Orange County. I don't want this responsibility or guilt. It isn't fair. *This would have happened no matter what,* I tell myself. But why am I the only person in the world who knew about it?

I turn and run from the stands to the parking lot, and collapse across the ugly mural on the hood of the car. I can't take this. Jessica might have tried to kill me, but I, without trying, am so afraid I failed to stop her from dying.

"Paski, are you okay?" Chris reaches out to me from the side of the car.

"No," I say. "I think I just killed Jessica Nguyen."

32

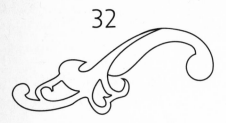

"She's not dead, thank *God,*" Haley's in the driver's seat of the Squee-geemobile, with her cell phone against her ear. We're still in the lot at the racetrack. She's on the phone with Jessica's mother. Chris is with me in the backseat, holding me. I can't stop shaking. He tries to calm me down by clicking his tongue the way mothers do with babies, and even though I am in a panic, I recognize how utterly sweet this is of him.

"Is Jessica okay?" Chris barks at Haley.

She holds up her hand to keep us quiet for another second while she listens. "Okay," she nods into the phone. "Thank you. Yes, I know. I will. Okay. Bye."

Haley turns to face us with tears in her eyes. All around us, fans from the stands are streaming to their cars in a concerned hush, mutter-ing about what's happened. Clearly no one can believe it. Haley tells Chris about the vision thing, and he listens without saying anything.

"It's all my fault," I moan.

Chris kisses the top of my head and squeezes my hand. "It's not your fault. She wouldn't have believed you even if she had listened."

"Jessica's in the hospital," Haley says, her lower lip trembling. "Her mom said she broke her legs and one arm, and she has a concussion because her helmet wasn't tight enough."

"Oh my God," I choke.

"Poor Jess." Tears roll down Haley's cheeks. "I should have told her about your vision, Paski. I'm so sorry."

"No," I stop her "It's my fault. I didn't do all I could to warn her because I was scared of her. Because she was mean to me. That's what happened. It's all my fault."

"It's no one's fault," says Chris. He hugs me. "This is awful."

Haley's lower lip continues to tremble. "I can't believe it actually happened. How did you know this would happen, Paski? It's freaky. No, I'm serious. It's totally freaking me out."

"I just *know* things." I say mechanically. "It freaks *me* out, too. Believe me. I don't want to know them, but I do anyway. I hate it."

Haley shrugs and looks tormented. "*I* didn't know. The whole thing with the visions and the psychic stuff. I'm not really into that."

"It's okay. I totally understand. Trust me, if some girl I didn't know came up to me and was all 'I have visions, you have to help me,' I would have reacted just like you did."

"I mean, I wasn't before. But now I totally believe you. It's impossible, but it happened. Beyond freaky."

Chris squeezes my hand again. "Both of you stop blaming yourselves, and let's just do what we can to support Jessica."

"I know," says Haley. She is now full-on crying. "I want to go to the hospital, you guys. I want to see Jessica. Is that okay with you?"

"I don't have a problem with it, though I doubt she wants to see me." Chris looks at me. "Or you. Now that, you know, there's a me-and-you kind of thing."

"I know," I say. Yet I am overcome with a sense that I should be at the hospital. A psychic "ability" kind of sense. I don't tell Haley this, however, even though she said she believes me. "We should go, though," I say, like I don't care all that much. Grandma has long told me that to exist in the world with my ability, I am going to have to learn how to act. Mostly how to act disinterested. To protect myself. So I shrug and add, "Because Haley should be with her friend, and right now we're Haley's ride." On the way to the hospital, with Haley driving because I'm still too shaken up to handle the Squeegeemobile, I try to sit up, but a piece of my hair is tangled in a gold chain around Chris's neck. "Ow?" I say.

He helps me untangle it. "Sorry," he says. "I almost never wear this thing. I just felt like it today."

All of a sudden, it hits me. The amulet. I haven't bothered to wear it. I've been too afraid. Or too ashamed. If I had worn it today, maybe none of this would have ever happened. I think of what Grandma told me when she gave me the necklace and how the universe rewards you . . . or not. I tell Haley we have to stop at my apartment before going to the hospital. I have to get it and I need to wear it, no matter how dorky Haley or anyone else thinks I look. It will guide me. It will tell me what to do. I know, I know, my dad will freak when he sees Chris. But I don't care. I am falling in *love* with this guy, and my dad is just going to have to deal with it. Besides, there are more important issues at hand. Spirit issues. Gift issues. Mine.

33

The tires of the Squeegeemobile rip across the asphalt of the parking lot at my apartment complex. Haley hurls the beast of a car into a parking spot, and only then do I notice that my dad is out on the upstairs balcony with Melanie and the twins, sitting in lawn chairs, all crowded together, playing cards. He looks right at us, and I don't think he's happy at all about the way his beloved car is being driven. I'm not too happy, either. I don't know why the sight of my dad hanging out with other teenagers makes me feel weird, but it does. They look like a family. It makes me a little jealous.

Dad scowls down at us in that angry-owl way he has, intending to make me feel guilty and horrible. I half expect him to screech like something out of a Harry Potter movie. He's that scary. But I don't care. Right now, I'm worried about Jessica.

"Wait here," I tell my friends.

I run up the cement steps, each making a hollow pinging noise when my foot lands on it, and my dad meets me as I open the door.

His arms are folded, like Mr. Clean, across the National Council of La Raza decal on the faded red T-shirt he's got on. He wears jeans, too, the big, baggy FUBU ones that make him look like the world's oldest, tackiest teenager. I hesitate before looking at his feet and regret it as soon as I do it. The gigantic basketball shoes he has taken to calling "kicks." Unlaced.

"What is that *girl* doing driving my car?" he demands. Yup. Still scowling. In my mind, I wonder how he thinks he can be both the world's oldest teenager and a stern dad. Does. Not. Compute.

"That *girl* is my *friend,* and her name is *Haley,*" I say. I push past him and charge up the stairs to my room. As I dig through my jewelry box for the amulet, my dad appears in the doorway, arms still folded. Chin still jutted out. Lips still tightly frowning. He closes the door behind him. He's boiling mad. He never would have shut the door if he wasn't.

"Pasquala," he says. He sighs. I hate that sigh. It provokes instant guilt in me. Even when I didn't do anything wrong. And he's doing the extra-deep-voice thing, to get more respect or something.

I find the amulet and put it around my neck. Instantly, it grows warm and emits a low sort of drone that I can feel but not hear in my bones. Like the universe is vibrating inside of me. I get a rush to my head the way you do when you sniff something with menthol in it, like Vicks VapoRub.

"Pasquala," he repeats. "Look at me."

I do, but with a rushed, annoyed look on my face, thinking that it would be a whole lot easier to look at him if he weren't trying to dress like Bow Wow. "I have to *go.*" The urge I had earlier to go to the hospital is much, much stronger with the amulet on. It's like an order from God, only I don't like saying it that way because then I start to sound like a lunatic. I just know that I *have* to get there. Now.

Dad holds up his hand. "Whoa. Wait a second there, *Chinita*. You are *not* the one who decides whether or not you have to go. I decide whether or not you *can*."

"But Dad!"

Dad sizes me up, like he realizes that I'm almost as tall as he is. Like he realizes exactly how much harder it's getting to boss me around now that I'm almost a grown-up myself. Like he realizes that if we were to, like, I don't know, get into a fistfight or something — which, for the record, would never happen — that I might actually be able to take him down. He says, "Fine. You can go. But first I have some questions that you need to answer before you're going anywhere. Understand?" He stands against my door with his arms crossed. He means business.

"Fine."

Dad uncrosses his arms and sits on the bed. He doesn't look so scary anymore. Now he just looks sort of saggy. I feel sorry for him but realize at the same time that this is what he wants. For me to pity him, like it's the last defense of a manipulative parent. He pats the bed next to him. "Sit," he says. What, I'm a dog now? Like a dog, I obey. Good girl. "First, why is that girl — why is *Haley* driving my car? You still haven't answered me."

In a voice that moves too quickly and shakes and quivers, I tell him about the accident at the racetrack and about how I had seen it but hadn't able to tell Jessica. I tell him how I asked Haley to tell her, but she didn't believe me. I tell him I was too upset to drive. I tell him I need to get to the hospital to make peace with Jessica.

"That explains *that*," Dad says, making a new face to let me know he thinks we've made *progress* in our communication, but that it hasn't been as easy as it could have been because of me. "But it doesn't explain what that boy from the party is doing in the car with you. I told you, I don't want you hanging around him."

"You don't understand. Chris is a really good guy."

Dad looks doubtful. Then he sighs through his nose but nods. "You're right. I have to trust you. You remind me so much of my mom, it's scary, actually." He's losing the will to fight with me. He always does. "So, where are you going again?"

"I have to go to the hospital to see Jessica."

"Why? I know she had an accident, Paski, but that girl is bad news."

"I don't know." My hand reaches instinctively for the amulet. "I think she's not that bad. I think she's okay. I have this urge to make up with her, to apologize or something. Just let me do it, Dad. Please."

"You can't go around telling people about your visions, Pasquala. You know that. Most people won't believe you. Haley didn't believe you. And now I think you really better keep it to yourself with Jessica. She doesn't need to know about any of this stuff. What's happened has happened."

"That is the exact opposite of what Grandma would tell me to do," I say.

"Your grandma isn't always right about things," says Dad, solemnly.

"Actually, she kind of is," I say.

Dad seems to think about this. "Oh, *Chinita*," he says with another sigh. "I just don't want you around the wrong kind of kids anymore. I think this Jessica is the wrong kind of kid. Chris, too. And maybe even Haley. You have to be careful who you hang out with."

"God, Dad, if it was up to you, I wouldn't have any friends at all except you! It's sick!"

"Just be careful. That's all I'm trying to say."

"I know, but it's too late now, okay? I have to go there and talk to them."

"Okay, Paski. But promise me two things."

"What?"

"That you'll drive the Squeegeemobile instead of Haley, because you're on my insurance plan and she isn't."

"Okay."

"And that you'll be careful."

"Yes. Can I go now?"

Dad shakes his head like he doesn't know what to think of all this, but he stands up, opens the door, and, to my horror, follows me down the stairs all the way to the garage. Chris sees him and looks like he wants to run.

"You," my dad says, pointing at him. "I just want to tell you right here that if anything, and I mean anything, bad happens to my daughter because of you, you'll have me to deal with."

Chris stares fearfully at him and for a moment says nothing. But then he does something that surprises me and makes my heart soar. With his voice quaking, he says, "Mr. Archuleta, nothing bad is going to happen to Paski. Sir, with all due respect, you should know one thing about me. I like your daughter a lot, and unlike the boys you appear to have me confused with, I fully understand that liking a girl means respect. My mother taught me that."

34

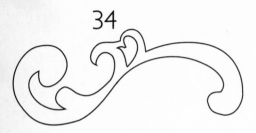

We arrive at the hospital and see television crews stationed outside from all the local networks and the national sports cable channels. "Oh my God, do you think this is for Jessica?" asks Haley.

"Pretty sure it is," says Chris.

"She's famous," I say as I turn in to a parking lot and find a space. I turn off the engine and open my door. Haley opens her door, too. In the backseat, Chris doesn't budge.

"Aren't you coming?" asks Haley.

"I actually think I'd rather wait here." He looks at me and says, "You should maybe wait here, too."

On my neck, the amulet begins to heat up. I focus on what it might be trying to tell me.

"I'm sorry," I tell Chris. "I have to go in."

He shrugs and moves to get out of the car. "In that case, I'll come, too."

We walk past the TV vans and into the hospital lobby. We follow signs to the emergency room area. Chris whistles a little. I think he's got mixed feelings about the whole Jessica situation. I can tell that he's really worried about her, but he doesn't want me to think he still likes her like that.

We get to the dreary waiting area, and Haley approaches the bored-looking fat woman behind the reception desk.

"We're here to see Jessica Nguyen. We're her friends. She's one of my best friends, actually."

The woman shakes her head. "No visitors."

"But she's my friend," Haley protests.

"Sorry."

"This is so unfair," wails Haley.

"Jessica Nguyen is under tight security," says the fat lady. "Not my decision."

Haley pulls me over to a bank of lime-green plastic chairs and pushes me down into one of the seats. She sits, too, and pulls out her cell phone. In the corner a television blasts the FOX News channel, and a bunch of unhappy-looking people sit around watching it. Chris joins us, picking up a copy of a golfing magazine from one of the cheap-looking end tables.

"This isn't fair," Haley repeats. "She needs us."

"Maybe she's not well enough to see anyone," suggests Chris. We consider this and share looks of guilt, fear, and sadness.

"Well, let's find out." Haley punches a number into her cell phone with a furious, determined look.

"Mrs. Nguyen?" She plugs her free ear with a finger to better hear. "It's me, Haley. We're here at the hospital, but they won't let us come up to see her." She pauses and listens. Then she says, "We're in the lobby of the emergency room. Oh. Okay. Thanks. That's fine. See you then." Haley disconnects and looks at us. "She's on her way down."

"Jessica?" asks Chris, glancing up from the magazine.

"No, genius. Her mother."

"Oh, right."

Poor Chris. He's very uncomfortable with all of this. But when I hear that Jessica's mother is coming to see us, I get a warm, fuzzy, and powerful sensation in the center of my chest. This is right. It is part of the plan. I know it.

A couple of minutes later, a very attractive Asian woman with a body that looks like a Barbie doll's comes out of the elevator. She's wearing the same kinds of clothes we saw earlier today at the Bebe store — sexy jeans, wedge heels, and a tank top. Her shoulder-length hair has been bleached almost entirely blond on the top and is black underneath. It's styled to flip up and out. Her makeup looks like it was perfect before she started crying, which she still is, in muffled sobs she tries hard to control. She has raccoon-smudge eyes and a red nose. She looks miserable. Tortured. I can see where Jessica gets her looks, though. They are both amazingly beautiful.

Jessica's mom rushes to Haley and gives her a hug. She hugs Chris, too. I feel so weird all of a sudden. Then, without really knowing who I am outside of Haley's introduction as one of Jessica's friends, Mrs. Nguyen hugs me, too.

"I'm sorry," she says. "I asked the doctors, and they said Jessica shouldn't have visitors right now. She's still heavily medicated and in and out of sleeping."

"Is she okay?" asks Haley.

"She's doing better."

"Good," I say.

"My poor Jessica!" Mrs. Nguyen's face twists in pain. "They say she's better, but she doesn't look better to me. She looks so weak. So broken. I can't believe this is happening to her."

"She'll be okay," Haley nods.

Mrs. Nguyen releases herself from the hug with me and looks around. "Jessie really needs your love now," she says. "She's going to need a lot of love and support from all of us."

Haley shoots me an awkward look and answers for all of us. "I know, Mrs. Nguyen. We're here to love her and support her. That's what friends are for."

Chris looks at me with a question in his eyes. It's sad how little parents really know about what's going on in their own kid's life sometimes. Mrs. Nguyen has no idea that her daughter tried to drown me. She has no idea that Chris and Jessica are hardly speaking anymore. And she has no idea that Jessica hates me or that I might have prevented this whole accident from taking place. She also has no idea that no matter how hard I try right now, I can't really feel much love for her daughter.

Mrs. Nguyen smiles at all of us. "You are such great kids. Jessie's so lucky to have friends like you. Thank you."

I feel the ethereal calm of the coyotes come over me, and the amulet grows cold and then warm on my neck, over and over, three times. I am being guided by spirits. I can feel them here, protecting me.

"I'm sure the doctors know what they're doing," Haley reassures her.

Mrs. Nguyen's face knots up with grief. "It's terrible." She starts to cry again. "She's broken in so many places. They have tubes in and out of her everywhere. She's unconscious." She sniffles into a tissue and breathes deeply. "That's why you can't come up to see her. I'm sorry. I know she would get a lot of energy from you being there, knowing you care about her." She starts to sob again. "They say she'll be okay, but I can't stand to see my child like this. It's horrible. I just sat there when it happened, I saw it happen, I saw my baby crash, and there wasn't anything I could do to help her."

Haley holds Mrs. Nguyen again as the woman's tiny body pulses with sobs. Not knowing what else to do, I put my hand on the woman's shoulder. Chris looks like he'd rather be anywhere but here, but he puts his hand on her other shoulder, then slides it over to mine and gives it a squeeze.

Jessica's mother gasps for air, the crying making it impossible for her to breathe properly. Haley looks at me over the top of Mrs. Nguyen's head like she doesn't know how to handle this. She looks like she might feel as guilty as I do. I feel sick with the images of Jessica broken and unconscious. And I realize that no matter how mean Jessica has been to me, she didn't deserve this. Even more than that, Jessica's mother doesn't deserve this grief. I should have done so much more to warn Jessica. To stop this from happening.

"I'm sorry," I say softly. "Please let Jessica know I'm here for her."

"Oh, I will," Mrs. Nguyen manages to respond. "Thank you."

She looks kindly at me with her wet red eyes, and I realize that inside every grown-up is a little child. I understand that Mrs. Nguyen is a really good person and that she really, really loves her daughter. Sometimes you have to be kind to people you don't like because of the good people who care about them. We are all connected in this web of life, of love, of hurt. This is why I was supposed to protect Jessica, even if she wasn't nice to me. Because protecting her would have saved this other person from *pain*.

I reach out and hug Mrs. Nguyen again, with feeling. I want her to know I truly care. "She's going to be okay," I say. I am certain that Jessica will recover as I say it. As certain as I was about her having the crash in the first place.

"I don't know. All I know is my daughter is up there fighting for her life." Mrs. Nguyen points to the ceiling, grief contorting her face. "And I can't do anything to help her."

On my neck, the amulet grows warm again. I am filled with a peace and understanding that I've not felt before, and I realize I must never again be irresponsible with my gift. Jessica is going to be okay. I try to transmit this understanding to Mrs. Nguyen in the form of another hug. "Don't worry," I say. "Be strong for her. That's what she needs now. And you have to believe me when I tell you she is going to be fine."

Mrs. Nguyen releases herself from my embrace, looks at me, and smiles softly. "You're right." She dabs her eyes and swallows her tears. "I shouldn't be like this. I should be strong for my baby."

I feel Chris grab my hand. "You're amazing," he says softly in my ear.

As Jessica's mother says goodbye and prepares to go back upstairs with a little more control over her anguish, I finally grasp what my grandmother has been trying to get me to understand. That I was sent here to look into Jessica's mother's eyes and understand that no matter what a person does in this world, someone loves them. All of us, haters and friends alike, are somebody's children.

"Do you really think she'll be all right?" asks Haley as we walk into the hallway, heading back to the Squeegeemobile.

"I'm convinced," I say.

"Convinced, like, as seen-in-a-Paski-*vision* convinced?" she asks.

Chris puts his arm around me and kisses my cheek.

I loop my arm through Haley's as the three of us walk. "Something like that."

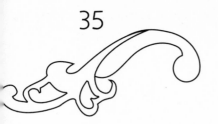

35

It's Sunday, and I'm waiting in line with a bunch of other OC people to have breakfast at a Coco's restaurant with my dad, Melanie, and the twins. Coco's is kind of like a slightly nicer IHOP, with muffins. I'm trying to ignore the twins' dear old dead grandma, who has decided to come along to gossip with me. In Japanese. Which I don't understand. Like I'm going to stand here in the waiting area of the restaurant and tell everyone about it. Uh, no. I learned my lesson from telling Haley about the visions. I don't need to give a roomful of strangers any reason to think I'm certifiably insane. I wish I knew how to say "go away" in Japanese. I'd do it right now. No, seriously, I would. I'm hoping she'll eventually get comfy where she is and stop using me as some sort of celestial Morse-code machine. I tune her out for the moment and try to pay attention to Kerani.

"Boom!" he cries. "Splat! It was insane, the way she flipped and splatted all over the track, man." He pancakes his hands together. An old couple in matching jogging suits moves away from him. I don't blame them. He sounds like a total psycho.

This is gross. Kerani can't stop talking about what happened to Jessica in a horrified but fascinated way. The crash has been replayed over and over on all the sports channels, in "slo mo," as Kerani says. It's probably going to end up on one of those "worst road disaster" shows that sick people watch. Jessica looks like a rag doll in the footage, flopping hopelessly off the bike onto the dirt. Every time he says this, it makes me think again about how I could have saved her.

"Archuleta, party of five?" calls the hostess.

"Oh, right here! Here!" cries my dad in a voice entirely too loud. We all follow the waitress to a large round table and take our seats.

"Dude," says Kerani as he opens his big, laminated menu with the photographs of the food just in case, I don't know, people here don't know how to read. "It was so messed up, the way she went splat."

"That's enough," orders Melanie. "I don't want to hear you speak that way about this again."

"Why not?" asks Kerani.

"We don't speak this way of another's tragedy," she says.

"I like that rule," says my dad. He nuzzles Melanie's neck.

"Eew?" I say under my breath. Dad ignores me.

Melanie turns to my father and says, "Do you know what you feel like having, sweetie?"

Kerani looks at me for support. I shrug.

"No one understands," he grumbles.

Actually, I do. I understand. But right now I just want to order a mess of French toast with a side of sausage and chow down.

Keoni, meanwhile, can't stop playing with his Game Boy. Dad can't stop mooning over Melanie. For the record, my dad has dressed like a psycho, in these weird cowboy-looking jeans with British flags on the back pockets and a flowered shirt with pearly buttons on the pockets. People stare at us as we wait in the vestibule. Melanie is really like a female version of my dad, now that I think about it. She's wearing ripped jeans and a funky old sweatshirt with hot-green canvas sneakers. Even so, I have a good feeling about her, and she asks me all the questions my dad always forgets to ask, like if I need money or how the school paper is going. Like right now.

"Made up your mind on breakfast?"

I smile at her. "French toast."

Melanie grins back and points at me. "A girl with good taste. Me? I'm thinking eggs."

At this, the grandmother starts in, loud. *Ohayou. Tadaima. Shinpai shinaide, Pasquala. Nakanaide. Hontou ni ureshii. Kangeki shiteru.*

As I try to ignore the voice from the Other Side, my father and Melanie kiss a couple of times, nothing sloppy, but still. It's sort of disgusting. While I'm normally not, like, super-excited to see a scary tattooed woman with overly bleached hair and a smoker's voice, it just so happens that this is what our waitress looks like, and I am relieved when she appears with her pad and pencil.

"What can I get you folks?"

Dad and Melanie stop kissing.

"Thank you, ma'am," I say to the waitress.

"For what?"

"Never mind."

"You need a few minutes?" she asks.

"No!" I cry. "Don't go. I'm ready. French toast, please. And a side of sausage."

Everyone else orders, too, and once the waitress has taken the menus away, my dad clears his throat in that way he has. "Kids," he says. "Melanie and I wanted to let you know we've fallen in love with each other."

Kerani, Keoni, and I all sort of stare at each other. I want to laugh, but I'm in control of my impulses. The twins, however? They *do* laugh. I blame their emotional desensitization on video games. But I like them for laughing anyway. I think they're pretty smart, and brave, and weird.

"Duh," says Kerani.

"I know you're probably wondering why we had the need to tell you this," adds Melanie, pretending her kids haven't just laughed at her.

"Not really," says Kerani.

"I was actually only wondering where my coffee refill is," says Keoni.

"What are you doing drinking coffee?" my dad asks him.

"Drinking coffee," Keoni answers. He and his brother chortle again.

Dad sighs. Melanie comforts him by placing her head on his shoulder. Ick. Dad says, "We wanted to tell you about us being in love so it wouldn't be awkward for all of us."

"Failed mission," says Kerani.

"Abort, abort," Keoni chimes in. They laugh again. They have their own strange twin sense of humor that I like.

Dad continues, "And we wanted to make sure it was okay with all of you before we take this any further."

"Eew?" I say. "Too much information, stop! Please stop!"

Melanie's mother butts in with: *Monku iwanaide.* She doesn't sound happy with me.

"*Emotionally,*" says my dad. "Take this any further *emotionally.*"

"Thank God," says Kerani.

"No physical details between parental units need be divulged at the breakfast table," says Keoni.

"Or ever," adds Kerani.

"We just wanted your blessing," says Melanie.

"Because," my dad finishes the thought for her, "we are planning to spend a lot of time together in the future."

Kerani holds up his hand like the pope and makes the sign of the cross over the table. Our parents ignore him.

Dad says, "Melanie and I both agree that even though we would like to be in a relationship with each other, our kids come first."

They look at us like they're waiting for an answer. I don't know exactly what they're hoping we'll say. Thankfully, my phone rings at this moment. I take it out of my silver handbag and look at the number on the caller ID. I don't recognize it.

"Don't answer that right now," says Dad. "We're having a serious discussion."

I press the phone on. "Hello?" Dad and Melanie share an exasperated look.

I hear a brief silence on the other end of the line. Then a familiar feline voice. "Paski? It's Jessica Nguyen." Again, she draws out the A at the end of her name, Jessicaaaaaaahhhhh . . .

Oh my God. Just when you thought a moment could not possibly get any more awkward and strange. "How *are* you?"

"I've been better."

"I'm so sorry," I say. I wonder if she has breathing trouble from the body cast. Poor Jessica.

"I was calling to say —" She pauses. Sighs as if she is agonized. "I'm *calling* to say I'm *sorry*."

"You *are?*" I fight the urge to swallow my tongue in shock. Across the table, Dad is staring me down. I know what he wants. He wants me to hang up and stop being so selfish.

Jessica coughs and laughs lightly to herself before speaking again. "My mom told me how you came by the hospital to see me. She said you were way nice to her, and you said nice things about me. So . . . I'm sorry for the whole thing with the pool."

"You are?"

Jessica pauses before answering, like this is very hard for her. "Yeah. My mom really likes you. So I'm considering calling everyone *important* from school to tell them you're *cool*," she announces cheerily.

"You *are?*" Is that a good thing? Or is it something that's only going to make me be more like the *that* kid I don't want to be?

"Haley swears you tried to save my life or something," she continues like she's bored stiff. "I don't know. But anyway, you're okay. You're not that bad. Everyone listens to me. So cheer up, you're going to be popular now."

"Uh, okay," I say.

My dad makes a hand motion like he wants me to hang up the phone. I hold up my hand to ask him to wait. This is important. Or at least weird enough to seem important.

"I also had a favor I wanted you to do for me," Jessicaaaaaaaaaah says. "A favor that's good for you and good for me. Mutually beneficial, as they say in the corporate world. But I want to ask you in person."

"At the hospital?"

"No," she says. "They sent me home. You have to come here. Today."

"I don't know if I can." I could, of course. But I'm still terrified of Jessica.

"If you care about your future, you will," she says. "Get a pen and write down my address. Now."

I do as she says, then hang up and look at my dad and the others. I am very curious about what Jessica has to say, but afraid. I want to tell Dad, but I know he'd refuse to let me see her.

"Everything okay, *Chinita?*" my dad asks. Melanie's mother, wherever she is, interrupts, and I end up repeating her words instead of my own.

"*Watashi wa kamaimasen,*" I say. Just to, like, shut her up. Because she wants me to say it. Melanie and the boys stare at me.

"My mother?" asks Melanie, a look of wonder on her face.

"I think so," I say, glad to not have to tell my dad about Jessica. I have to go see her. I feel it. But I know it's not smart to do so. But she *did* apologize, right? That's a big step. And I'd love to be popular. Who wouldn't? "She wants me to tell you *mattaku sono toori.*" I shrug and wait for the translation, adding, "She sounds pretty happy. Oh, she just said *Ii kangae desu ne.*"

"She is happy, yes." Melanie beams. She hugs my father and says, "She thinks we're doing the right thing. She likes you."

Our meals come, and even though I wouldn't want to admit it, I'm excited to sit at a table at Coco's on a Sunday morning with my dad and his girlfriend's family. I always wanted him to have a girlfriend, or a wife, and siblings could be nice. Oh, and a mom. I always wanted one of those, too. I mean, one of those who actually did things like call me "kiddo" and tell me nice things.

Dad cuts a pancake in two and folds the half in his mouth. Melanie watches and shakes her head. "Rudy," she says. "Smaller bites, sweetheart. There are people watching."

Dad smiles through the food and speaks with his mouth full. "Sorry."

"Swallow before talking, please," she adds.

Dad munches for a while, swallows, looks at me. "So you're okay with this?"

I smile at Melanie, the woman who might be the person to force my father to grow up. Things are looking up. I mean, Jessica apologized and Melanie told dad to eat like a human. "Yeah," I say. "It's cool with me."

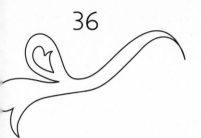

36

Two hours later, I pull the Squeegeemobile into the massive gated compound that is Jessica's home. It looks like a palace surrounded by flowing lawns and forests. No, I'm not just saying that. I actually call Emily and Janet from the curly iron bars of the front gate and describe it to them. I try not to sound like a squealy girl, but, you know. It's a phenomenal house. They're like, no *way,* not a *palace,* and I'm, like, *way,* and then I'm thinking, you know what? We *all* need to improve our vocabularies. *Way.*

"I don't think you should go in there," warns Emily.

"Why?" I ask. "Jessica said she's sorry, and now she wants to be friends. And her mom is way cool." Way again. Oops.

Emily sniffs. "Oh, Paski. You're way too nice sometimes."

"What does that mean?" I ask.

"It means you better be careful in there. That's what it means. Call me if anything happens. Or 911. Put it on speed dial."

"You guys, it's going to be fine," I say.

So, listen. This house? It's not just a palace but a white stucco palace perched on a cliff overlooking the Pacific Ocean. People *live* here? It looks like nuns should train here. Somewhere cloistered and distant from the real world. Do nuns train? I have never considered this, and it makes me laugh to think of them hurtling over high bars like athletes, in full skirt and whatever. Clearly I must be nervous.

The gate slowly opens with a chime of bells and allows me to drive into the compound. I ease the Squeegeemobile forward, hoping it doesn't contaminate the grounds. On either side of me, lawns stretch. Stone sculptures stand here and there, like this might be the grounds of a museum. The driveway is long, flanked by super-tall palm trees. I see a gardener driving around the grass on one of those mower things, and another couple of gardeners trimming hedges and flowers. Jessica has a fleet of gardeners?

Back home in Taos, we sort of had a backyard, but it was mostly dirt and weeds. Oh, and things like old mops and buckets and broken lawn mowers that my dad would leave back there to rust. I don't know why he did that, exactly, except that maybe he thought they were going to biodegrade down to dust and no one would know. Now and then my dad would get this idea that we needed grass, and he'd buy sod and lay it down. It would look nice for about a week, and then we'd both forget to water it.

After driving probably a quarter mile on a winding driveway, I'm at the front of the house. I park in the half-circle driveway and walk up the large stone steps, past the snarling white marble lions (money does *not* breed taste, apparently) to the enormous wooden door. I want to call my buds and tell them about the lions, but it wouldn't be polite to do that right now. I make a mental note to call them later with all the gory details. I ring the bell, even though the people inside already knew I was coming because I had to ring *another* bell down at the gate to have it opened. I'm not sure I ever want to have so much money that I need all these gates to keep people away. Security cameras above the door watch me. When I move, the cameras move. Creepy. A house with *eyes*?

Jessica's mother answers the door in a frilly white miniskirt and a matching white tank top. The skirt starts so low on her hips and ends so high on her thighs that I think it must be no more than, like, three inches long.

"Paski!" she says brightly, like we're old friends. She seems much happier than the last time I saw her. Relieved. I'm glad she's feeling better. It must have been scary thinking your child might die. "How are you?"

"Fine," I say. "How are you?"

"Good, things are good. Come in." She steps aside and makes a sweeping motion to the interior of the house. "I'm glad you're here. Jessica's expecting you."

I enter the house and look around. Mrs. Nguyen looks me up and down with a smile. "You are so cute!" she says. "You look adorable."

"Thank you."

"All you girls are so cute." She sighs and fidgets with the edge of her skirt like she wishes she wasn't as old as she is. I think the skirt is the same one Jessica wore at the party the night she threw me into the pool. Jessica's mother's belly is tanned and flat, and she has a diamond in her belly button. She looks better than most of the girls at school and must be at least twice our age. She's one of those moms all the guys at school dream about.

She closes the door after I step into the house. "Jessie and Bree are waiting for you," she says.

"Bree?" I ask.

"Brianna. Jessie and Bree are so excited to see you. They said you're new at school but that they've gone out of their way to welcome you."

They said that? I don't argue the point. I only smile and try not to look too stunned.

"That's the thing about Jessica," says Mrs. Nguyen. "She is so loving to her friends. And so generous. She's a great kid."

"Yeah, she is," I echo uncertainly.

"Follow me," says Mrs. Nguyen. She takes me to the living room and leaves me on the pale yellow sofa. "I'll just go make sure the girls are ready for company. I'll be right back, sweetie."

"Okay," I say.

After she leaves, I look around and allow my jaw to drop in amazement. The house is spectacularly large, and everything in it is pale, curly, tassled, golden, and expensive-looking. It reminds me of a TV set for that Spanish-language psychic, Walter Mercado, that my dad loves to make fun of. Windows take up most of the western wall, with incredible views of the ocean. The wall behind me is a fish tank. No, I mean the *whole wall.* It's like a city aquarium. I wonder if the fish get depressed, looking out the window at the sea.

I look around the room, amazed. I'm overwhelmed by the money these people have, but also by the fact that everything — and I mean everything — is covered in cheesy portraits of Jessica. There are photos. Paintings. Even a couple of sculptures. Of *course* she's the vainest girl on the planet. These people have taught her that she is the center of the universe. Jessica wakes up, walks in here, and sees that she is the most important human being to ever live. With all her money and fame, there's nothing to make her doubt her supremacy, not for a single second.

There's a fireplace and a sparkly gigantic chandelier, and the walls have shiny gold wallpaper on them. The furniture goes way beyond the norm, with little antique tables and chairs that don't exactly match but look like they were designed precisely not to. Everything goes together in unexpected ways. The gold, yellow, and cream curtains are really nice and look like they were hand-sewn. I can't be sure, but it looks like the fabric of the cords holding the curtains back is printed with tiny golden images of . . . Jessica's face.

Mrs. Nguyen comes back with a cheery smile and asks me to follow her. "They are so thrilled you're here!" We go down a long hall, past a half-dozen rooms that I wish I could wander through. I have never seen a house like this, not even on that MTV show *Cribs.* It's like a museum of all things frilly and scary. No. That's not quite right. It's like a shrine. To Jessica.

At the end of a second hall, we go down a curving staircase. At the bottom is another living room, this one done in a more modern style. Like the one upstairs, it has huge windows that look out to the sea. The creamy carpet is accented with a colorful modern rug done in squares and squiggles. Around the rug are two chairs and a sofa. They're very slick and leather. In the middle sits a coffee table that looks like a steel sculpture of something extremely bowlegged. On the wall behind one of the chairs hang three original paintings, each of Jessica's face at a different angle. They must each be six feet tall, and the colors are so bright you want to wear shades. My. *God.*

"This is Jessie's wing of the house," explains Mrs. Nguyen. Um, no kidding.

She leads me past a kitchen — a kitchen, Jessica has her own kitchen, with white granite counters and stainless steel appliances! — down another hall, past what looks like a miniature movie theater with red velvet stadium seating, to a large bedroom. Jessica waits inside, lying on a massive white bed. Brianna lies on her belly next to her, reading a *CosmoGIRL!* and snapping her gum. The bed sits on a simple dark gray platform in the center of the room. Strange. I have never seen a bed in the *center* of a room. The style of Jessica's wing is quite different from the rest of the house, which felt regal and stately in an English, Prince Charles, Vegas-stripper kind of way. This feels very lofty. It reminds me of a modern art gallery my dad used to take me to in Santa Fe.

"Hi," says Jessica in a soft, girlish voice. She points a remote at the wall, and a painting of Jessica's smiling face rolls down over the flat television she was watching. No more sign that there was a television there at all. Wow. She's smiling at me like we're really good friends.

"Hi," I say. Brianna smiles at me, too, but there's something weird about her face, like she doesn't understand exactly where she is or what she's doing. She reminds me of a newborn chicken, finding a whole new world before her every time she blinks.

Mrs. Nguyen kisses her daughter's head and speaks to her in the kind of voice parents use on babies. "My poor wittle girl," she says. "Does she need anything?"

Jessie looks at me and rolls her eyes. I guess we have something else in common besides motorcycles and Chris. We both find our parents annoying. If nothing else, we might be able to bond over that.

"I'm fine, Mom. Go away. I want to be alone with my best buds."

Brianna smiles at me again, like we actually are best friends. Like, if Jessica says it, then it must be true.

Best *buds*? Go *away*? She told her mom to go away? She called me her best friend? That's odd. All of it's odd. I know that sometimes I talk to my dad like this, but hearing Jessica do it makes me realize it doesn't sound very good. I should be nicer to my dad. I really should.

"How are you feeling?" I ask Jessica after her mother has tiptoed out of the room.

"Like dog crap," she says with a wry smile. Brianna nods as if she knows this to be true. Jessica waves me toward her. I go to sit on the bed. I'm on one side, Brianna on the other. Jessica grabs my hand with her free hand (the other is in a cast) and gives it a squeeze. "You are so pretty, Paski," she says. She turns to Brianna. "Isn't she pretty?"

"So pretty," murmurs Brianna distractedly, still flipping through the magazine. "But you're really pretty, too, Jess."

Jessica smiles and shrugs, like a queen. "I need to tan. But I can't, with the casts."

"You look fine," I say softly. Actually, she looks all bruised and battered, but you can still tell she's beautiful.

"I feel like I'm going to die," she says.

"She feels like she's going to die," says Brianna. Yeah, I think, thanks for the recap. Brianna, the master of repetition.

"I'm so sorry," I say to Jessica, apologizing for her pain but also for the tackiness of her house and the lack of intelligence of her friend. "I wish this never happened to you."

"Yeah, well, it did," Jessica retorts. "Freak accident."

"Yeah," I say.

"Anyway," she continues. "I'm the one who should say I'm sorry. About all that stuff with the notes and the pool and Chris." For some reason, her expression doesn't match the words. Her face is telling me she still hates me. Or maybe I'm just paranoid and still a little afraid of her.

"Jessie's really sorry," says Brianna. What is she, a *parrot*?

As Jessica stares down at the comforter, her expression seems a little bored, a little hurt, and a little devious all at once.

"Don't worry about it," I say, trying to sound relaxed. "I understand. The important thing is that we're cool with each other now."

She does not look up. "No," she says with a strange smile. "I *should*. I should say I'm sorry. I was a *total* bitch to you."

"You were," says Brianna to Jessica. "Like, *so* not nice. So cold." They grin at each other like being a cold bitch is a positive trait.

"I was petty and jealous," Jessica continues with a playful roll of her eyes. "Stupid, really."

"What?" My voice comes out higher and more pitiful than I realized it could. I look around this amazing room. "Why would someone like you be jealous of someone like me? You have everything."

Brianna says, "Yeah, Jess, you have everything. Except a tan. You even have a wheelchair now."

"Shut up," Jessica tells Brianna. Then she shakes her head and frowns. "No." She raises a single eyebrow, like Catherine Zeta Jones. How does she do that? I want to be able to make that face. "Paski, here's the deal. You got the only thing I really wanted."

"I did?"

She finally looks at me. "Five-ten, broad shoulders, six-pack, great smile, funny." She shrugs. "You know who I'm talking about?"

Brianna frowns and asks, "Chris Cabrera?" Like she isn't really sure.

"Shut up, Bree. I wasn't talking to you, okay?" snaps Jessica.

"Chris?" I echo. Jessica smiles and blinks really fast, like she's embarrassed to like him as much as she does. "He's just a *guy*," I say. "You have every guy in the world drooling over you!"

"*Every* guy, it's true," says Brianna.

Jessica tosses her hair back, then winces in pain. I guess it hurts to be snotty now that her bones are broken. "I know. I know that *now*. But I really care about Chris. He's my soul mate. I mean, he was."

I don't know what to say, so I keep quiet for a moment. "I'm sorry," I begin. "I didn't know it was that serious. If I'd known, Jessica, I wouldn't have. I mean, I don't know. I'm just sorry. About everything." I realize I've lied to her. But how else could I handle this?

"It's okay, Paski. Don't worry about me." An evil little smile creeps across her face. "I'm over him, pretty much. And I'll get back at him someday."

I look at her face to try to see whether she's joking. I don't think she is. "Get back at him?"

"Not him directly, but his memory. Not a big deal. Don't worry about it, okay? We're still cool. You can have him."

"Isn't that up to him?" I ask, sort of baffled.

"No, not really. If I really wanted Chris, I could have him back."

"She totally *could,* if she, like, *wanted* to," says Brianna.

I feel sick. I was hoping to actually maybe make peace with Jessica today, but I don't know how to respond. Did she bring me here to try and kill me again because of Chris?

Jessica smiles at me. "I mean what I said about being best buds. And about Chris. He's yours. I'm moving on."

"Okay," I say slowly.

"But the thing is, when you're friends with me, you have to play by my rules."

"You *so* do," says Brianna. "But it's worth it."

"I don't understand?" I ask Jessica.

"I'm saying that all will be forgiven and we can be friends, but you have to do what I tell you to do on matters of importance. So, rule number one is, when it comes to decisions for the group, I get final say."

"Oh," I say.

Brianna looks stunned for a moment, then starts to laugh like a hyena. Her eyes look fearful, though. Jessica holds up her hand in a way that tells Brianna to stop laughing, then she says to me, "That's rule one. Rule two is that you stop trying to race motocross."

"I'm not trying to race!" I cry. What does she mean?

"I heard from some people I know that you were practicing at the track with Chris."

"That was just for fun."

"Well, just don't do it anymore. Stay out of my territory, and everything will be fine. I mean, it's not that I don't want you to have fun. It's just, well, it's like this. My dad's in business, right?"

"Right," I say, wondering why she would need me to validate this statement.

"And in business, you don't want to have people in the same corporation competing with each other for the same work. You need to diversify your interests so that you increase your chances for success. We are like a company. Understand?"

I nod. I understand that Jessica Nguyen is crazy.

Jessica smiles and grabs my hand again. "In other words, you should find something else to be good at, the way Brianna is good at volleyball and I'm good at motocross and Haley's good at music. If two of us are doing the same thing, then it won't work as a company."

"I see."

"So you can't do volleyball or music, either," says Jessica. She looks at me like she's thinking. "We need to think of something really cool for you to be good at. Because that's the other thing about being part of our group. We're all outstanding. We are the hottest, smartest, coolest girls in Orange County."

"I know," I say, knowing I have to agree. I can't believe I'm going along with her, but as crazy as she is it seems unwise *not* to.

"Good girl. So let's think of something for you to be good at."

"I'm on the newspaper staff," I suggest. I wish I had the guts to get up and leave, but I don't. I'm ashamed to realize the thought of being a popular member of this group is intriguing.

Jessica wrinkles her nose. "Ugh, no. Way goofy. You need something cool to be good at, like fashion or skateboarding. Something. I'll figure it out. Don't worry. Meanwhile, there's something else important to talk about now."

"Uh, okay," I say.

"Brianna told me she saw you having breakfast with those geek twins this morning." She's scowling at me.

"Keoni and Kerani?"

"*So* gross," says Brianna, with a finger down her throat for emphasis.

Jessica stares at me like I've done something wrong. "The *geek* twins, Paski."

"And?" I ask.

She looks frustrated. "Hello? You want to be our friend, right? So, you can't be seen in public with people like that. What is *wrong* with you?"

"People like *what*?" I ask.

"Losers," says Brianna.

"*Total* losers," says Jessica. "We *really* want to be friends with you. Okay? You're cool. And I just know you're going to rock at fashion design."

"Fashion design?" I say. I have zero interest in fashion design.

"Yes. That's your cool thing that you do. But there are a few corporate laws you need to know about."

"Laws?"

"Laws," says Brianna. "Jess even wrote them down."

"If you want to go in public with someone," Jessica says, "you have to make sure it's someone who's going to improve our image. Not just yours. *All* of ours."

Brianna nods like a fool. I wish Janet were here, because she would slap these girls silly. Me? I can't speak. I don't know what to say. I mean, it's tempting to be part of their group. They're very powerful. But I don't want to have to change to fit in with them. I don't want to piss them off, either. I've been down that path already, and it almost got me killed. It's like being around a lion. You want to keep it well fed so it doesn't see you as food.

"The other thing is, I'm not so sure *four* is a good number for our company." Jessica looks at Brianna. They share a wicked smile. "So we're maybe going to replace Haley with you."

"*Replace* her?" I ask. "How can you just replace a friend?"

"She's getting a little weird for us," says Jessica. "All those beads and the whole turban thing. She's, like, *way* ethnic."

I can't find a word to say. What's wrong with ethnic?

"Totally," says Brianna. "Ethnic is *so* last year." I doubt she even knows what the word "ethnic" means.

Jessica nods and makes a face like it doesn't matter. "I haven't decided about it yet, so don't say anything to her. For now let Haley think she's still one of us. Anyway, so, you can go now, if you understand the rules and the laws."

"I understand them." I'm about to say I don't agree with them, but something stops me. The amulet in my pocket. It's getting warmer than ever. I'm in danger. I feel that very clearly. I have the urge to remain quiet and let this scene play itself out.

"But before you go, I have an errand for you," says Jessica. An errand? Like I'm her servant?

She snaps her fingers, and Brianna jumps up and gets a piece of paper from the top of the desk in one corner. She skips back to the bed and jumps on it.

"Ouch," says Jessica. "I told you no bouncing, Bree. God."

"Sorry. I forgot." Brianna clutches her breasts, as if they are the only thing in her universe capable of bouncing.

Jessica rolls her eyes at me. "Brianna forgets a lot of things. But she looks hot on the beach. She improves our image that way."

Brianna holds out the paper for me. I reach across Jessica and take it. It's a letter to her from the co-captain of Jessica's racing team, list-ing the name of the girl who is going to replace her in the regional fi-nals, which are going to be held next week.

"Obviously, I can't race. Lori McCafferty is my official substitute rider." Jessica rolls her eyes in disgust. "She's this total bitch from North County San Diego, Vista. Inland."

"We hate her," says Brianna.

"But she doesn't know that," says Jessica.

"What does this have to do with me?" I ask.

"So," Jessica grins viciously. "When I wiped out, it got me thinking. Accidents happen. You know? They don't always kill someone. But they *happen*."

I feel my blood slow into a thick, cold glue. "What are you saying?" The amulet warms more, and I get a fuzzy vision of a girl with long blond hair wiping out on a motorcycle. The fuzzy visions usually never happen, they're just powerful wishes on the parts of powerful people.

Jessica re-applies lip gloss in a mirror held by Brianna. "I'm not saying anything except that accidents happen and that our company might want to think about how an accident might happen to Lori. Nothing too bad. Just a little accident so she knows she isn't going to take my place forever."

Now I really don't know what to say. I want to dial 9-1-1. But that's not an option.

Jessica looks at me like she doesn't comprehend my reaction. "Don't worry. We do things like this all the time. No one has to know it was us."

"I don't understand?" I ask. "You want her to fall?"

Jessica looks at Brianna. "You know, Bree, I think we might want to keep these plans to ourselves until Paski gets acclimated to our corporation."

"Sure," says Brianna. "What's 'acclimated'?"

Jessica turns back to me. "Forget I said anything about Lori."

"Forget it?"

"Yeah. It was probably a bad idea." She yawns, but seems extremely alert to my reactions. "I'm pretty tired now, so if you guys don't mind, I'm going to take a nap."

"You want us to go now?" asks Brianna.

"Yes, please," says Jessica. "I'll catch up with you later."

"We have to go now," Brianna tells me. We get up to leave and walk toward the door of the room.

Before we exit, Jessica calls, "Paski?" I turn to see her smiling. "You know what? You're so much like me, I think it's better for us to be friends than enemies."

"Oh?" I ask, wanting so badly for it to be ten minutes from now.

"Totally," she replies. "Because if we're enemies, you never know what we might end up doing to each other. You *are* with us, aren't you?"

I close my eyes and wait for a feeling to come from the amulet. It's telling me to go along with this for now. To tell her I'm with them. "Yes, of course."

"You are part of our corporation?"

"Yes," I say.

"Excellent."

"Totally," says Brianna.

Jessica waves like a beauty queen. "Okay, bye-bye, guys. I'm so happy, Paski. As long as we're allies, it's all good."

I smile and nod, but what I think is: I might like to ride bikes, and I might be in love with Chris Cabrera. But other than that, I'm nothing like you, Jessica Nguyen.

As Mrs. Nguyen hugs me goodbye, I realize that this mother is the opposite of her daughter. I wonder if Mrs. Nguyen knows. I also wonder how it's possible for Jessica to be even more dangerous bedridden than she was when she walked among the rest of humankind.

37

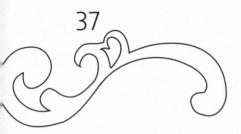

On Monday I ride my bike to school, and I'm surprised when Chris rolls up on a bicycle, too. He pedals up right as I'm locking mine and smiles at me from under his bike helmet. He's wearing jeans again, with a long-sleeved red thermal-underwear shirt with a white T-shirt over it.

"What are you doing?" I ask, ecstatic to see him.

"You inspired me," he says.

"I did?"

"Yeah, girl. Why waste gas when you can ride?"

He locks his bike up next to mine, putting his lock through my tire *and* his. I look at him in confusion, and he tells me that he wants me to teach him how to ride on hills after school. "You're not getting away until you show me all your tricks," he says.

"I can't do anything after school," I say.

"Why not?"

"I've got the newspaper."

"Oh, right. That's okay. I'll wait."

And then we walk through the humid morning air to the building, past the smoking Goth kids, past the chatting cheerleaders. As usual, we bump into each other, shoulders, hips, legs. Bump, bump. I feel like I can't get close enough to him. It feels like hunger or thirst, this thing I feel for Chris Cabrera. After the third bump, Chris laces his fingers with mine and holds my hand.

Gulp.

We walk across the courtyard and through the halls toward our lockers, holding hands, declaring to the entire school that we are officially an item. People stare and whisper. Chris is only, like, the hottest guy in school. My chest feels like it's full of light, expanded with pride and excitement. After we stop at our lockers, we go to Mr. Big's class.

We enter class holding hands, and I'm shocked and sickened when I see Andrew Van Dyke sitting in his usual seat, all spiked blond hair and pale yellow polo shirt with a pink-ribbon pin for breast cancer awareness. Is he trying to make a statement? What a weird thing for him to wear. He smiles at me like there's nothing different about him being here. Instinct kicks in, and I want to run away.

"Hey, dawg," he says to Chris. He twists his hand around like he's a gang member or something.

Chris nods at him, mostly out of surprise, but doesn't speak.

"Oh, it's like that?" says Andrew.

"Yeah, it's like that," says Chris.

Andrew slouches lower in his seat, spreads his feet wider, and laughs like it doesn't bother him, but I can tell it does. Everyone looks at him like he's diseased or evil. But I also feel almost sorry for him. I realize in that moment, that I am no longer *that* kid.

Andrew Van Dyke is.

After school, Tina comes flapping over to my locker in her oversize black trench coat, holding a framed photograph of her and her beloved Cesar. She grins like a crazy woman and leans to one side.

"Isn't he dreamy?" she says, sarcastic with the old-fashioned word but not with its meaning. She is completely in love with this guy. Why? What does she see in him? I look at the photo, and I swear Cesar looks brain-dead. I look at her nose. She has a new piercing. She now has studs in each nostril.

"You wanna go get coffee and visit him?" she asks. "He has a cute friend I could introduce you to."

I stash the books I don't need and put the ones I do need into my backpack. "Can't. Newspaper."

"Oh!" Tina hops up and down in her big red Doc Martens. I've never seen her so peppy. "I'm coming with you! I forgot."

I close my locker and start down the quickly emptying hall toward Miss Munn's room. Tina flaps along beside me like some kind of manic, hungry love machine. I don't understand her whole obsession with a grown man. It's sort of creeping me out.

"You don't need to protect me all the time," I tell her. "I'll be fine. You can go see Cesar."

"Please." Tina looks at me with a smile. "I'm not going to the newspaper for *you*."

"You're not?"

"Nah. I'm giving Sydney some cartoons."

"She talked you into it?" I ask.

"Sort of."

"That's great, Tina!"

We enter the classroom, and everyone glances up briefly before continuing what they'd been doing before. Whew. I am officially no longer that kid. I find Sydney curled over a proof of the upcoming issue, a red pencil in her hand.

"Hey, Sydney."

She looks up. "Hi, Paski! What's up?"

"Hello," sings Tina. She fishes through her huge black tote bag and pulls out a spiral drawing pad. "For you," she says.

Sydney takes the book, looks through it, starts to laugh out loud. "These are great!" She jumps up and hugs Tina. "Thanks!"

"So what's going on with you?" Sydney asks me.

I sit at the table with her. "Well, there's some news on the big regional race. This girl named Lori McCafferty from another school district is taking Jessica's place."

"And?"

"Do you still want me to cover it?"

"Sure."

"Okay." As I speak, I get an extremely vivid vision of the blond girl falling off the motorcycle, only this time I'm pretty sure she's dead. I shiver.

"What's wrong?" she asks me. "You okay?"

"What do you mean?" I try to smile. I don't want to tell people about the visions anymore. Not unless I know them really, really well.

Tina looks over at us. "She's having a vision," she declares. I now regret having told Tina about my "gift."

"A what?" asks Sydney.

"Nothing," I say. "So, I'll just go and start doing some research on one of the free computers." I try to sound totally normal.

But Sydney is perceptive. She stares at me. "There's something you're not telling me."

"No," I lie, thinking of Lori's motorcycle coming apart at the seams as she races. I think of how Haley didn't believe me about my ability. About how most people think I am crazy when I mention it. I'm not telling anyone about it anymore. I'm retiring from the psychic business. That's that. I say, "Everything's fine. Really."

38

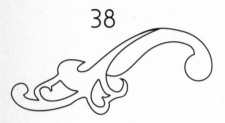

Chris and I ride along the path behind school, all the way to the canyon. He's as graceful on his bike as he is on the motorcycle. Until this moment, riding my bike has been a solitary thing, a time to think and feel, and for some reason, it has been the time I'm most likely to be in touch with my spiritual side. It's gotten hot out, and he's changed out of his jeans into shorts.

Chris is as playful and fearless on his bike as I am on mine, and the simple sight of him in his shorts and tank top, riding and smiling, his leg muscles flexing under his tanned, fuzzy skin, makes me crazy. He's amazing. How do you describe this feeling? It's like looking at something really delicious when you're starving. I want him. Big-time.

We get to the quiet place where the buffalo and coyotes revealed themselves to me, and without me telling him anything about it, Chris stops. He takes a drink from his water bottle and looks around. "How about here?" he asks. "Take me off the path. Teach me to ride like Paski."

I get chills. "Are you sure?"

"Entirely sure."

I lead him through the shrubs and over rocks, going easy at first. He's skilled enough to stay right behind me, no matter how fast I go. So I turn it up a little. And I keep turning it up. We cruise up the hills and fly back down. After two hills on which Chris even passes me, I stop. I straddle the bike and look at him with a huge smile.

"What?" he asks, smiling back and circling around me on his bike, a total show-off.

"You're such a punk," I say.

"Why?"

"Because you asked me to bring you up here to teach you to ride hills, but you're already good."

He gasps as if this were news to him, sarcastic.

"Why would you *do* that?" I ask.

He stands over his bike right next to me. "That's easy," he says. "I wanted to see you sweat." He touches my arm. "I like how your skin feels when you sweat. Kind of clammy, kind of slick."

The feel of his fingers on me is electric. "You're a punk," I repeat in a whisper. I don't mean to whisper, but honestly? I can't speak. I am completely overwhelmed with longing for this guy.

"I'm a punk who really likes you," he says. He kisses me, and the kiss lasts a long time. He looks in my eyes when we finish and says simply, "I want to spend as much time as I can with you. I wanted to come out here to watch you ride. There's nothing as beautiful in the world as *your* body on *that* bike."

My heart pounds like a million bird wings. I open my mouth, and the words come out small, in a hoarse whisper, truer than any I've ever said. "I think I might, uh, I mean I, I really like you, too."

"Let's go back to my house," he says. He moves in and nibbles my neck, kisses my shoulder. Heat fills my body. "My parents won't be home for a few hours."

I inhale deeply and listen to the wind. I listen for an answer. I look over Chris's shoulder to the top of the hill where I stood that day, alone with the visions, and I see the head coyote staring down at us with her warm yellow eyes.

"Okay," I say. "Let's go to your house."

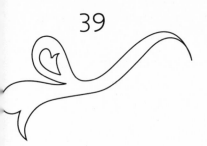

39

Chris lives in a beige, Mediterranean style house on a ridge with stables in the backyard and flowers and palm trees in the front yard. It's a very nice house, from what I can see so far. His parents have a lot of money; I don't know why this surprises me. I think it's because he doesn't carry himself the way the other rich kids do. He's more humble or something.

I follow him to the side of the house, near the garage, where he gets off his bike and punches a code into a black box. I hear the garage door opening. This thing is huge, like, for six cars, and it's got a gray floor that's all shiny. It has shelves and drawers and Peg-Board with tools and things all perfectly arranged. We walk our bikes to one corner, next to a bunch of other sports equipment, all perfectly lined up and organized, and I lean my bike next to his. My heart is pounding. I don't know what to do. I've kissed two boys, but I'm not exactly what you'd call an experienced girl. Something tells me Chris has a lot more experience than I do.

I follow him through a door into a small room with benches on the floor and coats on the wall. We take off our shoes, and stash them under the bench. The house smells good, like apple pie baking. There are cute paintings on the wall, of bunnies and things, with lines like HOME SWEET HOME underneath. Something a mom would put up. Something we'd never have in our home, only now, with Melanie coming along, we might?

We go from the shoe room into the kitchen. It's unlike most of the kitchens I've seen in Orange County so far, in that it's very modern and sleek. The others have been more country or something. I've never seen counters like this, and I run my fingers over them. He tells me they're made of stained concrete.

"It's really big in Europe. My mom's from Spain, so, you know, she likes to get everything from over there. Even her jeans. She's obsessed."

He gets a couple of glasses out of a cabinet and fills them with ice and water from the door of the stainless steel refrigerator. I thank him, and we stand at the island in the middle of the kitchen, drinking. I'm sweating so much it drips down the sides of my face. Chris is sweating, too. He grabs some paper towels and gives me some.

"You are so sexy, sweaty," he says.

"That's gross," I say.

"Nah, it's sensual." He leans over and sniffs me. He *is* European, I think. Don't they like body odor over there more than we do here? I can smell him, too, and even though he's damp, he doesn't stink. He smells like earth and ocean, actually. It's hard to explain, but it's like a clean sweat, with something chemical in it that makes my body tense up and fill with excitement. Chris sets down his glass and moves closer. He presses his body against mine. I set down my glass, too, and wrap my arms around him. His lips touch mine, and we kiss. And kiss. His kisses are gentle, searching, warm, amazing. I feel heat in my belly and between my legs. He presses against me harder, and I let my lips brush across his cheek, then his ear. As I nibble his earlobe, he lets out a little groan. I move my lips to his neck and taste the salt of him. Oh. My. God.

Chris pulls my hands and starts to walk backwards, kissing me. "Come with me," he says through the kisses.

I follow him through the kitchen, across a family room, up the stairs, down the hall, to his room. The whole upstairs smells good, like citrus and clean laundry. Chris's room smells like wood and men's cologne. It's a big room, with a king-size bed and nice dark brown furniture. He's got a couple of posters on the walls, but also framed paintings. Real art. And the few boys' rooms I've seen haven't been this clean.

Chris closes the door. Then he takes me to the bed. We sit on it and begin to kiss again. The kissing intensifies, and our hands begin to wander. He touches my shoulders, my collarbone. He stops kissing me to look at me. The grin is gone, replaced by a very intense expression.

"You are so beautiful." His hand slides from my collarbone to my breast, and he sort of traces it with his fingertips. "Wow," he says. "Amazing."

I close my eyes and focus on the feel of his hand on me. I feel like a coil that's being wound up, tighter and tighter, warmer and warmer. He holds me tight, and I think I'm going to die of wanting.

I grab Chris by the shoulders and push him down onto the mattress. He lies back and smiles. "I like an aggressive woman," he says. I can't control myself now and sit on top of him. I hold his hands up over his head, press them into the bed, and lean down to kiss him. My hair drapes across us, and I can feel his hips start to move beneath me. I feel like I'm going to explode. We continue to kiss, and our bodies move against each other like two sticks rubbing themselves into a fire.

Chris sits up a little and rolls me onto my side. He's on his side now, too. We're facing each other and kissing again. He takes my top hand and moves it down, to *there*. On *him*. It. I can feel *it* through his shorts, like a brand-new tube of toothpaste.

"Yeah," he says. He uses his free hand to unbutton his shorts and then places my hand inside them. It's weird, this thing that boys have. It's hard but soft at the same time? I glance down and see it peeking up at me. I laugh.

"*Hey,*" he says. "No laughing."

"No!" I say. "Don't take it the wrong way. It's just, he looks so *hopeful.*" I don't know why that seems so funny to me. But it does.

Chris grins. "Oh, he *is*. He's *very* hopeful."

I hold it like a baton, and he puts his hand over mine and moves it up and down.

"I've never done this," I say.

"I'll show you," he says. "Just like that. Not too hard."

My heart is pounding. I can't find enough air. Chris kisses me, and then he's lifting my shirt and kissing my chest. His lips are soft and warm, and I feel muscles in different parts of my body contracting without my permission. I have never been this excited in my life.

Suddenly I feel his fingers fiddling with the snap and zipper of my pants. I place my hand over his. "Don't," I say. I don't *mean* it, though.

I really *want* him to keep going. I just don't trust myself to know when to stop.

"Okay." He backs off instantly but looks at my eyes carefully. I have the eyes of a liar, I'm sure of that.

"You sure?" he asks. Very perceptive, this Chris Cabrera dude.

"I'm a virgin," I tell him.

"That's okay," he says.

"Are *you*?" I ask him.

He shakes his head. "Paski, we don't have to do anything you don't want to do, okay?"

I kiss him again, and take his hand, and put it back on my zipper. I open my eyes and see him smiling, like he finds me amusing and sexy all at once. He gets the zipper down without too much effort, and then his fingers sort of scoot down, past my underwear, until they're there. There, there. Yikes.

"Do you want to take this further?" he asks. He's panting a little bit, and his face looks red.

Uhm, yes. Yes. I can't think of anything I want more than to do that right now. But I remember the talk I had with my dad, and all the things he told me about being smart, making good choices. Going further would *so* not be a good choice. Not now.

"No," I whisper.

"Okay. That's probably the best thing anyway."

"Why?" I ask.

All at once he shudders, and my hand gets very, very wet and oozy. "Oops. *That's* why," says Chris with an embarrassed smile. He takes my hand off him and wipes it on his comforter. "Sorry."

"For what?" I ask.

He kisses me again and presses me down until I'm lying on my back. "Okay," he says. "Now, you just lie back, relax, and let me return the favor, okay?"

Oh. My. God. I try to relax as his hands wander. He asks me if he's in the right spot and asks me to tell him how to do it the way I like it. I tell him, and, unsurprisingly, he's a fast learner. Before I know it, I'm shuddering, too. It is the finest convulsion I could imagine, like being wrapped in a red velvet blanket on a cold day.

He grins at me. "Amazing," he says.

"Yeah," I say, out of breath and entirely, *stupidly* happy. "Pretty much."

40

It's the day before the big race, and I have an appointment to hang out with my new "best buds" at the mall. How is Jessica getting around the mall? I don't exactly want to go, but I can't say no being part of the "corporation" and all. I couldn't figure out what to wear, so I'm running late. I stood there staring into the deep dark shadows of my closet and tried to come up with just the right thing. When Jessica doesn't like what one of "us" is wearing, Haley told me, she is known to ask us to go home and change, in the name of the corporate image. In the end, I decided on a tight bright green Urban Outfitters T-shirt with a rainbow slashed across the front, a maroon zip-front hooded sweatshirt, and a pair of Seven jeans. I want to look good enough not to get sent home, but not so weird I don't feel like me.

So, anyway, I just got here and rushed to the food court. I spy Jessica in her wheelchair. Haley and Brianna sit with her at a table meant for handicapped people. Jessica wears a fur hat. Haley is in a bandana skirt, wraparound, with a tank and sparkly shawl. Brianna wears shorts with UGGs. Not sure I like the look, frankly. But trendy, for sure. They're drinking smoothies and looking at some shoes inside a Steve Madden bag. I approach, and they smile and wave like we're best friends. I feel happy when I see Haley, but scared at the sight of Jessica. Haley gets up to give me a hug.

"Paski, you are so cute in that shirt," Jessica announces.

"So totally cute," echoes Brianna.

"Where'd you get it?" asks Jessica.

"Urban Outfitters," I say.

"Sit down," she orders.

I sit.

"Now, Paski, Haley, I have to tell you guys, we've got everything set for tomorrow."

"What do you mean?" asks Haley.

Jessica looks so pert and adorable sipping her drink, it's almost impossible to imagine that this is the same girl who wanted me dead. "Okay," she continues. "But before I tell you, I have to ask you to sign this waiver."

She slips us each a piece of paper. It's some kind of contract on stationery with Jessica's name across the top. It says:

I, _____, agree on this date, _____, to keep everything discussed in this weekly meeting a complete and utter secret. If I so much as tell any of this information to a single soul, I understand that I shall be held fully accountable for my gross indiscretions, according to the laws of the corporation. I furthermore agree that if any member of the corporation should be discovered with regards to the actions discussed in today's meeting, by a law-enforcement agency or something of equal nature, that I will keep my vow to secrecy or face the harshest of consequences, including but not limited to expulsion from the corporation, public humiliation in the form of ostracism at school and in the community, and a fee of no less than one thousand dollars, payable in cash to Miss Jessica Nguyen, for contract broken. This contract is binding and nonnegotiable.

Signature _____

I read it again to make sure I understand if this is actually real. I look at Haley and see that she is already signing it. She looks at me and says, "Standard procedure for the corporation." When she finishes signing, she hands her pen to me. The pen has a pink powder puff at the top. I look up at Jessica.

"Are you sure you're ready to take this step?" She smiles wickedly. I nod. And then I sign. "All right. Good. Thank you both." Jessica snatches up the contracts, puts them in her large chocolate brown Prada handbag, and says, "Here's the deal. Brianna went over to the track a couple of hours ago, and she got Andrew to help her with the bolts on Lori's motorbike."

"She what?" I ask. I try not to gag or choke, or look as shocked and sick as I suddenly feel. Haley looks confused.

"Yeah!" Jessica claps her hands a few times in front of her, as if dusting them off. "It's all done."

"Totally done," says Brianna. "Andrew's a doll."

"Andrew?" I spit.

Jessica looks at me with sympathy. "I know, Paski. I know he put that stuff in your drink and everything. He's stupid that way. But he's useful to us in other ways."

"He knows a lot about motors. His dad has car dealerships," Brianna pipes up. She starts counting on her fingertips. "Mercedes, BMW, Audi —"

"Shut up, Brianna," snaps Jessica.

"What do you mean by 'help her with the bolts'?" I ask.

"Loosen them," says Jessica, like I'm an idiot. "What did you think I meant?"

Haley looks at me in alarm but doesn't speak.

"Uh." I start to panic. What if Lori is over at the track right now, practicing? I didn't think it would get to this. I mean, I kept waiting for a sign from the amulet, something that would tell me what to do. Oh my God. I have to do something. "You didn't really do that, did you? Tomorrow's the race, Jessica."

"Well, duh," she says with a broad grin. "And the race is where Lori's going to wipe out."

"No," squeaks Haley. "You guys didn't really do that, did you?"

"Totally!" says Brianna.

"You two don't have a problem with this, do you?" asks Jessica. It's not a question, though. It's a threat.

The amulet grows extremely warm on my neck. I have to call Chris, to warn Lori. It's so important that I don't mess up. "You don't think it's going to kill her or anything?" I ask, trying to smile. "So much more dramatic to just hurt her a little, right? I mean, that way no one goes to prison if we get caught."

"No one gets caught unless one of us blabs. Therefore, the contracts. Which, I will remind you both, you signed."

Haley picks at her pink manicured fingernails and says, "Yes, but I don't think we understood what we were signing about."

Jessica's eyes narrow at her, and I swear to God, I can almost see smoke coming out of her ears. Nostrils, too. "Do. Not. Tell me. You are going to cause problems."

Haley says nothing.

Jessica looks at me and Brianna. "This might be a good time to let you know, Haley, that I've considered corporate restructuring lately."

"What does that mean?" asks Haley, her eyes starting to fill with tears.

"It means we might have some layoffs coming up. I'm not sure. It all depends on worker productivity."

My urge to call Chris is tremendous. I have to do it. Now. Right now. I have to think of a reason to get away from here. I point to their smoothies. "Those look so good," I say. "Mind if I go get one and come right back? I am *so* thirsty. I've been riding my bike like crazy lately."

"Spirulina," says Jessica. "And ask for a protein shot. It's the best thing."

I smile and get up. "I totally have to pee, too. I'll be back. You guys want anything?"

Jessica and Brianna say no in a way that lets me know they have no clue what I'm about to do. Haley stares at the top of the table, glum, and says nothing. I dash to the restroom, lock myself in a stall, and call Chris on my cell phone.

I tell Chris about yesterday at Jessica's house. He listens.

"Jessica's kind of weird," he says when I finish.

"And the worst part is that she was talking about how she wants to make this girl Lori McCafferty, who's taking her place in the regionals, have an accident."

"Poor Lori. She's a great girl," he says.

"You know her?"

Chris says sadly, "You could say that."

"Why would Jessica hate her so much?"

Chris hesitates and says, "Because I used to go out with her in the eighth grade." He pauses. "She was the first girl I ever kissed."

"Really?" I ask. I try not to feel jealous.

"Yeah. And she's the one who turned me on to motocross."

"Jessica just told me that Brianna and Andrew loosened the bolts on Lori's motorbike. Someone has to tell her not to even practice on that bike."

"I'll call her," he says calmly. "No problem."

"Thank you so much." I breathe.

"Sure." He hangs up and I exit the stall hoping no one here has heard me talking. I wash my hands and try to stop them from trembling. "You're doing the right thing," I tell my reflection. "You can do this."

I go to the smoothie bar, get my drink exactly the way Jessica wants me to, and return to the table. "Yummy!" I chirp, hoping that no one can see me dying of nerves inside. "This is so good. You were so right!"

Brianna snaps her gum and says, "Jessica's always right. That's one of our company politics."

"Policies," Jessica corrects her.

"Right," says Brianna. "Company politics."

Jessica shakes her head and sighs. "Never mind. Okay, guys? Now we have to talk about our next project." She stares at Haley. "Making sure Haley isn't popular anymore."

Haley's eyes brim with tears again. "Why are you doing this to me?"

"You don't like our plans," says Brianna.

"Because they're dangerous!" cries Haley. "Because you're mean! It's horrible to want to hurt someone like that."

Jessica smiles. "That's the thing about business that you artist types don't understand. Good managers have to suspend empathy."

"What if I go to the police?"

"You can't. You signed the contract." Jessica smirks and holds it up to remind her.

Haley stands up. "The only contract I have that matters to me right now is with my *conscience*." She looks at Jessica her eyes wide with disgust. "You know, after you had your crash, I felt really sorry for you, Jessica. Like I should be friends with you even though I knew you were ruthless. I didn't want to be your friend after what you did to Paski at the party, but when you had your accident, I thought it might have changed you. It didn't. It made you worse." She scoops up her hand-bag and looks at me. "Are you with them?" she asks. "Or with me?"

I look at Jessica and Brianna and think about Lori McCafferty. I stand up, and side by side, Haley and I walk out of the mall without speaking.

We jump into the Squeegeemobile, and I call Chris again on my cell phone as I drive toward Haley's house. "What happened?" I ask him. I realize my voice is very loud.

"Well," he says. "Lori's okay."

"Thank God."

"But she's spooked, Paski."

"I don't blame her."

"She doesn't want to race this weekend."

"I wouldn't, either."

"And she asked me if I know anyone good enough to take her place. There aren't that many girls out there doing motocross at the level of Jessica and Lori."

"I know."

"So, like, I hope you don't mind, but . . ." He stops talking. I watch the freeway stretch out in front of me and feel the amulet resting comfortably on my neck.

"But what?" I ask.

"But I told Lori that you should take her place in the race."

"You did?"

"I hope you don't mind."

"I don't know how to race!" I protest. But even as I say it, I know it's not completely true.

"You'll be fine," he says. "Lori already gave the team your name."

"What?"

"But you have to promise me you won't hang out with Jessica and Brianna anymore."

"Why?"

"Well, as we speak, the police are down at the track, getting Andrew's and Brianna's fingerprints off Lori's bike."

41

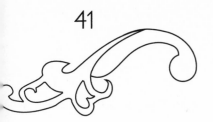

It's the day of the regional finals, and Brianna and Andrew are on their way to jail. Yup. That's right. Jail.

Brianna confessed that Jessica was involved in the plot, but Jessica has denied it all. She's going to let Brianna and Andrew take the fall for her. I know this because I was lying in bed, waiting for Dad to tell me the waffles were ready, when Jessica called to tell me everything and to ask me to reconsider my "resignation" from the company. I have the phone to my ear, listening to her. As she talks, my eyes dance over the photos of Taos and New Mexico pasted on my bedroom door. The images give me strength and connection to the universe. The majesty of the landscapes also makes everything Jessica is saying seem trivial and extremely superficial.

"You really are a good fit for this company. You know that deep down inside, you're just like me," Jessica says again. "Together we'd be unstoppable."

"What about Brianna? You're just going to let her go to jail for you?"

"Eh," she breathes as if it means nothing to her. "Brianna won't even notice she's not at home. You know how she is. A loaf of bread is smarter than that girl."

"Is that how you talk about your friends?"

"Sometimes. Only when they deserve it."

"So what do you say about me behind my back?"

"You? Nothing."

"You know what, Jessica? You're sick."

She laughs like I've meant this as a compliment, which I haven't. "Ah, but the truth is, you're are just as sick as I am. You're just like me."

"I should let you know who's going to replace Lori in the race today."

"Who?"

"Me." There's a long, long silence, during which I imagine she is sharpening the blade of some kind of huge, deadly knife, specifically for the act of stabbing it into my heart.

"But you can't do that!" she responds, simply and without detectable emotion. "Motocross is my special thing. Not yours."

"No, Jessica, cruelty is your special thing. You're very, very good at it." I hang up. Around my neck, the amulet feels like it's starting to glow, and I sense its low, comforting vibration in my bones.

I think of my grandmother's warm gaze and use her energy to calm myself before going down to breakfast. I am so nervous about this race, I could throw up. I've been practicing every day after school with Chris, riding at the track until sundown and then going to Starbucks to hang out with Tina. We all sit in the corner of the shop on the puffy chairs and drink decaf Frappuccinos while we do our homework. It feels good, and right, to have these two people in my life.

These two friends. I'm happy to say Chris and Tina really get along, even though neither one had spent much time with the other before. Chris is amazed by her drawings, and he wants to show them to his art dealer mom. Tina has started calling me "the diplomat," because she thinks I'm even better than she is at building bridges between different cliques. She's also the only person in Orange County I have told of my plan to build an even *bigger* bridge with Chris. I mean, big. He's the one. I'm going to lose it to him. I've already made up my mind, but I want to be sure I do it right, meaning that I'm protected. I told Emily and Janet, too, and they're really excited for me. Emily has been e-mailing me tips that border on the obscene, from this about.com Web site.

Finally I get out of bed and put on a pair of jeans and a plain old T-shirt, clothes from my other life, back in Taos. They feel really comfortable and good. I open the door of my room and head downstairs. I find my dad sitting at the table alone. I'm surprised. Lately Melanie has been here with him, and the twins have taken to running in and out of our apartment as if it's their own. They've even hooked up their spare Xbox 360 to our television.

"Hey, *Chinita*," he says. "Ready for waffles?"

"They smell great," I say. I sit at the table, and Dad hops up to get a plate for me. He sets them down in front of me, and after I drizzle fresh maple syrup, I attack the food. Dad stands watching for a moment, and then I notice he's beaming. That's right. Beaming. Like he's so super-proud of me.

"Why are you looking at me like that?" I ask.

"Did you forget?" he asks.

"Forget what?"

"Today's a special day."

"I know. The race is today."

"Ah." He sits back down at the table. "But before that, there's your appointment."

"My appointment?"

"At Planned Parenthood," he says. He clears his throat and blushes. Oh, God. I did forget.

"That's today?" I ask absently. I don't want to talk about this with him. I really don't. Thankfully, he seems as uncomfortable about it as I do.

"Yup. In an hour. Go get ready after you eat."

I stare at the plate of waffles, and suddenly the food doesn't look as good. "I'm done," I say.

"But you didn't eat."

"Guess I'm not hungry."

An hour later, my dad drops me off at the Planned Parenthood office and drives away. He wanted to come in with me, but I was like "Uh, no. I don't *think* so." He wanted to make sure that I wasn't scared. Scared of what? The only thing that was scary was the fact that my dad wanted to go in there.

I open the door and see the waiting room. A bunch of other women sit there, mostly older than me. No, wait. All of them older than me. I don't know if I'm supposed to feel weird, but I do. At least I'm alone, though.

I give the receptionist my name and appointment time, and she signs me in. She asks for my insurance card, and I hand it to her. My dad has this great insurance now, or at least that's what he says, thanks to some screenwriters' guild or something. Anyway, I try not to shake as I take the card back and put it in my wallet. I say a silent prayer that the receptionist won't, like, ask me why I'm here or something, because I truly do not want to have to answer that in front of all these people.

I sit in a chair in the waiting area and flip through a magazine. For some reason it's all about golf. That's what they have here. I look around for something else, but all the good magazines have already been taken. I notice a couple of the women are here with men, but they hold hands and kiss, so the men are obviously not their dads. I wonder how many girls my age have dads who would make them an appointment at a place like this. Probably not too many.

A few minutes later, a hippie-looking lady in purple clogs opens a door and, after looking at a folder in her hand, calls my name. I set down the golfing magazine — such a struggle, I know — and join her.

"How are you?" she asks me.

"Okay."

She takes me to an exam room, and she sits in a chair while I sit on the table. She closes the door and then asks me what I'm hoping to get out of my appointment.

"Uh," I say. I blush. "I don't know." Duh! What a stupid thing to say. I'm an idiot.

She smiles at me in a comforting way. "Your dad, when he called, said you might want to look into some birth control options."

I feel the blush turn into a full face-fire. "He did?" I choke.

"You're actually lucky he's looking out for you," she says. "You'd be surprised how many parents don't want to think about it, and how many kids get into trouble as a result."

I look at my feet. She pulls out a booklet called *Your Choices* and starts flipping though it, showing me all the different *options* out there for me. I listen and think they all sound *barbaric*. Did you know an IUD is a wire they stick in your uterus, and that it works because it irritates your body into thinking you're pregnant already? Awful.

"You can think about these options while you undress," she says.

"Undress?"

"The doctor will be right in to talk to you more about all this."

She tells me to take off my pants and underwear and to sit up on the table with a sheet over me. I've had pelvic exams by my regular doctor, so this isn't that weird, but the whole thing of being here to talk about the fact that I'm thinking about having sex soon is a little much for me right now.

The purple-clog lady leaves, and I do as she requested. I sit there on the table wishing I had something to read so I could distract myself from the fact that I'm here, naked, on a piece of butcher's paper on a table with a thin, ugly sheet over me.

The door opens, and a tall, black woman doctor with short, dyed-blond hair and red trendy eyeglasses comes in. She looks nice with a relaxed and pleasant face. She asks me a lot of the same questions the other lady asked me, which makes me wonder why I had to talk to the first lady at all. But whatever.

The doctor tells me to put my feet in those stirrup things and to scoot my butt to the end of the table. I do it, staring up at the fluorescent lights and pretending I'm somewhere else. It's not like it's painful or anything. It's just awkward. It's not first on the list of things I'd like to be doing, let's just put it that way. She does an exam and tells me that everything looks fine but the lab results will say for sure. Then I sit up again, and we talk. There's something very uncomfortable about this. I mean, she was just sticking stuff up there, and now she's sitting here talking to me like we're having coffee somewhere.

In the end, I decide on birth control pills and condoms. The doctor observes me calmly and tells me she thinks I've made a good, healthy choice, and she writes me a prescription. She gives me a free pack of the pills to start but tells me they won't be effective for another month. A month? I have to wait a month? I go back to the waiting room and call my dad to tell him to come pick me up.

He tells me to come on out; he's been waiting for me in the parking lot.

42

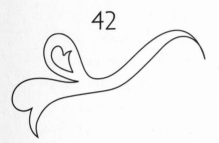

I stand over my bed, peering into the white cardboard box of racing outfits. Lori, who happens to be my size, gave them to Chris, who dropped them off with Melanie while I was at the Planned Parenthood appointment.

I reach in and remove the pieces of clothing one by one. They are all leather, heavy, protective in the way that motocross racing clothes have to be, but they range in style from a basic black outfit to a sexy white-and-hot-pink one. I try them all on and assess the results in the slightly rusted mirror on the wall in my room. I eventually choose the sexy one. It looks the best. I *know* it will probably give my dad a heart attack, the way the white leather pants lace up the front like a football with hot pink laces, and the way the jacket has cutouts that accent the shape of my breasts. But I also know that a lot of people are going to be watching this race, and that one of them is going to be Chris.

I finish off the outfit with Grandma's amulet, tucked into my shirt beneath the racing jacket.

Trying not to look too sexy, I lumber down the stairs in the stiff leather pants and shuffle into the living room. My dad is sitting on the sofa with Melanie again. She's over all the time. They might as well get a big yellow tube, like in a hamster cage, and just connect these two apartments already. That or knock down the wall and make it official. They look up. My dad's mouth tightens at the sight of me, and I know he doesn't like the outfit. Melanie smiles at me, though, and tells me I look great.

"Doesn't she look great?" she asks my dad. He says nothing. Crosses his arms. "I said, doesn't your daughter look beautiful?" Melanie elbows him until he agrees with her. She's softening my dad in certain ways that I really like. I could get used to having her around. "You know what?" she asks me. "I have the perfect shade of pink lipstick for you. Come with me."

Melanie grabs my hand and pulls me over to her apartment. She's wearing flip-flops and has this funny way of dragging her feet that I think is cute. The twins sit on the couch, still in their pajamas, playing video games, and smile when they see me.

"That's an awesome outfit," says Kerani.

"Superhero outfit," says Keoni.

"Moto-Girl, Master of the Universe."

"Mistress of the Universe."

"That doesn't sound right."

"Motocross Madness."

"Moto-Mistress, mad at the universe," says Kerani. They laugh. They continue with this word game. I stop listening.

Melanie leads me into her room and starts to dig through the clear plastic makeup tub on her wooden dresser. I assume she made the dresser herself. She makes almost all of their furniture. After twisting the caps off a few tubes and analyzing the shade, she finds the lipstick she was looking for.

"Pucker up," she says. I do, and she puts it on me. I don't think I've ever had another person put makeup on me. I feel her breath on my cheek as she fills in my lips carefully, and I get chills. So this is what it feels like to have a mom, I think. I could get used to it. Yes, I could. "There," she says. I look at my face in the mirror, and sure enough, the lipstick looks really good with this outfit.

"Wow," I say.

"It's one of those all-day kinds, too, so it won't come off no matter what."

"Glad it was the right color, then," I joke.

"Oh," she says. "The thing is, if it had been wrong, we could have taken it off quickly. It's only after it dries that you can't get it off."

I like this, the motherly makeup advice.

Melanie considers my face, knits her brows together, and says, "Here, sit down."

I sit on the edge of the bed, and she proceeds to give me a full makeover. Foundation, blush, eyeliner, shadow, mascara. The whole thing.

"There," she declares, smiling. "You're beautiful."

I stand up and look again in the mirror over the dresser. I like what I see. I have chills. I want to cry. I have never in my life had a grown-up woman help me with girlie stuff like this. She notices my tears and pulls me in for a hug.

"I never had a daughter," she says. "And I always wanted one. This is so much fun. We're going to have so much fun together, Paski."

"Thanks, Melanie," I say.

"Of course. Hey, how about after the race, we go shopping? Celebrate your win?"

"I might not win," I say. I'm also thinking that Chris and I already have plans for a date after the race, but I don't want to tell Melanie because she might tell my dad, and he's still not thrilled about Chris.

Melanie laughs and puts a hand over her heart. "I highly doubt you'll lose. But if you do? You're still a winner. Remember that."

43

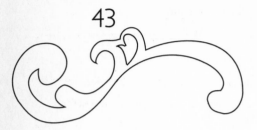

Dad drives me to the race in the Squeegeemobile. Melanie, Keoni, and Kerani come, too. We kids are all crammed in the back. My dad and Melanie hold hands over the stick shift, and I have a powerful sense that their bond is going to last a long time. These two were meant to meet. I wish I had such certainty about the race. I am so nervous, I haven't eaten since the few bites of waffle this morning.

We get to the track and it's packed. There are TV crews and lots of riders. The air smells of sausages and onions. We go to the registration table, and I sign in. Lori McCafferty is working the sign-up table, and I meet her for the first time. She's beautiful, with a deep tan and long blond hair — the same girl I saw in Jessica's wish-vision.

"Good luck," Lori says, hugging me. "I know you can do it."

Then I get directed to an area where the rest of Jessica's team is meeting. My dad, Melanie, and the twins go to the stands and find seats. The other riders are friendly but seem a little suspicious. They've never heard of me, and there's a lot riding on this race, no pun intended. If I win, I get instant notoriety, and go on to nationals. One of the other team members tells me that Jessica is in the stands with her mom and dad.

I can't believe it. "Why did they let her in?"

"Her dad brought a lawyer and said this was a free and open event for the public," says the other racer.

I search the crowd and find them. Jessica waves at me with her one good arm, a nasty, sarcastic look on her face. She's in a wheelchair.

I feel a tap on my shoulder and turn to see Chris. I'll be using his old bike to race, and he was going to get it tuned up and bring it to me.

"Wow," he says, looking at the tight white leather. "You look hot."

"Thanks," I blush.

He leads me to the bike. But instead of the old one, I'm shocked to find a brand-new yellow Yamaha women's bike, the kind all the top racers are using. "What is this?"

"A present," he says.

"A very expensive present," I say. I hear a screeching sound over our heads. I look up and see a white seagull circling directly above. As I watch it, three others join it, circling me.

"My mom and dad gave me some stocks when I was a kid, and I can do what I want with the money," he explains.

"You can't give me this."

"I can. And I just did. You know. Just in case. It's right out of the shop, mechanic-checked and good to go."

Chris kisses me and walks away, looking over his shoulder with a smile. I realize he's leaving me with no choice but to take the motorcycle. I'm stunned. He calls out, "Kick much ass, Paski!" and raises a fist in the air.

I hop on the bike and can't believe how supple it is, like it was made for me. I join the other riders in our area and then follow them to the starting line. I can feel the power of the earth, of animals, of the spirits, with me. The amulet warms on my neck, and I can't tell if it is meant as a reassurance or as a warning. I'm afraid.

Finally the announcer calls us to line up. I stand with my bike alongside the other girls and wait for the gun to sound. And then we're off. I try to calm myself and listen to my instincts. I pretend I'm alone on my bike in the mountains of Taos, and I just focus. I don't even know if I'm ahead or behind. I ride. That's all I do. It feels like flying when I take the jumps. I relax a bit and lift my legs off the bike in the sixth jump, and I sail through the air. I hear coyotes howling, and I feel the flutter of the seagulls above me. I enter a mental space that feels like a tunnel. And then, before I know it, the race is over and I'm braking. The crowd is roaring, and Haley has hopped the fence and is running up to me, congratulating me.

Telling me I won.

44

Keoni and Kerani sit on the sofa in my living room and stare at me. I'm trying to find a cable sports channel that might have something about today's race. I mean, I know I won. But at the same time, I can't believe it. It's like I need to see something from outside my little universe to confirm that I really did it. My future brothers breathe through their mouths and keep staring.

"What?" I ask them. "Why are you looking at me?"

"You're like a god," says Kerani.

"Goddess," I correct him.

"Whatever," says Kerani. "I mean, you totally iced everyone out there. You are the messiah who has come to dethrone the evil Jessica."

"Whatever," I say. My dad and Melanie are in the kitchen, cooking dinner. They've asked me to eat with them, but I declined, saying I have a date. With Chris. I totally told my father, and he was so happy about the race that he didn't seem to mind. Weird.

"Okay, guys, I'm going to go get ready." The twins stand up when I do, and both of them bow down to me, laughing. "Cut it out," I say.

"Hail Queen Paski," they say in unison. How the heck do they do that? Talk at the same time? Bow at the same time? Sometimes I wonder if they share a brain.

I skip upstairs to take a shower. I take my time shaving my legs and armpits, just in case things get intimate with Chris. I scrub myself, then just sort of stand there in the comforting spray of hot water and let myself relax. I have the powerful sense that I am finally in the right place.

When the hot water starts to turn cold, I get out and towel off. I wrap myself in another towel and hurry to my room to find something to wear. I close the shades, drop the towel, and stand naked in front of the mirror, inspecting my body. It certainly looks like a woman's body. I'm not a kid anymore. I mean, legally, sure, I'm still a minor. But the body in the mirror is full-grown. I've been having periods for almost six years now. That's almost a decade.

I open the closet and start the never-ending search for the Right Outfit. It seems so much more important here in California than it was back in New Mexico. I consider going the cute and girlie route, but I think I'll be at my sexiest if I'm comfy. The problem with skirts and all that stuff is that you spend the whole time worrying about whether your underwear is showing or something, and you can't really focus on being present, in your body, in your mind, listening to your companion speak. Companion. I get a chill thinking of Chris in these terms.

I decided on a pair of ripped jeans I got from the Urban Outfitters catalog, with a long white tunic-style shirt over a white cami-tank, and big wooden beads I borrowed from Haley. I think her style is wearing off on me. I wear black wedge Vans sneaks with pink stripes, and a new perfume I got from Melanie as a present after the race, the Cool, by Ralph Lauren that everyone's wearing. After that, I apply a tiny bit of makeup, some blush and mascara mostly, and blow-dry my hair straight.

Once I'm dressed, I sit on the bed and flip through a *CosmoGIRL!* until I hear the doorbell ring. Then I check my hair one last time and go back downstairs to find everyone seated around the table. My heart bucks in my chest at the sight of them. The family. My family.

"You look nice," says my dad. Melanie beams at him in approval. "Have fun."

I open the door, and there stands Chris in a pair of khaki pants and a dark gray T-shirt. He wears a white beaded choker around his neck and smells like wood and ocean.

"Wow," he says when he sees me. "You look great." He leans in and says hi to my dad.

"You, too," I say. I feel my cheeks flame from the blood rushing to them, and I turn to my family. "See you later," I say.

"Hi. Be home by midnight, or I'm calling the police," says Dad.

I step out of the apartment and close the door. I follow Chris down the steps to a parked silver Toyota Prius.

"It's my mom's," he says. He opens my door and waits until I'm in to close it again. Very thoughtful. The inside of the car is spotless and smells like Chris's delicious cologne. He opens the driver's door and folds himself into the seat.

"This is so weird," I say, looking at him behind the wheel.

"What's that?" he asks as he starts the engine.

"I don't think I've ever seen you drive a car," I say.

He grins. "That's probably true. My parents don't think I need one." He eases the Prius out of the parking space.

"Why not?" I ask. "I mean, it's not like they couldn't afford it."

He nods and pulls onto the street. "It's an environmental thing."

"Oh," I say.

"My dad, I don't think I told you. He's an environmental lawyer. He's big on public transit. That's like his mission in life, to get good public transportation in So Cal."

"That's cool," I say.

Chris punches the stereo buttons, and the new single by Coheed and Cambria comes on. I love this song. Then he reaches for my hand and drives without saying a word, all the way to a juice bar.

"This cool?" he asks.

"Sure," I say.

"I've been craving a mango smoothie," he says. "Then the movie, then we can get dinner."

"Sure."

We go in and order. Then we take our drinks and sit on high stools at a counter, looking out of the front window. We talk about the race and about how weird it was that Jessica was there, waving at me like we were friends.

"I don't care," I tell Chris. "She makes me sick, actually. I kind of feel sorry for Brianna, though. Taking the fall for her."

"I don't," says Chris.

"You don't?"

He shakes his head. "She did what she did. She made that decision herself."

"Yeah, you're right," I say.

We finish the smoothies and go back to the car. Chris takes a different route than I expected, and before I know it, we're pulling up to Haley's house.

"What are we doing here?" I ask.

"I forgot to tell you, Haley has a present for you," he says.

"A present?"

"Isn't your birthday next week?"

"Yeah. How did you know that?"

"She told me. She's going out of town and asked us to stop by."

We get out and walk up to Haley's front door. Haley herself answers and invites us in. She tells me she's written me a song. I get goose bumps. It's one of the nicest things I can imagine anyone doing.

She sits in a chair in the slightly darkened but very white room, positions the guitar on her lap, and starts to play. The song is about finding yourself, standing up for what you believe in, and the true meaning of friendship. I feel like I'm going to cry, standing there, holding Chris's hand, and listening to this amazingly talented girl. Why is the house so quiet? Where are her parents? Why is the room so dark? Why does it smell like pizza?

When she gets to the last part of the song, I hear other voices in the next room, singing along, and then the dark room is suddenly light, and people start streaming in. There's Tina with her boyfriend (man-friend?), Cesar, Sydney and the rest of the newspaper staff, Tyler, Keoni and Kerani, a few people I know from other classes, casual acquaintances, Mr. Big.

"Surprise!" they shout when the song has ended. Then my dad leads them all in the hokiest rendition of "Happy Birthday" you've ever heard.

I'm stunned. I can't breathe. I look around the crowd. Even my dad's here. With Melanie. He *knew* about this? He pretended he thought I was going on a date when he knew I wasn't? At least that explains why he was so happy to let me go, right? But that's not the weirdest part.

The weirdest part is that Emily, Janet, and my *grandmother* are here. So is my grandmother's stinky hippie boyfriend. My best friends were the last to come in, and they're coming toward me with their arms out for a hug. They look so cute, just as cute as any of the girls around here, but with their own style. I feel my body relax at the sight of them, like I've come home. Am I hallucinating? Is this a vision or reality? I blink and realize my mouth is sort of hanging open.

"What is this?" I ask Chris in a half-whisper. I don't want to believe I'm actually seeing my two best friends in the whole world coming toward me. If it's not true, I'll be so sad.

"An early surprise birthday party," he says. He shrugs like it's nothing, but I can tell he's being funny.

Emily and Janet run over to me, and we hug. They're *real*. My grandmother lingers near the back of the crowd with my father, watching with intense pride in her eyes. She doesn't say a word, but I know what she's thinking: that she is proud of me for finally honoring the gift I was given. I'm pretty sure she's also gloating a little because she'd always told my dad I'd be a great rider, and he'd always been too afraid to let me try.

"What are you guys doing here?" I cry to Emily and Janet. And I mean *cry*. I'm sobbing. I can't believe they're here. I'm so happy to see them, I'm sloppy and weird. Haley and Tina stand with us, smiling. I love them, too. I feel like I have four best friends, two I've known forever and two I want to know for the rest of my life.

"Your dad called our parents and told them about the race, and he offered to fly us out for the weekend, and here we are!" exclaims Emily.

"Do you know how hard it was for me to not tell you we were coming?" asks Janet.

"She was a mess on the plane, too," says Emily, rolling her eyes.

"My first flight ever," laughs Janet.

I look over at my dad. He's holding hands with Melanie by the kitchen counter, and he waves. I mouth "thank you" to him, and I can see that he's trying not to cry.

"I can't believe you're here!" I shriek, and I hug my friends again.

"We had to come," says Janet.

"We totally knew you'd win," says Emily. "I mean, we really knew. Your grandma saw it and told us she knew you would. But she told us not to say anything about it to you."

So they knew I'd win. Why didn't Grandma tell *me*?

"You *won*!" screams Janet, and we hold hands and jump up and down. I know we're acting silly, but that's the best thing about having best friends you've known all your life. You can do things like this.

When we stop jumping and screaming, everyone else in the room comes over to give me hugs and congratulations. I am so happy, I could float away. There's food, and people start to fill up their plates.

I introduce Emily and Janet to Tina and Haley, but they say they've all been here for about an hour and that everyone knows everyone else already.

"Except Chris," says Janet.

"Chris," says Tina suggestively. "The beautiful Chris."

"He's also a great guy." Haley smiles.

Emily looks behind me and whispers. "That must be him."

I turn around and see that he's standing nearby, smiling at me and listening to Tyler. Janet turns and looks at him, not very subtly, either.

"Oh my God!" she cries, typically Janet. "You are *so* hot!" She says this last part directly to Chris. He blushes.

"She's hilarious," Haley tells me. "I like her."

"A girl direct and honest," says Tina. "Imagine that. In Orange County."

"Get *over* here," says Janet to Chris. Shy, she's not. "Let's get a look at you."

Chris comes over and shakes hands with my pals, a total gentleman. "It's good to finally meet you two, I've heard a lot about you."

"We've heard a lot about you, too," says Emily to Chris.

He puts his arms around me and kisses the top of my head. "I'll leave you girls to catch up," he says. "I'm getting some soda. You want anything?"

We say no, and when he leaves, Emily says bluntly, "He is *so* the one."

"Yeah," I say, low, hoping my dad isn't listening. "I want it to be him."

Emily, Janet, Haley, and Tina grin at me, and Emily says, "You have to tell us everything."

"Totally," agrees Emily.

"Every detail," insists Tina.

"All of it," says Haley.

"Don't worry," I say. "I'll tell you guys *everything*."

Well, I think, maybe not *everything*.